HER DARK PROMISE

Bria Rose

SERPENT & ROSE PUBLISHING LLC

IMPORTANT NOTE

I invite you to experience this story with an open mind and heart. I do not condone any situations or actions that take place between the characters. Please be advised that this is a work of fiction, meant for entertainment purposes only.

This novel contains dark and mature themes including, but not limited to: graphic violence and torture, explicit sexual content, strong language, and emotional manipulation. **Other trigger warnings** include: attempted suicide, sexual assault, CNC, depression, bi-sexual situations, self-harm, dub/non-con, and panic attacks.

Some **specific kinks** include, but are not limited to: knife play, bondage, breath play, voyeurism, and degradation.

If you want to see the full list of trigger warnings before reading, please visit my website at authorbriarose.com/book

Your mental health matters! Please proceed with caution if any of the above content is triggering for you.

For the scarred souls,

May you find the strength to heal and embrace those who cherish every fragment of your being.

CHAPTER ONE

The sounds of their footsteps pattered along the mushy soil of the earth, their whispers filled the night. "Hurry up, Merrill. This place is giving me the creeps."

I stared at the figures from the top of my balcony, clutching the blanket wrapped tightly around my shoulders as a harsh wind blew around me, leaving chills along my skin. The weather had been slowly changing from the blazing summer heat to the chill of fall. I could see it in the ever-changing trees and smell it in the air.

This was my favorite time of night. I found a strange peace in watching how nature changed, even in small ways, undeniably envious of decaying leaves. They could grow, wither, and die, while I was...me.

I needed this moment, however small and fleeting, before I tried to sleep. And yet, here were two humans sneaking onto my lands, pilfering it from me. It had been many years since someone had the audacity to pass through my front doors.

I eyed them curiously. It didn't matter who they were. Not their status in life, nor their circumstances. I only cared about their purpose. Purpose was everything, and it defined if they'd live or die.

The intruders' hunched forms stalked through the rose garden, opened the heavy front doors and slipped inside. I lazily pushed my way from the balcony archway and out my chamber doors, wondering what poor, unfortunate souls had stumbled onto my lands. A smirk pulled at my lips at the prospect of having new toys to play with. It had been too long.

I clung to the shadows, observing them from a distance. Their faces lit up in awe as they gazed hungrily at my desolate castle in the middle of the dense forest. The gray coloring of the castle against the eternal fog cast an ominous feeling that should have sent any sane human running in the opposite direction. The points of the castle were so high that they couldn't be seen from the ground, soaring above the fog. Moss and vines had taken over the exterior of the stone walls, bringing the only color to the bleakness that was my home.

I narrowed my gaze to find that their clothes had numerous patched holes, their skin was littered with dirt smudges, and their shoes had more patches than I could count. They hadn't bathed in months. How they made it all the way out here in the first place was a mystery that I didn't care to know.

I was about to step forward when I felt a presence behind me. Turning, I found Emilia staring blankly over my shoulder at the unwanted guests. It was a far-off look, the kind that told me she may be here, but her mind was not.

I slid next to her, resting my arms over the railing, and said in a lazy voice, not bothering to turn toward her, "I haven't decided if I am thrilled to have new playthings or if I am annoyed to have to deal with them at such a late hour."

She turned toward me and gave me a small smile. "You haven't had visitors since Callum came ten years ago."

I thrummed my fingers on the railing. "Has it truly been that long? Feels like only yesterday since my little bird came to live with us." I smirked to myself, thinking of just a few hours ago when his cock was buried deep inside me.

I gave Emilia a sidelong glance and saw her cheeks redden as if she knew where my thoughts had lingered. I huffed a laugh as she asked, "What kind of a night do you think it's going to be?"

I thought for a long moment and then responded, "They have yet to do anything salacious. Though, personally, I hope they do something to warrant punishment. I've been rather bored lately."

But as the words slipped from my mouth, I instantly regretted them. Emilia and Callum were enough, especially when I considered all the years I'd spent alone, bound to this castle with nothing but my memories to keep me company.

I couldn't explain why I felt a yearning, a want for more. I didn't know where it came from, and I hated it.

"It could be fun," I continued on with a wink.

She began to laugh before her hand flew to her throat, and she winced in pain. Her eyes widened as she looked away, attempting to hide her pain from me. I didn't want to embarrass her further so I tapped her on the shoulder, brought my hands up, and signed, *You don't suppose they committed such a heinous crime as to require dismemberment? I have yet to do that.* I smirked playfully. Emilia looked back over and seemed to assess them with that sharp gaze of hers. Then, she turned back to me, brought her hands up, and signed. *Per your rules, your majesty, they must have to commit such an atrocious act so as to warrant capital punishment.*

I smirked at her. "I am not worried; look at them: they reek of evil." I cocked my head. "What do you think they have done?"

Emilia scoffed. *At the very least, they have proven themselves to be thieves.*

We focused on the two guests; the female bounced up and down on the balls of her feet and screeched, "Can you believe this? Claude, we won't have to eat scraps anymore."

I was taken aback by her words. Were they just here because they were desperate to make ends meet? Did they just want food in their bellies?

Claude was walking around the entrance, looking into every nook and cranny as if he expected someone to jump out at them at any moment.

"Merrill, I don't have a good feeling 'bout this place."

Merrill rolled her eyes and walked over to him, slapping him on the back. "Oh come on, if someone were here, they would have already made their presence known."

"I don't think—"

"Stop worrying, would you? A find like this doesn't come often."

He grinned at her, the tension slightly leaving his shoulders as he wrapped his arms around her and pulled her flush against his chest. His hands made their way down to grab her ass as he drawled, "And here I thought the biggest find was that little old woman at the edge of the forest."

Emilia and I straightened at his words, waiting to see what he meant. That longing for something interesting shifted almost violently—I didn't want them to finish their story.

Merrill threw her head back in laughter. "That old bitch didn't know what hit her. I loved the sound of her flesh when my blade sliced her throat."

Any sympathy I would have had was erased in the blink of an eye, and rage filled me, so familiar and welcome.

What shall you do now, Callie?

Not her. Not now. Get out of my mind! Sometimes her voice felt so real. I'd spent so many nights covering my ears, trying to talk myself into the truth—she was just another memory haunting this place, and she didn't have any power over me.

Testy... I thought I taught you better manners.

I didn't have time to worry about her. I squeezed my eyes shut and cast her from my mind.

That never keeps me away for long, Callie.

Red lined my vision as I concentrated back on the murderers as the man rubbed himself all over her, moaning, "Merrill, you make me so hard when you talk dirty like that."

She threw her hands around his neck and sloppily kissed him. "You can fuck me after we clean this place out." She pushed off of him and made her way over to one of my paintings, running her nasty fingers across it.

I knew everyone who lived on the outskirts of my forest. There weren't many, most were afraid to venture too close, but not her. The old woman, Mariam, in the little house with overgrown brush and a litter of stray animals lingering about. Mariam, who had never harmed a hair on anyone's head. Who was alive mere hours ago, was now dead.

Violet shadows surged across my skin, the only indication of me having any emotions left at all. I had been numb so long that even the brush of thrill at the thought of punishing them made me feel alive again. Humans had not changed over the last several centuries. Their cruelty had no limits, so why should I be merciful?

Their purpose was to steal, and perhaps I could have let that go, but now I knew too much.

As I moved away from Emilia, she signed one last thing, *Make them suffer.*

I stared at her for a moment longer than intended. It had been years since she had said anything violent. There was fire in her eyes. We both had grown fond of Mariam. She was nothing to the villages, a cast-off, but not to us.

I nodded and moved away from her, my own temper flared. Adrenaline coursed through my veins at all of the ideas running through my mind of how I was going to punish them for their crimes. It was almost too much to contain. Not only against me, but against every single person that they had robbed and murdered.

Claude went back to stuffing whatever his clammy little hands could find into a bag. He kept looking around as if he was sure that he was being watched. He should have listened to his instincts.

He called out to her over his shoulder, "Merrill, we need to leave. I don't like this."

She let out an exasperated huff and yelled, "Can you just do as your told and shut your mouth for once?"

Merrill was an older, short woman with hair that looked as though a comb hadn't run through it in years. She was putting her dirt-covered hands on everything in her sight.

My ears almost burst as she screeched to the male, "My bag is almost full. Grab that blanket and put whatever you can in there." She took a moment to look around. "I'm shocked all of this is still here. That no one else has looted it."

They kept talking as I walked around, tuning out the rest of their conversation. I had already made my decision. They were never leaving this castle alive.

I looked up and found Callum had joined me in looking down at them from the other side of the landing.

He walked over to me, bowed slightly, and said, "Your grace, it looks like we have guests."

"Indeed. Soon, I'll go and welcome them."

"What's giving you pause?" Those beautiful light brown eyes were looking at me curiously.

I narrowed my eyes, not knowing how to respond. I didn't want to tell him the truth, that Emilia's words left me with a slight hesitation. I'd only ever wanted her to be different than me—better. I didn't want her to see anything, hear anything.

"I take it you have already decided?"

I didn't bother to glance at him as I replied, "Yes, for what they have done."

He must not have heard what the female said, otherwise he wouldn't have been curious about my reasoning. He paused and then asked. "Can I be of any assistance? I could hold your blades and hand them to you when needed."

I smirked, still looking at the couple, "Don't try to seduce me right now, little bird, I need to focus."

He looked down, blushing, and turned to me, bowing, "I will leave you to your guests, your grace. If you should need me for any reason..."

"I don't need to look too hard. You're never too far away."

I ran my eyes over Callum's body as he walked away. Desire for his hard cock had my insides turning to liquid, but I had one thing to do before I could give myself over to it.

I turned back to the couple who had made quick work in grabbing most of my possessions near the entrance. I gripped the railing in an attempt to calm the raging storm inside of me, not wanting to make my presence known until their bags were completely filled. It had been so long since anyone had found my castle, much less done something to deserve my punishment.

I was itching to get my hands on them, my shadows begging to be released.

The looks on the faces of humans when I appeared were comical. I never tired of the confidence humans had before they realized their mistake. They were always confused that a living soul would ever reside here. Cold. Desolate. Isolated. And for a woman to be here was even more unusual, to say the least.

They looked around, and Claude said, "Merrill, we can disappear with this loot. Let's go."

She sighed, caving into his paranoia. "Fine. At least we know this is here if we ever need to come back."

Claude nodded enthusiastically at her. The pride he felt for finally succeeding in something was almost laughable. They really were pathetic. I knew they wouldn't be challenging for me—no one was.

They were making their way out of the castle as I walked around and descended the staircase leading to the South Wing.

I called out to them, "Please Merrill, help yourself to my things. Like this ornate egg that you forgot." I picked it up from a nearby table and turned it in my hands. "It isn't like I am getting any use out of them."

She dropped the items that she was holding and screamed, "What're you doing here?"

I sighed, still looking at the egg in my hand. "I don't think you have a moral reason to ask me what I am doing in my own home," I stopped and looked at her, "though I do know exactly what you are doing."

Her face had gotten red from what I could only assume was utter shock at my sudden appearance. Merrill quickly grabbed a blade from beneath her tattered shirt and held it up, pointing it directly at me. "If you know what's good fer ya, you'll leave us be!"

I put a finger against my lips and whispered while looking all around the main entrance, "Merrill dear, you must be quiet. You wouldn't want to wake the beast, would you?"

She cocked her head and looked at me in disbelief, "Have you lost your mind?"

I widened my eyes dramatically. "Oh, have you not heard of the stories?"

Claude had approached his wife, staring at me with his mouth agape. "*La bête*? So, the rumors are true?"

I turned my attention to him, giving him a most sincere expression, "Of course they are. The beast has held me prisoner here for so long. It lurks in the shadows, waiting for any unsuspecting person to walk into its territory. Waiting so patiently to allow their prey to relax, make them think they were safe, and then..."

Claude had moved his arm around his robust wife and leaned closer to me, wanting to hear the rest. "And then?"

"The beast attacks, leaving nothing left for anyone to find," I said, barely above a whisper.

Merrill laughed, "Good story, but none of that is true!"

"Oh? How would you know?" I tapped my finger to my chin. "Isn't it true that long ago, a group of hunters entered the woods, but only one returned with all the pieces of his friends? He told the story of the beast, the hungry creature of the forest."

Merrill scoffed. "There are rumors, but if there were such a mighty beast then someone would have seen it by now. You are spewing nothing but lies, wanting to scare us off so you can have this all to yourself!"

"I told you that this is my home. All of these belongings are mine."

Merrill huffed a short laugh while her husband had not moved his eyes once from my body. He gulped. "And your here all by yourself?"

I wrapped my arms around my body, feigning sadness, "Unfortunately, I am trapped here. All alone..." I dipped my head so that I could look at him through my lashes.

I could see that he had licked his lips and as I looked down, his trousers had started to become engorged. Merrill followed where my eyes were looking and then looked back at me with disgust filling her sunken eyes. "How dare you stand in front of my husband and force us to see your near naked body! You're vile! Whore!"

I contemplated that for a moment before I shrugged, the fabric of my thin robe falling off my bare shoulder, "I have been called worse."

Merrill turned to Claude and slapped him, and yelled, "Stop starin' at her, you damn fool. Let's kill her and then leave this godforsaken place." He snapped to attention as he nodded quickly at her. I took a step forward and she turned her blade on me once again. "Stay away, wench! Actually come here and stand still while I gut you like cattle."

The look in her eyes was wild; she was determined to do as she promised. I looked over at Claude, who hugged both bags tightly to his chest, making sure not to drop anything. With the items securely in place around one arm, he used the other to grab a blade from his waistband and pointed it at me. He slowly stepped in my direction, thinking that I would back up at the threat of the both of them. "You heard my wife! Get out of here before I—"

I swiftly moved to him, grabbed the blade from his weak hand, and sliced his arm from shoulder to elbow. He screamed out in pain, dropping the bags, and fell to his knees, clutching his arm as blood pooled around him.

I backed away as Merrill rushed to his side, eyes bulging out of her sockets at the unsuspecting violence.

I smiled sweetly at her as she shrieked at me. "How dare you! Claude, can you get up?"

He grunted to her as an answer and she helped him to stand on shaking feet. "Kill—kill her, Merrill."

"Come now. You are going to make your wife kill me? Didn't know that she was the one with the balls."

His ears and cheeks burned red at the insult and spat out, "You'll pay for that!"

I threw the blade in front of their feet. They looked at me, confused as to why I would give them back a weapon, as I said, "I have a better idea. Let's play a game. Cat and mouse. Catch me, and you can have it all, but if I win, I will take your souls."

I didn't wait until they answered as I turned around and took off.

I could hear the rest of my possessions clanging to the floor as Merrill yelled, "After her!"

I ran down the hallway barefoot, my robe flying behind me as I passed by portraits coated in dust. My heart was beating wildly at the little game I had come up with. Foreplay before the actual fun began. I smirked at the thought of what their faces would look like once they realized who—what—I was.

I could barely hear them behind me, so I slowed down and walked past closed doors, rooms that I had abandoned long ago. The memories within them weren't worth remembering.

I ran my hands over them as I continued walking and called out, "You're awfully slow…" I smiled as I could hear their screams of rage getting louder, closer.

I rounded a corner and stopped in front of a worn wooden door that led up to the tower. It was my favorite room in the castle, the one place where I could truly be myself.

I waited until they saw me, opened the door, and rushed up. Round and round and round. Up and up and up. The steps felt like they would never end as it was the tallest building on the premises. It used to be where top-secret meetings were held, but now it was my own personal oasis.

Once I reached the top, I entered without being out of breath, having climbed these stairs countless times over the last few centuries. I waited for them to barge in, but they never came. I was growing impatient by their delay, ready to sink my claws into their flesh, until I heard their labored breathing, the harsh sound reverberating around the room.

The door was flung open, and Claude charged me. I could only assume that this newfound act of bravery came from my comment about his wife.

"I got her Merrill!" He had a look of pure determination on his face. Spit flew from his mouth as his voice rang off the walls of the tower.

I could only wonder if this had been the dynamic their entire marriage. The wife made all the decisions, and he merely went along with her. And this was his moment, the moment where he was going to finally prove to her that he wasn't as incompetent as he had been throughout their entire miserable marriage. I could appreciate his gumption, but it was futile. He was no match for me.

He clumsily jabbed the blade toward my throat, but I easily dodged it and tripped him. He screamed out when he landed on the arm that I sliced open, hollering in pain. I could hear Merrill entering the doorway as he hurried to stand back up, cheering him on. He raised the blade above his head as he strode back over to me as if that were a better approach. I had grown bored of him, so I reached out to grab his throat tightly. Before he could register what was happening, I snapped his neck so roughly that his head severed in several places, almost falling off completely.

His blood splattered over my face and body. I hung my head back, smiling at the sound of his body hitting the floor at my feet. I raised my hand in front of my face, the purple shadows danced across my skin, giving me the added strength needed to kill the pathetic human. I brought my blood-coated fingers to my nose, inhaling the intoxicating scent of death.

I turned toward her, rubbing my bloodied fingers together as her piercing scream invaded my eardrums. I waved my hand, and her body was forcefully propelled back into the chair. Her hands and legs were tightly bound to the sides, rendering her immobile. The wind was knocked out of her by the force of magic. She was gasping, trying to wrap her mind around what had just happened. She truly thought that they would overpower me.

Humans were just as dense as ever.

I sighed at the rush of adrenaline that the kill always brought to me. It was one of the few, rather only, moments that brought me as close to pure happiness as I could get. Punishing those that deserved it. Punishing those who thought they could take advantage of the weak. Punishing those who thought they could betray me and get away with it.

No. I am not there anymore. I am fine.

I took a deep breath, cleared my mind of the past, and slowly made my way over to the table that had various devices that I had accumulated over the years for torture. I picked up my favorite rusted pruning shear and made my way back over to her. I stopped directly in front of her and watched her writhing around. Loving the way her hair was in disarray, her tear-stained cheeks, the way the ropes cut into her skin, causing them to bleed, and last but not least, the terror. Pure terror clouded her eyes. The terror was so palpable in the air that I could taste it.

I even made a show of licking the air and moaning in delight.

She thrashed around, trying her best to get as far away from me as possible, which was fruitless. She would never be escaping this prison with her life intact.

I walked over slowly to stand in front of her, using the tip of the shear to lift her chin to look up at me. She swiveled her head away from the chill bite of the tool and did her best to avoid eye contact.

I rolled my eyes and grabbed her chin, forcing her to look at me. "You know, you shouldn't steal from others and then attack them in their own home. It isn't very nice, is it?"

"Fuck off!" She was going to fight me until the very end. Good.

"Tsk tsk tsk." I released her chin and grabbed onto her finger.

"Wh-what are—" I giggled at her guttural cries of pain as I dug the tip of the shear underneath her nail bed and slowly pushed in toward the cuticle and scooped, effectively severing the nail from skin.

"You are a guest in my home. Do not use such foul language while addressing me." Tossing the ripped out nail bed to the floor.

"How're you any different from us! You killed my Claude fer no reason!"

I laughed dryly. "No reason? Weren't you just boasting about an elderly woman that the two of you murdered in cold blood before arriving here?"

Her eyes widened. "So what if we did?"

I towered over her, and gritted my teeth as I demanded, "Tell me what you did to her, Merrill."

"Get away—"

I lowered my voice and repeated, "Tell me what you did to her, Merrill."

My powers afforded me the luxury of twisting minds to do my bidding. It was all a matter of finding the right buttons.

She blinked rapidly, and then the truth started to slip out of her. "I—well, we needed more money to pay off someone we owed. We were out looking fer something to steal and came upon her home.

"That woman had nothing but herbs, handmade blankets, and books made of roots and flowers. She was simple."

"Gold, she had gold," she panted the words, sweat beading down her face.

The gold I had paid her over the years, buried in one of her floorboards. I felt my chest tighten.

"She should have stayed in her bedroom, but she didn't. She came out with a broom and—"

Merrill tried to clamp her mouth shut, confused as to why she was telling me all of this. It didn't matter, she didn't have a choice once I used my powers to force her to tell me, "and I used my blade to cut into her throat." She clenched her teeth together and gritted out with a smile on her wrinkled face. "And I watched the light fade from her eyes. And I enjoyed it."

I nodded slowly and asked, "So, her only crime against you was to protect her home from intruders?"

"She should have stayed out of our way!"

I could feel the rage steadily building inside of me with every word out of this wretched woman's mouth. To think that they believed they had a right to kill someone weaker than themselves. But not just someone, one of the three strays I'd collected over the years. That was not something that could go unpunished.

I squeezed the arms of the chair so hard that my knuckles began to ache. I knew that my eyes had begun to glow purple by the look of fear in her eyes. Shadows, a dark purple that nearly appeared black, skittered along my skin, a reaction to the burning emotions flowing through me.

"Can I tell you a little secret? You and I have something in common. I love murdering humans, hearing their screams, seeing the blood drain from their skin, and watching the soul leave their bodies...but I have rules...only those that deserve it, and you signed your death warrant when you killed Mariam."

"Who?"

"The old woman you killed!"

She ignored me and instead begged, "You don't have to do this. I will leave, I'll tell no one you're here. I swear it."

"Thank you, Merrill, I needed this. I needed you." I leaned my eyes close to her face, tears ran down her cheeks as she screamed in terror.

I grabbed her hand and began the same agonizingly slow pace of extracting the rest of her fingernails. She tried and failed to yank her hand out of my grip, which only caused me to tighten mine. I squeezed her hand so hard that I could hear bones snapping and continued the pattern over and over again until both of her hands had not one fingernail left. Until her blood was running down the wooden frame of the chair.

I leaned back and tilted my head, observing my work of art. I smirked as she said while hanging her head in defeat, "Please...please, I can't handle anymore..."

"Well, I did win the game. I did warn you what would happen if you lost." Her cries began to get louder at the realization that it wasn't a matter of whether she would die but of when. Her cries turned into an all-encompassing scream of anguish.

"If you could please stop screaming in my ear drums. You'll burst them if you continue," I said sweetly.

This time, she made eye contact and stared at me like I had lost my mind. She wasn't wrong—I lost it years ago.

"Please, spare me."

I knew this was coming. It was always the same. First, it started with anger. They would always scream at me, calling me every vile name they could think of until they saw my powers and realized that they were no match for me. After that, they would resort to crying and then bartering. Their tears had no effect on me, it didn't matter what they did or said after I made the decision that they would die.

I rolled my eyes as the woman continued to badger me to spare her life. "Did Mariam plead for her life, as well? Did you take the time to consider sparing her for even a moment?"

Her only reply was more tears. I tuned out her cries as I slowly moved around her, contemplating how I would make her suffer for her crimes.

Humans were such depressing creatures. They always acted tough when faced with a weaker opponent, not realizing that there was someone out there who was bigger—more dangerous.

Someone who reveled in their pain. Hearing their screams. Seeing them squirm. Begging me to stop.

I never would.

In these woods, I was the apex predator.

La bête.

I stopped behind her, reached forward, grabbed her by the hair, and yanked her head back. The pathetic woman cried out at the unexpected pain and stared at me with bloodshot eyes.

"How should I kill you, Merrill? Any suggestions?" She didn't answer. I scoffed, looking away. "I have spent centuries torturing pathetic humans, so I have a few ideas. Let's see... I could cut you in various areas of your body and watch as you slowly bleed to death." I looked back at her. "No? Hmmm... How about I rip you apart limb by limb? Or I could kill you exactly how you had killed Mariam."

I wrapped my hands around her head and was flung into her mind. I thought of the woman and was transported to two days ago. Mariam had come out of her bedroom, broom in hand, and screamed at them to get out of her house. I could feel Merrill's sick elation at seeing the woman, and wasted no time in grabbing a knife from her boot. Mariam retreated back into her room, but Merrill was quicker and kicked the door open. Mariam fell back and shuffled away as Merrill strode to her, plunged the blade into her neck, and then stood back and watched her slowly bleed out.

I let go, and Merrill strained to say, "Please let me go. I won't do it again."

I cocked my head to the side, wondering if she would ever own up to her crime. "She must have screamed and begged you to stop, just as you are doing now. What makes you different? What gives you the right to live when she doesn't get that chance?"

"Oh yeah? And what makes you any different from me? You say you're going to kill me. That makes us the same."

I leaned down until my face was inches from hers, breathing in her putrid breath as I said, "There is a difference. I have never pretended to be anything that I'm not. But you... You keep spewing lies, and honestly, it is disgusting."

I raised my hand to let a blade form from my shadows and plunged it into her neck, just like they had done to Mariam. Her blood squirted in my face and down my hand, but I held still as I watched the life drain from her eyes until her soul had left her body.

Silence.

I took a deep breath, happy to never hear their shrill voices again. I considered sending Callum to Mariam's house to find her body and bury her properly. It would be the right thing to do. She didn't deserve to rot there alone without a proper burial and send off into the afterlife. Not that it is something that I necessarily believe in, but maybe she does.

I stared at the woman for another moment, wishing that I had prolonged her suffering, but there was nothing to be done about it now. Not even my powers were capable of bringing someone back from the dead once their soul had completely left.

I gathered my powers one last time and waved a hand over their bodies, shadows cascaded down from my hands intermixed with bright golden sparks, and the moment it touched their bodies they burned. Ashes replaced flesh.

I made my way out of the tower, and Emilia was waiting for me there. I had saved her about twenty years ago from a fate worse than death, and out of thanks, she designated herself as my official guardian. She ensured that my basic needs were met and that the castle was in near-perfect condition. It took me time to adjust to her presence, but now, I wondered how I'd ever gotten along without her.

"They are taken care of. Mariam can rest easy knowing that her murderers will burn in the pits of Hell for all of eternity."

She nodded, raised her hand, and rubbed her throat. Her injury must have aggravated her because she had brought her hands up and signed, *They got what they deserved. Do you need me to clean the room?*

I shook my head. "I took care of it."

She looked up as if she could see through the walls and floor and into the room where their bodies were nothing but ash on the wind. I followed her gaze toward the tower which was located at the back of the castle and was so high that there was a severe drop in temperature once you reached the top. It was a perfect place for torture.

From its current state of desolation, no one would guess that we were once a happy, peaceful kingdom that took care of its people. Where I could walk around without a worry of an attack. The people who I knew would lay down their lives for me, their princess. But that was before the execution...

Before *her*.

I gave Emilia another nod and left her, heading back to my chambers. It was a rather eventful night, and I was ready to wash their blood from my body.

I entered my chambers, not even bothering to close the door, and walked to the open window like I did every night. I grabbed my wrap from the chair next to me as the sting of the cold air bit into my skin.

I heard a noise behind me, but didn't turn around as Callum wrapped his strong arms around me, squeezing me to him. I let my head fall back onto his chest as we stood there, looking at nothing in particular.

"How was your night?"

I knew what he was asking and turned my head until I was looking directly into his eyes. I knew what I must have looked like, but he didn't balk at the blood. His love for me didn't waver as he brought his mouth down to mine.

I said in an icy voice, "You know the rules, Callum."

He stopped immediately, and closed his eyes in defeat. In a quiet voice, he replied, "Yes?"

I watched his retreating form move to the middle of the room, and then he knelt with his hands on his knees, head bent, naked.

Good little bird.

I had fucked Callum every single night for the last ten years that he had been here. The way that my body reacted to the feel of his cock in me was nothing short of a revelation. I felt a connection with him the moment I saw him. There was something that was so broken about him and when our eyes met, he looked as if he was ready to die. He welcomed it, and that's when I knew that we were alike. Two tortured souls finding each other.

Before the curse, I'd only been intimate a few times. Whenever things inside the castle became too much to bear I would find anyone who could help me to satiate my needs. Yet, I knew so little about men, about myself, and he welcomed my curiosity. He'd awakened something in me I might have been shameful for in the past—a desire I didn't care to fight any longer.

I walked over to him and ran my fingers through his bowed ruffled head. A moan escaped his lips. I yanked his head back by his hair to look me in the face, his eyes heavy with lust, breathing rapidly. A thrill ran through me at the thought that he would do anything that I asked. No matter the request.

"How shall I fuck you tonight, Callum?"

He whimpered, and I couldn't hold out anymore. I was done playing games for the night. "Get on the bed," I ordered.

He was more than happy to oblige. Getting up, he walked over to the bed, getting on in the middle while I walked around it. Stripping off my clothes the closer I got, his eyes glued on me.

I knew that he wanted to kiss me, but I felt as though it were too intimate. A boundary that once crossed, would completely shatter everything that I had built over all these years.

I'd made a promise to myself not to grow too fond of my strays, and I'd already broken it with Emilia. I couldn't possibly give myself to him, not entirely, because like all humans that had come and gone since my curse, he'd wither away and die.

And you will watch, her voice haunted my mind, daring to ruin the moment.

I cast her out, not paying her any mind. Completely naked, I climbed to the top of the bed and spread my legs for him. I slowly dragged my fingers from my breast down my stomach all the way to my sex. My back arched as I made slow circles around my clit.

His eyes were hungry, waiting for me to give him permission. He slowly moved up and down his length, squeezing hard, staring directly into my eyes.

"You are beautiful, your grace," Callum moaned.

I smirked at him, making slower circles. "Even with their blood still on my body?"

"I would fuck you whenever and wherever you wished. I am your consort and yours to do with as you please."

"And you are fine with being a body for me to use whenever I wish?"

"If my only purpose in life is to bring you pleasure, then I would consider that a well-lived and full life." I scoffed because I knew that he meant every word.

Tired of talking, I leaned back, rested my back against the headboard, and called him over with a flick of my finger.

He gave me a sly smile and crawled over to me like the good little bitch he was, and placed his head between my legs. He hovered above my pussy and tentatively licked all the way up in slow lazy movements. I ripped his head up and commanded, "Faster."

With that, he inserted two fingers and pounded them into me while sucking my bundle of nerves. My breathing turned ragged. He was stretching me, but I needed more. What I wanted was more than sex—it was primal.

I threw him off me, grabbed him by the shoulders, and pushed him onto his back. I straddled him and moved my hands over his bare chest. The feel of his muscles sent heat down to my core. I could feel my cum pooling on his stomach. I leaned forward, grabbed his cock between my slick legs, and lowered myself onto him. He groaned in ecstasy, his thick cock filled me. I jerked my hips forward and got into a rhythm.

He tried to touch me, and I bent over, pinned his hands over his head, and whispered breathlessly, "You want to touch me, little bird?"

All he could do was nod, not able to find his words. I leaned down to his ear, biting it hard enough to cause him to whimper.

I smiled and whispered, "Be a good boy and show me you deserve that honor."

I let go of his hands, and he grasped onto my hips and fucked me so hard that I had to grip the headboard or else I would be propelled off. It didn't take long for us to find our release at the speed he was going, hitting that spot with each thrust.

I let go of the headboard and collapsed on top of him. We laid there for a moment, our breaths intermixed. There were only two things that made me feel any kind of emotion and one of them was when his throbbing length was deep inside of me. Even then it was a feeling that wouldn't last, a fleeting moment.

Princess, do you really think he wants you for anything other than sex?

Circe.

Would she ever not invade almost every moment of my damned existence. Always reminding me of my shortcomings?

I replied to the voice in my head, "Get out."

"What?"

I sighed as I sat up, looking down at his flushed face, and couldn't help but think about the way they killed Mariam. About how she was no more.

Another dead body, taunted Circe. *How many more will die because of you?*

I squeezed my eyes shut as I slid off of him, and rolled over to get out of bed to go to the bathing chamber. He knew what I wanted, knew what our arrangement was.

And he was right. He was my consort. Nothing more and nothing less.

Chapter Two

The distant sounds of bells chimed three times, alerting me to the witching hour. A time that I had become accustomed to living in. I had laid in bed staring into the night sky long after Callum had departed. I hadn't dared to close my eyes, knowing that the nightmares would come once again and I couldn't bring myself to allow them to find me.

The rage had yet to die down. Thoughts of Mariam lying in her cottage pulled at a part of me that I barely acknowledged. I killed that couple too quickly, and now I was left with this pit in the bottom of my stomach. An indescribable ache that, no matter how much I tried to cast it from my mind, wouldn't go away.

I threw the covers from my body when it was clear that I would be getting no sleep tonight and glided out of my chambers, and down the hall until I was in front of large oak doors. I pushed with little resistance to an empty library as a loud creak rang in the silence.

I picked up the candle and lit it with a single word. "*Incendu.*" It blazed until there was a circle of light twirling slowly around my body.

The library was grand. My ancestors had taken great care when designing this room. During the day, natural light filled the room with its floor-to-ceiling windows and thick columns in between. There was a spacious rug in the middle of the room with intricate patterns that was gifted to us by a famous artist whose name I couldn't remember. Sliding ladders attached to the bookshelves lined every wall filled with thousands of books on various subjects from mathematics to personal journals from great scholars worldwide. Though I always favored books that spoke of far off places: of spices that I had yet to taste, the chilling bite of the ocean air on my face, or seeing monuments that touched the heavens.

It was once said that our library was the largest of all the kingdoms on our continent. And at one time that was most likely true... Over three hundred years ago. But now? Now, I stood in the middle of the Great Library in perpetual silence. Was it still grand if there was only me left to see it?

I took a deep breath, shook off the foreboding feeling that washed over me, and strode past the mantle that spanned the length of three windows. There was a blank space above the mantle that once held a family portrait, but I couldn't bear to look at it after what had happened so I moved it to one of the many deserted locked rooms.

I made my way to the far back left corner of the room with a particularly deep alcove set, where even light was unable to penetrate this far back. This was just one of many alcoves within the castle that led to various secret rooms, hallways, and even outside. My ancestors wanted there to be multiple escape routes in case anything were to happen.

Even though I couldn't stand to look at the portrait above the mantle, I kept a smaller one in this alcove to always remind myself of all I lost. I deserved nothing less. I spared them a sidelong glance and stopped in front of the section that housed the books on wars that have come and gone, their victors long forgotten.

I located a book with a worn green spine. Nothing was outstanding about it, other than it being empty. I pulled the spine toward me, causing a small door to slide open. I opened the door to reveal a small room that used to be privy to the most secret of meetings, ones that the royal family didn't want anyone to see or hear, beside the tower, and the books that didn't exist to outsiders.

Belle and I found it when we were searching for a new book to read. I loved listening to her read. She was such a smart girl, and could read complex books at the small age of five. Not even I did that at her age.

I remembered the day. Belle was a little short and was trying to reach on her tippy toes to grab a book when she pulled on something and fell backward as the door swung open. We were both shocked that a door opened revealing a hidden room. It wasn't terribly large, about as big as one of our servant's bedrooms. The walls were nothing but shelves which were lined with books that were coated in a thick layer of dust. The books ranged in differing sizes, shapes, and colors. The room itself had a table in the middle with a used candle and a chair sitting on top of concrete flooring as if it were an afterthought. As though the people who made this room had no idea of the knowledge that would need to be hidden from the rest of the world.

We walked around it and soon found out why it was kept a secret. *Magic.* All of these shelves were lined with books about magic from different regions around the world. They weren't in any particular order, a scattered collection. We had walked around, taking it all in when I looked over at the table.

"Magic?" Belle's eyes lit up in a way they shouldn't. Our father hated witches, and forbade magic. Yet, everything inside her body beckoned her childlike curiosity to know more about it.

"I wish you wouldn't say it like that." I rolled my eyes dramatically.

"Like what?" She blinked her large, doe eyes.

"Like it's some adventure," I said. "Magic is forbidden for a reason. We shouldn't be in here."

Belle bounced on the balls of her feet, ignoring my pleas.

There were three open books taking up the majority of the space on the table. *The Anthropology of Witchcraft and Demonology. A History of Witchcraft and Varying Anathemas. Anathema: A List of the Most Notorious Witches in History and their Wrongdoings.* I flipped through a few pages skimming through the sentences and had to look away when I flipped to a gruesome photo of what looked like a snarling wolf with horns.

I looked around the table once more, and Annabelle picked up a familiar leather-bound book with writing inside.

Father's.

I cast my mind away from the past and focused on the present.

I sighed, dust particles dancing in front of my vision in the flickering of the candlelight. I set the candle on the top of the worn table and sat in one of the two chairs that were placed on either side. I looked down to find my quill, ink, and journal where I had left them.

What would I write about tonight?

I always came here when there was something heavy weighing on my shattered heart. Put my thoughts down on paper and then locked them behind closed doors.

The pain returned and I swiftly picked up the quill, opened the thick journal to the next blank page, and began writing.

October 1761,

Two strangers came to steal from me. That is not new, though it hasn't happened in a decade. What is new is that they arrived after having murdered the old woman. She had been in my employ since she was young.

I gripped the quill hard enough to snap as I had to take a few deep breaths. Breathe in. One. Two. Three. Breathe out. One. Two. Three.

My mind cleared slightly, but not enough to rid myself of my anger. I continued writing.

They killed her in cold blood. Though there is no need to worry. She was avenged. She can rest peacefully knowing that her murderers were in pain in their last moments. My single regret is that I did not make it last longer.

I closed my eyes and sat back. I imagined Mariam's smile was wide every time she came to gather another child, knowing that she was doing something meaningful with her life. That is what she told me when she asked to be the one to shepherd the children away from that horrid village. It was one less thing for me to fret about, so I obliged. I made it seem like a simple, unimportant task when I should have told her the truth. She was essential, and good, and very much needed.

I opened my eyes and the ache eased slightly. I must have gotten out all that was necessary. I was about to close the journal until something stopped me. The book had worn with age as I had only ever written in this one.

My magic allowed me to continually add page after page without needing another. Meager fickle magicks that any child could learn regardless of their affinity.

"You truly love to torture yourself..." I said to myself as I flipped back through the journal until I found the page I was looking for.

I closed my eyes and was brought back to the day Emilia was brought into my life.

The night before, I had consumed an entire bottle of venin to rid myself of Circe's voice. Naturally, I had overslept, completely forgetting about the Reaping. I looked toward the window and found that it was still bright enough to tell me that the sun had yet to fully set. I hurried outside despite the ache that roared in my head from the poison.

I had barely reached the gate and was about to start calling the child when I saw a small, frail figure lying face down in the mud. Something sank inside me, and I ran toward it. I dropped to my knees in the mud and couldn't comprehend what I was seeing—the child's clothes were in tatters.

But they had always taken special care of the children. The chosen sacrifice was given a good meal and clothes before being tossed into the forest. I didn't understand why this one was different. I cursed myself when I realized that she was right outside of the perimeter that kept me away from the rest of the world. I was about to use a stick to drag her to me when I heard screaming down the main path. Mariam was by the child's side in an instant, panicked, out of her mind. Mariam quickly picked her up and brought her to me so that I might examine her.

I had yet to see her face, as her long blonde hair was covering it. It wasn't until Mariam sat her down and I turned her over that I was disgusted by the sight. Mariam gasped beside me as we beheld the bruises and wounds along her body, but the most hideous of all the wounds was the large bruise around her throat.

I had to bite back the bile threatening to escape my lips. The child was incredibly malnourished and looked no older than nine years. Her heartbeat was faint—alive, but barely.

Her mouth opened, and out came a croaked whisper, "They hurt me."

I shut the book as I opened my eyes. I usually tried not to think about that night as it brought back feelings of rage so deep that I knew I would unleash all of my power on the despicable humans who had dared to lay a finger on her. But I couldn't give in to the rage, fearing that I could harm Emilia, so I suppressed it.

Though honestly, perhaps Emilia didn't need my protection as much as I assumed. She had always told me of her desire to take over after Mariam became too old to shepherd the children. But since the day I found her in the mud, beaten and assaulted, her eyes bled revenge. This anger never seemed to boil over, but was simmering, waiting for the right moment. Would she do her duty and take care of the children? Or would she leave and find the men who hurt her?

I looked over, out into the library, and found that it was still dark. I must not have been here for long. Time escaped me, the days often bleeding into the nights.

I tapped my foot under the table, unable to decide whether I wished to attempt to go back to sleep or...

I smirked as I stood, pushing the chair back and rushing out of the room barely remembering to lock it behind me. I quickly exited the library, winding around the various halls until I reached his door. I never came to his chambers, never needed to until tonight. After everything... I needed more.

I pushed the door open to find Callum sprawled on his bed fast asleep. I could see from the doorway that his chest was bare, and the sheet was pulled down enough that the only thing it was covering was my favorite part about him. I glided over to the side of his bed and watched his chest steadily rising and falling. I cocked my head to the side and smiled as I thought about how easy it would be to end him. A simple thought and he would cease to exist if I wished it.

Luckily for him, I did not.

Luckily for him, he was incredibly handsome. His brown hair was wild, shrouding half of his face from me. I gently swiped a stray piece of hair away from his eyes so I could look at him, as I had never watched him sleep. I always sent him away after we fucked, never having a desire to share his bed. Never needed that amount of intimacy.

I ran a single finger down his jaw, over his chest until I reached the top of the sheet right over his flaccid appendage. I didn't want to wake him, so I retracted my hand and stood there staring down at him.

I was reminded of the time we met. He was a lost little thing. He was with three other men who had stumbled upon my castle, thinking they could loot it. I stood in the shadows and heard Callum plead with the men to leave. The largest man, presumably the one in charge, hit Callum in the face so hard that he flew back into the wall. I then watched as all three men beat him for just trying to do the right thing.

He was a victim.

I smiled to myself, thinking about what I did to his abusers. How I used my shadows to form a blade and slit the throat of the one closest to me. His blood splattered all over me, and the sounds of his gurgling sent tingles down my body. I threw my shadows at the next one before he could realize that I was there, hitting him square in the chest. The shadows dispersed and he dropped to the ground.

The last man heard the sounds of his friends and whipped around toward me, but before he could avenge the fallen I simply thought about him dying and his neck snapped. I always liked a challenge, and taking my time, but fury spread through me at witnessing them beat poor Callum who was cowering by the wall.

I walked up to him slowly and knelt in front of him. His arms were wrapped around his knees that were pressed tightly into his chest. His clothes were too large for his sickly frame and I could clearly see varying hues of purple and yellow, indicating that he had been beaten more than once. Callum was crying so hard, assuming that he would be next, that he winced from the pain.

This helpless creature was no match for the men that he was with and was malnourished.

He finally looked up at me when the killing blow didn't come and asked, "Are you going to kill me too?" His voice was so quiet that I had to strain to hear it.

He was like me. A lost soul trying to survive. "What is your name?"

"Callum."

I informed him that he could stay until his injuries healed and he got a belly full of food and then he was free to go. I stood, and he moved to follow me but hissed and held on fiercely to his side. He must have broken bones if merely moving was causing him pain.

"Please. Don't make me go back there. I will do anything you ask. Please..." There was a sadness in his eyes, but it had been so long since I allowed anyone to stay since Emilia came, let alone a man. I couldn't trust him, not just because he was a man, but because my castle wasn't a place that I would allow just anyone to stay—it wasn't a home. Though, I took a moment to really look at him. I could see that even though he was skinny he had a good build, shaggy brown hair, and a handsome face. But he looked dull as if he was ready to give up. Ready to die.

I could understand that feeling.

"Fine. You can stay."

I do not know exactly what made me agree, but I just had a feeling that I should. I scratched his chest from his collarbone down the length of his breast. Blood dripped from the wound and I leaned forward, licking the trickle that fell down his chest. Shivers ran through his body. I leaned back so that our faces were next to each other and whispered, "You are mine now."

I am being rather nostalgic tonight...

Coming back to my senses, I looked at him one more time, deciding if I wanted to wake him, but decided against it. I got up and walked out of the room.

CHAPTER THREE

"**M**iss Emilia, how are you feeling?"

She cleared her throat. "I am well, thank you for asking. And how many times do I have to tell you to please call me Emilia," she scolded gently.

I could barely listen to the two of them talk as I thought back on yesterday. Something didn't sit well with me. I could feel something in the air, something foul. But I couldn't place my finger on it.

I drummed my nails against the goblet of wine as Callum laughed. "I don't think I could do that, Miss Emilia. It is customary to show respect to one's elders."

They were talking to each other from across the table, Callum to my right and Emilia to my left. I focused on the food that Emilia had prepared for us this morning. There was a platter of flaky chocolate croissants and blueberry brioche. Next to it was the fresh bread and butter plate. An assortment of smoked salmon, capers, onion, and hard-boiled eggs beside it. Emilia drank lemon and ginger tea while Callum preferred coffee. I always drank wine.

A meal fit for a queen as she would always tell me. A queen indeed.

Even though she knew that I would barely touch it. My body preferred to live on the hatred that coursed through my body every second of every day. My temper had yet to ease after everything from the day prior. Though I knew I hadn't allowed their pain to last as long as it should have, the memory of the sounds of their screams put a smile on my face.

Emilia rolled her eyes. "I am only older than you by four years." His only response was to shrug playfully while grabbing a piece of bread and biting into it.

Sometimes I envied their ability to be casual with each other; I could never relax enough to fully let go. Before them, life was easy but incredibly lonely. I carried on with little to fret about, and then they arrived, securing a place in my home—my life—and now I felt anxious daily. What if my powers got out of hand and I harmed them? What if I had to protect them from outsiders and ended up killing them?

"And what about you, your grace?" I heard Callum ask. "How was your hunt?"

He knew just how much I loved a good chase, but he had never seen me in action. I glanced at him over the top of my goblet from my peripheral and smiled triumphantly. "They suffered, but not nearly enough to satiate my appetite." I took another sip of wine.

You simply can't control yourself, can you?

I closed my eyes and tried to cast Circe's voice from my mind when Callum asked, "What was their crime?"

"They murdered Mariam."

His eyes widened from the shock as he went wholly still. "What?"

"They killed her for the gold that I had been giving to her over the years." I squeezed the cup tightly. "They boasted about what they did to her, and I didn't do her justice in making sure that they suffered more than she did. I suppose we'll just add her to the list."

"List?" Callum inquired.

I shook off my collective madness. "Nothing. Take a shovel and go to her home on the edge of the forest. Go down the path until you hit the river, and take a right. Follow it until you see her cottage. Give her a proper burial."

How many more will die, Callie?

"Enough!" I said it loud enough for the wrath in their eyes to soften into pity and worry.

The sound was unbearable. I rolled my eyes and finished the rest of the wine. I had yet to touch my food, having completely lost the desire to eat.

Callum leaned forward—he always moved on whenever I answered that voice inside my head aloud—and said, "I am glad they are dead. They deserved nothing less."

I held his stare, mutual understanding shown in his eyes.

My heart skipped a beat thinking of Mariam lying in a pool of her own filth, the blood having already dried on her wrinkled skin. I swiftly stood and ordered. "Go now, Callum."

"I'll leave right away. I will take care of everything," he assured me.

I knew he would. I didn't respond as he left.

"Are you going to let me take over?" Emilia asked. A hopeful look spread over her face.

"I am considering it," I said.

"What is there to consider?"

My head began to pound. I wasn't calm enough to have this conversation with her. "Many things."

She stood in a rush, her knees knocking against the table, causing the china to shake. "You've been training me for this since I was a child. I know what to do, how to find them, how to care for them, which towns to take them to."

She sounds so much like little Annabelle. Will you lie to her too? I used the palm of my hand and thrust it against my head to quiet the voice. Why was it getting so worse lately? And yet, how could I deny the truth in Circe's words?

I folded my arms across my chest. "You know how to do everything Mariam did. I am not concerned with your ability to serve. I know you will do right by those children. I am more concerned with what you will ask them, or what they will say to you. I mention that town and you shiver, Emilia."

She glanced down at her arms involuntarily where little bumps began to rise.

"You want to find the men that hurt you. You want revenge."

"I have earned it." This time, her eyes did all the talking for her. Dark, fox-like, seething with that rage I knew she lived with every day.

"But your revenge is not more important than those kids," I said defiantly, and regretted it rather quickly.

Her eyes dropped, and she sank back onto her chair, fingers curling into the cloth of her dress.

"I need to know I can trust that you will not disappear on some hunt for them because I can't protect you if you do, and if something happens to you, Emilia," I paused, realizing my voice had grown weak, shaky. I cleared my throat and pulled back my shoulders. "Who will take Mariam's place then?"

Her body slumped into the chair, and she began to eat quietly. I wanted to reach out and touch her and give her some kind of reassurance, but I couldn't soften this moment any more than I already had.

"You will have your revenge," I promised her, the same one I'd made since the day I found her. I wasn't sure how, but I'd keep that promise.

I wrapped myself in my favorite black robe, not bothering with any other clothing as I watched Callum from the front steps of the castle leave with a shovel and other essentials in a bag slung over his shoulder.

Anger flooded as I watched Callum turn into a speck in the distance. The fact that I couldn't follow him did nothing to help my already foul mood. Anything could happen in those woods. And if he—

I grunted, flew down the stairs, and walked around the castle until I spotted my greenhouse on the North side. I needed to calm my nerves and the only way to do that was to stick to my routine.

Wake up. Eat. Garden. Eat. Fuck Callum. Sleep.

This routine was the *only* thing that kept me sane enough to not harm the two souls whose lives I promised to watch over. To keep my powers at bay. I only used enough to purge any excess energy. Though it made my life incredibly monotonous and predictable, it was a necessary evil to ensure that I didn't lose myself again.

I couldn't get lost in my magic again.

Something that I hated more than showing my feelings was the loss of control over my life. Feelings were nothing more than a distraction; an unnecessary emotion that clouded all judgment. And that's when mistakes were made, that's when you put everything that you have ever held dear to you on the line...because of *feelings*.

And for that reason, I found them to be repulsive and insignificant—a weakness.

I wrenched open the doors to the expansive greenhouse that was about nine feet tall and twelve feet wide. The walls were made of a special glass that I created with my magic that would allow me to see the outside world, but kept anyone from seeing inside. I didn't want anyone to be able to see me while I was off in my own little world.

I had built the greenhouse when I read books on herbology years ago after nearly destroying my home. It only started with a few plants, but as my knowledge grew, so did they. It looked like a jungle, things that I used to read about in books. At least, what I imagined a jungle to look like.

I had unintentionally created a place where the voices couldn't reach me. *That* voice couldn't penetrate the glass walls. I wasn't sure why. Sometimes I wondered if she was showing me kindness, a small moment in the day where my madness couldn't haunt me. After all, she was kind once.

I cleared my mind as I held up a piece of the *euphorbia milii* in my hand that had thorns all over the stem, and thoughts of last night invaded my mind again. The smug look on their faces as the miscreants boasted about exactly how they murdered Mariam.

Fuck.

How the look of surprise made them light up with glee at the fun they were going to have. The sound their blade made when they sliced her neck open. The pure blood lust for anyone whom they could overpower.

Just like that day...

I felt something wet running down my hand—blood. I was so focused on thinking about the couple that I didn't realize the thorns had cut deep into my hands from squeezing so tightly. I didn't move as I stared at my cut-up palm as the sting of the pain went away along with the closing of the wound. As if an expert healer had stitched me up good as new. Not a trace left.

I grabbed a cloth off the work table on the side of the greenhouse facing the back of the castle. I yelped when I found Emilia to be directly behind me, my own personal little ghost. My bloody hand dug into my chest as if I could reach into my chest and grip my beating heart.

Once my breathing had slowed, I said, "If I didn't know any better, I would assume that you took at least a tiny bit of joy in scaring both of us with your antics."

"You were lost in thought. I didn't want to bother you."

I glanced sideways at her and tilted my head. "Oh really? So, all those other times?"

She looked down as her cheeks reddened. I scoffed, knowing that I had caught her in a lie.

She was the only one that I allowed such informalities.

She bowed, walked to a large pot on the work table, and got busy tending to one of the plants. We worked in comfortable silence as the sun sped across the sky from behind the thick plume of fog. I could barely focus on the dirt beneath my fingernails as my foot couldn't stop its incessant tapping.

Callum should have been back by now. Unless…something went wrong.

No. Now wasn't the time. Worrying would do no good.

I could feel myself spiraling and I closed my eyes as I heard Emilia clear her throat. "I thought about what you said." I slowly opened my eyes and looked at her. She was staring at her fingers. "You're right."

But I didn't want to be right. I wanted to give her what she wanted, but not at the expense of the children. They did nothing. They were just names drawn from hysterics to be sacrificed to a forest to appease *la bête*.

She took another deep breath before saying, "Let me take over for Mariam, and I promise you, if I should find any information about the men that hurt me, I will bring it to you before doing anything brash."

I waited, and let the words settle. I wanted to trust them… I did. I hesitated and she saw it.

"You promised me revenge."

"I know I did, but—"

"They took everything away from me. That town. Those people. Not only was I left to die, but they... They..." She held her throat as she had that far-off look on her face as if she were reliving that moment all over again and signed, *I will* never *forgive them.*

Of all the things I thought she would say, this was not one of them. I swallowed, contemplating what she had just said and thinking about what that would mean. "Where is all of this coming from?"

She was trembling, and I could feel the fear and anger. Against my better judgment, I placed a hand on her shoulder in an attempt to bring her some sort of comfort. "I know. Not a day goes by that I don't think about what happened to you. We will get them, we just have to be wise about it."

She nodded her head in quick, deliberate movements.

"You understand that you would need to live away from this castle in order to create relationships with the villages to save the children."

She finally looked me in the eyes, "It would only be for a few months out of the year."

"And you would need to speak to many humans."

She set down the tools that were in her hands and walked over to me. I could see the resolve on her face as she said. "You saved me. You saved Mariam and Callum. Every single year you save the children from the horrors of the forest and send them away to live elsewhere. You are—"

"Don't say it," I said more sternly than I intended, but I didn't need her telling me that I was a savior. I wasn't.

She bowed her head and then looked away. "It is my turn to give back the gift you have given to me for all these years. A home. A place to heal."

Awkward silence ensued. I didn't know how to respond to her. I couldn't imagine her out in the world. She had only known this castle and before that...

"Just like you said earlier, if not me, then who?" Emilia asked after another moment.

She was right. If not her, then who else would take over the role? I was cursed to roam these lands, unable to cross the invisible barrier.

"Callum could." The moment I said it, I knew she would agree with my decree, but the hurt in her eyes made me reconsider. I sighed. "I will consider it. We still have time until the Reaping."

She gave me a small smile and a bow before returning to filling another pot with fertilizer.

CHAPTER FOUR

We didn't speak again for the next few hours, and I finished the row of plants that needed to be repotted.

Garden. *Check.*

Do you not care for that bird of yours?

I straightened at hearing her voice. No, not here. *Give me this moment, you old hag.*

That is rather rude, Callie. Respect your elders.

"You don't have a right to ask for such a request," I answered aloud.

I heard rustling and remembered that Emilia was still in the greenhouse. She set aside her tools and quietly exited through the front door to give me privacy.

Once the door had closed, I addressed her again, "You are merely a figment of my imagination. You have no power over me."

That doesn't take away from the little fact that he has yet to return.

My eyes widened as I looked up at the sky and realized that she was right. Callum would have immediately sought me out if he had returned.

Oh, that's right. You don't care about him or anyone else for that matter.

"I don't care. You saw to that yourself."

I only gave you exactly what you deserved. I wonder what Callum deserves...

I calmed my racing mind. "The only apex predator in these woods is me. I am the one to fear. No one would dare enter these woods so close to the Reaping."

I could hear her scoff behind my ear. *And yet...two arrived last night. Who is to say that it won't happen again?*

"You're wrong." And even to my own ears, I could tell that I was lying. I didn't know anything about the couple or where they came from. She was right, but I would never admit that to her. I sucked in a fast breath.

I could almost feel her shrugging as her voice faded. *Maybe you're right. Though you know what happened the last time you believed you were right.* And then she was gone.

I tried for another moment to focus back on the task in front of me, but she had won. I couldn't stay in there any longer as my beating heart wouldn't cease its erratic rhythm.

Ever since that day, the sun could never fully penetrate the overcast sky, but I could tell that it was well on its way to its descent for the night. I tried to take a few calming breaths and center myself. And when that didn't work, I cursed into the sky and stormed to the front of the castle. He should have returned by now, the pest.

Why wasn't he back? Did something happen?

I shook my head at the absurdity of that thought. Of course, he was fine; he was more than capable of taking care of himself.

But...it wouldn't hurt to go see. If I went to the gate, I would see the moment he returned and I could release some of this pent-up anger right there in the forest.

I strode through the rose garden and over the long, winding bridge that was now covered in vines and leaves that had fallen from the forest. It was dense, having overgrown throughout the centuries. Though for me, it was so familiar, I could walk it blindfolded.

I made my way through the forest until I reached the rundown gate that had one of the sides ripped off a hinge and rested on the ground. The other side of the gate had fallen to the ground long ago, vines growing around it all, threatening to consume it entirely.

I walked forward until I could feel the buzzing energy of the barrier, I lifted my hand toward it and tapped. The force of the magic zapped my finger, causing it to burn my skin. I rolled my eyes at the predictability of the curse. At the beginning, I'd run into this barrier about a hundred times, burning my body, screaming through the pain. I wasn't going to stop until I found a weak spot.

There wasn't one.

I dropped my hand and took a step back, stared out into the distance, and loathed Callum for a moment, for the ability to travel beyond the barrier. If I had to kill every single human in the world to be able to walk off of these grounds, I would without a second thought.

I heard a rustle not far from the gate, and I disappeared into the shadows of the woods. I breathed a sigh of relief. He was back, safe. I stalked the shadows, wishing to scare Callum, loving the squeal he made whenever I caught him off guard. I let out a breath, my muscles relaxing at the sound. I smirked, ready to see the look on his face when I emerged behind him, and see how high he would jump this time.

The rustling got closer, but the movements didn't match Callum's footsteps. No, Callum's were loud, and he would have walked the main path straight up to the gate. These footsteps were soft, and I could barely hear them. They stalked like I stalked, as if they didn't want to be seen or heard. A hunter?

Was he with the others that had come? Or sent to find them?

I stepped back further into the darkness, becoming one with my surroundings, and waited for the human to appear, to see if my assumptions were true.

No matter how much they wanted to avoid the path, they had to walk through the gate to come onto my land. I could hear their footsteps pause before finally taking the first step out of the thicket of trees.

I narrowed my eyes at the sight before me. The human turned out to be a man studying the path. There were multiple blades strapped around his body and another larger weapon tightly around his hip. He was too far away to make out his face, but that didn't matter. The moment he stepped foot onto my land, I would attack. I would find out if he was an accomplice with the couple from last night.

He slowly made his way over to the gate, but before he stepped over the threshold, he stopped. I cocked my head, wondering what was going on in his mind.

Just one more step, human, then you'll be mine.

His curly black hair covered his face while he stood, assessing his surroundings. He was alert, quiet.

Finally, he took a single step over that invisible line. I was about to attack, but before I could make a move, he threw a blade toward me. The blade lodged into my shoulder, and the pain from it fueled my rising anger. I yelped, startled by the action.

He was quick, quicker than any human I had encountered before. To catch me off guard was a testament to his skill, but I would make sure it didn't happen again.

I ground my teeth together and pulled the blade out, gripping the handle so tightly that my knuckles had turned white. I wanted to rip him to shreds, but I refrained and slowly walked out of the thicket of trees and watched his eyes go wide. He stood staring at me, mouth agape, in utter disbelief that it was not an animal he attacked.

His eyes were a bright emerald green scattered with flecks of gold around the irises, so piercing that I would have been drawn into them if they weren't attached to a leech of a male.

I stopped a few feet from him. "What did you wish to accomplish with that stunt?"

If he wasn't confused before, he was now. I could see he was at a loss for words until his eyes looked over to the blood dripping down my arm. Unbeknownst to him, the wound healed the moment I pulled the blade out of my shoulder.

Instead of saying anything, he quickly threw his bag onto the ground and bent over it, searching for something. I prepared for another attack when he pulled out a few supplies that had me puzzled.

He barely paid me any mind as he started to walk toward me, barking orders, "Miss, please take a seat on that stump. I made an ointment that will heal your wound before it becomes infected. And—"

"Stop right there." My voice rang out, cutting through his incessant rambling.

He stopped mid-step, supplies in his hand. His eyebrows knit together as he said, "I am not here to harm you. I apologize greatly for injuring you. I would never harm a woman."

"Oh, how comforting," I mocked.

"Honest," he said. "I thought you were an animal." I took a demanding step forward. "Stories your people tell children to scare them."

"My people?" He gave me a guarded look. "Where are you from, miss?"

"Do you believe women are weaker than you? That they don't have what it takes to fight? Is that why you would never harm a woman?"

Men were all the same. Useless. Never stopped to listen to what anyone with a cunt had to say.

"What? Of course not. I would never hurt anyone without just cause. Please, miss, we need to go to the castle that is just beyond these woods, it isn't safe for us here."

Interesting... I continued to entertain him, to see where he was going with this.

I widened my eyes as if his words scared me and asked in a hushed tone. "Not safe? And what are we not safe from?"

He scanned the area with that expert hunter's eyes, ready for someone or something else to jump out of the woods at any moment. "You know, there are rumors about this place."

"Rumors?"

"Yes, they say that there's a beast that prowls the woods, taking men who dare come unto these lands." He looked back toward me. "There's an infamous story about the first surviving hunter who spoke of a beast in these woods. In my village, they tell the story every year."

"During the Reaping."

He looked at me, confused. "You know about the Reaping?"

"Yes," I confirmed. "I know about the hysteria of the beast, and your town thinking sacrificing innocent children to the woods will satisfy the monster's hunger."

He cringed with distaste. "It's worked so far, has it not?"

Strangely enough, he had a point. Long ago, when I'd torn apart that hunting party, I'd only done it because they were simply in the wrong place at the wrong time. It was one of the days that I was using my magic against the barrier, and they attacked me. I ended up killing them all except for one.

I planted a fake memory in his mind and sent him home to hopefully keep others away, but it had the opposite effect. Others came to hunt down the monster that had mauled their friends, and I killed them as well. Resentment festered inside of me until one day, the men stopped coming and instead, there were children. They had deemed me *la bête de la forêt*—a god.

Never, in my wildest dreams, did I think they'd start feeding the forest with a child once a year to appease their new god. And in my silence, my lack of action, I'd given them all the reasons to continue their awful tradition.

I played demure. "You're hunting a fairytale in the woods. In all my years here, I have never seen such a beast."

"You are right. If there were such a mighty beast, then someone would have seen it by now, but here I am. If I find nothing, I'll report back. If I find something, maybe I'll end it all then..." he paused, leaving the words hanging. "Wait, all your years? Do you live out here?"

I turned my back to him and shrugged over my shoulder. "I needed a place to live, and it was empty." Then I stopped because something he said struck me rather violently. I drifted back to Merrill, who'd uttered the same words. *If there had been such a mighty beast, then someone would have seen it by now.* Are my intruders connected? Was the hunter lying and looking for his friends?

He stepped closer, eyes narrowing. "Aren't you afraid of the beast?"

I narrowed my eyes. "Maybe I am the beast."

This time he laughed, and it made my blood boil. Though he wouldn't be laughing for much longer.

He lowered his defenses, continued for a few more moments, and then took a deep breath, trying to calm down. "Thank you for the laugh. I needed that. Now, if you would allow me, can we please go to the castle so that I may tend to your wound?"

He stepped toward me again, oblivious to my rising anger, and tried to grab me when I swatted his hand away. He took another step back.

"Miss, you must let me help you!" He growled in annoyance. Such a short temper.

"Tell me your purpose here, boy."

"Boy?"

"Don't make me repeat myself."

"I am hunting," he uttered strongly.

"There's nothing to hunt," I countered. "You're intruding on my land, just like your friends did."

"Your land? My friends?" His face pinched together in confusion.

I was done. I threw the blade and saw his eyes widen at his weapon barrelling through the air back at him. He barely jumped out of the way as I shot out my hand, grabbed a hold of his neck and threw him against the cold metal gate.

I bared my teeth and demanded, "Tell me why you're here."

I could feel my power rising to the anger flowing through me, the shadows flew around us, balking at how close we were to the barrier.

I tried to calm down my powers, not wanting to kill him yet, but the anger wouldn't subside. His eyes bulged out of his head as he was barely able to get a breath from the way I was squeezing his throat. He stared at me, as if he couldn't understand what he was seeing.

I released him slightly, threw him harder against the metal, and repeated, "Say it, hunter."

He took a moment before croaking out, "Why can't I move? What the hell is this..." He cursed when he saw the shadows, "Witch!"

I narrowed my eyes, and eased up on my magic, not letting him go, but allowing him enough space to speak. "I'm waiting."

His eyebrows knitted together, clearly confused about his current predicament. His eyes traveled from my face to the blood on my shoulder.

He remained silent, so I continued, "You have three seconds to say something of value to me, or I start removing body parts." I looked down at his trousers and then looked back at him, smirked and said, "I know which part I would start with."

I could feel his throat bob under my hand. My eyes never left his, waiting for him to seal his fate just as his friends did before him.

"I was hunting in the forest when I came upon this path and followed it. I'm hunting the beast."

"Liar."

"What?" He questioned.

"I can feel your heartbeat, boy. It beat faster the moment that lie left your lips." I took a step closer, staring down at him despite our significant height difference. "How about I take a little guess? You and your friends came into the forest looking for weaker humans to steal from. You found an innocent woman in a little shack and thought she would be an easy target. Your friend told me how much pleasure she took in taking her life. Somehow, you got separated, and you followed them here. I have bad news for you, I killed them for what they did."

The question was... Were there more of them? I could take them on, but I wasn't sure Emilia and Callum would make it. I couldn't guarantee that I could hold in my anger and not kill them in the process. I needed to know how many more were coming.

"Friends? I don't—"

"Don't worry, I won't kill you, yet. Tell me what I need to know, and I will make your death swift." I grabbed his chin between my fingers.

"I didn't come with any friends," he ground out, "but you should kill me, because the second you let me go, there will be no stopping me from gutting you just like your ancestors."

Just like they did to me, Callie. I gasped at how loud her voice was, and my hand loosened around his throat. *He reminds me of someone... Your father, perhaps?*

Tears began to fill my eyes. I squeezed his throat until his face almost turned blue and then finally let go of him. He fell to the ground, coughing hard, trying to catch his breath. And as he looked up at me, the expression on his face was no longer that of worry, but of rage.

Good. That was something we had in common.

I used my shadows to infiltrate his mind and bend his will to believe that he didn't wish to move. Little sparks of gold floated around him, my eyes glowing a bright violet. Always did when I used my magic.

It was my turn to smirk. Smirking at his stunned expression, I walked closer, nose to nose, and said in a low voice. "As I have said before, I am not afraid of the beast. I *am* the beast." I waved my hand in front of him. "*Somnum.*" I blew powder that I kept in my pocket in case Emilia had one of her spells into his face.

His body immediately slumped to the ground as I had placed him under a sleeping spell. I walked over and stood directly above him. "You will answer my questions."

I waved my hand over him. My shadows moved until it was directly underneath him. I bent down, touched his shoulder, and thought of the destination and my magic did the rest.

We were transported directly to the tower while my prisoner slept. Too bad he wasn't going to be getting much sleep after today. I preferred the open environment of the tower because it was completely vulnerable to the elements as I had smashed out the windows long ago when converting the space.

The stone heightened the temperature of the weather. When it was winter everything in the room would be unbearably cold to the touch. In the summer, the stone could get so hot that your core body temperature would rise so high that you would die from heat exhaustion. Sometimes I would see what would kill them faster; the weather or starvation.

I chained him up to the wall with his wrists above him.

I stood back waiting for him to wake, but he was out cold. I didn't think I had given him enough powder to be out for more than a few minutes. I scanned my eyes down his body. His hair was curly and wild, draped over his face. I walked closer to him and raised his chin up so that I could see his face better. His forehead had creases as if he was in a constant state of stress. He looked tired.

His body on the other hand looked like it had been sculpted by the gods themselves. I knelt down and ran a single finger over the grooves of his arm, which was hard to the touch, and he wasn't even tense. This was someone who could inflict an immeasurable amount of damage under the right circumstances.

A hunter... Just as I thought.

My core clenched together, seeing this male tied up against the wall... It did things to me. I would have to do this to Callum later. My thirst had yet to be quenched. I blinked a few times, coming back to my senses, and realized that I had leaned into him, my face dangerously close to his. I pushed from the ground and let out a shaky breath.

I was just about to rouse him with cold water when the boy started to wake, clearly dazed and confused as he was slowly coming to.

"Hello, you."

He snapped his face to me. He didn't say anything, but pulled on the chains, testing their strength and when they wouldn't budge, he yelled, "What is this? Let me go right now or so help me when I get out of he—"

"You will what? Kill me?" I threw my head back and laughed. "You are my prisoner and you will answer my questions."

"I told you already! I have no idea what you're talking about." He was pulling harder at the restraints, attempting to break free, the sweat gliding down his body. If he wasn't in league with them, I would already be licking that trail of sweat. He was that handsome.

"I have already told you I would free you of your earthly bonds and kill you once you tell me how many more people are in your band of miscreants."

"I have traveled here for no such purpose!"

"We will see about that."

I walked to the wall and spun the wheel that slowly pulled on his chains until he was standing and then hanging from the ceiling while I informed him, "I killed your friends quickly. Don't think that you will get the same luxury."

He blasted a string of curses at me. He had such a colorful mouth and a rather large vocabulary for someone who conspired with urchins.

"I will let you down if you tell me the truth, hunter."

"I have tried to tell you the truth, but you refused to listen."

Surprisingly, he did not plead for his life. I walked over and strapped weights to his feet to stretch him as far as I could. He took the punishment as his arms strained to try and hold himself as still as possible to not tire himself out so quickly.

After a few rounds of this, he smirked, but weakly. "Is that all you got?"

My anger soared through my veins, and I knew that if I stayed here any longer, I would end up killing him before I got the necessary information. He wasn't broken enough to talk yet, but that would change very soon.

"I think a little alone time up here will do you some good." I released the weights with a snap of my finger as I walked out and down the stairs to find Emilia outside the door. Without looking at her, I said, "That man is in league with the two from the other night. He doesn't eat, and no one goes into that room until I say so."

Before I turned from her, she raised a hand and I stopped, barely turning to look at her.

She signed, *Callum has returned.*

I walked into my chambers without calling for Callum because I needed a moment to think, and began to pace. I couldn't sit still. If I didn't find out fast, it could be too late, but if he wasn't willing to talk, then a little isolation would do the trick. No one could last in the tower for long, especially being hung from the ceiling like that. I could use my magic and get into his mind, but it was too dangerous to do that while in my current state. I might kill him before he told me anything.

I needed to release my energy more than I ever had before. I snapped my fingers and a full glass of wine appeared. I drank it sloppily, some of it dripping down my chin. I wiped my mouth with the back of my hand, breathing hard, but it wasn't enough. The rage was still boiling under my skin, I screamed and threw the glass across the room at the wall. The pieces shattered all over the ground. I needed more.

The sun had fully bid farewell as I yelled, the sound vibrating through the walls, "Callum! My chambers, now!" Even if I hadn't yelled, I knew he would have heard me. He was never too far away.

It didn't take him long until he entered. "Yes, your grace?"

My fingers were itching to punish him for how that boy continued to lie to me. Golden sparks flying everywhere. There was no holding back my powers tonight. If I didn't hurry and fuck this anger out of me, then I ran a high risk of losing control.

I strode over to him and ripped his linen shirt to shreds, the material hanging from his wrists and the hem of his pants. I ran my fingers over his chest, scratching him all over. He hissed as each nail dug into him and then moaned as I licked up the trails of blood and then bit his nipple.

Flashes of the hunter chained to the wall came back to me, helpless and completely at my mercy.

"Get on the bed."

He did as I commanded, and I chained him to the bed, both hands and legs. I wasn't in the mood to have him touch me, and I didn't want to give him a chance to get out of what I had in store for him. Though I knew he would never ask to stop, always craving my depravity.

Once I had him chained to the bedposts, I took a moment to look him over. He had filled out in the last ten years of being here, with lean muscles, shiny hair, skin healed from the horrors of his previous life, and eyes full of life. That look he gave me had me pooling between my legs, ready to ride him. I stood at the edge of the bed and started undoing my lacing. Slowly pulling on the string until it was loose enough to pull off. Shrugging my dress off, giving my breasts room to breathe.

Left in just my skirt, breasts bare, exposed to him. I turned to the side and slid my skirt over my hips, bending forward slightly, exposing myself to him, and I could hear him panting. I loved the way I affected him. I climbed up slowly onto the bed and over him, straddling his lower stomach.

I could feel his erect cock pressed against my ass. I leaned forward, dragging my nails over his chest, drawing a little bit of blood, and he hissed. I stood up, which surprised him. His body arched, yearning for more. I moved my feet so that they were between the headboard and his chained arms when I saw the look of recognition and lowered myself down on his face.

The moment that my core met his face, he started sucking and licking as if his life depended upon it.

A starved man.

I gripped the headboard and started rocking back and forth. We had a steady rhythm when his body started writhing, I knew that he was running low on air, but I couldn't stop myself. I sat down lower on him, giving him my full weight, not allowing him to get away from me even if he wanted to.

I wanted to punish him. The desire was so strong.

He was in a frenzy, but still, he kept licking me and then stuck his tongue inside of me. Causing me to squeeze my legs around his head as I found my release. I screamed Callum's name.

Once he had licked up all of my cum, I leaned a little forward giving him a chance to get some air into his lungs. He sucked in a huge breath, panting.

I thought he would be done when I felt him lift his head, running his tongue from my ass to my clit, and purred into me, "Again."

My daring little bird.

Chapter Five

Callum had elicited a few more orgasms out of me until my body could no longer handle it, legs shaking, sore enough that I laid in the bath longer than I normally would have. I was aware that my sexual appetite was strong. I could never seem to get enough, but Callum's could possibly rival my own. He fucked me enough to quelch the fury inside of me at that bastard's words, if only momentarily.

I lathered a sweet-smelling tonic in my hair and sat against the back of the tub allowing the hot water to soak in my skin, melting the tension from my body. I took deep breaths and prayed that time could do my bidding for once and slow down so that I could evade sleep. My bathing ritual after fucking Callum was the last task of the day; the last task before I tucked my body within the confines of my bedding and closed my eyes only to be accosted by the nightmares.

It was always too much to handle and I would stay awake for the remainder of the night until dawn once again greeted me with its presence and the cycle would start over again.

Day and night. Night and day.

The days bled together and the only reason why I gave a damn was because of the two broken souls that resided with me. I had promised each of them that I would keep them safe so long as they followed my rules and did as they were told. And since they had, they'd made themselves essential to my life.

Both served a purpose and continue to prove their loyalty and usefulness. I treated them like my subjects, but respected their wishes...to an extent. If I kept them at arm's length then they couldn't make me weak.

And yet, I felt it now. A strange vulnerability, a lack of control. I didn't know if the hunter had friends, if they'd storm my lands. How many more would come? I needed to know.

To sulk away in a dark corner. They'll die like all the rest have.

"No Circe. They won't," I rubbed my hand against my face, annoyed that she would invade my thoughts so soon after the last time.

That hunter in the tower? Will you kill him?

"He may be a hunter, but he is still just a human. He will die once I get the necessary information out of him." If I didn't find out how many more were on their way, my humans could perish. That couldn't happen.

What if he is innocent? You can't keep him here. You're to kill him or he'll tell everyone your secret.

She was right, just like always. I couldn't deny it.

"Will you just leave me alone for one fucking moment?"

Such vulgar words. What would your dear father say?

I immediately stiffened at the mention of my father. I gripped the edge of the cast iron tub until pain radiated throughout my hands.

I closed my eyes and ground my teeth together as her laughter rang throughout the room, so loud that I had to hold my hands against my ears to try and stop the noise. No matter how hard I squeezed my hands, the sound wouldn't stop. She kept on going and going, getting louder and louder until I snapped my fingers and a full glass appeared in my hand.

My *venin.*

I didn't waste any time and downed the entire glass in one go. The moment I finished it, the voice started to fade away into the background. As if there were an invisible wall that shut her out instantly.

That never keeps me out for long.

I took a deep breath, once again met with nothing but my thoughts to keep me company. I opened my eyes as I brought the glass up to my face and turned it over, staring at the remains of the red liquid. I knew that one sip of this drink could kill a human the moment the liquid touched their lips. I brought the glass up to my nose and inhaled its toxic scent. Praying to a worthless god that this one glass would finally do its job and take me away from this never-ending hell.

I still drank poisonous wine every day. Though *la venin* was only used when I needed my mind to calm. When the raging in my soul couldn't be stopped by fucking or killing. When the nightmares were so palpable I would wake drenched in sweat.

I sighed as the rest of the effects began to work. My body began to melt into the tub and my fingers started to tingle. I dropped the glass, hearing it shatter in the recesses of my mind as I slowly blinked, loving the numbing effects of the poison, and sighed, looking around the room that I had come to memorize.

The ceilings were high, with intricate patterns coated in the most expensive gold dust that money could buy. The flooring was made of ceramic, the most coveted material at the time. Three windows traveled the length from floor to ceiling directly in front of the tub. The windows were my favorite feature as I could look out over my rose garden and think about the fond memories of my past. The only memories I cared to hold onto with every fiber of my being. And past that was the Forbidden Forest—a name not to keep others out, but me in. The dense forest loomed around the border of my land, mocking me and reminding me of my eternal imprisonment, the invisible tether that bound me to these lands.

As much as I loved my home, I had dreamt of more once upon a time. That was before the curse—before that day. The curse that was placed upon me was legendary, yet no one remembered it. The enchantress was true to her word—only I remembered the truth.

Before I knew it, the water had turned cold. I got out and stumbled to bed for the one hundred thirty-five thousand and fiftieth night in a row.

After the effect of the wine had faded away, I tossed and turned all night long, my thoughts going back to Emilia. Worrying about how this was going to affect her. She had been tormented by that town and now there was a male here from it. I massaged my fingers into the sides of my head, a headache coming on from the stress.

I looked over toward where I knew the tower was and narrowed my eyes at the male as if I could see him. It hadn't been long since I left him, and I didn't want to return too soon. He needed to believe that I could leave him up there until the day he died if he didn't tell me what I needed to know.

Yet, it was almost unbearable waiting. I was never good at being patient. As a child, I was scolded for it constantly and after all these years, nothing had changed.

I needed to do something before I completely lost my mind, more than I already had. I got up, threw on a robe, and headed to the library to do a little reading, but I paused as I passed by the large oak door leading to the tower. He wasn't in there long enough to make a point, but then again, I didn't have any time to waste.

I growled as I wrenched open the door, stalked up the stairs, and through the small wooden door. I entered the room, and a shiver ran down my spine again seeing him dangling from the ceiling. "So...are you ready to play nice and tell me what I want to know?"

His muscles were so tight from having his arms raised above his head for so long. He was dirty and haggard, a stark difference from the rugged hunter from the woods. His head was hanging to the side as if he tried to get comfortable, shaking from the cold night that he had just endured.

He lifted his head, voice cracking, "You can't treat people like this."

"Like what?" I asked innocently, clasping my hands together behind my back.

"You imprisoned me without just cause. I did nothing to you." His teeth clattered together so hard that he could hardly get the words out.

"As I have told you before, I will let you go once you give me what I want. And what I want is to know how many more of you there are." I walked over to the table with the weapons and ran my fingers over them, thinking about which one would make him talk.

"And I have tried to explain that I don't know who you are speaking of. I think all of this was a big misunderstanding."

"And *I* warned you not to lie to me again. That there would be consequences." I could feel my magic stir under my skin, and I knew I was right because his eyes bulged out of his head.

He didn't have enough strength to struggle. His voice was breathy when he said, "I am not lying."

I watched as the veins in his arms became more visible while he tensed, his muscles pronounced. I quietly studied him. Could I be wrong? Was he telling the truth?

"*What* are you?"

"You said it yourself, a witch." I could hear the numbness in my own voice.

I raised my hands up to my face and looked at the vibrant shadows twirling along my hands. I could see how petrified the poor human was, and I was delighted by his fear. Unfortunately for him, I was about to get even more terrifying.

"I have magic flowing through my veins, magic so strong that I could kill you with just a squeeze of my hand." I focused my eyes on his leg and began to slowly squeeze. He screamed out in pain as the shadows surrounded him and did my bidding. I squeezed just enough for him to get the point and smiled. "As you can see, it would be in your best interest to tell me the truth before I break every bone in your body, heal you, and then do it all over again and again until you can't take anymore."

"I am here alone!" He spat.

I rolled my eyes, and he hung his head, knowing this would be going nowhere at this rate, and sighed in defeat. "Nothing I say is going to prove my innocence. Nothing I say will make you believe me."

"Well, I have a rather brilliant idea!" I clapped my hands together, excited to finally dig my fingers into him. I walked until I had to crane my head to meet his eyes above me. "And I will even give you a choice."

He questioned, "A choice?"

"Yes. Would you rather I use my instruments on you?" Lifting a large clamp that was rusted from the many years of use. "Or magic?" I lifted my other hand with the shadows.

I could see him tense again. "And do what with them?"

I ran a single finger over his taut stomach, teasing. He shuddered. "Choose fast. One... Two..."

"Magic!" He blurted.

I grinned, excitement coursed through my veins.

I swiped my hands toward his chains and unbound them, he crashed to the floor with nothing more than a grunt. I knew that his muscles ached from being suspended. Before he could try to move, I cast my magic into his mind and forced him into thinking that he had to stand up and sit in a chair in the middle of the room.

His body moved, as exhausted as it was, into the chair, and laid his arms on the armrests. He stared straight ahead, and I looked down to find that he was gripping the armrest so hard that his knuckles were white. I laughed to myself as I grabbed a few pieces of rope, and strapped his hands, feet, and torso to the chair. I walked around him until I was positioned behind him, bent over, and whispered in his ear, "Wrong choice."

My hands moved to either side of his head. I closed my eyes and pictured myself entering his mind until I was in a dark, endless space except for the presence of floating images swirling around the room. I walked through his memories, seeing every moment of his life. From his birth to his first kiss to his first fuck.

When I walked in someone's mind, I could feel what they felt in that moment like it was my own. It was the only drawback to doing this, but desperate times called for desperate measures.

I walked past so many images until the room started to spin, and I was thrown into a rather mediocre-looking home with two small children playing a game together. I took a few steps closer to get a better look, and I could see that my chained-up prisoner was the oldest of the two. He had the same black curly hair covering his eyes and that serious expression he seemed to get when concentrating. He moved a piece on the board and yelled in excitement at his victory. And the other boy with blonde hair kept staring at the board as if he could change it through sheer willpower.

I moved around the room and walked to a door in the far-left corner and opened it to enter another memory. Even though I knew messing with memories had no impact on what actually happened, my rules still applied.

I walked into another memory of him as a teenager with a girl with beautiful blonde hair that was done up in an assortment of braids sitting atop her head. They were in the shadows of a building, and she was leaning against a wall while he caged her in with his body, his head bent forward to whisper sweet nothings into her ear.

Ah, finally... Something fun.

I whispered into the memory, focusing my energy on the girl, and said to her, "Go over to the counter and grab that knife." She smiled up at the hunter, playfully pushed his body back, and walked seductively over to the counter on her right. He was looking at her like he was ready to devour her.

He stalked toward her until he saw her picking up the knife. I walked over to where she was, standing directly behind her, and whispered into her ear, "Stab yourself in the heart."

She tilted her head at him, still smiling seductively, and drove the knife into her chest between her breasts, blood spurting everywhere. The hunter screamed and moved to stop her, but it was too late.

I stayed where I was, and saw the look of horror as she gazed down at what she did and started crying hysterically, crumbling to the floor as he ran forward and caught her.

I focused on her once more and said, her mouth forming the words at the same time I was talking, "Why would you kill me? Why would you do this to me? It is your fault." She choked on those last words and relaxed into his arms, eyes glazing over. Dead.

He was breathing rapidly, tears in his eyes, chest heaving, hugging the lifeless woman to his chest. Looking around, trying to find the answers in the room. I knew that he was crying in the chair because the emotions that he was feeling in his memories were the same ones that he would feel in reality.

I would break his spirit for making me feel his heartbreak. Would make him beg me to put him out of his misery by the time I was done with him. He would rue the day that he stepped foot onto my land.

I made my way out of the room and into another that was so bright that I had to shield my eyes. I stood in a beautiful meadow that was outlined by a thicket of trees. Animals were frolicking about, birds chirping, and bees buzzing around feeding on the flowers. The first thing I noticed was that I could feel the heat from the sun's rays against my skin. I had never been more thankful to feel one's emotions while in this state.

I lifted my head up to the sky, drinking it in. I hadn't seen the sun like this in so long that I almost forgot what it felt like. It was so serene that I was almost lost in its beauty when I heard a piercing scream coming from my right. I turned my head and saw a woman and a young boy with black curly hair. My prisoner. He looked to be around five years old here.

I walked over to the two lying on a blanket and found the woman tickling the brat as he tried his best to get away from her, but you could tell that he was enjoying every moment.

I narrowed my eyes at the scene; this wouldn't do. As much as I was enjoying myself, I had to remember my purpose. While I couldn't harm the boy, the woman was fair game.

A flash of Mariam's face flitted across my mind, reigniting the anger over everything that had happened, and the newfound threat this man posed. I refused to allow him to bring anyone else here.

You think you can save your pathetic band of misfits, Callie?

Fuck. Not her again.

I said aloud into the meadow, the two humans below me none the wiser, "Leave me alone. Stay out of my head."

What? Do you not enjoy our talks?

"No, I don't particularly enjoy talking to someone who is no longer alive."

Ha. You were always quick-witted.

I tried to block her out, but she was relentless. No matter what I did, her voice kept getting louder and louder until it felt like it was all around me.

I couldn't take anymore, I let go of his head, and I was transported out of his memories and back to reality.

I backed away from the chair and leaned against the wall in an attempt to catch my breath.

I only looked up when the man yelled, "Is that the best you got, witch?"

Yes, Callie, is that the best you got?

My rage was in full force as I strode past him without another word. I unbound him from the chair and placed a long chain around his ankle so he could use the pot I put in the corner of the room. I didn't care to clean him up if he soiled himself.

"Next time, I would recommend choosing the instruments."

I had barely walked down the steps when I snapped, and a glass of *la venin* appeared in my hand. I drank it and threw the glass down, barely registering anything past the need to rip him apart.

I could still hear her trying to talk to me, but soon her voice faded. I called out to Callum and met him at the bottom of the staircase leading up to the South Wing.

I paid him no mind as he walked a step behind me and asked, "Your grace?"

"I am not in the mood, Callum."

"Of course." I could feel his eyes on me, concerned about what was going on. He waited a moment before he asked hesitantly, "If I may... Is there anything you wish to talk about? "

I stopped in the middle of the staircase and spun around. "And what gave you the impression that I had anything to talk about?"

I could tell he was nervous. So nervous that he spit out, "It's nothing! I just–"

"Never mind that." I stopped to rub my hand against my head and remembered what I had sent him out to do. Putting my anger aside, I asked, "Tell me, did you succeed?"

Callum recovered quickly and said, "Yes, her garden was impeccably kept and I knew it was the one place that she made sure was perfect. I felt as though that is where she would like to be buried if given the choice."

"Good." I continued up the stairs.

"Your grace, if I may, I was a little surprised that you wished for me to give her a burial."

"Oh? Why is that?" I mused.

He widened his eyes and stood straighter. "I don't mean any disrespect. I think it was kind of you to want to give her a proper burial."

"You think I'm kind because I took pity on the old woman? I had you bury Mariam because I owed her a debt, that is all."

"I—well, yes." He ran a hand down his neck, a nervous tick of his. "And you killed her murderers. They will never be able to harm another person again."

If I was doomed here forever, punishing the wicked was the least I could do.

"I haven't heard someone call me kind in a long time." I cocked my head to the side.

His hands were dirty from digging her grave, and smudges of dirt peppered his face. He was so handsome, and I wanted to fuck him more now that he was a little dirty. There was something sexy about a man having just worked outside that caused my insides to stir.

I sauntered back down the stairs to him, brought my hands up, ran them slowly up his stomach, and stopped at his neck. I leaned forward and ran my tongue up the side of his now exposed neck. I could feel the shiver that ran through his body as his breathing increased. "Am I kind when I open my legs for you?"

"Uh—" His neck had started to turn red.

"Was I kind that one day where I bent you over the dining room table and fucked you with my shadows until you were begging me for release? Edging you until there were tears streaming down your face."

He gulped, and I could feel his cock growing by the second. I didn't think I would be able to last for much longer, even my own words were making me wet.

"In this world, we do not have the luxury of being *kind*. Mariam was kind and look where it got her." I paused for a moment and saw that he knew I was right, but I was done talking. "You're the next item on my list for the day, Callum. So, should I edge you again or bend you over this railing and fuck you? Or both?"

He nodded enthusiastically, ready for whatever I had planned.

"Unfortunately for you, I am rather impatient today." I let go of his neck and pushed him hard against the railing, not waiting until we got to my chambers. I pushed him down onto the steps and climbed on top of him, straddling his waist. "And angry."

I couldn't hold back any longer. I bunched up my dress as Callum undid his trousers and lined up his cock at my entrance. His cock stretched me, and the feel of him was nothing less than intoxicating. I moved my hips back and forth, and quickly found my release.

I slid off of him, but before I could completely turn away, I could see the confused look on his face. He had yet to find his release.

I turned away fully and walked back up the stairs, calling over my shoulder, "How's that for kindness, Callum?"

Fuck Callum. *Check.*

The rest of the day was spent following my damned routine, but it wasn't as productive as I wanted. Emilia and I had worked in silence again as I couldn't think straight. She did her best to keep her distance, but it was obvious that I was not going to be the best of company this afternoon.

I stopped what I was doing and glanced in Emilia's direction as I recalled a memory many years ago.

"You have to kill it," I told her, watching her hold the rabbit in her small arms. She'd been with me for months and still couldn't manage to properly hunt. I knew I could do it on my own, shield her from it, but when she decided to leave here, what would she do to feed herself? I had to teach her something. I had to teach her how to survive.

"Emilia," I said, growing impatient.

She held the rabbit tightly, and it seemed to nuzzle in her arms, making my job all the more difficult.

"It will make a good dinner," I said. "We put it in a stew, and we'll be able to eat for days. Don't you understand? This is how you survive. You kill it and eat it."

"I've named it," she whispered. "You can't expect to kill something I've named."

"You just found it. How have you already named it?"

"His name is Chip," she said, using her fingers to lightly play with its feet. It sat still, calm.

"That's a silly name."

"He'll hear you," she shushed me.

A smile was creeping up, almost daring to break my carefully placed mask. But this was no laughing matter. "You already have the cow—don't think I don't know about the cats you hide under the bed."

She gasped, eyeing me seriously. "There's only two."

"Three," I corrected. "Do not lie to me."

"Please," she begged. "Don't make me kill it."

"How will you eat on your own?"

She lifted the fat rabbit up, looking into its dark eyes. "I will survive on berries."

"You will die, then."

She rolled her eyes. "Why do you keep preparing me to leave? I don't want to leave."

"You won't always feel that way. I cannot give you a life here, not one that means anything. One day, you will want to see the world,"

"I don't like the world," she said flatly. "The world was cruel to me. I want to be here, with you."

The urge inside me to fight her eased a bit. Perhaps it was too soon to talk of her future, her life outside here, when she'd only just started to feel safe again—and sleep without nightmares.

"I will find us something else to eat, but you cannot keep the rabbit. Set it free."

She hesitated, and opened her mouth in protest.

"Emilia," I said sternly.

She leaned down and freed the rabbit from her arms; it was long gone in minutes.

I was brought back to the present with the thought that if anyone were to come here to try and kill me, then there was a high probability that Emilia would be a casualty. No matter how hard I tried to keep her out of it. Or I could agree and allow her to leave, but would she even be able to make it on her own?

Though her feelings at this moment were the least of my worries. Her feelings wouldn't matter if more humans came. If there was a fight. If she died…

I had been pacing in my chambers for the last hour, wrestling with myself on what was the best course of action. I could feel my power vibrating right under my skin, just itching to get released. The temptation was intoxicating, but I never allowed it the freedom I knew it craved when my emotions were heightened.

I paused by the large balcony doors and closed my eyes, trying to relax my mind and body. Breathe in. One. Two. Three. Breathe out. One. Two. Three. I walked outside to feel the chill of the air on my heated skin and gripped the railing to hold me steady.

I quieted my mind the best I could. Silence—the lack of sound that had kept me company for far too long and now just a reminder of what I had to lose.

I took a breath before focusing back on the task at hand—finding out the pertinent information from that man. I knew that I should wait a few more hours, leave him to starve a little longer before continuing the interrogation. I growled, opened my eyes, and slammed my fists against the stone surface. It didn't matter that I fucked Callum a few hours before; that prisoner was the only thing on my mind. The voice had been successfully cast out of my head for the time being, but even as the effects were starting to fade, I knew it was only a matter of time before she came back as well. She never left me alone for long.

This wouldn't do.

I pushed away from the railing, and stormed out of my room, down the stairs, and straight to the tower's door. I hurried up the spiraling staircase, taking two at a time. Without needing to catch my breath, I threw the doors open and found him exactly as I left him.

I waited for his quick wit and was almost disappointed until I heard him say, "So witch, back for more?"

I narrowed my eyes and walked toward him without a word. I could see that he had something in his hand to use against me, but I flicked it away and forced him to kneel on the ground. I stood behind him as he tried to squirm away from my hands, but grabbed a hold of either side of his head and squeezed tightly.

He screamed as I commanded, "You will tell me what I wish to know."

I closed my eyes and dove back into his mind aggressively, not caring that the sudden intrusion would cause immeasurable pain.

The darkness surrounded me once more as I filtered through his memories, searching for any image that showed him with those two murderers.

Nothing.

I had grown tired of staring at the images and focused my mind on the memories from the past few days. After finding one that looked promising, I dove into the image by mere thought and was immediately transported into it.

The estate was close to town, as I could still hear the noises in the direction of what I assumed to be the town square. I took in the two-story, stone building in front of me. It had two sets of windows in the front that were evenly spaced out on either side of the large, wooden door, with steps leading down to the neatly paved dirt path upon which I stood. The grounds were expansive which made me wonder exactly what family my prisoner came from.

It was nothing to boast about, but then again this was my first time seeing an estate. We didn't have anything like that in my kingdom. It must have been a modern way of building homes. I didn't have to dwell on it long before the prisoner came riding on the back of the horse at such an alarming speed that I jumped out of the way or else he would have rode right through me.

He dismounted and strode up the steps, and I followed along behind him. He hurried through the house and stopped outside of a door. I expected him to knock, but he continued staring at it. He lifted a hand before knocking, and a deep male voice called for him to enter.

I followed closely behind as he opened the door and walked inside. We entered a spacious room that was full of shelves lined with volumes of various types of books, from finances to history. In the middle of the room, a closed window let in some much needed sunlight. The rays made the dust particles in the space much more evident. The room was incredibly stuffy.

"So, have you come to tell me what is on your mind, son?"

I was so preoccupied with looking around the room that I didn't notice a man standing in the corner, looking at a book on one of the shelves.

The man walked over to the desk and sat in the chair behind it, commanding the room without the need to stand. He had peppered hair, a full beard, and clothes with not one wrinkle. He was immaculate.

If he hadn't just called my prisoner 'son', I would have assumed they were related somehow, as they looked exactly alike with only minor differences.

My prisoner stiffened at his father's words, back straight and hands at his side. As furious as he was mere seconds ago, he reeked of nervous energy; he was afraid of this man.

I walked over to his side and stared at him, willing him to continue and give me something I could use.

Finally, he found his courage, and the hunter said, "Father, this madness *has* to end."

The man didn't even bother to look at him or say anything as he continued reading something written on parchment. He clearly couldn't be bothered with this apparent nonsense.

The hunter raised his voice as much as he dared. "*La bête de la forêt interdite* is a myth! So why do you insist on continuing this tradition?"

My back straightened. They were talking about me.

His father lazily looked at his son—really looked at him. His eyes ran over his haggard appearance, and he took his time in answering, knowing that the delay would anger his impatient son more than whatever he had to say.

When he deemed that enough time had passed, he said, "Just because we have not seen the beast doesn't mean that it is not real. You know the stories of *l'homme tailladé*. The group of men was shredded to ribbons, the survivor's skin grotesquely marred from having to be stitched back together. We are preventing that from ever happening again."

"And yet it continues."

His father shrugged. "No deaths in years, son. Why should we stop something that is working?"

"It is a ridiculous superstition. The Church of the Beast, which you head, believes it. Has made it into a deity that you believe warrants yearly sacrifices."

"The sacrifices are not the only reason to continue on..."

My face paled, no, it couldn't be true. I tried to calm my breathing.

"What do you mean?"

I held my breath.

"You will soon learn the intricacies of leading this town."

"And what intricacies are those?"

A sly smile played on the man's lips. "Through fear."

My mouth had gone dry, and I didn't have to look at the hunter to know that his skin had gone pale. I could feel the disgust run through him. He was the son of the leader of the village, the village that tossed Emilia to the forest.

I had the son of the very man who sealed Emilia's fate...and all the children before her.

My prisoner squeezed his hands tightly by his side and replied, "You are willing to sacrifice your daughter just to continue inciting fear in your people?"

"It is an honor to be one of the chosen! Joséphine knows what is expected of her."

"She is five years old! She doesn't understand any of this."

His father's lips pressed together, and I thought I might have seen a flash of emotion in his features.

His voice dropped to a whisper. "I am devastated, Bastian, but plenty of families have given their children to the forest over the years. I don't have a choice in this."

His sister was the chosen one this year. How could a father accept this fate of his own child?

Perhaps, the same way yours did.

I gasped when I heard her, glancing around the room at the father and son, feeling like she was inside the memory with me.

Two similar fathers, willing to murder their children for the cause.

A chill ran through me as the room shifted, and my own father took the place of the man behind the desk for a split second. His face was cold, and distant, staring at me as if I were a creature. A beast.

I shook my head, and the memory went back to normal.

"Then save her," he begged. "Throw her to the forest. I'll find her, and take her somewhere else. I will run away with her."

"You will not," he ground out. "You are needed here."

"If you think I'm just going to watch you kill her—"

His father surged to his feet, walked around the desk, and punched his son so hard that he fell to the floor. His father stood over him as he yelled, "I expect this piss poor behavior from Soren, not you. My word is law!" Spit flew from his mouth. "Now leave."

The man walked back to sit at his desk, his face still red from what his son said to him. He picked up some papers and shuffled them around as he said, without looking at his son. "Before I forget, you are to meet with Boniface's daughter, Mary."

"No."

The man stopped mid-lick of his thumb to turn a page and asked, "What did you just say?"

"I will not marry that woman." The hunter spit blood onto the plush rug. "I will no longer cower beneath you. I will not allow my sister to be your next victim in your inconsequential quest for power."

"You are my successor, the next head of the town council, and will marry a woman of equal status. Either you choose within the month, or I will choose for you."

"You are a coward," my prisoner said as he stood, wiping the blood that dripped off his chin with the back of his hand.

"I think it is humorous that you believe you have a choice in any of this."

He scoffed. "I do have a choice. And I am choosing to go out and find this beast of yours and kill it. I will even bring back its head so you can mount it on your wall of trophies."

The man's eyes narrowed. "I can see that your mind is already made up. You are as stubborn and pig-headed as your mother was."

I could feel the anger radiating off of my prisoner, energy so thick that it could rival my own. "Do *not* speak ill of her."

His father quickly stood, slamming the book closed. "Remember who you are speaking to." My prisoner lowered his head in submission. A look that stirred something deep inside me. I looked over at his father, who continued fiercely, "I am warning you, if you decide to do this and something were to happen, nobody will come looking for you. I will make your brother the head of the house and you will be nothing but a stain on the family name."

"As you wish, Father." With that, my prisoner turned sharply around and stormed out of the room.

I was shaking with anger. This was the man who was responsible for the last set of children. Not because he truly believed in the myth but because he wanted to control the people of his village. I was so angry that I could hardly breathe. My heart was racing, thrumming violently inside my chest.

Before I allowed the memory to fade, I strode over to the man and punched him through his chest, ripping his heart out. "I promise you this. I will find you and I will kill you."

The memory faded, and I was back into the main part where his memories were stored.

I was seething and yet confused. My prisoner seemed to loathe his father and despise the Reapings. If he was that against it, why would he team up with Merrill and Claude Or...maybe he didn't.

Panic swept through me at the thought. I couldn't believe that. I hurried and swiped through the memories until my face came into view at the gate.

No...

It couldn't be.

There was not one trace of Merrill and Claude anywhere in his memory. But, how could that be? I was sure that he had something to do with Mariam's death. He had arrived not a day later than them; it couldn't have been a coincidence. He couldn't have been telling me the truth.

But, if he was, then...I just tortured someone that didn't fit the criteria. I had just tortured an innocent man.

I dropped my hands from my tight grip around his temple and stepped back. He hung his head the moment that I let go, and I was, for the first time in centuries, at a loss for words. His body slumped to the ground. He had passed out from the rest of his remaining energy being completely drained.

I hadn't slept at all that night.

I could have sworn that he had something to do with both of those murderers, that there were others.

Now the question was... What do I do with him? And how to tell Emilia? Should I tell her?

"Your grace?" Callum had pulled me from my thoughts as I was slumped against my chair with a grape pressed lightly against my lips. Callum and I were sitting at the table in the dining hall, having breakfast.

I slipped the grape inside my mouth and asked, "What is it, little bird?"

"Is everything alright?"

I leaned forward, grabbed my glass, and took a long drink from it before getting up and leaving the dining hall.

Before I exited the hall I called out, "Emilia!"

I had too much on my mind to deal with Callum right now.

I walked toward the kitchen doors and as I passed by the tower doors, it opened.

Emilia appeared. "I know that you told me to not feed him, but if you are going to continue to torture him, he needs the basic nutrients to keep him alive."

I couldn't stop staring at her, wondering how I would bring up the information I had learned last night. I thought that I was going to know what I was going to say to her when I saw her and called for her to get it over with, but I was, again, at a loss of words.

I hesitantly reached out a hand and placed it on her shoulder.

Her eyes widened. "I am sorry that I went against your orders. I will never disobey you again."

I shook my head. "It's not that. I walked through the hunter's mind last night and I found some harrowing information that I felt the need to share with you." Best to push through. "I found out that his father is the man who is in charge of the Reaping."

Her face paled and her body fell to the floor in a heap too fast for me to catch her. I didn't know what to do as she asked in a gravelly voice, "What?"

"His father is—"

"Gerard Corleone," she whispered, eyes staring off into the distance.

I bent down so that I could look into her eyes. "The hunter did not approve of his father's actions. He is innocent." I didn't know why I felt the need to say that to her.

She wasn't crying or anything. Her face was blank, like she wasn't really there.

"Emilia?" I shook her a little. "Emilia!"

Her eyes met mine slowly as she swallowed hard. Her hands shook as she signed, *I don't remember.* Tears appeared at her water line, lips trembling. *I don't remember anything from that night.*

Her admission took my breath away. I couldn't help her. Not with this. I wish I was better at this, and I had to look away.

I felt her tap my hand clenched on my leg and looked back as she signed, *Can you... Can you look into his memories and find the man who hurt me?*

I took a moment to come up with the right words to tell her, but the only thing that came out was, "Of course."

I knew there was a slim chance of successfully finding anything because that would mean that the prisoner would had to have been physically around when that particular event happened, but I didn't have the heart to tell her that. The answers for what happened to her would be in her mind, but they had been sealed away to protect her sanity.

I gave it one more moment before standing and asking, "Did he eat anything?"

Without looking at me, she shook her head.

What was that fool thinking by not eating? How long had it even been? Time had always seemed insignificant as I had an endless supply of it. How long could humans go without food and drink?

Killing innocent lives now? Circe mocked.

Shut up, no one was talking to you.

Her laughter rang in my ears and slowly faded away into the background as I rushed up to the tower.

Chapter Six

I didn't know what to say to him. I had tortured him for days, not caring about his needs. I was so sure he was guilty that I couldn't see past the rage that blinded me from possibly discerning the truth earlier. I felt my breathing grow ragged and my heart thundered in my chest. I was getting sloppy, reckless.

Now I had to decide what to do with him. I could kill him and be done with it, but that was against the rules. His purpose here was to hunt the beast, stop the sacrifices, and save his sister. None of that warranted death. But if I let him live, he could return with other hunters. I knew he would, even if he promised that he wouldn't. Humans weren't to be trusted and I had given him every reason to hate me.

I took a deep breath before pushing the door open and heading into the room as a thought passed through my mind.

Or I could keep him...

Take my time in deciding how to take care of his father.

I narrowed my eyes and made my way over to him. Since he was no longer a threat, I allowed myself a moment to look at him—really look at him. His black hair was shorter than the men's from my youth, but the way it looked on him was nothing short of remarkable. My gaze lingered on the chiseled edge of his jaw, strikingly sharp as if it were sculpted from stone. His muscles bulged beneath his ripped shirt, and sweat beaded on his skin.

I thought back to a few days ago, about my hand wrapped around his neck and how he towered over me. To anyone else, his demeanor could make anyone fearful of the damage that he could inflict, but not me. No, nothing scared me anymore.

I sighed and lifted a brow when I saw one of his muscles tense. "You can stop pretending to be asleep now."

He opened his eyes but didn't move. His muscles must have been atrophied. "Are you happy now?"

I raised my eyes until we were staring at each other. I tilted my head, hair falling in front of my face, and asked, "Why would I be happy?"

"You got what you wanted, didn't you? Found out I was telling you the truth? If not, then I wouldn't be breathing right now."

I scoffed, set down the plate full of food I had taken from Emilia, and brought it up here for him. "You're right about one thing. If I had found out that you were a part of their group then you would be dead...eventually. No, I would have drawn out your suffering for years until your body finally gave out and killed you out of mercy."

He widened his eyes and snapped his mouth shut, seemingly shocked by my admission. And I swear I saw a shudder of fear pass over his body, one that I knew he tried to hold back but couldn't.

"But that is not why I am up here." I looked away, lost in thought. "I have yet to decide what to do with you."

"What do you mean? You found out the truth! Now, you do the right thing and let me go."

"The right thing?" I pondered, finger tapping my chin.

"Yes!" He exclaimed. He was getting more and more agitated by the second.

And the more agitated he got, the more the vein on his forehead became apparent. I wanted nothing more than to poke it and see exactly how angry he could get. I had never had someone defy me as much as this male, and it was profoundly entertaining.

"Well, answer me!"

I guess I was taking too long to reply to him.

I focused my attention back on him and completely ignored his plea. "I saw what was in your mind. I know why you came in search of the beast and, unfortunately, you will not be able to accomplish your task. You are well-known in your community and there is the possibility that others might come for you.

But...if you were to stay, as your father said, no one would come for you. He would make sure of it."

I continued when it was apparent that he couldn't form a coherent thought. "I know of the rumors. No one returns when they venture out into the forest in search of slaying the beast. And to keep up appearances, it doesn't matter what I decide; you can't go back."

Finally finding his voice, he asked, "And why would you care about the rumors? Unless... Unless you... Oh god. You?"

The pieces were finally fitting together in his mind.

"You aren't the brightest in your family, are you?"

His mouth dried as his question turned into more of a statement. "You're the beast."

"Thank goodness that face of yours is so handsome," I said, smirking.

"You—you can't do that." His throat sounded scratchy, he was parched. "You can't keep me here. I have a family, I have—"

"In a hurry to get back to your betrothed? Or take over your family's business of tossing children to the forest?" I scoffed at the idea. "Yes, it sounds like you have so much going for you."

"My memories, what you saw, that doesn't decide who I am. I still have a choice and you're taking it from me." He looked shattered and horrified.

I shuddered at his words, begging Circe to not choose this moment to haunt my thoughts and force me to feel my own memories all over again. I didn't want to break into hysteria here.

A choice. I was never given a choice. But, I never asked to be a magic born. Never wished to be cursed. Never wanted to be immortal. I stopped cursing a worthless god and realized that life was unfair. We all do what we must to survive.

I looked down, ignoring his words. There was still a full plate of bread and cheese sitting right next to him. "You haven't eaten."

"Tampered with, no doubt."

Understandably, he didn't trust me, and I didn't trust him, but this was exasperating. "If I wanted to kill you, I could have done that numerous times already. You can trust that my servant did nothing to your food."

He eyed it hungrily, but warily. He didn't move.

I sighed and walked closer to him, causing him to tense. I raised the hem of my black satin dress and slowly pulled it up, exposing my thighs, and knelt down, straddling him. He sucked in a breath as I sat my bare pussy on his lap—utterly sinful.

He gave me a sly smile but grunted when he tried to move his arms to attack me, thinking it the perfect opportunity since I had gotten so close to him. I smirked as he narrowed his eyes at me when his arms wouldn't move. My shadows, once again, invaded his mind.

I smiled to myself as I leaned to the side, took the bread, and sniffed it. It was full of the flavor of the herbs from the garden, light and fluffy with a crunchy exterior. I brought the bread to my lips, flicked my tongue against it, and slowly took a bite, moaning in delight. I could feel his length move at the noise, stiffening. His breathing grew deep—heavy.

I gasped at the sensation, chills running through my body. Salacious intent danced in my eyes as shame washed over his features.

I waited a moment before responding: "See... No poison." I brought the food to his lips, waiting for them to part, but he refused. Closing his mouth even tighter. Stubborn male.

I grabbed his hair, yanked his head back, and shoved it into his mouth until he had no choice but to bite down.

I threw the bread down onto the plate and grabbed his chin making sure that he didn't spit it out. "Chew."

After a few moments, he slowly began to chew, then swallowed. Looking over my face, a thousand thoughts were clear for me to see. He wasn't sure what his next move would be. Would he try to kill himself? Or play my games?

I rolled my eyes and shifted on his lap as he continued to grow beneath me. He closed his eyes, concentrating on anything but me sitting on him. "You will eat. You chose not to do it yourself so now I will do it for you."

I went to pick the cheese up when he said, "I do want to eat, but I need my hands to do so."

"Then why didn't you eat earlier?" I raised a brow.

"There was a possibility of it being poisoned." I just kept my brow raised as he continued to stare at me. "How do you expect me to eat if I can't use my hands?"

"I suppose you do have a point. And, if I unchain you, then you will eat?"

"Yes," he rushed out too energetically.

I knew what he was trying to do. I had been around long enough to know that when a wounded animal was backed into a corner, they would do all they could to fight their way out. Though, I never gave anyone a chance, growing bored with the others, but this one... This one felt different, a feeling that I couldn't place quite yet. No matter, he had piqued my interest.

"I suppose you do have a point."

He smirked, feeling triumphant that his plan was working.

I flicked my wrists, and his chains unlocked and the moment it did he moved quickly, lifting my body up and pinned me down to the ground, straddling my stomach. One hand wrapped around my throat and the other had both of my wrists pinned above me. I couldn't help but feel shocked that he had moved so fast as it looked like he didn't have an ounce of fight left in him.

This human was full of surprises.

"Wrong move, witch."

I smiled up at him. "Harder." A look of surprise crossed his features that made me want to laugh uncontrollably if I wasn't pinned down. "You think this can hurt me? Think again."

"Shut up! After I kill you, I am—"

That struck a nerve. The laughter died in my throat.

"You wouldn't be the first to try and guess what happened to them? I killed them all." I clenched my teeth together, then got a funny idea. "*Si hoc incidas, tunc valde stultus es.*"

I laughed at my own joke, he growled, "What did you just say?"

Loosely it could be translated to our language to mean, *If you fall for this, then you are dull-witted.*

I replied, "You will never leave this castle. I have placed a spell on you binding you to these lands. You can't leave."

He squeezed my throat tighter. "You're lying!"

I continued to smile at him as a chill ran through me. Everything about this was exhilarating. I knew I shouldn't be enjoying it, but I was.

"No, I'm not." My voice was so low that I wasn't sure if he could hear it.

He was desperate, so desperate that I could feel it, as thick as the fog outside.

"If I kill you—"

"I can smell the desperation on you." I laughed in his face, as much as the restricted movement would allow. "I can't die. You think I haven't tried over the years?"

I squirmed a bit under him to test exactly how strong he was and he didn't disappoint, but I could tell that he was still weak. He wasn't strong enough to fight me in his current condition.

My words changed his features and softened them for a moment, but he quickly shook it off. "I could beat you with one hand tied behind my back," he seethed.

"I think you are too weak to fight." It was slightly difficult to talk around my throat being constricted like a snake.

I could see that he was determined and wasn't likely to take no for an answer. I was curious to see what his next move would be.

"I want to fight," he growled.

"I have magic." I was surprised that he would propose such an asinine idea.

"I am *not* afraid of your powers."

"No, it seems like you aren't." I saw something in him I liked, perhaps a bit too much. "Even if you kill me, I have placed a spell on you so that you can't leave." I could see that he was fighting with himself, his grip loosening, wondering if I was telling the truth. "Sure, I could be lying, but is that something you are willing to risk?"

He took a moment to think about what his next move was. His thighs gripped my stomach tightly, his large form hunched over mine.

I stared into his moss-green eyes and waited when he finally asked, "Care to make a wager?"

This male had officially piqued my interest. This was the most fun I'd had in a long time.

"A wager?"

"If I win, you're dead and I am free to go back to my village."

"And if I win?"

He narrowed his eyes at me. "That won't happen, so there's no use in worrying about that outcome."

"It's only fair that we talk about the *slim* chance I have at beating you."

"Coin."

I looked at him pointedly. Was he slow-witted? He seemed to realize that would not be something I could want and sat silently on top of me, his hand still firmly on my throat.

"The wager is off. You have nothing to offer." I didn't move from under him, too curious about what he would say next.

He closed his eyes out of frustration, tired of wasting more time, and gritted out, "You win, you can do whatever you want with me."

The fight in this one was foolish, but at the same time, invigorating.

"Anything, you say?" I closed my eyes and pretended to think about it and asked, "So, if I win, then you will stay here as my pet?" I narrowed my eyes, studying him. "I will use you. I will hurt you. I will break you."

A shudder fell over him. He seemed to take a moment to consider the wager, or perhaps contemplate my words and what they meant.

"We have a deal, but no magic. We fight fair."

"Very well," I tsked. "I accept the terms of the wager, but first you eat."

"Stop wasting time and let's get this over with."

"You are obviously too weak to fight. I can feel your hand trembling. It's no fun hunting a wounded animal. Eat."

He hesitantly let go of my neck and bounced back on his heels, standing up and raising his fists in a fighting stance. "No, we do this now."

"You need to eat." Nothing. He didn't back down. I sighed. "Fine, I did try to warn you."

I rolled my eyes, got up from the ground, wiped myself off, and stood there waiting for him to make the first move.

He waited a second before he rushed toward me, fist flying through the air. I waited until the last second to move my head just enough to evade his attack and sidestepped him, tripping him in the process.

He landed hard on his stomach and knocked his head against the stone floor. Even I winced from the sound and knew that he was badly injured.

"Foolish egotistical male."

I went over to him and, to my surprise, he began to get back up. I allowed him to, and he used all of his strength to throw multiple punches at me and missed every time. He was panting, using the wall to hold himself up. He wiped sweat off of his forehead with the back of his hand. He pushed off the wall and approached me, his movements slowing down, growing lethargic.

He must have used the last bit of his energy when he pinned me on the ground.

His body was giving out, the fool. I warned him. Had he been at his full strength this would have been much more enjoyable. I just needed to wait him out. He stumbled forward and just as I was about to catch him, he reached under his shirt and pulled out something shiny. Before I knew it, I felt something sharp slice through my side.

"I told you I would kill you," he panted.

I looked down and saw blood dripping down my sides, soaking into my dress. I rolled my eyes and looked back up at him. His eyes had brightened as if he knew in his heart that he had succeeded in killing me. I stepped back, pulled the shard of glass out without flinching, and threw it to the ground.

"You'll have to try harder than that. And you cheated."

His eyes widened, clearly confused, and just as I was waiting for another attack, his eyes rolled in the back of his head, and he fell forward. I reached out and caught him, and if it hadn't been for my magic, I would have fallen along with him.

I dragged him over to the wall, placed him down next to the food, and said, "If I were a better person, I wouldn't say this, but unlucky for you, I'm not human so... I told you so."

He shouldn't have fought me when I entered his mind, nor hit his head that hard against the ground. That coupled with no food or drink and being suspended for endless hours could even bring a talented hunter to near collapse.

I took a deep breath, coming to terms with the new addition. "You've lost. Now you'll eat." He barely opened his eyes and narrowed them at me though I was done with his games. "Or I will force the food down your throat."

He knew that I meant what I said, and without sitting up, he reached for the cheese and nibbled a small piece. He closed his eyes, savoring the taste. And before I knew it, he was scarfing down the food as if his life depended on it. In his case, it did.

I stared at him and pondered what him being at his full strength looked like. This was a pathetic excuse for a fight. His body was moving out of sheer will and nothing else.

He leaned up on his side just enough to be able to drink the entire goblet of water and guzzled it down sloppily. He dropped the cup with a loud clang and collapsed onto the ground, exhausted from the fight.

"You're mine now, but you can worry about that tomorrow. For now, rest."

"No, I can—"

"*Sonum,*" I said as I blew the powder in his face.

I crouched next to him, sliced the pad of my finger, and pressed it against his lips. Allowing just enough to enter his body to heal any life-threatening injuries, but not enough to replenish all of his strength. He was a hunter, after all. I couldn't let my guard down even with my powers. He needed uninterrupted rest if he was to fully heal from his injuries.

You mean the injuries that you caused.

"That's beside the point."

He has a lot of fight in him, doesn't he? Remind you of anyone?

"Leave it to you to find a way to talk about yourself, again."

If I don't, then who will?

I ignored the pest and walked out of the tower, placing a locking spell over the door and windows, ensuring he couldn't escape.

"Sleep tight for tomorrow the real fun begins."

CHAPTER SEVEN

*T*he sun was so bright in the sky that I had to squint my eyes against it.

"*Dreadful.*"

"*Your highness, the food is ready.*"

I turned to find one of the servants bowing, the smell of fresh bread hit my nose from behind her. My mouth was watering as I rushed to the amazing picnic underneath the shade of the oak tree they had set up for us: mother, sister and me.

Our kingdom used to be quiet and simple. We thrived, our people were happy, and the days were boring but so very peaceful.

As a girl, I used to dread the routine of it all. My father only had two daughters, meaning every day, I was being trained in something new. Something I could use to help lead the people when he was gone. I complained often about it, but now, with my father's war on magic, I longed for those simple days again.

He was often in the war room, his advisors preaching hysteria, traveling from village to village outside the castle grounds to hang the accused. My mother sat so beautifully on the ground, picking at the greenest of grapes on her plate, savoring the juices, while women, children, and men were swinging in town squares.

Sometimes at night, I could hear them screaming.

I gripped the handful of flowers that I had picked and handed one to each of them before sitting down. Mother smiled before bringing them up to her face, inhaling deeply.

"What a thoughtful daughter I have! Lovely of you to join us." Mother's voice was as lovely as a lullaby. So lovely that I could listen to her talk every second of every day.

"Let me smell, Mama!" Belle looked just like our mother, voice just as lovely, but with father's strong will. A dangerous combination.

Mother lowered the flower down to Annabelle's face and she inhaled just as deeply as mother had and sneezed.

They laughed, and I did try to smile with them.

"Your tutor tells me you're daydreaming more often lately," my mother observed. "What's wrong, my darling? Is it the arranged marriage proposal? Your father would never make a decision without your approval. And it's not for almost an entire decade. You have time to get used to the idea. Don't fret."

"It's not that," I said, but that wasn't entirely true. I had no interest in my suitors because my interests lied in books, travel, and...magic. Three things my father would never tolerate. "It just seems like the hangings are getting worse." I swallowed, carefully navigating the topic. "I've read some of the documents on the accused. The things they are executing people for are just," my voice dropped to a whisper, "silly. They hanged a man for witchcraft because he used a tonic of his own invention to save his newborn babe from a sickness."

My mother's body straightened. "You shouldn't be sneaking into your father's office and reading that."

"I shouldn't?" I challenged her. "I'm going to be queen one day, aren't I? Is Father expecting me to travel from village to village and hang people without proper evidence? I've read the books on magic, Mother. It is not tonics or strange looks, or even people who behave oddly."

Her mouth went agape. "Stay out of the forbidden rooms."

We both heard a noise, a cough. A strange woman that seemed to appear out of nowhere stood beside my mother. Mother looked over her shoulder and sighed with relief.

"This is Circe, and starting today she will be your governess. I am certain you are in good hands, and she will help with all this daydreaming."

"Another one already?" The last one didn't last but a month. And the one before that had disappeared into the night after looking after me for an even shorter amount of time. I knew my mother was desperate, but I couldn't allow this one to stay, couldn't let them find out my secret.

The woman smiled at me and bowed. "It is a pleasure to make your acquaintance, your highness."

Our eyes met, and the connection did something to me. Something odd. The feeling I had before, panic and anger over my father's choices, eased a bit. Could I trust this one? I desperately wanted to. I was tired of suffering alone.

She was older than my mother or was she? I could not place her age, but she was beautiful. Her skin was pale, but she had a glow about her, with light brown hair braided behind her back that reached to her hips. Her dark eyes were bright and kind. I got the sense she was going to be a tougher egg to crack.

"I don't think you will rid yourself of this one so easily."

I turned to my mother who had a knowing look on her face. A look that I couldn't quite place.

I looked away from them both.

The governess took a seat beside me in the grass, with little grace, crossing her legs over the other. "It is an honor, your majesty."

"Perhaps you will not think so after a few short weeks," I muttered.

My mother scowled in response.

"I think you'll come to find I am not so easily scared off, your highness."

Now

"Your grace?"

I surged forward out of the bed and landed upon someone, one hand wrapped around their throat and the other lifted, ready to strike a fatal blow.

"Your grace!" Someone squealed out.

I blinked rapidly and looked down at the face under me. Callum.

I squeezed my hand, extinguishing the shadows that had encompassed it.

"I could have killed you. I was about to *kill* you!" I couldn't keep the anger from my voice.

He still couldn't talk as I was still squeezing his vocal cords too tightly. I released his throat slowly.

He sucked in a huge breath as he coughed. "It's Emilia."

"Where is she?" I finally took a look at him. He had deep scratches across his face, blood smeared. This episode had to be bad if this was the outcome.

"The chapel."

I retreated, ran down the steps of the South Wing, and went through the halls so fast that they were a blur. Why was she there? Were her nightmares back? It didn't matter, I needed to hurry before she harmed herself. If she died, then I would have failed again.

Better hurry then.

I hissed and ran faster until I burst through the chapel doors to find an ungodly scene. Emilia was standing behind the altar with a blade raised above her head. Her mouth was moving, but I couldn't hear what she was saying.

"Emilia?" She continued as though she didn't hear me. I hardened my voice. "Emilia."

She paused and looked at me, cocked her head to the side, and she continued to say something that I still couldn't hear. Her grip on the blade was so tight that I could see her hand shaking from the intensity of it.

Now that I had her attention I walked up to her tentatively, not wanting to make any sudden movements.

"Put it down." She narrowed her eyes at me, but I said calmly, "I order you to put the blade down."

I made it to the steps. I was almost there. I was close enough that I could hear what she was saying, but it didn't make sense. It wasn't a language that I understood. I didn't think that was possible. It sounded old.

A noise behind me told me that Callum was there to help. "Oh my god. What is she—"

"Do not move, Callum! She hasn't had one of these nightmares since she first came. I don't want to startle her while in this state."

I didn't dare take my eyes off her as I walked up the stone steps until the only thing that was between us was the altar. The moment I touched the altar her eyes rolled into the back of her head and she brought the blade down, cutting deeply into her forearm while she said, "You will pay for what you did to me."

A chill went down my spine.

The blood dropped onto the blade and then she was falling. I pushed the table aside and barely caught her as her body dropped to the floor. I cradled her head in my lap as I heard Callum running toward us.

I gently laid her down as I put my hands over her arm. Fuck. I could see to the bone. Blood ran over my hands and I ran a nail over the skin on my wrist and pressed it tightly against her lips. She drank my blood deeply, and it wasn't long before the laceration began to repair itself until there was no evidence that there was a wound to begin with.

I bowed my head, not understanding what just happened.

"Why would she do this?" I looked up to find Callum kneeling on Emilia's other side, his face horror-stricken. "Has she ever done something like this before?"

I nodded. "Yes. Though it was many years ago. I don't know what could have possibly prompted this."

Then my eyes closed as I remembered the prisoner in the tower and where he was from. I had told her earlier today who his father was.

All you ever do is cause others pain. What a sad, miserable life.

"Leave!"

I don't know if Callum thought I was talking about him, but he didn't move. "May I please help carry her back to her room?"

I took a deep breath, and before I could reply to him, Emilia's eyes fluttered open. She tried to speak but then she swallowed. Her voice must have been strained from what just happened.

"Don't speak. You're fine." Her eyes roved around and then widened in worry. "We are in the chapel where Callum found you, but you are safe. Everything is alright now."

Her eyes landed on mine as she brought her hands up, *What did I do?*

"Nothing of significance. Just a nightmare." She screamed out in horror at the sight of the blood on her hands. I waved my hands over them, manipulating her mind to think the blood was never there until I could get her to her bathing chamber to wipe away all evidence.

She blinked as her body started to shake.

"Callum, carry her." He nodded and lifted her in his arms. She pressed into his body as she became so still that one might think she was a statue. I had to look away as she looked too fragile.

We reached her chambers and when I entered, it was just as organized as it was when I came in here the last time. It was the room that my cousins would stay in when they visited. It was grand. Her four-poster bed was against the wall to the left with sheer curtains draped around it. The window was open, the curtains billowing in the wind.

Despite it being the beginning of fall, the room was freezing.

Callum followed me as I flung open the bathing chamber doors and began to fill the tub with hot water. Her eyes were open as I looked back at Callum standing behind me, awaiting instructions, but she wasn't saying anything. I wasn't sure if she was conscious, but she was awake enough to stand on her own.

"Set her down." He did as I instructed and left.

I felt the water to make sure it wouldn't scald her and then lifted her nightgown over her head until she was completely nude in front of me. "Get in."

She did as she was told and sat down, head bowed.

Without saying a word, I picked up a tonic, rubbed it in my hands, then lathered it thoroughly in her hair. I let that sit while I picked up a bar of sweet-smelling soap and rubbed it over her shoulders, down her back, and arms. I moved around the tub and lifted each leg, taking care to not scrub too high. When I had finished washing her body, I looked back into her face to find her crying. I reached out, took her face in my hands, and began slowly rubbing away the blood with my thumbs until there was not one trace of blood left.

I never knew what to do when she cried. I would rather take action and kill whoever had caused her harm, but I couldn't do that now.

"I'm sorry." Her voice was so soft.

I stood up to grab the towel that was on the side of the water basin and said with my back to her, "I know this happened because of what I told you earlier, but I looked through his memories, and there is nothing about what happened to you."

I had searched through all of his memories; tore through every part of his mind because I thought there was a chance that the couple was there. I would have remembered seeing Emilia, but I didn't.

Her eyes met mine and she nodded.

"Aren't you going to ask about what I am going to do with him?"

She closed her eyes. I assumed it was to beg me to kill him, but I was surprised when she shook her head. "I would never ask you to explain yourself, nor do I have the right to make any requests."

"Even for a male who is the son of the one who did this to you?"

"Even then. You would *never* allow anyone to survive if they were anything less than innocent."

She was right. I would kill him if he was guilty of this crime or any other. Unfortunately for me, he was not a threat. He wished to kill me, but I saw a glimpse into the boy he was and I was certain that he wouldn't hurt my humans.

She was also right that I didn't owe her an explanation. I didn't owe her anything, but I found myself telling her all the same, "I am keeping him. He is the first born son to that monster and though he is an egotistical brute of a male, I cannot in good conscience kill him as he has done nothing wrong. It wasn't for lack of trying either. I couldn't even find anything in his past to warrant punishment. You know my rules." I couldn't punish him for his father's crimes. "His father will not come looking for him which is why I must keep him. If I sent him back, they would surely send more. This is the only way." I sighed. "I will instruct him to not approach you."

"You are too kind, your grace."

I handed her the towel. "Dry off and head to bed."

I didn't wait for a response as I exited the bathing room to find that Callum had shut the window and started a fire for her so that she wouldn't be cold. Good, now I didn't have to. I kept walking out of the room and leisurely walked back to the South Wing.

What could she have meant when she said that I would pay for what I did to her? Or was she even talking to me? She was looking straight at me, but maybe she was seeing someone else. I could go into her mind and pry, but I had learned that Emilia's memory was fragmented because of what happened to her and so I wasn't sure what good it would do. Not when what I would witness might not even be a true memory.

I suppose it didn't matter. She was awake, and if it were to happen again, I would handle it like I always did.

I absentmindedly ran a hand through my hair, and it was sticky. I lowered my hand in front of my face to find that there was dried blood in my hair. I stopped in front of a mirror in one of the halls and was taken aback by my appearance.

There was blood everywhere. My face was smeared with it. I didn't even remember touching my face. My hair was matted, but the brown was so dark that you wouldn't notice the blood in the dark.

The blood was a stark difference to my pale-brown skin. I had lost the glow I was so proud of when I was a child, something which my mother wouldn't stop commending.

Despite the pale skin, I was striking.

I didn't eat much which honed my features from any extra fat that I might have had and sharpened them. My brown eyes were at times so dark that they appeared black. They were hollow, dead, which was appropriate for how I felt on the inside. I finally had to look away, not caring to stare at the creature who ruined everything.

Reminiscing again, are we?

"There's nothing to reminisce about."

I would beg to differ. We had fun.

"*We* didn't have fun. You're dead. Just like the rest of them."

She clicked her tongue at me as if she were disappointed. *Don't you find it rude to speak to your governess like that?*

"You are not her. You are nothing to me."

It was silent for a moment and I thought that she was gone, but alas... *You did this to yourself.*

By the time Emilia had calmed down and I had taken yet another bath, I was too awake to think about attempting to go back to sleep so I went to the tower as the sky was starting to lighten.

He has a lot of fight in him, doesn't he? Remind you of anyone?

I cocked my head to the side. "If you are insinuating that we are the same, then you couldn't be more wrong."

I narrowed my eyes at him as I stood over his sleeping form, still under the spell. He had his arms under his head as a makeshift pillow, his knees folded into a tight ball to stave off the chill of the air. I suppose I could have given him a blanket, but it never occurred to me as anyone who came into the tower never left.

I made a face as I took him in and heat pooled in my core. I wasn't blind. He was one of the most handsome men that I had ever seen in my existence. And that mouth... All of the vulgar things he said about me only fueled the desire. I would need to find Callum soon.

Already wanting to fuck him?

"So would you if you could." She laughed at that.

I looked over his injuries and found that he had a rather nasty cut along his arm—no, multiple cuts around his body. Indents in his skin where my nails dug into him. Dried blood on the back of his head where he hit it on the ground. All of these injuries were just from the fight? He was in worse condition than I thought.

I scoffed, the fool. I tried to warn him to wait until he got his strength back before he tried to fight me head-on.

I nudged him with my foot, ready to play, but it didn't work. I allowed him to sleep for an entire day which was more than enough time. At this point, I was being generous. I knew he wasn't dead because I could see the faint movement of his chest rising and falling.

I took a step back and continued to ogle him.

I couldn't help but rove my eyes further down until they stopped on the appendage beneath his trousers. I could see its outline through them and had to bite my bottom lip to keep from moaning. My thoughts grew darker by the second.

I was a mess, a filthy mess. I'd just tortured him, and now wanted to undress him to get a better look. Could I handle another plaything? He was stronger–willed than Callum. He'd be a problem.

I'd have to break him.

"What to do with you first?" I pondered.

I hadn't thought further than making the choice that he had to stay. I couldn't give him the same allowances as the others. He wasn't necessarily my prisoner, but he wasn't exactly free to choose to leave.

Such a conundrum.

I kneeled on the ground and slapped his cheek hard enough to sting.

I chuckled as he was startled awake. "So, have you given up then?"

He narrowed his eyes. "I gave my word that if you won then you could do whatever you want with me. I am nothing without my word."

He shuffled around, and reached for something near him when he thought that his words had distracted me enough.

"So, that isn't a weapon clenched in your left hand just waiting for me to let my guard down?" I asked while pointing to the hand closest to the window.

He tightened his hold. "I can't be too careful around you. I don't trust you."

"Neither do I. Lucky for you, you don't have to trust me as you are my new pet, and I quote, 'you can do whatever you want with me.' And believe me, the possibilities are running rampant through my mind." I lowered my voice as I took a step toward him. "Let's test it."

"Test what?"

"If you can do what you're told, like a good boy. Take off your clothes." I licked my lips and found him following the movement.

He did as he was told and lifted up his shirt until it was no longer tucked in. He grabbed the hem and pulled it up and over his head, dropping it to the floor.

I looked down at his trousers, and I could see him begin to snarl, but he did as he was told.

I rubbed my legs together and could feel my breath shortening. I wondered if he felt the same way. I turned around and exaggerated my hips as I walked to my chair. I looked over my shoulder enough to see that he was breathing rather heavily, looking me up and down. With a smile, I sat down.

"On your hands and knees." We stared at each other, but he still didn't move. "If you won't listen to simple instructions then—"

Without another word, he got on his hands and knees without taking his eyes away from mine.

"Crawl to me." He gritted his teeth together so dramatically that it was a wonder that he didn't chip a tooth.

He crawled. One hand and foot in front of the other. His hips swayed as he moved, muscles shifting under his weight. He crawled until he was directly in front of me. I reached down next to the chair where I had set a collar down and fastened it around his neck, which was connected to a leather rope. His eyes widened, and he tried to back away from me when I grabbed the leash and pulled him back to me until our mouths were almost touching.

"Bark."

He growled. "Fuck you." I leaned forward and bit his lip hard. He hissed. "Do your worst, girl," wincing from the pain as blood appeared.

I licked my lips and swallowed his metallic blood.

"Girl? You clearly don't know who you're talking to."

"Enlighten me, because I think that I am looking at someone completely out of their mind."

I smiled at him. "I lost it years ago." He snapped his mouth shut, not knowing how to respond. "Well, since you are going to be here for the foreseeable future, I think introductions are in order."

"You first."

"That mouth of yours is going to get you into trouble, more than you already are. I could find other things for you to do with that mouth," I said seductively, "but I will humor you just this once. I am the stuff of nightmares. The story parents tell their children to make them behave. You may call me 'Your grace'."

"Your grace?"

"Yes, I am the queen, after all. It only makes sense," I said coyly.

"Queen? There has not been a queen here in centuries. What's your name?"

"You don't need to know that, as you won't be using it. Your grace... Your majesty... Mistress... *Lover...*" I smirked. "Any of those will do. Now, what is your name?"

"If you won't give yours then there is no reason to give mine."

I scoffed and looked away; the nerve of this human was insurmountable. "You are just begging to be punished, aren't you?"

Before he could move, I spun us around and pushed him back into my chair as I used my shadows to secure ropes around his wrists, legs, and stomach.

He pulled at his restraints, testing them, but every time he pulled, they tightened.

"I wouldn't do that. You'll cut off your circulation and I am not done playing with you yet."

I sauntered around him slowly and stopped at the side of the chair, calling forth my power, and reached into the shadows and extracted a knife from the kitchen. He eyed me warily. I grazed the tip of the blade across his bare stomach, down the material of his undergarments, and over his thigh, causing it to get dangerously close to his most sensitive area. He hissed and stared at me with pure disgust in those moss-green eyes, but maybe with a hint of something else. His cock hardened even more under the pressure of the blade which only confirmed my suspicions.

Did I have a masochist in my grasp?

"If I didn't know any better, I would assume that you enjoyed the feel of the steel against your skin."

He jerked his leg from what I can only assume was the bite of the cold blade, but didn't say another word, just continued staring at me as if he were challenging me to truly do my worst.

"I will give you one last chance. Tell me your name."

His eyes dropped to his lap, and said in a tone full of disdain, "Never."

I walked around until I stood in front of him.

"I may look young to you, but I promise that I have more experience than anyone you have ever met. So, I know a couple of ways to get the answer out of you." Something came over me and all I wanted to do was feel the strength of his thighs under me again, his cock growing for me. I situated myself on him again. "Do you like the feel of my pussy on you, hunter?"

I wiggled my hips in slow, precise movements. Leaned my head back, moaning out loud.

I leaned forward and whispered in his ear, "Do you have any complaints?" And bit his earlobe causing him to buck into me. I gasped when I felt his massive erection hitting my entrance, the material causing a delicious friction.

I laughed and leaned back. I ran my hands through the hair on his chest; he did not disappoint. His father may have wanted him to become head of the household, but this man wasn't made for such a sedentary life.

He tensed when I licked up his neck and whispered, my hot breath against his ear, "What is your name?"

He leaned forward, as far as the restraints would allow, and said, "You can call me anything you want, harlot."

His anger was so palpable that I could taste it.

Two could play this game.

He was getting on my last nerve. I reached down and stuffed my hand in his undergarments, grabbed his balls, and lightly squeezed.

Speaking against his neck, my nose brushing under his ear, I said, "I don't think you are *grasping* the position you're in. You are mine to do with as I please. I decide your future... You can live here peacefully like the others, or you can be stubborn, and I will leave you locked up here permanently and play with you whenever I want. So, let's try. One. Last. Time." Squeezing even harder, emphasizing the words. "What. Is. Your. Name?"

His breathing had shortened, and he kept swallowing hard. He still had not uttered a single word. After a few seconds, I pulled, causing him to groan, arching his back, his bare chest pressed against mine. I would be lying if I said his reactions weren't making me feel a certain way.

I needed more, needed to see if I could feel anything else. I withdrew my hand a moment and saw surprise enter his features until I licked my hand and grabbed onto his cock, firmly stroking his cock agonizingly slowly. He shut his eyes and angled his head back, exposing his neck to me.

He was enjoying this and surprisingly, so was I. He was determined to not say anything, but I would get it out of him one way or another. I leaned forward and ran my nose along his neck, causing him to stiffen even more and hold his breath. And then I licked the ball at his throat.

"What is your name?" I nibbled along his jaw.

He tried to suppress another moan, but he couldn't. He had grown even bigger. I could feel it pressing even harder against me. I surprised myself when I started to move back and forth with the motion of my hands on him as if he were fucking me.

"Bastian Corleone," he breathed out the words.

The moment his answer left his lips, I stood up, leaving him wanting more. He would never admit it, but his body didn't lie. He wanted me even if I did have him tied up in my tower.

He licked his dry lips and looked at me with hooded eyes. The mere possibility of sex could drive sane men to insanity, and I wanted to know exactly how far I could push him until he broke.

His eyes roamed my body. I had chosen to wear a floor-length satin gown with a plunging neckline that hugged my curves—revealing and easily discardable. Something I was sure the women of his time did not do.

I shrugged it off until I was completely naked in front of him. I wasn't shy and would often walk around the grounds in the nude, loving the way it allowed me a little piece of freedom. I also wasn't naive enough not to see the way my body made men react and would use it to my advantage when necessary.

I despised the way women were always made to feel bad about having a body that made men weak in the knees or women sick with envy.

In my opinion, women should use the assets that the gods gave them.

Mmmm... Bastian...

His eyes were heavy with lust. I knew what he was thinking, but I wouldn't give him the release his body so desperately needed. He needed to learn his place and know when to shut that big mouth of his.

"Watch and learn."

I called Callum.

"Yes, your grace?"

He stopped dead in his tracks when he saw me naked in front of the prisoner. He kept his eyes on the stranger, and Bastian's eyes were on him. I knew he was confused, but not for long.

I walked over to another chair, brought it closer to Bastian, and sat down on the edge. The look on his face as I spread my legs open, allowing him to see all of me, was exhilarating, a mix of arousal, disbelief, and shock. I lifted one knee up, licked my fingers tasting him on me, and rubbed them up and down my pussy.

I looked at Callum and said, "Show our prisoner how to properly treat a queen."

He looked over to Bastian and then back at me, smiling, and knelt in front of me. With one more look at my face, waiting for approval, I nodded.

He wrapped his arms under my legs, pulled me closer to him, and started playing with my clit with his tongue. He pulled away and sucked on two fingers before inserting them inside. He resumed his position of playing with my clit with his tongue.

My eyes never left Bastian as I started moaning, one hand gripping Callum's hair, pushing him further into me, and the other holding onto the top of the chair, back arched. Callum and I had never had an audience and it was revolutionary. I wondered how long it would take for Bastian to give in to his desires and take me as well. To have Callum watch us. I closed my eyes and imagined Bastian's head between my thighs. I pinched my nipples and imagined Callum sucking them, biting them.

How hard would I need to work to convince Bastian to join us?

I opened my eyes and met his heated ones. Maybe I wouldn't have to try so hard, I smiled to myself. Callum curled his fingers and hit that spot in my inner walls that always had my legs shaking, squeezing his head with my thighs. I was panting as I called out Callum's name and reached my climax. I was so sensitive while Callum cleaned me with his tongue, causing me to groan a little more.

Once he was finished, I stood up and walked over to Bastian, leaning forward and running my hands from his knees to his hips. His cock twitched, begging to be touched. I knew that he was in pain from being worked up with no release and he would not be getting one tonight.

"Let this serve as a lesson to do as you are told. I don't enjoy asking twice." I turned away and left, not even bothering to put my clothes back on, with Callum in tow.

I left him strapped to the chair, not wanting him to touch himself, and smiled as I heard him yelling a string of harsh words directed toward me.

I returned to my room to bathe when Callum rushed in front of me to start my bath. I knew he was dying to know what that was all about, and I didn't really know myself. I hadn't meant for it to go that far, but it was as if I wasn't in control of my body. I could attribute it to being in the heat of the moment, but when we looked into each others' eyes, it was as if my body simply reacted.

I didn't care what to call it, all I knew was that for the first time in years, I felt...excited.

And what the queen wants, the queen gets.

I could feel Callum staring at me.

"Go on, little bird. Ask me."

Looking me up and down with hunger in his eyes, this man would never be satiated, and neither could I; we were a perfect fit.

"I do not have any right to ask you to explain yourself. I am yours to do with as you please. And that includes fucking you where ever and in front of whomever you wish." He moved to stand right in front of me. "I belong to you."

I reached out to touch his face, and he leaned his head into my hand. "You would do anything for me, wouldn't you?"

He reached out to me, wrapping his arms around my body, hands roaming over my heated skin. He pressed his hips into me to show me just how ready he still was for me.

"I would lay down my life for you. You are my salvation. There is nothing I would not do for you."

He dragged his hands back up my body and caressed my face. There was that look in his eyes. A look that proved that his words were true.

He swallowed as his eyes looked down at my mouth. He then slightly leaned in but stopped at remembering the rules. He was never to kiss me. It was too intimate, and made me too vulnerable. I would never again be weak.

I gave him a short nod, staring at him for another moment before walking past him and into the bath.

CHAPTER EIGHT

"Your majesty, can I get you anything else?" Emilia was sitting next to me, looking completely uncomfortable.

I had decided to have breakfast outside today because everyone needed the fresh air, especially Emilia. She would still be locked in her chambers if I hadn't ordered her to come outside. I worried about her and at the very least wanted to keep a better eye on her. I didn't want what happened to ever happen again and her staying locked in her room was a recipe for disaster.

I leaned forward to pluck a grape off of the small table next to my chaise lounge that I made Callum bring outside. From the back, one could see for miles and miles and miles. Sometimes I loved to sit out here and pretend that everything was normal and that I could venture out into those rolling green hills to see what lies beyond.

But I couldn't.

I plopped another grape into my mouth. "Just relax for a moment, Emilia. There is no one to impress by keeping the castle clean. No royals to entertain. No musicians to play my favorite songs as I dance the night away with different males vying for my attention. No one. So sit back and relax."

She quieted down after that. I think my tone may have come out too harshly, but she was ruining the joyous mood I was trying to create. I sighed as I pinched off a piece of freshly baked *kouign amann* and ate it, savoring its sugary taste.

I settled my attention back on the scenery as my mind wandered to the hunter in the tower. He was not what I expected, though I didn't know what to expect.

That's not true.

You're right. I did know what to expect. I was going to kill him and be done with it and now, I replied.

Then kill him.

You know I can't. I was growing more agitated.

Your sister is dead.

Don't speak of her. Not you.

She continued as if she didn't hear me. *Your promise to her means nothing.*

"I have grown tired of you. Leave." I could hear rustling beside me, and found Emilia standing to leave.

I must have spoken the words aloud and calmed my tone, "I didn't mean you. Sit."

I could see that she was conflicted about what to do. Whenever I began to talk to myself both Callum and Emilia would leave me to my thoughts. They had no idea that I was speaking with my dead governess, and I'd never tell them. It was devastating enough knowing I'd never be able to fully get rid of her.

Even in death, she was a constant companion, no matter how much I loathed her.

A constant companion? How sweet. I think we deserve each other, don't you? I could hear the disdain in her tone.

I took another bite of the cake and ignored her as I sat straight up at the sight before me. I must have been truly distracted by Circe to not have heard the commotion because a blonde-haired male was being hauled over to me with his hands tied behind his back and a blade to his throat. His nose was bleeding, and I could see discoloration peppering his skin that would soon turn into bruises.

"Callum, what is this?" I stood, alert.

"Your grace, forgive the intrusion, but I found him staring up at the castle as I was out gathering berries for tonight's dinner." The blonde one was squirming in Callum's arms, still not looking at me. "Bow to her majesty!"

Callum whipped him around and pushed him to his knees. Our eyes met. I stared at the boy for longer than necessary, studied him just as hard as he seemed to be studying me. His eyes were a bright blue, brighter than the sky on the sunniest day from what I could remember. So bright that they were almost transparent.

His eyes widened in amazement, *no*, recognition. "It's you."

I was taken aback by his comment. "I have never seen you in my entire existence. Who are you?" I demanded.

"How do you look exactly the same?" He was speaking more to himself than to me.

"Show a little respect when speaking to her." The blade bit into his skin and blood trickled down as he stilled.

"Please. Help her," he said desperately.

Now he had my attention.

"Stop." Callum stilled but didn't let go of the boy. I descended the stairs and walked up to them. "What are you talking about?"

I needed answers because nothing this boy said was making any sense. The only thing I did know about him, something I could perceive quite rapidly, was that he was harmless. He wasn't here to hurt anyone. No, he needed me. But for what?

I had to look down as Callum had him on his knees, but his head still came up to right under Callum's chest.

The boy was panting and didn't say anything for a moment, collecting his thoughts.

"I need you to save my sister, your, erm, majesty."

I pinched the bridge of my nose in raw annoyance. "Who is your sister, and why would I have anything to do with that?"

"I know that you save the children who are sacrificed in the Reaping, and I need you to save my sister."

I took another good look at him, and a shudder ran through me. I knew exactly who this boy was, but I needed confirmation.

"Is your sister's name, Joséphine?"

"How did you know that?"

I chastised myself until I remembered that his father said no one would be coming to look for him if he didn't return. That was the entire reason I decided to keep him here and not allow him to leave.

Was it all for nothing? Did I now have two of them to consider?

Though he had yet to ask about his brother. Was he even aware that Bastian was here? Were there others?

I tried not to let the panic break my voice. "Callum, did you see anyone else?"

"No, your grace, just him."

We would see about that. I reached out both of my hands and dove into his mind. I could faintly hear him screaming, but I didn't have any time to waste. I couldn't take my time like I did with his brother.

I quickly went through his memories of the last twenty-four hours to see if he had rallied anyone together to come join this little escapade of his. I was thrown into the middle of a room as he hurriedly ran around, throwing varying possessions into his satchel. A few weapons, a couple of apples, cheese and bread, and a leather-bound book with a quill and ink. A strange combination.

"Please, don't weave me."

The boy and I both straightened and turned. A little girl around the age of five was standing in the now open doorway in a pink nightgown with white lace that stopped at her ankles. Her brown hair cascaded down her back and pieces were tied back in white ribbons to match the lace. Her eyes were filled with tears.

The boy gripped his satchel tightly against his shoulder and walked over to Joséphine, kneeling in front of her. "I have to leave."

"Bast is gone. If you leave, I'll be all alone."

He leaned forward and kissed her on the forehead, squeezing his eyes together. Then looked back into her wide eyes, eyes that had yet to understand the horrors of the world she was bred into.

How I envied her naivete.

Though she was about to learn about those horrors if her father got his wish. It was just another reason to detest that vile human. They were all the same, or maybe not. So far, the hunter had proven himself to be a better human than I had met so far. And I had met quite a few over the years.

I focused back on the siblings as he was finishing his goodbye.

"Be strong. Everything will be alright, Jo. I love you." He left without another glance back.

I followed him out of the house. Disappointment ran through me as I realized the sun had just set and I missed it. I hated to admit it, but I missed the sun. I pushed past the feeling of displeasure and continued to follow him down the street and into the woods. His steps were hurried and he didn't falter as if he knew exactly where he was going. As if he had walked this path before, many times.

I took a chance to look around because I realized that it was my first time being outside the barriers of my land. Yes, I had been outside in Bastian's mind, but I didn't think about it until now, didn't take the time to bask in how it felt. This was my first time feeling free of the constraints of my curse. I looked over to him as he started talking to himself.

"She has to be here. I don't know what I will do if she isn't. But if she isn't then hopefully someone else will be able to help me." He took a breath and then rolled his eyes. "And where the fuck did Bast go? What if he got himself killed after he stormed out of the house?" He paused and seemed to ponder what he said, then shook his head. "Oh, he's not dead, certainly the world would quake once the great Bastian perishes and all father's hopes and dreams for the family die with him."

Interesting... Did they not get along?

He kept trudging along, and after a while, I sped up the memory to right before he got to the castle.

I could tell that it was getting closer to morning as the sky had slightly lightened.

He paused right at the gates, just like his brother, took a breath to gather his courage, and then took a step over it. He walked up the dirt pathway, past the trees, over the stone bridge, and stopped walking when he was in the middle of the rose garden right in front of the stone steps.

He wasn't there long before I saw Callum silently walking up behind him, placing his blade into his side, and said in a lethal voice, "State your business."

The boy straightened. "I am here to see the woman with dark brown wavy hair, and she was standing next to an older woman. Are either one of them here? I need to—"

Callum hit him in the side of the head with the blunt end of the blade, and the boy fell to the side. "What do you want with her grace?"

He groaned from the pain. "I told you, I just want to speak to her."

Callum had tried to get answers from him and punched him a few times to make a point, but the boy didn't fight back once. Interesting. The boy kept reiterating that he would only speak to the dark-haired woman. Me.

I exited his memories because I knew the rest.

"Let him go."

"But—"

"I said 'let him go'." I narrowed my eyes at Callum and dared him to defy an order. He dropped the boy immediately.

"What was that? Why do I feel lightheaded? My body heavy?"

I ignored his questions and commanded, "Tell me your name."

"Soren Corleone and I came with no one. I am here to ask, no, to *beg* for your assistance." He flinched at the pain in his head and body after I assaulted his mind.

I squatted in front of him, an elbow resting on my knee, chin on my palm as I drummed my other hand against my arm. I tilted my head. "I already saw what happened in your brother's mind. I know that your father has condemned your baby sister to be sacrificed to the beast."

His eyes blinked with recognition. "Bast is here?"

"Is that the only thing you took out of what I just said?"

"Wait." I could see that everything I was saying overwhelmed him, and I wasn't giving him a chance to process anything. "Saw everything? Were you there?"

"Nevermind that. If I allow you to survive, then we can go into specifics. But, for now, you came to ask me to save your sister from dying, did you not?"

He looked relieved and nodded his head, his tense shoulders eased. It was so odd, being a relief to a stranger. He wasn't hunting me, he needed me. My stomach grew lighter, but I ignored the feeling.

"Why would I do such an act of kindness when I have no reason to?"

He blanched. That was not what he expected me to say.

"I saw you. Is this not what you do? You save the children."

"Says who?"

"You," he whispered. What was he talking about?

He tossed a sharp gaze between Callum and I.

"My best friend was sacrificed when I was nine years old."

I opened my mouth to reply, but no words came out. That was not what I was expecting him to say.

"I followed her into the forest later that night as soon as I could sneak off. I wanted to save her. I was going to run away from everything with her. I tracked her to this castle and hid in the shadows as I saw you and an older woman talking to each other with her standing off to the side with a blanket around her shoulders. I heard you both talking."

How could I have missed a boy spying on me? A young, inexperienced boy at that. I must have been so engrossed in Mariam's conversation that I simply didn't notice. How many others had also penetrated these walls without me knowing? A dread ran through me at the possibilities, but it was something that I could think of at a later date.

I tried to deflect. "I am not sure what you are talking about."

He looked tired, his eyes were rimmed in red and he started to sweat. "I remember that night clearly. You told her you were tired of the sacrifices and hated humans. You were so passionate about your disdain for what was happening in my village that I—" He cleared his throat. "That isn't relevant. You instructed the woman to take her and that you would see her the following year for the next Reaping. I left my best friend in your care because I knew she would be safe. I have not worried once during the Reaping because I believed that you would protect them."

My breathing hitched, and I crossed my arms over my chest. "If you believe wholeheartedly that I would protect them then why come now? Are you lying? Or did you really come to save your brother?"

"I didn't know Bast was here. I needed to make sure that you were still here, and that you would help her."

I heard his heart beat faster. He lied. But why lie about something like this? I'd believed everything he said until this point, which meant I couldn't trust him. Either way, I'd get the truth out of him soon enough.

I noticed that he had yet to ask about his brother.

"Come. This will be fun."

The moment we stepped inside, Bastian raised his head and went white as a sheet.

"Nononononononono... No! Soren, what are you doing here?" Soren was looking at his brothers' haggard appearance. In his short time here, he had lost a little bit of weight, his cheeks were more pronounced and hollow, and his eyes were bloodshot from lack of sleep.

"Well, what the hell are you doing here?" Soren retorted.

I knew this was going to be fun, so I sat down to watch and Callum came to stand next to me.

Soren walked over to his brother, brows knit together. He lightly ran his fingers over his brother's bruises which were still a deep purple and tried his best not to flinch when Soren poked too hard. I could explain why he was heavily bruised, but I didn't care to.

This boy, Soren, already knew too much about me. More than I'd ever want him to. He didn't also need to know I felt some remorse over the unfair fight, or that in too many sick and twisted ways, I wanted to make his brother's cock stir again.

Soren stared at his brother in disbelief. "What did she do to you?"

He was surprised by this, and I felt a tinge of discomfort at his shame in me. And that pissed me off.

When they both looked my way, I smiled and waved at both of them.

"Be careful. She has magic flowing in her veins. She is not to be trusted," Bastian warned.

Soren set his satchel down on the ground and began to rifle through it. Callum tensed beside me, ready to strike, but the boy surprised us by bringing out that notebook, ink, and quill. He dipped the quill in the ink and began to write.

The room was silent as we watched him write, ignoring everyone, lost in his world.

"Oh no, don't let us interrupt you."

He looked up and asked me, "Is that what you meant earlier by seeing everything? Did you somehow go into my mind? Does it always hurt when you do that?"

Bastian gave him a patronizing look. "Is that truly what is pertinent, Ren?"

He set his notebook down before trying to pull at the rope.

"I wouldn't do that, the more you pull, the tighter they get."

He turned his head swiftly toward me and asked in an exasperated tone, "What is that supposed to mean?"

"Exactly what I said. If you continue you will end up cutting his hands off and that would be a shame. I have plans for those hands."

"Does that mean they are spelled?" He stopped trying to free his brother and reached down to write in that notebook again.

Was he taking notes about me? What a curiously weird human.

I wasn't struck speechless often, but I didn't understand how this boy could not care that his brother was strapped to a chair, practically nude.

The hunter must have been thinking the same thing because he said through his teeth, "Soren, put that fucking notebook down and pay attention!"

He lifted his finger, finished whatever it was he was writing, and then said, "From my calculations," he pushed the brim of his round glasses back up his nose, "you came out here to kill the beast to placate father and end the Reaping, but instead you found her and pissed her off enough to land yourself in this situation."

This boy was quicker than I thought, and far more intelligent than his brother.

"Wait, if you're here then who is looking out for Joséphine?" Bastian panicked and started struggling against the ropes. "You can't leave her alone with him! He is going to sacrifice her! You have to go back and stop it! Take her away! I don't care, but get her away from him."

"Stop moving." He was going to injure himself even more if he didn't calm down.

"Why do you think I'm here?"

Bastian stopped struggling. "What are you saying?"

"I told you she was real."

The hunter widened his eyes as they fell back onto mine. "*This* is the woman you were talking about when we were kids?"

Soren nodded his head. "I came to beg for her to help, Jo."

"And he has yet to explain why," I interjected. "Why would I help you when you lied to me?"

"I didn't lie."

"Oh, yes you did. Well, not all of the truth. Your sister is not the only reason why you came to see me after all these years. So, why?"

I saw the ball in his throat bob as he carefully thought about what to say next. "I came here for you. I have been wanting to return since the day I saw you." Soren walked to me and knelt, bowing his head. "I will do anything to save my little sister, but I wanted to see you again."

"Me?"

"I've wanted to see you and this place since I was a boy."

I gave him a smile that I hoped felt condescending. "Am I supposed to be flattered by finding out I've had a child stalker for years?"

"I'll do whatever you tell me to do, be whoever you want me to be, if you save my sister."

A slow smile spread across my face as my eyes met Bastian's, who was devastated by the turn of events. I put my eyes back on the bowed head before me, just like his brother yesterday. However, this one was way more submissive. I loved seeing a man on his knees.

I leaned forward, grabbed his chin between two fingers, and raised his face to mine. His eyes were so transparent that I could read him so easily. He meant every single word he said.

"And if I asked you to kill yourself for her, would you?"

I raised my hand without looking at the boy, indicating to Callum that I wanted his blade. He handed it to me, and I presented it to Soren. Without hesitation, Soren grabbed the blade and brought it up to his neck. Bastian was screaming behind him, a stream of incoherent sentences.

"As you wish." He sat there waiting for me to give him a signal to do it, but I just sat there contemplating.

What are you going to do, Callie?

What was I going to do? I focused on the facts.

This boy was innocent, more than innocent. He was going to sacrifice himself to save his sister. That was something that I could empathize with. It was almost comical that any of this was happening. Here were Joséphine's older brothers ready to give up their lives to protect her. What a lucky girl. If either brother had left well enough alone, their sister would have been spared regardless. Though they didn't need to know any of those details, not when I had them in my clutches.

I was wet just seeing Soren on his knees, so willing to do as he was told. A good boy. I loved a good fight, but there was something about a man giving himself fully over to me. That was why Callum and I had such a fun time together. Could I handle the two of them?

"There is no need to kill yourself when I think you would be of more use to me alive." I sat back. "You came here for me? Fine. I will save her life for yours. You have my word."

I could see his throat bob. I had him. And so did Bastian.

He yelled, "Do not listen to her, Soren! She will do anything to keep you here!"

"I wasn't talking to you. Actually," I waved my hand and unbound him. I smirked at the stunned expression on his face, speechless for once. "I set you free."

Bastian stood on shaky legs. His strength still had not returned fully.

I clapped my hands together and said gleefully, "What fun we are going to have."

Soren swallowed, not completely understanding what he happily walked himself into.

I flicked my finger at the door, flinging it open. "Get out," I said, still staring at Soren.

"I am staying." Bastian was stubborn as a bull.

"I don't remember offering that option to you," I teased. "You and I both know what our arrangement is."

"I am your slave in exchange for Joséphine's protection."

"Actually, the deal was that you would do whatever I said and I am telling you to leave."

Bastian wasn't backing down.

"Then why offer this to me?" Soren questioned.

I slid my eyes to Bastian and gave him a sly smile as he answered, "Because she wants me and she knows that I would never leave you alone with her."

I didn't deny it.

"She loves her games." Bastian stood on shaky legs and walked over to us. "You think you are so smart. That you are the only one who sees everything, but you're not. I see how much you enjoy it when I defy you. How much it turns you on when I threaten to kill you," Bastian seethed.

I narrowed my eyes. Maybe he was smarter than I gave him credit for. He scoffed and looked down at his brother. "I will be home soon. It won't take long for me to find a way to kill her."

I looked over at Bastian. "If I wanted to play games, I would have asked if you wanted to make a wager. Then I would have asked how long you think it would take until your little brother's heart gave out from lack of oxygen."

I shot my shadows toward Soren's throat, wrapped around it, and squeezed lightly as his eyes widened. He was too stunned to move and while inflicting pain on others always brought an immeasurable amount of joy to me, this felt wrong. I felt nothing but disgust for harming an innocent, but I was quickly learning that they were the same. They would do anything to protect the ones closest to them. Predictable. I just needed to hold out a little bit longer until...

"Let him go!" Bastian roared.

He took a step forward, ready to charge me, knowing full well that he was outmatched.

I let go of my grip on Soren as he crumpled to the ground and stared up at me. He looked up at me with not a trace of anger in him. No, that look in his eyes was awe. I ignored him as I looked back at Bastian.

"I said, *if* I was in the mood to play games. Luckily for you, I am not."

"I will stay," Soren said defiantly.

Bastian raged. "No, you won't."

"You don't own me. I can make my own choices."

"You don't understand!" Bastian exclaimed.

"You heard your brother." I turned my attention to the fiery blonde. A thought came to me and I ripped his shirt open while maintaining eye contact and ran a nail down the length of his breast then sliced the bed of my finger and pressed it against his wound.

I winked as I brought my bloody finger up to my lips and sucked his blood, and faced Bastian. "And now he is spelled to stay with me until I die or if I give permission."

Bastian cursed and punched the top of the chair that he had been strapped to. His hands were pulling at the little hairs on the nape of his neck.

"Beg me to stay."

He wasn't looking at me, but at his brother behind me, his eyes pleading. Whatever silent fight they were having with their eyes ended with Bastian sighing.

"Well, pet, what is your choice?"

He hung his head and said, "Please, allow me the honor of serving you until I become a shell of the man I once was until the reaper takes pity on my soul."

He was so dramatic.

"Don't want to leave him with the big, bad beast?"

"No."

"No, what?"

He sighed. "No, your grace."

I moved closer to him, whispering into his ear, running my hands through his chest hair, allowing myself this small reprieve from the growing heat between my legs. "This will be a lot more fun. Don't you think?" He had fought me at every turn. Throughout all of the torture, he always had a witty retort. "You will behave yourself. Do You. Understand. Me."

He nodded. His chest was already exposed, so I ran a finger down the same spot as his brother, pressing down as he hissed. I sliced my finger back open, and placed it over his chest.

"This cut will ensure that neither one of you leaves these lands ever again."

I could tell by his expression that he regretted ever coming here. I could also tell that he would keep his word in trying his best to kill me the first chance he got. He would fail, but it would be fun to watch.

I stood back and said, "Oh, and since we are going to be living together for the foreseeable future, I suppose I will let you in on a little secret." I smiled down at him. "You could have escaped if you were to make it out of the tower. There was no spell binding you to my lands."

"What?" His skin paled.

The only answer I gave him was a simple shrug.

I walked to the middle of the room so I could address them both. "If you are starting to hesitate and regret your life decisions, it no longer matters. You both belong to me."

I turned to walk out of the room when Bastian spoke up. "I will stay up here and continue upholding our end of the deal. I will never complain, and I will *never* try to escape. I am yours to do with whatever you please. Just...let my idiotic brother go."

He is quite persistent, isn't he?

"No."

I ignored Circe, and continued staring down into the eyes that wanted to murder me in the most gruesome of ways. There was a twitch in his jaw that gave him away, despite trying his best to speak to my human side. They would learn that the human side of me died out long ago. All I had left were two humans to protect, and now both brothers stood to jeopardize the sliver of peace I'd managed to obtain.

He took a few deep breaths and said, "Then please, I beg you, don't torture my brother. Whatever you have planned for us—I will take both punishments."

Soren was confused by his brother's actions.

"No need for dramatics, yet. If you both are useful to me, obey me, then there's no need for torture."

CHAPTER NINE

It was well past noon by the time we left the tower. I had them following me down the halls, and into the dining hall to get something to eat. I knew that Bastian would have his mouth watering in no time once the smell of fresh food hit his nose.

No one said a word as we walked, but I could tell that Soren was staring at everything before muttering absentmindedly, "Did you know that this castle was constructed in 817 AD? And look at her.. Still standing after all these years."

"Ren..." Bastian said tersely.

"Oh! And did you know that the labor to construct these walls was so rigorous that people were said to have died right on the spot?" He placed his hands on the cold walls as if he could hear the past. "It's rumored that they were buried within the walls because they didn't want to take the time to bury them in the ground. I suppose there were too many bodies to worry about."

"Why do you always jest in the worst situations?" Bastian questioned. Soren shrugged and Bastian walked up to him and slapped the back of his head. "Say another word about the stupid castle and I will bury you within these walls myself!"

"Okay, sorry," He said, rubbing the back of his head.

We entered the dining hall. "The seat to my left belongs to Emilia. She is the only other female that resides in this castle. Callum's seat is directly to my right. You both can sit next to him, I don't care which seat you occupy." We were walking toward the table as I finished explaining where everyone's place was. "Sit."

I had assumed that they would want to sit as far away from me as possible, but Soren went to sit next to Callum. Bastian intervened at the last moment and sidestepped around him, forcing Soren to sit three seats away from me.

Callum entered with a couple of trays full of food.

"Hunter, be a doll and help Callum fetch the rest."

He stood and left with Callum without another word.

Now, it was just Soren and I, and he didn't waste a single moment before asking, "Are there any other people living here?"

"No, just the three of us. And you two." I leaned back into my chair. His tone and demeanor reminded me of a child. What other questions would he ask? My head was already starting to pound.

Callum set the rest of the platters down and took his seat.

"Is Emilia going to be joining us?" Soren asked.

I didn't want to give it another thought, but she should have been down by now. I didn't know where she went after I left, and I hadn't sent Callum to get her because I had never needed to in the past. Maybe she just needed a little more time to come to terms with Bastian. Though, I would have to have a conversation with her right after lunch.

It didn't go well the last time, and now with the addition of Soren... I shook the thought away. I could already see her face pinched together with distaste.

"She will join if she wishes. However, you are not to approach her unless she approaches you first. Is that understood?" They both nodded.

I reached forward and took a few blackberries from the platter, giving them the cue to dig in. They all filled their plates as I sat back and slowly plopped the berries into my mouth, staring at the two newcomers.

I could see Bastian doing his best to ignore me, only side-eyeing me occasionally. But not his brother. Once he realized that I was looking at him, he stared right back. His gaze was intense, so intense that I almost looked away.

I cleared my throat and said, "Let's get introductions out of the way. These two are Soren and Bastian, my new pets." I pointed a sharp nail at Callum. "And this is Callum, my consort."

"Consort?" Bastian questioned bluntly, but then seemed to swallow his tongue.

I was about to continue when I saw a look cross both of their faces that made me pause.

"Do you have a problem with a woman using a man for sex?" They both looked away from me, and I continued, "Or is it because I am not a male that I should think higher of myself and not fuck anyone other than my husband?"

Bastian spoke up, "It is just not something that is talked about so openly."

"Spin your judgment however you like; you are still looking down upon us for enjoying each other sexually. You will learn that within these walls, we fuck whenever we want and wherever we want. There are no rules here, no standards. We're just...us."

The idea perplexed Bastian enough to stare off for a long few seconds, considering the idea.

"How freeing," said Soren, as if he were reading Bastian's mind.

"Rules are in place for a reason," Bastian snapped back at him. "If there are no standards, no rules, what makes us any different from animals?"

I ignored their bickering and continued, "And then there's me. I am the Queen of these lands and you will address me as *your grace* or *your majesty*."

With a grumble, Bastian whispered to himself, "I will never call you anything, but a—"

Callum threatened, "I would think long and hard about your next choice of words if you want to continue breathing."

"Settle down, boys. We have more pressing issues. You both need a role here."

"A role?" Bastian asked.

"I can't just keep you around for that pretty face of yours, can I?"

"I just thought—"

"Everyone has a role to play. If you aren't going to be an asset then I have no use of you. And if you're of no use then I may as well kill you now so there is one less mouth to feed."

He snapped his mouth shut.

"So, what are your strengths?"

He thought about it for a moment before he answered, "I am a good hunter and—"

I cut him off. "Go deeper. Tell me something I am not already aware of."

He contemplated for a moment before he said, "I enjoy cooking. Though, I never had a chance to because of obvious reasons."

"What is obvious about that?" I asked, clearly confused.

"Is it not a woman's place?"

I stifled a laugh.

"I think a woman's place is wherever she wishes. It seems your village thinks very little of their women... Some things never change, do they?" I rolled my eyes at the thought. It was good that he could cook because that would give Emilia a break. I knew she was spiraling and a break from her daily routine might be enough to snap her out of her stupor. "You will then cook every meal for us, starting tomorrow."

He nodded.

"And you?" I looked at Soren.

Without hesitation, he said, "I am a scholar. Before you decided to keep us, I was going to go off to university to study."

He held his head up; he was very proud of his profession.

They may be related by blood, but they couldn't be more different.

"A scholar you say?" I was intrigued, but not surprised. "Nothing else?"

"Is there something wrong with being a scholar?" He asked, not defensively as I suspected he would.

"A scholar isn't a skill that I can utilize so you will clean the castle every day. You'll start on one side of the castle and then slowly make your way through it. If a door is locked, then skip it."

"Clean?" Soren repeated the word as if it were foreign to him.

"Yes. I mean, I could find other ways for you to occupy your time here, though it doesn't matter to me how you get on your knees." I knew that would get a reaction out of Bastian. I would do anything to torture him, get under his skin. He was gripping the silverware rather tightly, mouth in a grimace. "I don't enjoy repeating myself. As I said before, you will earn your keep here or you will die. I don't have time to take care of two useless humans."

He smiled at me, a wide smile that held nothing back. "Humans... The way you say it, it's as if you're not one. If you're not human, then what are you?"

"I've had enough of your questions today, scholar. You will clean. Have I made myself clear?"

"As you wish, your grace."

I blanched. Was he not going to fight back?

"May I at least have run of the castle? For research purposes, of course. You mentioned some doors would be locked."

"There are very few places that I don't allow you to venture into. Stay out of the West Wing, South Wing, and the greenhouse. You may go everywhere else: the kitchens, library, any of the other rooms and the grounds. Of course, stay away from the main gate and don't wander too far into the forest. I wouldn't want to assume that you are trying to escape... Not like you could even if you tried," I said teasingly.

"The library?"

I think he heard me say 'library' and then tuned out everything else.

"Yes, the library which I know you will love since you are a self-proclaimed scholar. Tomorrow you can start there."

His eyes lit up and he nodded enthusiastically.

I narrowed my eyes at him, dumbfounded, as Bastian asked, "What the hell are you so excited about?"

Soren cleared his throat and gave him a shrug. "What? Am I not allowed to smile? It is a beautiful day, is it not?" He gestured outside to yet another gloomy afternoon.

Bastian went right back to eating his food when Callum scoffed.

Bastian set his fork down aggressively and turned to Callum. "Actually, what about you? Your only job can't be to fuck her."

Callum smirked, though I assumed he would have gotten upset over what Bastian just said. "My duty is to service the queen with all of her needs, as you saw a few nights ago. And if I remember correctly, you rather enjoyed the show," he teased, rubbing his thumb across his bottom lip.

I interjected, "That reminds me, hunter. Callum hunted a few days ago and we are running low on meat for tonight's meal. So, that's your job for today."

Without looking away from Callum, he said, "Yes, your grace."

I knew he was only using my title to demean me. Bastian was a horse in need of breaking, and soon.

"And I will join you."

All of their heads turned toward me simultaneously, mouths agape.

Callum swallowed. He looked at Bastian suspiciously and then back at me. "I understand why you would want to go with him, but hunting is not a job for a queen such as yourself. Let me go in your stead."

I leaned forward, skimmed my fingers along his jaw, and said, "You worry too much, little bird." And then sat back in my chair, looking at Bastian. "We will go after I garden."

Bastian did his best not to roll his eyes, but I could sense the tension radiating off of him.

Instead, he said too sweetly, "Callum is right, hunting isn't for a woman of your stature. Not to mention that I wouldn't want anything bad to happen to you. What a shame that would be."

I knew what he was saying, could read between the lines. "Yes, what a shame that would be. Though I wonder...what mischief we could get into with a rifle all alone in the woods where sound goes to die?"

He didn't take his eyes off mine for a second, stuck in a war of our own making, waiting for the other to look away. He finally realized that it wasn't something he would win and conceded. "As you wish."

We all heard a noise at the door as Emilia entered. My back straightened at seeing her sudden appearance, and I realized that I should have checked on her earlier. Her hair was a mess, her eyes were bloodshot as though she had been crying for hours; she looked completely disheveled.

She stormed up to the table, slamming her hands down, causing the fine china to tremble. Her throat bobbed, and I knew it was sore, but she spoke as loud as she could, "You are the spawn of the devil! Curse you and your entire fucking family!" She blindly grabbed whatever was within her reach and began to throw the items as hard as she could at both of them.

Everyone was out of their seats. The brothers shielded themselves from the onslaught of food and drink. I stood there in shock as I had rarely seen even an ounce of anger from her in the past twenty years. I had come to my senses and found that Callum had rushed around the table and grabbed her by the waist to haul her away. He whispered something in her ear that no one else could hear.

She wasn't listening to anything he said, thrashing in his arms, doing everything in her power to get away from him and back to the brothers.

The sound of her screams disappeared as they rounded the door, and he took her back to her chambers, I presumed. The entire ordeal left me stunned, my ribs tightening around my chest and heart.

What do you think? They seem to be causing quite a bit of chaos to the very humans you vowed to protect. Are you going to give into your true nature and kill them in their sleep?

"Enough," I said, loud enough for everyone to look at me. I remembered where I was and breathed out a sigh of aggravation, changing the subject. "Callum stays in the East Wing, as will the both of you. There are ample rooms so pick whichever ones you want. I couldn't care less. Every day you will be at this table before I arrive at half past eight. I don't recommend being late."

I needed to hurry and check on Emilia.

"Why did she attack us?" Bastian asked. "She doesn't even know us."

"Is she alright?" Soren asked at the same time.

I didn't have time for this. "Clean up this mess and meet me outside of the greenhouse at half past seven," and stormed out after Callum.

I ran through the halls back to the South Wing and up the stairs. He was opening her door with her still thrashing, begging him to let her go as they entered her room.

I followed closely, watching him set her down, and she crashed onto the ground crying. I rushed to her side.

"Emilia, what happened?" Her sobs wracked her entire body. I calmed my voice, sending her into a trance-like state that always seemed to work whenever her emotions got the better of her. "Emilia, tell me what happened."

She looked up at me and signed, *I don't want them here. Please. Please. Please.* Her hand was balled in a fist, and she kept circling it around the middle of her chest, begging me to listen.

"Her episodes have been few and far between, but ever since Bastian stepped foot into this castle her mental health has dramatically declined."

I shot my hand out and wrapped it around his mouth.

"Wait for me outside." He left without another word.

I took a deep breath in. One. Two. Three. Deep breath out. One. Two. Three. Then, I turned my attention back to Emilia who had dropped her head to the ground.

I escorted her over to her bed and sat at the edge with her. "I will explain everything when you wake up." I blew a powder into her face and caught her as she fell backward.

I needed her to sleep, and wake up renewed and calm before we discussed the brothers. I knew why she didn't want them here, understood it deeply, but I also knew I had to keep them or kill them. I massaged my temples and closed my eyes, her earlier idea lingering in my mind. Maybe staying in Mariam's cottage wasn't such a bad idea after all.

I opened her door to find Callum pacing, his hands constantly rubbing his arms up and down, his nervous tick.

He turned to me when he saw me shut the door and knelt before me. "Forgive me for speaking out of turn, your grace."

I didn't know what to think. Nothing I decided would make anyone happy. My hands were tied. "Stay with her."

My mind was clouded when I walked out of the greenhouse to find Bastian waiting there with his rifle, his hair ruffled as if he had been running his hands through it all morning.

I was left to my thoughts after leaving Emilia alone, but there was nothing left to do until she woke up, and that wouldn't be until tomorrow.

He stood when he saw me and barely nodded his head as a greeting, until he saw my

appearance and cocked his head to the side, clearly confused. The simple long black gown that was immaculate this morning was now covered in a light layer of dirt. I walked over to him, my baby hair wildly framed around my face, dirt under my nails, and on various parts of my body.

I teased, "What? Do I have something on my face?"

He coughed, trying his best not to look at me. "No, I just didn't expect you to look…"

"Radiant?"

"Dirty."

He was rather direct, but his statement was true nonetheless.

"You know exactly what to say to make a girl melt. How lucky am I?" I moved past him with a shove. "Let's go; we haven't got all day."

We walked in tense silence with him slightly behind me, I wasn't worried that he would attack me, not yet anyway. Even though I couldn't leave my lands, they were vast enough that I could walk for miles in every direction. Our current path was heading northeast to where there was a small meadow that I knew the deer enjoyed grazing this time of day.

Bastian finally broke the dreaded silence. "You didn't need to come with me. I meant what I said: hunting is not something a woman should be doing." Then he teasingly said, "What if you were to scratch that perfect skin of yours."

I smirked. "Oh darling, I have more scars than you would ever be able to count in your lifetime." I stopped right before the clearing, using the shadows to our advantage. "And I don't trust you not to do something idiotic that would surely get you killed."

He had gone rigid and hissed, "I would never abandon my brother to the likes of you." He walked a little closer than I would have expected, and I heard the sound of metal scraping against fabric. I sensed his movement and motives, which were all rather predictable.

The tip of a sharp blade was pressed tightly against my neck.

I sighed. "I thought we had *just* talked about you not doing anything reckless."

His hot breath was against my ear as he said, "I don't trust you, witch."

The way he said it, the hardness in his tone, reminded me too much of my father. His war on magic, on anyone different. The countless people he burned out of fear. Times had changed, but the hysteria remained. Good looks aside, I wanted to kill him right here and now. Spare myself the trouble of having to explain to Emilia that I had no choice. I had to keep these strays if I wanted to keep her safe.

"Is that the best insult you have? Come on, you can do better."

"It's the only insult I need."

"You fear what you don't understand, and you understand nothing."

He pulled me against his body, his hand grabbed my stomach so tightly that I knew if I didn't heal immediately then I would have had a bruise. If I so much as moved my head, the blade would cut into my skin, causing me to bleed all over my already dirty dress.

I could kill him now, but my body betrayed me. I didn't want him to stop. My skin had heated over our position. No one had ever treated me so callously, with such disdain that I could taste it whenever they were near me. *Touched* me.

And I wanted more.

He was punishing me, hated me, and I liked it because punishing myself felt fitting.

"Shut. Up."

He still hadn't decided if he was going to kill me or not because my blood was still tucked safely away in my body.

I asked, "So, what was your plan here? Kill me and then run off into the sunset with your brother?"

"That about sums it up."

"Then fucking do it, coward, if you think that will indeed break the spell that I cast on you both." If I could have moved my hand I would have pointed when I said, "That scar on your chest proves that you now belong to me. Just ask Callum; he has the same one."

"You already lied once, and I will try anything to get away from you. To protect my family."

I couldn't focus on his threat when I could feel his hard chest at my back and thought about how it would feel to be pressed beneath him once more. I couldn't deny that I was attracted to him and wanted those large, calloused hands to roam over my body. I wanted more, oh, I wanted so much fucking more.

So, I gave in, and I moved my hips in small motions at first from side to side, grinding into him little by little.

I knew he wanted to fuck me, saw it in his eyes when I grazed that blade across his thigh. He was excited.

A shudder ran through my body as I thought about his hatred toward me and how rough he would be because of it. I welcomed it while he held my waist, his grip tightening, his cock hardening. I left him that night in the tower after getting him all worked up and he had yet to get a release. And something told me, something I didn't quite understand yet about Bastian, that he needed this more than I did.

We were so different, and yet, the same. Did I want to break him? Would the fire leave his body as soon as I did?

At that moment I decided that he would be mine. Even if he was thrashing, tied to my bed, he'd be mine. And eventually, he'd learn to accept the part of him screaming for it.

I was brought back to reality when I could hear him trying to suppress a moan, but failed drastically. If it was even possible, the hold he had on me tightened and I sighed in bliss at the feeling. It was unbearable to continue our little dance, but I wanted to see if he would make the next move.

"Stop moving," he breathed.

"That wasn't very convincing." I could feel his cock hardening the longer he had me in his arms, the longer I swayed. "You don't want me to stop."

He skimmed his nose along my neck, and it was my turn to suppress a moan as he said, "You think I don't know what you're doing?"

"Trying to distract you enough to disarm and then kill you for your insubordination?" I teased as I continued swaying my hips in slow circles.

"Oh yeah?" He said breathily. "You think you're in a position to be killing anyone?"

"I could kill you without moving a single muscle."

No sooner had the words left my lips, he pushed me roughly against a nearby tree, my body getting scraped by the harsh bark, the blade finally dug into my throat as I felt blood dripping down my cleavage. "There is no world in which I would *ever* want you."

I laughed as much as the blade allowed. "Your head might think that, but there's a part of you, a part you hate, that wants nothing more than to fuck me."

"Shut up!"

Stubborn male. I wasn't done playing.

"You're right. You probably couldn't even get me off if I drew you a map."

"You would want that, wouldn't you?"

"Just stating facts. Could never elicit these sounds from my lips." I then proceeded to give the performance of one of my lifetimes and moaned while lifting my dress and touching myself.

I saw the blade pierce the trunk of the tree as he braced his hand on the skirts of my dress, lifting it. I stopped laughing as his other hand moved over mine, making slow and deliberate circles around my clit.

"What was that you, little slut? I can't hear your filthy mouth anymore," he growled.

"If you think that is going to work, then we will be here all night."

Neither one of us wanted to admit that our most primal instincts wanted to take over and devour each other. We didn't need to like each other to be attracted to the other, but if he wasn't going to admit it, neither would I. Two could play this game, and I never lost.

I moved my hand to the trunk of the tree to brace myself and have a better grip, better control over wiggling my ass all over his cock painfully straining in his trousers.

We were both silent for a few seconds while he kept rubbing me and I grinded on him.

I relished the feel of his hand on my pussy, but laughed and asked, "Is that the best you can do?"

Admittedly, the words came out as more of a whimper than I'd have liked.

I knew I was egging him on, but I needed more friction.

He fit a calloused finger into my pussy and started pumping in and out of me, causing my legs to shake.

We were both caught in another war with each other, holding out until the other admitted what exactly was happening. He'd die before he admitted it.

"Is this what you wanted? Me fucking you with my finger? Or do you wish it was something else?"

I scoffed, breath quickening. "If this is what your cock is going to feel like, then I should have killed you on the road. Or rather the lack of feeling..."

"You fucking bitch." He wasted no time in bracing a hand on my throat and inserting another thick finger, moving them so fast that I couldn't help the moan that escaped from my lips. I lied when I said I couldn't feel one, but two at once was nothing short of euphoric.

I couldn't even pay attention to anything else except where those fingers were. I clamped my thighs together, doing my best to not allow him to give me an orgasm, to not allow him to win. But his next words, breathed right into my ear, sent me over the edge, "Come for me, your fucking majesty."

No. No. Not so soon.

His lips found my ear, and for a moment, his voice softened a bit. "I want to feel it."

I stilled as a tidal wave of pent-up anger over the last few days ran through me. If he hadn't had me pinned against the tree I would have collapsed to the ground.

What the fuck just happened?

I believe you are exactly what he said, my dear... A whore.

Fuck off, Circe, I cursed.

It took a moment to realize that he was still behind me, his fingers still inside of me. I quickly reached down and grabbed onto his wrist, my cum sliding down his fingers and onto my hand. I pushed his fingers out of me and slowly turned around to look into his eyes. I had never expected things to go that far so soon. I never thought that he could get me off with just his fingers.

Those words sent me over the edge.

When I looked him in the eyes, I was surprised that he was just as out of breath as I was. His hand was still braced on my throat, and we were so close that our breath intermingled. We stared at each other, caught in a trance that neither one of us realized we were stuck in. He brought them up between our faces and rubbed his coated fingers together.

My eyes widened as he brought them all the way up to his mouth, stuck out his tongue, and licked his fingers. Moaning as he closed his eyes, savoring my taste. He opened his eyes and the spell was broken.

"Fuck." He ran his fingers through his hair and then made a grunt as he turned around and started walking off.

I called after him, "Where do you think you're going?" Still using the tree to hold me up.

"Leaving."

"You still have to hunt. This... It meant nothing. Shall I punish your brother for your insolence?"

He stilled the moment I threatened his brother. So predictable.

He marched back toward me, not daring to get too close. "Don't you dare touch him."

"Then go do your fucking job and I won't have to."

"This is all your fault."

"I don't remember asking you to put your fingers in me, *lover*. You did that all on your own."

"If you would have just let us go to begin with then none of this would be happening."

"Are you done sulking?" I nearly rolled my eyes. "You are under my command. *My* control. Do I need to remind you of our little wager?"

"Control! You want to go another round, *my queen*?" He said my title, dripping with sarcasm. "Want to see how many times that control of yours breaks?"

"Who says that I would allow you to touch me again?"

"Well, seeing as you can't stand without the help of that tree. Then it can only be assumed that you will be the one begging me to fuck you. Obviously, Callum hasn't been able to satisfy your needs as he boasted."

"Callum's cock is the least of your worries... Unless you want to be worried about it?" The look of pure disgust on his face was priceless. "I could describe it to you in perfect detail, seeing as I fuck him every single day."

He seethed. "In your dreams."

"Oh, that image will definitely plague my dreams tonight, thanks for that. Do you think you will dream of my scent still on you? Wake up with your fingers in your mouth, your dick so hard that you can't wait until you can do it all over again the next day?"

This entire exchange had me wet all over again. Wanting more than just his fingers inside of me, but I wouldn't be the one who gave in first. He would be begging me in no time.

"That only happened because I knew you would use your magic on me if I refused, witch. I would never touch you under any other circumstances."

"Excuse me?" I was truly offended by what his words meant. What he believed. "Contrary to what you may think, I would never force myself onto another. It's a vile act, justifiable by death. But if that's what you need to tell yourself to help you sleep better at night, then fine. Make me the monster that you want me to be. But we both know what actually happened." I scoffed. "You're still panting."

"So are you."

Damn. He was right. Instead of acknowledging that fact, I said, "I won't ask you again to do your job."

He mumbled something under his breath as he walked around me, bringing out his rifle, and went off to do exactly as I instructed.

I called over my shoulder as I made my way back to the castle, "Same time tomorrow, then?"

Chapter Ten

I had just finished a rather silent breakfast, no one being in the mood to speak. Not even Soren was in the mood to pepper me with questions. Callum could tell that I was angry and opted not to say anything, knowing that if I needed to let off a little steam, I would seek him out. Which I was sure wouldn't be long as I was itching to dig my claws into something.

The aggravation that riddled my body could also be due to lack of sleep. I kept waking in the night once my *venin* wore off and the nightmares wouldn't stop plaguing me. The worst part about the nightmares? I remembered every single *fucking* detail. Each one. Every single night.

I moved the porridge around my plate with fresh berries that Callum had picked earlier this morning, knowing that I liked them right off the vine. This was the first time that Bastian had cooked for us without me having to intervene and force him to comply. I was glad that I didn't have to threaten him so early in the morning. I truly didn't have the energy.

I had checked on Emilia earlier and she was still asleep, which was worrisome. I had hoped to talk to her last night, but I couldn't think of waking her until her body deemed her well enough to wake.

I lifted a small spoonful to my lips and nibbled at it. It tasted divine, but I just wasn't hungry, though I wouldn't tell him that. My appetite was nonexistent from the nightmare.

Sighing, I stood up from the table and left without a word.

Wake up. *Check.*

Eat. *Check.*

I spent the rest of the morning with my hands in the soil of the greenhouse, lost in my own thoughts. A pinch of regret lingered. I shouldn't have let him touch me, let him see that there was a softness in me. How would he try to use it against me moving forward? Again, I thought about killing him, how burying them both in the dirt would save me all the trouble.

You'd be no better than your father.

I started to yell at Circe, but it wasn't her in my head this time, just me. My consciousness, somehow alive after all this time.

Garden. *Check.*

By the time I emerged from the greenhouse, I could tell that the sun had made its way far across the sky. I had been in the greenhouse longer than originally planned. No matter.

I began to head over to the library, wondering how much Soren had cleaned, and wanting to return to a little bit of normalcy since yesterday's events. I crossed my hands behind my back as I made my way there. The door was ajar and a strange noise came from the other side of it. I opened it slowly and saw something that made me pause.

Soren was on his hands and knees, covered in sweat from head to toe, making a noise that could only be described as a mix between grunting and cursing.

"Scholar, you're not being very kind with your words."

He jumped the moment I spoke, knocking over the pail full of water, soaking my bare feet and his clothes even more. So lost in his own mind that he didn't hear me enter.

He clutched his heart. "Your grace."

"Scared you, did I?"

He replied, "I didn't hear you."

"Clearly."

I looked around the room and saw puddles of water in various sections on the ground. The shelves were patchy with areas still covered in dust. I walked over to the fireplace and picked up a vase made of brass, full of fingerprints.

"I had no idea that one person could make a space that was already moderately clean, dirty again."

"As I told you—"

"Just because you're a scholar doesn't mean that you can't be good at other things. Even someone as smart as you knows that."

"It is not expected of men to take part in cleaning the home. So there was never an opportunity for me to learn."

"Your poor mother," I muttered. "Everything was left to her, then?"

He thought about it, longer than I expected. "I suppose it was."

"Well, I am not your mother. Until I find use for your knowledge, your hands will find use."

I walked to one of the bookshelves. "And what do you think of the library?"

His eyes softened in fascination as he took in the room and sighed. "It is my favorite room in the entire castle. It's surreal that I finally get to see it in person."

"You seem to know much about this castle. Why?"

"I'll answer your question if you answer mine."

There it was. Back to the questions.

"I don't have time for any of that," I said while picking up a random book and walking over to my chaise lounge. "You have much to clean."

"Your grace, I believe we have nothing but time." He gave me a crooked smile, his glasses sliding down his nose a little.

How right he was. However, it was *I* who had all the time in the world, and for them, it would be short-lived.

I didn't answer him verbally. Instead, I sat, raised the book up, and began to read, or pretend to read while he resumed cleaning the floors.

I pondered while watching him. None of my usual tricks were working on him, no. It seemed as though the crueler I was the happier he became. So unlike his brother. So happy to please.

Do you think that his mind is simple?

No, Circe, I think that he is anything but simple, I answered in my head.

I focused back on Soren, who looked over at me right at that moment and patted the spot next to me.

He looked so gleeful, that I was surprised I didn't see a wagging tail behind him. He stood, untucked the shirt from his trousers, and wiped the sweat from his face.

I stared at him. How he could get his hair wet while mopping the floors was unknown to me, but I loved how it forced him to pull it back out of his face. Every sharp curve of his jaw was on display. The water clung to every inch of his muscles on his stomach, dripping down the skin that was showing. If it were up to me, I would have him drenched in water constantly. My eyes roamed down to his trousers that had stuck to his lean thighs, showing me just enough of him to make me want to see more.

I wasn't blind; like his brother, he was fairly handsome. Met all of the requirements that I needed to want to see every inch of him. Just another plaything, but I didn't need to overcomplicate things further. Not after what just happened with Bastian. And yet, I took pleasure in unabashedly staring at his physique, until he coughed, once again garnering my attention.

"May I please go and change? It is uncomfortable and I would rather not sit on this antique chaise lounge soaked through."

"I don't care. Sit."

He looked hesitant and instead of sitting on the lounge, he opted for the floor.

It was awkward for a moment because I had never had a normal conversation with anyone who wasn't Callum, Emilia, or Mariam in many years. And even then, I always kept them at a distance, never wanting to get too close. But now—now I felt slightly nervous.

I called him over, thinking I could tease him and get back at everything his brother made me feel yesterday, but now I couldn't think of anything that would work. I looked away to collect my thoughts, and when I looked back I saw Soren thrumming his fingers against his leg. He was itching to say something.

I sighed and waved my hand in his direction. "Out with it."

He smiled wide, grabbed the quill from behind his ear and the leather-bound journal from under his shirt, and began to write furiously in it. He wasn't even looking up as he shot out a list of questions at me.

"How exactly does your magic work? What are the extent of your powers? The cut on your hand healed within seconds of mixing our blood—does it do that often? You look to be the same age as you were when I saw you fourteen years ago. How old exactly are you? Is this a result of your magic? Is there anything you can't do?"

I sat there staring at him, overwhelmed by him. He didn't seem to care that I had magic nor did he seem afraid, rather I was more of a science experiment that was completely at his disposal. It was both perplexing and terrifying. I had lost control with Bastian, and now I wasn't even sure how to handle Soren.

"Why do you care to know so much?" I couldn't help but ask.

He shrugged. "I want to know everything about you."

I rolled my eyes and scoffed at his confidence.

"Humans are strange creatures indeed."

"Humans?" He inquired, then mumbled to himself, "She said that yesterday." He looked me directly in the eyes and asked, "What do you mean by that? Do you really not consider yourself human? If you don't, then why?"

I had no words. I was growing agitated the more he spoke. I could feel my nostrils flaring. I wanted to hurt him to quiet him, but I resisted the urge with great effort. He wasn't his brother. He'd done nothing to insult me yet.

He laughed as he rubbed the back of his head. "I apologize. Sometimes I get a little carried away." He set the leatherbound book to the side of him on the floor. "May I please ask you a question, your grace?"

Changing tactics, are we?

I gave him a guarded look. "Now what?"

"Bastian said that you both made a deal. May I ask what that entails?"

I smiled, seeing this as my chance to rile him up a bit. I leaned forward, resting a hand on my knee, placing my chin on my palm.

"When he first arrived I thought that he was here to bring harm to this castle and its inhabitants, but it turns out that it was all a misunderstanding. Though as you know that doesn't matter, so he made a wager. We would fight, and if he won, he would leave with my head, but if I won, he would stay...and be mine."

He contemplated everything I told him, and I waited, staring at him to catch his disgruntled reaction, but it didn't come.

"Why didn't you make a similar deal with me?"

"I didn't need to. You were already willing to stay to save your sister."He nodded, then asked, "Could we make a deal?"

"You have nothing to offer me." He placed a hesitant hand on my knee, the knot at his throat bobbed. "What do you think you're doing?"

"Is this the deal that you made with my brother? Isn't this what you want?" It all felt mechanical. He was hesitant, not knowing what to do, as he lifted onto his knees and leaned toward me. "I would like to be your whore."

He was shaking. I knew that he was infatuated with me, his eagerness gave him away, but this felt wrong. I placed my hand on top of his to stop him and asked, trying to redirect the conversation, "And what would your brother think?"

He lifted his hand from my thigh and bowed his head. "Take me instead of Bastian. He—" There was a pause, heavy, lingering. "He doesn't need another reason to hate himself."

What the hell did that mean? Did I sense self-loathing in Bastian? Yes. But I didn't understand where it came from, and why it continued to grow in my presence.

"You are presumptuous. I'm well satisfied with Callum."

"If that were true, you wouldn't look at Bastian the way you do."

My mouth went agape. "I look at him and you the same way. Inconvenient little deer that wandered onto my property, and every day I contemplate gutting for meat." I stood from the chaise lounge and was about to leave when his hand flew out and he gripped me around my wrist.

"Wait." I looked down and raised an eyebrow, waiting for him to continue. "I have nothing to offer you. All I have is my mind, my intellect."

His mind.

I remembered what he said yesterday about traveling the world. I briefly imagined it—all the things he'd seen that I couldn't. Maybe he did have more use.

"Your mind, you say?" I turned my body around to face him. I placed my hands on his shoulders, pushed him back against the back of the lounge, and lifted a knee to rest against one leg.

"I thought you didn't want me as your whore."

"I don't. But this," I rested the other knee against his other leg, straddling him, and roved my hands up his neck and into his hair. "I want this."

"My hair?"

He was so smart and yet so simple. I laughed.

"Your mind." He opened his mouth to ask me to elaborate but then shut it as my hand covered his. "You want to make a deal? Fine. Mind for mind. I will answer one of your questions if I can see your memories willingly. One question for each memory."

I dropped my hand.

He asked, "What are you hoping to see?"

I felt myself slip; my gaze lost. "Everything. I want to see what you've seen during your travels. But you will keep this between us. A word of it to anyone, even your brother, and I'll—"

"Gut me for meat?"

I gave him a nod of approval.

"Is that part of your powers?"

"Is that your question?" He scolded himself, realizing his mistake, and shook his head. "Seeing into one's mind is one of my powers, yes."

"Wait! That isn't what I wish to know!"

"Calm down, little scholar. Let's just count that as an explanation of what I plan to do to you and not a question."

He let out a breath and smiled.

What is wrong with him?

If he was freaking Circe out then there might actually be something wrong with him.

"Why are you so happy?" I couldn't help but ask him, I was growing weary of it.

He blinked back his surprise. "I am just happy to have something that you covet."

It didn't explain everything, but it seemed as though that was all I was going to get out of him for the time being.

So instead I asked, "What is your question?"

"I need to ask you now?"

"I suppose not." I lifted off of him completely. "We will meet back here at this time tomorrow. Have your question prepared."

I walked out of the room without any more interruptions, leaving him to finish. I knew I should go and see Emilia. She had to be up by now, but I wasn't ready to face her. Not yet.

This is who you are.

"Will there ever be a day when you leave me alone?" I asked curtly, back leaned against the wall, wrestling with what to do about Emilia.

I wouldn't count on it.

Just a little bit longer, then I would go and see Emilia, I promised myself. I kicked off the wall and headed to the kitchen.

I took the stairs down to a lower level of the castle where it was considerably colder, following a delicious smell I couldn't place. The walls were made of stone. There were a few tables in front of the sink and counter space for the larger animals to be butchered. Only a few windows lined the tops of walls, allowing in much needed light and fresh air.

I found Bastian gliding around with his back to me. This was the most carefree I had seen him.

The light cascaded down from a small window toward the ceiling and hit his front, highlighting the bulging muscles under his shirt, sleeves rolled up his forearms. Bastian was the shorter brother of the two, but he was stockier than Soren.

I licked my lips, hungry for more than just food, but I told myself that I would make him beg me before I ever fucked him or let him touch me again. He would lose at this little game, but that didn't mean I couldn't play with him.

And yet, I also cursed myself for wanting him in any way. For even thinking about complicating things further.

You've never been good at self-restraint, Circe tsked.

I opened my mouth to respond but resisted.

I was about to walk over to him when I heard him humming to himself, a familiar tune.

"A cook and a singer? A man of many talents."

He jumped high and turned toward me, his arms clutching a bowl of something tightly to his chest.

He answered, out of breath, "It was my mother's favorite song."

"How sweet."

"Don't patronize me, witch."

I smirked. "Back to the name-calling, hunter?"

"I don't see a reason to call you anything other than what you are."

I didn't have a witty retort because he was right.

Bastian had since thrown a towel over his shoulder, curly black hair falling over his eyes, wanting to go back to cooking. Actively dismissing me, yet I found myself coming closer to him. When I was a foot away, he asked, "Is there anything else I can help you with?"

"What are you cooking for us tonight?" I asked, genuinely curious.

He had something brewing over the stove, a bundle of rosemary and thyme were tied together with twine next to chopped vegetables set to the side, and he was currently washing some fresh raspberries, blueberries, and pears.

He ignored me. I sighed and walked over to stand next to him, and he stilled with the knife in hand, halfway cutting through one of the pears. He set the knife down and moved over to the large stone oven to pull out a fresh loaf of bread. I sniffed the air as the smell permeated the room. He set the bread down and then checked on whatever was boiling in the pot.

It was obvious that he was doing his best to ignore me, but I wouldn't make it so easy for him.

"Did your mother teach you how to cook?" He didn't reply, and we stood there in silence for a few moments. The only sound was our breathing until

I surprised myself and said absentmindedly, "My mother didn't have to do anything related to keeping up with the castle. But she loved to make us *tarte bourdaloue*."

I had turned away from him as I thought about the last time Mother had baked for us, and before I could spiral into despair, he said, "I loved watching her cook in the kitchen. She would always show me each step she did and why she did it. What spices went with what foods. It was the only time..." He seemed to come back to his senses and proceeded to go back to ignoring me.

I rolled my eyes and eyed a bowl of cream on the other side of him. I smiled to myself and reached past him, brushing my breasts against his arm. I placed my finger in some of the cream that he made for dinner and brought it to my lips, sucking it off. I made a little moaning sound which made Bastian lean toward me involuntarily.

"Tell me something. Did you suck on your fingers last night? Could you still taste me on them?"

He looked away, but I looked down at his pants as they began to swell and then smirked up at him. "I don't even have to touch you to get a reaction out of you. You want to bend me over this counter and take me, don't you?"

"You would let me, wouldn't you?"

I swallowed, praying my nerves weren't visible. He was getting too good at saying just the right thing.

"I wouldn't."

It was his turn to smirk and lean forward into my side, whispering in my ear, "Tell me, if I put my hands under your dress, would you be dripping?" He ground his hardened length against my body.

I returned to stare at him and we both knew it was true.

"Do you want me to touch you? Admit it."

"No," he snapped, as if all his senses had come back to him. "What you do to my body...it's magic."

I bared my teeth at him. "I already told you that I don't do—"

"Maybe it isn't something you're doing, but it's something about you. Something I have no control of." His voice began to edge with frustration.

"When I'm around you, I feel like I don't even know who I am. You make me hate myself."

I opened my mouth to reply, but the words rested on my tongue. In an instant, I felt every shattering emotion I'd buried for years. Once upon a time, I was alone, seeking acceptance wherever I could find it. I was weak then, but not now. Why did his words burn me so much?

"Anything else you need, your grace?"

I gripped his chin with a strength he didn't see coming, squeezing the bone and forcing him to look me dead in the eyes.

"Father didn't raise a good boy, did he? Good boys don't disobey or give in to fleshy temptations. Good boys follow the rules." I laughed richly. "You don't even know who you are, but I'll show you."

I pushed his chin away from me, and a muscle in his jaw ticked.

I walked back up the stairs into the dining hall, ran my hands down the red silk chemise with nothing on underneath that hugged my curves, my nipples peeking through the fabric, and leaned my hips against the edge of the table, hands resting at my sides, waiting for Callum to enter as it was sunset. I didn't have to wait long to hear the sound of footsteps outside the door, until it was opening to reveal both Soren and my little bird. They both stopped and stared at me, most likely confused that I had arrived before them.

"Run along, scholar, I don't think you'll want to partake in the game I am about to play with your brother."

"But it's time for dinner," he said dumbfoundedly, clearly confused.

"Don't worry. I'll let you back in when we are done."

Soren was still staring at me, so I flicked my finger, forced him backward until he was in the hallway, and slammed the door shut.

"Hey! I'm starving! Can you at least—" I created a small opening with my shadows and set down a platter of bread and berry jam next to him. "This is not what I meant. I mean, it's, well..." His voice grew muffled. "Oh, this is excellent jam."

I tuned him out as I looked back toward Callum, who was walking to me, eyes roaming my body hungrily. He was smiling large enough that his dimples were showing.

"Your grace, you are as ravishing as you were this morning."

"You're just saying that because you know you get the privilege of helping me out of my gown." He looked down, red staining his cheeks; even after all of these years, he could still get flushed when simply thinking about fucking me.

He looked back up and asked, "So, a game? What are we playing tonight?"

At the same time, Bastian was walking up the stairs carrying a platter of food and stopped to stare at the two of us.

"Where is my brother?"

"Take a seat."

He narrowed his eyes, but did as he was told, and set the platter of food on the table and sat in his chair.

While looking into his eyes I commanded Callum, "Help me with my dress."

His eyes became hooded; he knew where this was going. Like he said, he was mine to fuck where I pleased, in front of whomever I pleased. And this pleased me.

Callum undid the back of my dress, and I slipped it off slowly, standing bare with both of their eyes drinking me in.

Bastian hadn't moved an inch, but I could see his hands grip the sides of the arms of the chair. I knew he would move the moment I got close enough to him, so I waved my hands in his direction, sending my shadows into his mind.

"Fuck! Not again."

"Let's do some self-discovery, shall we?"

Neither male said anything.

"Come on…admit it…" I smiled at his silence. "Very well. You asked for it."

I climbed on top of the table, widening my legs so close to him that if he only were able to move freely and lean forward, he could run his tongue over me. The thought made me shiver in anticipation.

"Callum, show this pet what true devotion means."

"As you wish, your grace." I moved my legs until I was kneeling on the top of the table and bent forward, never taking my eyes off Bastian. I could tell that he was uncomfortable because of the growing strain in his pants that he was unable to touch.

We continued glaring at each other until I heard clothes being discarded on the ground. Bastian's eyes left mine, looking to the right at Callum. His breathing quickened, pupils dilating, cheeks crimson. He hastily looked away as Callum climbed onto the table laying on his back, feet moving under my legs so that I was straddling him. Placing one hand on my hip and the other gliding his cock to my entrance he stuck the tip barely in, coating his length on my already dripping pussy.

"Oh, hunter…" Bringing his attention back to me.

Callum pushed inside me without warning, pain interlaced with the delicious feeling of elation coursing through me as I screamed out Callum's name, staring at Bastian the entire time. His throat bobbed as his eyes never left mine.

Callum stilled inside me and rolled his hips in the way that made my toes curl. He wrapped his hands around either side of my waist, bending his knees slightly, causing me to hold onto his legs for stability.

He then quickened his pace, slamming into me as I scraped my nails up his legs trying to gain some traction. I could feel raised skin where my nails had dug into him over the years and though I could have healed them, he insisted that I leave them. He said he wanted to wear these marks proudly, proof that he belonged to me.

I was brought back to the present when Callum squeezed my hips hard enough to make me groan deliciously at the pain.

Callum was relentless, hitting my cervix with every thrust which caused a little bit of pain, but I didn't care—I reveled in it. All I cared about was that Bastian was here to watch. Heat flooded my system even more when I thought back to that first time in the tower.

Tied up.

My blade against his thigh.

My hand wrapped around his cock.

The thoughts ran rampant through my mind as I could feel my orgasm fast approaching while listening to my favorite sound. Flesh against flesh.

I was right. Having an audience was even better than not.

In a moment I was being flipped around, back hitting the table, my feet being lifted until my legs rested on Callum's shoulders, and before I was about to protest, he moaned, "Fuck. You feel so fucking good."

My orgasm shot through me, and I screamed out Callum's name as he continued to pound into me relentlessly, his arms securely wrapped around my knees, holding me to him, as the orgasm waned, finding his own moment after mine. He leaned his head on the side of my foot, still resting on his shoulder as he caught his breath, slowly pumping in and out. He pulled out of me after a moment and readjusted himself until his clothes were back on his body. My legs were weak, and I was still trying to catch my breath, confused about what had gotten into Callum when my entire body shuddered. I looked down and found Callum's face between my legs, licking me clean.

"Enough." I sat up as he got off the table to lean against it, his own legs shaking slightly.

I smirked in Bastian's direction as Callum's cum dripped down my legs and asked, "Did you like the show?"

I still had him restrained, while he moved his eyes down my body and to the mess that Callum and I had made of the dining table. Heat rushed his features and I knew without having to look that his cock was so stiff that it was painful.

But his only response was, "You expect me to eat my food on this table after that pathetic display?"

I laughed as I put on my dress that was haphazardly tossed on the ground. That mouth of his would only continue to get him into more trouble, but I was ready to deliver the pain he obviously desired.

Callum stood straight at that, leaned forward, grabbing Bastian by the collar of his shirt. "I warned you *not* to speak to her that way!"

He brought his fist back.

"Stop!" My voice rang through the room. I could see Callum's hand wavering, still not letting go of his shirt. "Callum, I gave you an order. Let go of him."

He turned to me and asked, "What is wrong with you?"

"What?"

He paused for a moment, gathering his courage.

"Ever since these parasites came, it has been nothing but chaos, yet you do not kill them. Emilia is in ruins because of their mere presence here."

I squeezed my eyes shut. "They've done nothing to deserve death."

But his comment on Emilia wasn't lost on me, and the guilt that I had been trying to suppress all day began to spread throughout my body. I should have gone to her sooner.

I always knew you were such a coward, Circe teased.

"I saw what happened when you came in from the hunt yesterday. You kill them and everything goes back to the way it was."

"Like it or not, this is our new life."

He squeezed his eyes shut and gathered himself before speaking in a softer tone. "Please... I know you are growing fond of them, or rather, you are having fun, but you can't allow them to live and leave Emilia to her madness."

"Enough." My voice was barely above a whisper. Anger radiated from my body. I opened my eyes and knew that they were a stark violet as mist swirled around me. Callum effectively stopped talking and bent his head, shaking. I grabbed the plate that Bastian had brought in from the kitchen and threw it whizzing past Callum's head.

My my... Look at that temper...

"Shut up, Circe!" I waved my hand in the direction of Soren's chair, removing the top part of it, and splintering it into thousands of pieces.

I had finally caught my breath when I saw that tiny pieces were in Callum's hair, and some had cut into Bastian's face and arms as he got hit with the brunt of the force.

I bit into my hand hard enough to draw blood and shoved my palm against his mouth as he gagged, trying his best to not swallow it. Once he had swallowed just enough, I stormed out of the room and found Soren sitting on the ground with an empty platter at his side, head resting on his elbow, bored.

"Are you quite finished with whatever it is you were trying to prove?"

I left him sitting there because if I didn't leave right at that instant, then I would have killed him just to spite his brother.

As I was about to turn the corner, I could hear Soren exclaim, "What the hell did you guys do to my chair!"

It was almost sunset by the time I made my way back to my chambers and walked to the balcony to bid farewell to my nemesis, the sun. A beacon of hope that would never come, my castle meant to be forever isolated and covered in fog.

When I was a child, I was so full of life that I never knew a day of turmoil. That is until Circe. No. I would try and go on one moment without her consuming my mind.

I stripped my clothes off and let them fall on the ground, walked to the chair on the balcony, and sat down, loving the feeling of the moon's rays licking my naked skin, even if it was through the fog.

Callum entered, walking next to the chair, and asked, "May I speak freely, your majesty?"

"I wouldn't stand too close, Callum. I can't promise that I won't kill you where you stand at this moment."

I could hear his shuffling movements, and when I looked over, I saw that he was kneeling again next to my chair, his head bent low to the ground.

"I beg for your forgiveness. I just do not trust those two and I was upset that they came in here and began to make your life a living hell. And Emilia..."

He looked up just as I stood up from the chair, grabbed his neck, and pushed him against the railing of the balcony.

"Who the fuck are you to tell me what constitutes a living hell? Do you even comprehend the word?" I was squeezing his neck so hard that he was writhing in pain, begging me with his eyes when his voice wouldn't work. I knew that I needed to let up on his throat, but I couldn't stop. "To have every single person in your life *die* right before your eyes. To live alone for hundreds of years, with no one else but yourself! Now, tell me, do you know *anything* about hell?"

His eyes began to droop, life slowly slipping from them.

I think your little bird has had enough, Callie.

"Fuck." I let go of him and he crumpled to the ground.

Good Callie.

"Say another fucking word and I will end you. I am not in the mood for your antics tonight," I cursed Circe aloud.

I turned my back to him and sat back down, thrumming my fingers against the arms of the chair.

There were a few moments of silence until he whispered, hesitant, "I should have spoken with you privately about Emilia. I am thoroughly concerned about her health. I heard her crying throughout the night."

She did? Circe was right. I was useless.

I rested my palm against my forehead, rubbing my temples. He was right. He was always fucking right.

"Why are you avoiding her?"

I crossed my arms. "I am not necessarily avoiding her. I just..." I grumbled, trying to find the right words. "I don't know how to talk to her. I don't know how to comfort her. I am not good with emotions."

"Emilia thinks highly of you. I am sure she will understand. Is killing them really not an option?"

"The brothers aren't their father. You should understand that better than anyone." I paused, allowing it to sink in. "I will speak with Emilia first thing tomorrow morning."

"I don't want anyone to die. I feel guilty wishing death on another, but I want to protect what I have found inside these walls. I will do anything to protect you and Emilia."

"I understand."

He turned around to stare out into the forest. I stood up and ran my hands up his back, leaning into his strength. "I will forget that dinner and this conversation ever happened. Let me remind you that they are both staying, and that is final."

"You are too..." Upon seeing the look I gave him, just as he was about to use *that* word, he changed course at the last second and said, "Generous. I don't deserve it."

"No, you don't. But I know that you will do anything to try and live up to my expectations."

Chapter Eleven

"Emilia?"

I had gone up to her chambers almost immediately after Callum left. He was right. I had avoided her for too long.

I pushed the doors open and was surprised to find the curtains drawn, as she usually enjoyed having them open to stare out of the windows. Not even with my sharp eyesight could I make out anything in her room.

"Emilia?" I called out again.

Purple shadows surrounded my hand and lit up the space enough for me to see Emilia huddled on her bed, hands wrapped around her knees, eyes staring straight ahead at nothing.

I walked swiftly to the bed and sat down next to her, not touching her. I didn't want to startle her out of her trance. I sat there and looked her over to see if she harmed herself. I didn't find anything wrong, and as my eyes made their way back up to her face, I found that she was looking at me.

"I am so angry. I have never felt so angry before." Her face was hard, full of fury.

"I know." I did know. I knew exactly what she was feeling, and I didn't want that for her.

"I hate them." Her voice was full of menace.

"You hate their father," I corrected.

"Are they not a product of their maker?"

"Are you?" I shouldn't have been as harsh, but I needed her to know that they were not him.

Her eyes widened, taken aback.

I sighed. "You need to find a way to come to terms with this."

"I don't think I can."

"You must try." She didn't answer me, her eyes downcast. "I've been inside their heads, Emilia. Both of them have been victims of their father in different ways...both hate the Reapings. They share blood with a monster, but that doesn't make them one."

My own words wrecked me, and I thought of my father. The burnings. My eyes began to sting. What was happening to me?

"When I look at them, I see *him*."

I reached up, wanting to push some hair back behind her ear, like I used to do with Belle, but resisted. Emilia rarely liked being touched. I sat with her until she fell back asleep, both of us breathing the tense air without another word spoken. I watched her slumber like I did when she was a child, her chest rising and falling. I should have let Mariam take her to a village to find a new family, just as I had with all the other children. Instead, she reminded me of Belle, and I kept her like a doll. A play thing. I'd done the same to Callum.

You spread misery, Circe said.

I got up and left her room, wanting the balcony—the night air. Too much had happened in such a short amount of time that I had barely taken a moment to think about the ramifications. I constantly went back and forth between letting them go and doing exactly what Emilia wished and kill them.

I aimlessly walked through the halls of the castle, not bothering to pay attention to my surroundings. I had been here so long that I could navigate the passageways blindfolded.

So, I did just that. I closed my eyes and let my body move freely, wherever it wished. I didn't know how long I kept my eyes closed until I was done and ready to head up for a bath, but when I opened my eyes I was shocked.

Why was I here?

I dropped my head and ground my teeth together, rooted to the spot, unable to move my feet. Why would my body bring me here?

I took a deep breath, staring down at the bottom step of the staircase leading to the West Wing. I roved my eyes slowly up, taking in the intricate circular carvings engraved on the wood, doing my best to avoid the inevitable.

And when there were no more carvings to look at, I raised my eyes even more and found myself trembling under the heavy gaze of the corridor. A place I hadn't been in hundreds of years, I didn't even dare pass by these steps, avoiding the area completely.

I turned away and started back toward my chambers, telling myself that too much had changed. I wasn't ready to reopen old wounds that I would rather stay scarred. I was down the hall before I stopped, my mind not allowing me to take another step.

Was there a reason that I was supposed to come here tonight? Little Annabelle, were you trying to tell me something?

I reluctantly moved back toward the staircase. Staring up into the abyss, the darkness of my past. I could see that day so clearly which was the main reason I stayed away. I didn't want to revisit that moment. The running. Screaming. Pleading. Killing. Devastation. Chaos.

It was all too much. I took a few deep breaths, clearing my mind. And placed one foot on a step. My heart was beating so fast that it would have beat out of my chest if possible. I almost conjured my *venin*, but if I was going to go there again, I wanted to attempt to stay clear-headed. Respect for them—for her.

I slowly made my way up the staircase, staring at my feet the whole way up, too ashamed to hold my head high. I made it up to the landing, and I felt lightheaded, took a few deep breaths to try and get my bearings. I was stronger than this. They were dead, and I was alive. Immortal. I was stronger than this, wasn't I?

I took another deep breath and started walking. Nothing had changed.

I made my way over to her door. If I thought that walking up the stairs was hard enough, opening her door made me want to burst into flames. My hands were shaking as I pushed the door open, an audible squeak filled the room.

The room itself was shrouded in darkness, the only light coming in was from between the curtains. The daunting shadows cast throughout the room had me on edge. I dared not touch a thing, not wanting to tarnish her memory. I conjured a ball of purple shadows in my hands and walked around. Nothing had changed besides a thin layer of dust that coated every surface.

Her four-poster bed was against the far left side of the room in the middle of the wall, drapes hung down from the posts. She had a vanity that was situated in front of the window across from her bedroom door. She loved to look out over the grounds. Her bathing chamber was across from the bed and her boudoir to the right of that. She had a couple of shelves that held all of her most personal items. Her walls were covered in the paper that adorned this entire wing; gold-plated leaves of varying sizes.

I left it just how she had it when she died. I left this entire wing the way it was after that fateful day and moved myself to the South Wing. It was the furthest point away.

As if my mind conjured it, figures materialized out of thin air. Mother had rushed into Belle's room and I heard coughing from the bed. I heard Annabelle's voice and gasped, clasping my hand over my mouth.

People rushed all around me. It was pure chaos. There was no other word for it.

I remembered this. Was this a manifestation of a past memory? Everyone looked exactly as they had. What was happening? This couldn't be real!

A trail of blood littered the floor all the way to Belle's bed, where she was bathed in it. No one had been able to staunch the bleeding and the doctor was on his way here.

"Is she alright?" I could see myself asking.

No one listened.

"Is my sister alive?" I was still being ignored.

Father rushed past me. "Someone tell me what happened now!" Everyone stopped what they were doing, flinching in the process. No one spoke up. He looked to the man who brought her in. "Tell me."

The man bowed. "We found her in the forest. An animal attack."

"Why was she alone?"

No one answered. She wasn't watched, and now she was on the verge of death.

I looked over to the doorway, knowing what I would see.

I watched as Circe grabbed my younger self on the shoulder and dragged me slightly behind the door, but not far enough away that Annabelle wasn't visible.

I walked over to them and heard myself whisper just low enough so that only she could hear me, "Save her!"

She narrowed her eyes. "You know I can't."

I pleaded, "Please!"

She hushed me. "Enough."

"I will do anything."

She looked away and sighed. She wasn't going to do it.

Her eyes met mine again.

"If she miraculously heals, then they will know it is magic. I will die."

"But...it's my sister. *Your* princess."

Circe regarded me with kind eyes, but her expression was stern.

"Belle walked in on you using your magic, and what was the first thing she said?"

"That I was an animal... That father would burn me like all the other animals." I was crying now, rather hysterically. "She didn't mean it... She's just a child. I know she didn't mean it."

"And yet, you were not the animal she needed to fear." Circe frowned, and I waited for her to tear up, like all the other weeping men and women around us, but she just stared forward.

"What did you do?"

Circe bowed her head, but the corners of her mouth barely lifted before settling back into a grimace. But I caught it. I was too in shock to know what it meant at the time, but I caught it.

I knew everything that would happen next, but my body went numb, and I tuned everyone out beside *her*. I left the vision of me and Circe, walked over to the side of Belle's bed, and sat down. I had panicked last time and could hardly look at her as she laid in this bed, but this time I would take it in. Memorize her beautiful little face.

I reached my hand out and began to rub away the blood, but my hand went right through her face. I snatched my hand away, not wanting to disturb the image before me. I hesitantly reached out my hand and hovered it right above her cheek. Blood was smeared everywhere. It was probably over her entire body, but the sheet covered her enough that I could only imagine what it looked like.

Her eyes fluttered open and stared straight ahead—straight at me. My heart dropped as it looked like she could see right through the mirage and was truly here. In the flesh.

And then the next moment she closed her eyes and her chest ceased to move.

"Why isn't her chest moving?" I heard myself ask.

Chaos ensued. Though I didn't care as the image slowly faded away into nothing.

The last of my childhood, my innocence, left the moment she drew her last breath. I felt something wet on my face and brought my hand up, wiping away tears that had escaped.

Something inside me snapped.

I screamed out, not caring who heard me. Needing to purge the emotions that had started to make their way to the surface. I picked up a candelabra from a nearby desk and threw it at the wall causing a large tear in the fabric of the paper. I clamped my hands over my mouth and held onto the bed column for support. More tears formed in my eyes, my entire body shaking. I blinked them back, rushed out of the room, slammed the door, and dropped to the ground. The door held me up as I sat there, cursing myself for disturbing Belle's room. I would fix it later, but I couldn't go back in there right now. Not with all of these wretched emotions so fresh in my mind.

I hurried down the steps, not wanting to be there any longer. The anger had slightly dissipated and all that was left was the guilt. I knew just what I needed to make myself forget about everything. I went in search of Callum's room.

I didn't find him in his chambers, so I went to the only other place where he would be. His favorite place in the entire castle—the battlements facing North.

It didn't take me long to find him sitting atop one of the edges of the battlement on the castle's Northside, staring off into the distance. I approached him, rested my hands on the flat surface next to him, and followed his line of sight, still in his peripherals.

I knew why he enjoyed coming up here:. the view was endless. Rolling green mountains went as far as the naked eye could see, littered with trees and valleys. The castle was situated on the summit of a large hill and aside from the strategic reason for its placement, the panoramic view was spectacular.

Years ago, when the sun wasn't hiding behind the fog, it was one of the most beautiful things I had ever seen. The way that the sun would cast its light across the varying passes and turn everything into magnificent hues of oranges and yellows.

A sight to behold.

"You should have seen it when the sun graced us with its presence."

Callum jumped so high that he was millimeters from falling to his death, just as I grabbed him and ensured that he didn't.

"Your grace!" Callum gripped the edges hard as he tried to calm his rapidly beating heart. He didn't waste another moment before he hurried down from his seated position and stood next to me, his chest still rising and falling quickly.

He looked exactly how I felt on the inside. Though I had calmed down and was completely drained of energy. I didn't even have the desire to fuck him. Intriguing.

I looked back over the view and stood there while he hesitantly stepped closer. We didn't say anything for a long time and just stared.

Feeling a little scattered?

Yes, I answered her truthfully, in my mind. Lying to her would do no good, she was a part of my subconscious.

I felt like I was out of my element, even more so when I took a step to Callum's side, searching for his warmth. He didn't move and instead allowed me to lean into him, use him once more, but in a different way. A way that I knew he had been craving ever since he decided to stay.

The breeze blew past us, chilling the air to near-freezing temperatures, yet he didn't move though I could feel his body trembling. He tried to hide it, to prolong my touch, but I straightened, ready to go back inside.

I turned when he asked, "May I ask you something?"

I dropped my head slightly, unsure if I had the strength, but then nodded and turned back to him.

"What is it about Bastian?"

"There is something about him that is hidden from us. Something that he is keeping a secret even from himself. Why do you ask?"

"For many years, it has just been the three of us, and while I hate to admit it, I am a bit jealous. But my love for you is not fickle. If you wish to take another, I will continue to stand by you. Join you even."

"Oh?"

"I've thought about it," he admitted. "It's been on my mind...and you are always so honest with what you want. Why shouldn't I be?"

He was pouring his heart out to me.

With a sigh, he continued, "Does Bastian mean something to you? If so, then I will do everything in my power to help him transition into his new life."

Does he *mean* something to me?

"I don't know what he is to me. I am just as tempted to kill him as I am to fuck him. Eventually, we will both understand each other, but until we do, things will be tense."

"And Soren?"

I grinned at the thought of him.

"I think he'll be happy with the library for the next fifty years."

Callum laughed at the thought.

"He's different. His mind works so frantically, but there is some brilliance in it, I suppose. He never stops talking about his travels, either."

"We will never bore between the two." I paused and blinked slowly. "What happened with the chair... What I said..."

"I haven't the faintest idea what you're talking about, your grace."

My chest warmed, and for a moment, with the memory of Belle so fresh, I let myself give him a weak smile.

I left him to gaze at the sights some more as I went to go see a few of my own.

I entered Soren's chambers, considering his travels more seriously. He was lying back against his headboard, reading a book next to the flickering flames of candlelight.

He sat up in the bed and put the book next to him. "Your majesty?"

I reached the bed, lifted my dress to my knees, and crawled over to him.

"What—What are you doing?"

I placed my hands on either side of his head and commanded, "I do not wish to go searching through your memories. I do not have the patience. So, I need you to think hard about your favorite place that you have traveled to."

I gave him just less than a minute to think before diving in. It took a moment to truly understand what it was that I was seeing.

The sound hit me first, a sound that I had never heard, and I didn't have the vocabulary to accurately describe. But it was loud. Booming.

I was standing next to Soren on a wide expanse of what I could only imagine was sand. An enormous amount of hard sand squished beneath my bare feet. I was blinded while trying to make direct eye contact with the water from the way in which the sun was hitting it.

I heard the loud booming sound again and looked to my right to find that there were cliffs on which the water was pounding. Slowly chiseling away at the landscape with how hard the water was crashing. Particles sprayed everywhere. I almost wanted to stand under its shower and taste it.

I saw movement next to me and turned back to find that Soren was wiping a single tear from his eye. I knew he agreed with me. This. This was the most beautiful view that I had ever seen in my entire life—no, existence.

I could feel emotions of awe, shock, love, sadness, happiness; an array of feelings all bottled into one and all for this experience. It was overwhelming, and I soon followed suit, with tears slowly forming in my eyes. I couldn't help it. I sank to my knees and just watched the water reach my fingers and then retract, only to do the same dance over and over again.

Is this what was out there? *This* is what I had been missing?

What brought me joy a moment ago brought nothing but pain. And regret. And then the anger was back. I would never see this for myself. Never experience this for myself. I thought that I would be able to see the world through his mind, but it was just another reminder of something that I would never have.

I left his mind abruptly and sank back on my knees, sitting there as he caught his breath, drained from me going inside of his mind.

"Did you find what it was you were looking for?"

"Yes."

"And?"

"Was that the ocean?"

"Yes, that particular mass of water is located in France's southern region. That was my first time seeing it, and it was magnificent."

The past hit me violently, the way it often did. Everything I'd lost then, and everything that never was. If I had never discovered my magic, never met Circe... Though it wouldn't have mattered, I would have been married off to whomever my father wished and been stuck in another type of prison. Forced to fuck and produce more heirs, continuing the cycle.

I didn't wish to talk about it, so I asked, "What is your question?"

He was learning quickly as he didn't push the conversation further and answered my question, "I thought I had more time. I am not prepared."

Lies, Circe sang.

"I do not enjoy being lied to, scholar."

"It is not necessarily a lie, rather, I have too many to narrow it down to only one."

"Tick tock. When I leave this room our deal is over."

"What is your name?" He said without wasting another moment.

I was dumbfounded once again. Would I ever not be at a loss for words around this male?

"Out of everything that you could possibly ask, *that* is what you wish to know?"

"I have been wondering about your name ever since I was ten years old."

I gripped the poster of the bed and said without turning around, "That is information you don't need to be privy to. You will only ever address me as *your grace* or *your majesty*, so my name is irrelevant."

"But–"

"I don't need to explain myself to an impudent boy like yourself and—"

"Stop calling me boy. You know my name. You're not that old, anyway."

"I am far older than you can comprehend."

He narrowed his eyes, not in anger but in thought.

"Is that why you don't consider yourself a human? I thought it was your magic," and then panicked, "That's not my question."

He sat back, crossed his arms, and stared at me some more.

I lifted my eyes to the ceiling, tired. I was so tired.

"If that is all, then I will take my leave."

"You have yet to answer my question per our agreement."

"Then ask me anything else, but my patience is running low," I warned.

"Her name was Léna. She was one of the chosen from my village when she was eleven years old, and I was ten. They sent her out and I was going to follow her and save her before the beast got to her." He loved this girl, however much a child could love another child. I narrowed my eyes at him as he continued, "She was short, had thin brown hair that reached just below her chin, and wore a white dress with chiffon around the edges."

"You remember her dress?"

"Yes."

I had looked through his memories that first day he came and knew exactly what girl he was talking about. Léna... The small girl who had shown up in a beautiful dress and had such polite manners. I remembered her well.

"So, what is it that you wish to know?"

"Where is she?"

"Why? Do you wish to see her?"

His throat bobbed. "I just wish to know what happened to her. Is she being taken care of?"

A pang of jealousy coursed through me. They were mine the moment they stepped on my land, and now he wants to leave for *her*?

Circe tsked. *Everyone always leaves you. It is inevitable.*

I bit back my retort, focusing solely on Soren.

I could tell that he saw a change in my demeanor, so he held up his hands, not knowing what to do.

He tried to explain himself. "I do not wish to seek her out. I merely wanted to satiate my curiosity and worry. I never found out what happened after you found the children, and before I could investigate, I was shipped off to a private boarding school."

Still, I said nothing, considering what the information meant to him—how long could I hold it over his head? But then I thought about Annabelle, Emilia, and what I would do if I were in his position, hunting for the truth. I would stop at nothing; I would need to know what happened.

I sighed, my resolve waning. "I remember your friend. She had a birthmark on her upper arm that was visible out of the bottom of the sleeve of her dress. I normally don't remember the children, but she stuck out." I clasped my hands behind my back. "I sent her with Mariam, my liaison for the children. There are little towns all over. Mariam would spread them out to orphanages or families looking to home them."

He swallowed. "She could have been sent to an orphanage?"

"Better than dead in the woods, wouldn't you say? I apologize for not having an extensive book of eligible families looking for sacrificed children in my library, Soren."

"Why couldn't you have kept her," he whispered, just loud enough for me to hear.

"What did you say?" I said loudly, my voice snapping.

His eyes found mine, and there was a hint of defiance. "You could have kept her, just like you did Emilia. At least then, I'd know she was safe."

I stared at him like he had two heads. "How did you know about Emilia?"

"It was a guess," he said simply, "that you just confirmed."

I blinked and felt the rage inside me simmer. He didn't know what his father did to Emilia before he left her for dead.

"Emilia is special," I told him without shame. "She has seen horrors, horrors your sweet little Léna never had to endure. You cannot understand why Emilia is a part of my soul, and for that, you should be grateful. You have spent your life soaking up the privileges that come with the second-born son. You have never understood what it is like to be an outcast... To be truly different, and have the entire world hate you for it—to be chosen to suffer. You do not understand horror or true loss." I stopped, feeling the rage shift inside me, twist there until a sadness overcame me.

"I overstepped."

"You talk too much," I said sharply. "Your head paints a rather beautiful image of the world, Soren. Wouldn't you like to keep it that way?"

He didn't respond.

"Keep that in mind before you ask your next question."

"I overstepped," he said again, slowly. "Thank you for what you did for Léna. You have no idea how much that has been weighing on my soul all this time."

Something changed in him at that moment. He wasn't just looking at me as though I was a mystery he wanted to solve, but rather, something precious. Someone worthy of his affections. I had tried to scare him, and it hadn't worked.

I removed myself from his gaze and was about to head to the dining hall when Soren asked, "I have a request."

"I have told you that you get one question," I snapped, my temper shorter than normal.

"Not a question. A request."

"Hurry up."

Just then, we both heard his chamber doors opening. Bastian said, "Ren, let's go to breakfast before the witch scolds us with her venom for being late."

At that same moment, I felt something sharp glide across my arm. I didn't even flinch at the pain that radiated as the object made contact. I swung my head back to find Soren holding a knife dripping with my blood and a small cut on my upper arm.

"Ren!"

I could hear Bastian yell as I grabbed the knife from his hand, gripped his hair and yanked it back, exposing his throat, and held the point of the knife there. The room went silent and I seethed, a sense of betrayal washed over me. Moments earlier, I'd shared a tender moment with him.

"Do not think that just because I have allowed you to stay here, *alive*, means that I won't kill you."

Soren's eyes widened. "I was only—"

"Let him go!" Bastian demanded.

"Hunter, order me around one more time and I will slit his throat and force you to watch him die in front of you." I could see him take another step forward, so I pushed the blade further into Soren's throat. "Do not test me."

Soren swallowed, wincing as the knife nicked him, and held his breath. After a moment, I lowered the knife and dropped it on the bed.

Soren took in a large breath, hand covering his throat, and whispered, "You aren't human after all... Fascinating."

"You fucking bastard!" Bastian wracked his hands through his hair, pulling at the ends.

What was wrong with him? His brother was right, he was completely unhinged.

Chapter Twelve

Then

The sun was shining bright as I looked down from the window in my chambers, seeing all of the carriages pulling forward with people streaming out of them—members of royalty with their many entourages.

I didn't want this. I knew that I was going to have to marry someone soon as my father needed to secure an alliance with a larger kingdom that had more resources than we did. While we were thriving on our own, we were small, and my father feared that the magic born would retaliate and there would be a war.

I didn't realize that I was fiddling with my hands until my mother came over and placed her hand atop mine.

"Darling, let's make haste."

She was in the most elaborate dress that I had ever seen her wear, adorned with an outrageous amount of jewels. I suppose they already had someone in mind for me to marry if they were insisting on wearing such outlandish attire.

The dress I wore had so many layers of petticoats that I wasn't sure how I was going to sit in it. They even brought out my tiara and placed it upon my head, securing my hair around it in complex braids.

"Mother..." I didn't know how to tell her that I didn't want to go. This entire night had me on edge. I had been working with Circe for years to control my magic, but I had already lost control multiple times with Circe whenever I thought about this night. I couldn't do it. "Just tell them I am ill and choose a suitor for me. We all know that it doesn't matter if I approve of the man or not."

Her brows knit together as she responded, "Where is all this coming from? I thought you would be excited to be around girls your age and dance the night away. You love to dance."

I squeezed my hands together behind my back, not wanting her to see just how much this was affecting me. Never wanting to disappoint her, always wanting to be the perfect daughter, but I was far from it. If they knew who I truly was they would hang me.

That thought wasn't helping my nerves.

Just then, someone interrupted our conversation and said, "Your highness, you look stunning. I apologize for my tardiness on such an important occasion."

My mother turned around to find Circe curtseying. Mother sighed.

"Talk some sense into the girl. We need to leave now before the guests start speculating on our absence."

"Of course, your majesty."

The moment Mother walked out of the room, I grasped Circe's hands and begged, trying to hold back the tears. "I can't do this Circe. Too many things could go wrong. I don't want to marry. I don't want to be queen. I don't want any of it!"

She placed her hands on my shoulders.

"You will get through this. You do not have a choice in the matter, but I will be with you always Callie. Remember what I taught you? Deep breath in. One. Two. Three. Deep breath out. One. Two. Three."

I followed her instructions, her voice soothing me, helping me to count and when I opened my eyes again I felt a calm wash over me. I was always shocked at how well that worked.

"I can do this," I said, a little more confident, but not by much.

"You can do this," she said sternly but lovingly.

We left to meet Mother and Annabelle in front of the ballroom doors. Mother held up her hand to the guards to give us a moment.

She turned to me and asked, "Are you ready?"

I took a breath and looked toward Circe, who gave me a curt nod. I looked back at my mother.

"I will make you proud."

She cupped my cheek and then spoke to a guard, "Open the doors."

They made their entrance, and then it was my turn. I took one last breath before stepping into the expansive ballroom. There were columns spread throughout the sides and in between the columns were windows. In the daylight, you could easily see for miles in every direction, a view we were quite proud of.

Rows of tables were set on one side of the room adorned with our finest tableware fit for any king to use. Only the best for my soon-to-be husband. Whomever he may be.

I stood at the top of the staircase, with my spine straight and my chin lifted. I would play my part and play it well...for my kingdom. I slowly descended, crossing my fingers that I wouldn't fall on my face in front of everyone. The thought almost sent me into a full-blown panic. No sooner had panic begun to set in, Father was at my side, offering his arm for support.

He leaned over to whisper, "My daughter... You..."

Words seemed to escape him. He just smiled and kissed my forehead gently as we reached the table.

I exchanged pleasantries with everyone that my father introduced me to, and all of the names were immediately forgotten the moment they left my lips. All of these people supported my father's war on magic, and I was disgusted that they could be filled with so much hate. If only they knew who it was they were really speaking to, I was sure their smiling faces would be replaced with a different kind of emotion.

I almost smiled at the thought.

I focused back when we made our way to our seats at the head of the table, and everyone sat down to listen to a lengthy speech by my father, thanking everyone for being there. Once the formalities were complete, the servants began to bring out the feast. The smell had me salivating: smoked chicken, geese, mutton, pork and beef. Sturgeon and whale, the most expensive seafood, were placed on several tables. And even more exotic were the peacocks that were served last, along with goblets of ale, apple wine, and water. No expense was spared.

There was nothing on the table that didn't smell divine, but I needed to remember my manners. I made idle conversation with Belle when I had the weird feeling that someone was looking at me, but when I looked around I couldn't see anyone who was. I tried my best to eat and not look around, but it was hard not to.

Dinner finished, and the dance began. Mother was right, dancing was one of my favorite parts of my grueling school schedule. It didn't matter, as long as I was on the dance floor. My dance card was full of the eligible princes, and I could see them all staring at me, as though I was a prize to be won. That if they put on their brightest smiles and had dashing good looks, then I would choose them. As if I had any say in whom I would marry. I knew how this game was played, though I thought I would be spared from this fate. That I could find someone that I cared for and who loved me in return. The kind of love that my parents had, even if it started out as an arranged marriage.

I looked over at Annabelle, who was with her entourage of girls hoping to get into her good graces. I worried that soon it would be her turn. Did she want to be married off like I was about to be?

She should have been the eldest sister; she was kind to all, proper, never raised her voice... Everything I wasn't. She was so intelligent, and I would often find her in the library reading rather than getting enough sleep. I would stay up with her just to keep her company, but oftentimes she would read things that made absolutely no sense to me.

I looked over to my right and found a group of men looking me over, their eyes undressing me as they scanned my body up and down. Not even hiding the fact that if I allowed them, they would take me right then and there.

I wasn't naive enough to not recognize that I was a rare beauty: smooth, russet skin, and dark brown wavy hair that flowed down to just above the middle of my back. Large, dark, brown doe eyes that knew nothing of the truths of the world. Innocent. Allowed others to control her. Even though I would be the next queen, I still would hold no real power. My husband would.

I didn't want this life for her. I didn't wish this life on anyone.

I walked out of their line of vision and spotted Circe speaking in low tones to a few servants that I had never seen before.

I quickened my pace to her when I overheard someone say, "King Jean just executed a teenage witch who, rumor has it, was performing her witchcraft deep in the woods. Then not long after, the baker's daughter fell ill and died!"

"Good. Let her perish. She got exactly what she deserved. I wish I could have been there to see her burn."

My skin heated with their words. They were laughing over the tragedy. Didn't see the girl as a human but a monster. I knew who they were talking about; Circe had told me that the girl would go into the woods to get away from her abusive family every night and was caught dancing around a fire.

She wasn't even magic born. Someone had accused her, and she was burned the next day. I almost cursed them for saying such inconsiderate and hateful words. But, I looked over at my parents who were laughing with more of their supporters, and at that moment, I hated them. Hated what they stood for. Hated them for unknowingly hating me. The one thing they did right was hiring Circe to care for me. She was the only one who knew the real me and didn't fear it.

I straightened and was about to join in on their conversation until my father walked out of the ballroom with Lord Padden. I remembered where I was and the shame it would bring upon my family. Not only that, but it would lead to unnecessary questions.

I remembered what Circe asked of me a month ago about trying to spy on my father and his private conversations. I loathed it, but we needed to know which group of people would be targeted next.

I had successfully infiltrated a few meetings using the old tunnels that I discovered while playing as a child and that hadn't been used in years. I kept them a secret until I told Circe, thinking that she could use them to sneak out of the castle. And I was right.

This knowledge allowed us to save over twenty magic borns over the last few weeks. Circe had decided that once I was old enough, I would be the one to sneak through the inner walls of the castle and spy on my father because I wouldn't be punished if I were caught. At least, not as harshly as someone else. I had already been lying to my family ever since I found out about my powers, and if this lie aided in saving lives, then it was worth the risk.

I had turned my back on the group upon my father's arrival, grabbed a glass from a passing servant, and followed them out of the ballroom. Based on their direction, I knew exactly where they were heading. I hurried through the tunnels and got into position just as my father and his council of advisers situated themselves in one of the secret rooms in the castle.

"I heard from my spy that they are planning a rebellion. And soon," Lord Padden said.

A rebellion? Circe had told me no such thing. The lord had to be spewing lies or else I would have known. Circe would have told me.

"Have you heard back from King Ewan? How does he feel about your proposal?"

"He has agreed to marry his son to Calathea."

Father nodded in response. "The alliance with Ewan is crucial. With his help, we will have the numbers and the resources to eradicate the covens from existence once and for all." Eradicate? My breathing had become labored, and the walls suddenly felt too close to me, but I needed to focus.

"They say his son is," Lord Padden's voice lingered. "A bit wild."

"A challenge for Calathea, perhaps, but she will adapt," Father added. "She's come of age, and if we can make her marriage beneficial and strengthen her reign, she will understand."

I pushed past the pain building in my chest as I heard Lord Padden ask, "It is not a secret that your daughter has spoken against you for the executions. Will she fall into line?"

I gritted my teeth at their blatant disrespect toward me and expected him to be put in his place, but Father simply said, "Rumors. My house is in order, and my daughter will do her duty." I couldn't hear anymore and rushed as silently as I could out of the walls, hurrying to the wooden door of their room to wait impatiently for them to finish deciding my future.

The moment they opened the door, I demanded, "Father, I must speak with you."

Father's spine had straightened, and he excused his council with a shallow nod, escorting me into the room.

"Please tell me it's not true. Please tell me you're not actually considering marrying me off for politics and warfare?"

Father looked at me as if I had grown two heads; this was not what he expected me to say. "How did you—"

"Tell me it isn't true! Please tell me you wouldn't do that to me, knowing how I feel about your witch hunt!"

"Enough!" He roared, voice so loud that I recoiled away from him for the first time in my life. "You will marry him, bed him, and give him children—as is your duty as a princess. You will secure your role in his kingdom to save ours."

"There is nothing to save if you would stop killing innocent people!"

One moment, I was standing in front of him, and the next I was on the floor, my face stinging from where his hand had struck me. I saw the look of regret on my father's face, but he simply straightened his back and said in a slightly calmer tone, "You will understand when you get older. I am only doing my job as king of this country and as your father. This war isn't going to end, it's only going to get worse. Can't you see that, child? If you are weak, if you are," he paused, and swallowed, desperation clinging to his voice, "too soft, you will destroy everything."

I said not another word to him as I took a moment to collect myself and strode from the room. It was well past sundown when I stormed into the stables and found Alexei putting away the reins of one of the horses. I had often sought him out when I needed small reprieves from everyone, even Circe, when my heightened emotions became too much.

All we did was kiss. I knew that I could never sleep with him, never risk someone finding out I had soiled myself. The price of my virginity, a silly little thing that made me soft, as my father said, would be my crown. He wanted me pure? I wouldn't give him that. I wouldn't marry a prince who wished to kill more of the people that I had vowed to help Circe save.

My people.

He turned around, too stunned to speak as I pushed him hard against the wooden wall, hard enough to make the walls rattle. He made a small noise at the movement, and something ignited within me: a feeling of heat pooling near a part of myself that I had denied. A feeling that had me laying in bed wide awake because there was an ache within me that wouldn't go away.

I wasn't ignorant about sex, but I had been raised to believe that you only had such relations when you were married and only to have children. It was not something to be enjoyed.

I didn't know what I was doing but allowed my body to take over. I ran my hands through his hair and watched as his mouth fell open.

"Your majesty—" I brought my lips to his as I always had, and I hesitantly rifled with the shirt tucked into his trousers, pulling at it haphazardly.

He smiled against my mouth and aided me in freeing his tucked shirt, pulling it over his head and throwing it to the ground, never taking his eyes off mine.

I looked around him and found a back room that housed the hay. I pushed on his chest until we were inside and kicked the door closed. His chest was heaving as he realized exactly what I wanted from him when I started to pull at the strings of my corset, attempting to get out of the contraption that is women's fashion. It always felt like a walking prison. I despised it.

I saw him coming over to help me, but I needed him and I couldn't wait another moment. I walked to the table with different shaped tools laid upon it, and used one to cut the laces of my gown, nearly cutting my skin in an attempt to pry the abominable attire off.

I stood completely nude in front of him and had never felt more free; the way Alexei stared at me with his lips parted, eyes hungry, made me want to convulse right there.

"Take them off," I commanded.

He nodded and nearly tripped over his feet, ripping his trousers off of him. When his appendage sprang free, I knew exactly what would help that ache inside of me.

But I felt a wave of anxiety. I was never taught how to be intimate with a male, and while I knew what body parts went where I was completely out of my element, and I hated it.

He could tell that something was a little off and hesitantly ran his hands up my body.

"You are so beautiful, your majesty." Sweet words that I was sure would make anyone swoon, but I didn't need him to be sweet. I didn't want him to shower me with kisses.

I wanted him to fuck me. I wanted him to make me scream and make me feel something other than pity and self-loathing. I wanted him to ruin me and see the look on my father's face when he learned of my indiscretions. I wanted to hurt him just as badly as he had hurt me.

"Stop talking." I swallowed as I grabbed him and copied what I had just seen him do to himself which seemed to make his once smaller cock grow at least a few inches. And judging by his shudder, he seemed to enjoy me touching him like this.

Then it all happened so quickly. He lifted me onto a table and rammed into me without warning. The pain was blinding and my head felt dizzy. Tears pricked my eyes. I didn't know it was supposed to be painful—why didn't they warn girls about that part?

Instinctively, when the pain became overwhelming, I bit into his shoulder, which seemed to get a reaction out of him because he pounded even harder into me. The pain subsided and was soon replaced with an intense feeling that had my inner walls gripping him, begging his cock to stay inside of me. Our moans filled the room. He tried to stare into my eyes, but I didn't want that so I pressed his head down, forcing him to suck on a nipple. That seemed to be my undoing because I screamed at an intense rush running through me—legs shaking as I felt something wet escape me.

My cheeks reddened as I thought about what that could have been, when I felt him jerk and then something filling me inside. He stilled, our breathing intermixed.

He kissed my shoulder before he pulled his head back. "You are incredible."

I scrunched my nose, not knowing how to respond. Shocked that I had actually gone through with something that I had wanted for a change. I knew I had ruined myself and I couldn't have been happier. And I wanted to do it again.

I pushed him off of me, grabbed his dark cloak from the floor, and wrapped it around my shoulders in an attempt to be inconspicuous.

As I walked out of the room, I said, "Same time tomorrow."

I smiled to myself as I walked back to the castle.

Chapter Thirteen

Now

I used my shadows to form into a makeshift cock.

"Open your mouth," I commanded, guiding it to Callum's mouth.

He was on his hands and knees, hard and naked, begging for me to fuck him. After what happened with Bastian and the nightmare last night, I needed a brief respite from my bleak reality.

I found Callum in his study. A room on the lower floor that wasn't used for anything from what I could remember. He had his nose in a book in another language. He loved learning, having come from a poor family that didn't have the resources that I did. As outdated as those resources they were.

Callum was too happy to oblige and licked my pussy, getting it nice and wet for him.

I brushed the hair away from his face, grabbed a handful of it, and guided him at a slow pace, his eyes never leaving mine.

Fuck. I don't know why it was so hot, but I loved seeing Callum in this position—this vulnerable. I pushed his head further along the shadowy shaft and held his head there until tears started to slide down his face. Only then did I let go.

I did that a few more times, which left both of us dripping when the doors flew open and Bastian said, "Callum, I—"

He stopped when he realized what he walked in on.

I lowered my eyes and gave him a lazy smile. I shoved Callum's face back onto my length and held him there. I stared at Bastian and said, "My little bird is busy right now. We are playing a game. How long can he hold his breath before he dies?" I looked down, and cocked my head, and asked, "Should we see if you can beat your record of sixty seconds?"

I could tell that Bastian was still slightly intoxicated; had been since I effectively crushed his spirit a few nights ago. Since then, he has clung to Callum.

"Get off him."

I could tell that Callum was running low on breath, but wouldn't move until I let him go. He would die right there if I wished for it.

"I promise you he would die a happy male if I chose this to be the moment he left us."

Red crept up Bastian's beautiful face, and I could tell that he didn't like what I was doing to his new friend. I rolled my eyes and pushed Callum a little further until I knew I was at the back of his throat. Once Callum gagged, I let go.

He coughed and sucked in copious amounts of air as he leaned on his heels, not embarrassed at being exposed to Bastian. There was nothing left to hide as he had already seen everything.

"Are you going to keep allowing her to degrade you?"

Callum dipped his head and then looked back up at Bastian. "Bast, you don't understand. I would let her trample over my dick if it made her happy. I would even fuck you if it brought her joy. Everything I do is for her."

He took another breath and stood, walking to Bastian, his cock swinging between his legs. I eyed Bastian and swore I saw his eyes dip down and his throat bob, but he diverted his gaze fast enough that I couldn't be sure.

"I do not desire men," Bastian tensed.

Callum put his hand hesitantly on Bastian's shoulder as I said, "You don't have to desire men to have fun with us."

It was easy to tell that Bastian was struggling to respond to Callum.

When he didn't say anything, I piped up. "We could have fun together."

Bastian glanced back down at Callum, who was looking at him, breath shortening. I brought my hand up my body, needing the friction as flames ignited inside of me. I had often fantasized about the three of us together, but I never imagined that Bastian would agree. The thought was almost enough to make me combust.

Whatever spell had come over the room was broken when Bastian knocked Callum's hand off his shoulder aggressively, stepped back, and then retreated from the room.

"He will come around when he's ready. Now, come here and bend over the desk." Callum obliged. He bent his body over, widened his legs, and spread his cheeks with each hand. "If you move your hands, then everything stops. Do you understand?"

He nodded vigorously.

I said not one word as I guided the shaft to his ass, slowly rubbing it around his opening until I sank slowly inside of him. Callum hissed in pain, and I paused to let him get used to the size.

He held on, begging, "Please keep going, your grace. Don't stop."

I smirked as I continued to ease into him at an achingly slow pace until I was buried in him all the way, and my hips were flat against his ass.

"Tell me, who owns you?" I asked, teasing him by grabbing his balls with my shadows.

He tensed under my powers, not wanting to cum so soon, and said immediately, "You, your grace. Always you."

I moaned at hearing his response. "Say it again." Squeezing tightly.

"You own me."

When hearing those words, I pounded into him while squeezing him at the same time, my other hand on his shoulder for added stability.

"You own me. Only you. Always you." Callum repeated over and over again.

Fuck. Yes.

I was relentless, and every time I pulled out, I would widen the girth of my shadow cock and watch as it disappeared back inside of him. I loved feeling his walls tighten around my length, able to feel what my shadows felt. They were always calm after fucking Callum, so I was never afraid to use them around him.

It didn't take long until I felt him engorge and then tense as he came. I didn't stop until his entire body had stopped shaking from the orgasm. I let my powers disappear while inside of him, and grabbed his hair from behind, forcing him to arch his back.

"Tell me."

"I am yours."

I let go of his head and conjured a wooden chair to the middle of the room. It was a normal chair with a hole in the seat, a contraption that I heard about from a far-off kingdom and had to try. Callum scurried over to the chair and laid beneath it ready and waiting. I could feel myself dripping down my leg with how wet I was.

I sat down and Callum didn't wait a moment before his mouth was on me. Licking. Sucking. I had to grip the arms of the chair to keep myself from moving too much. I threw my head back and moaned as his tongue penetrated me and had me squirting all over his face.

I stood and got rid of the chair with a wave of my hand and looked down at him. It was a work of art, and he was mine.

"Look at you, little bird, covered in me."

He gave me one of those smiles that would melt anyone else. How would it have melted me before all of this? He stared at me, eyes wicked with excitement as he wiped a finger against his face and then brought it to his lips, sucking.

Fuck.

My eyes darkened, and I was on him in a flash, and we fucked and fucked...then fucked some more.

I made my way to the library. It was cold and empty. I conjured a ball of light in my hands as I made my way through the stacks of books. I walked to the back of the room, touching a panel that opened a hidden room next to our family portrait.

Every year on the anniversary of Belle's death I would come into this room and write her a letter about what had been going on in my life. This year I had much to tell her. Though I wanted to leave out all of the darker details: how the nightmares had come on stronger, Circe was speaking to me more often, Emilia seemed to be on the edge of a mental breakdown, Mariam was murdered, and vivid memories had begun to play themselves for me in my waking hours.

It was all too much. And I didn't think she needed to be privy to that information.

Do you ever think that maybe she doesn't want to hear from you?

I couldn't talk about her, not to Circe. Instead, I opened the book to the next blank page, dipped the quill into the ink, and got ready to start writing.

It is all your fault.

I ignored her and put the quill to the parchment.

November 1761,

Hello dear sister,

Much has changed the past week. Two males have decided to stay in the castle with Callum, Emilia, and me. The transition has been smooth—well, as smooth as it could be. I will admit that it did not start out on the best of terms, but

I stopped writing. It was all the same. I never talked about anything of substance, nothing that truly mattered. I thought that if I shared my thoughts with her, she would see me as she did in life—a monster.

All I had ever done in my life was lie to everyone I loved. Everyone who once mattered. I didn't want to lie anymore.

I started anew.

Dear Belle,

I have been lost for centuries. I am still here in this castle because of my curse, a curse that I don't believe I deserve to have broken.

You were right. I am the animal Father wanted to purge from this world.

This was how I would pay my penance. And even if I did find a way to break the curse… What would I do?

The thought was once exhilarating but had lost its luster when it wouldn't be with her. When we were younger, we begged Father to allow us to visit neighboring kingdoms, but he outright refused for fear of the magic-born people possibly harming us. He always said that he could protect us from within these lands. So we would lay in bed at night and make a game out of telling each other where we wished to go if given the chance. Belle always said that she wished to try out all the different flavors and spices around the world. I chuckled to myself, remembering how her little face lit up whenever she talked about a new food that she read about.

Then she would look up at me as I told her all about my desire to immerse myself with people of different cultures and live a life free from the pressures of being royal.

But was that still something I craved?

I was still sitting as I looked around the room that was still coated in dust: two chairs, two candles, and two stacks of books. Books that were useless in helping me find a way to break the curse and venture outside of these lands.

The stack to my left were the books that I had already gone through multiple times. The middle stack was books that I had given up on. My eyes slid over to the stack of books I couldn't decipher anything useful either, as they were written in a language that I had no idea how to read, an ancient language long forgotten. Circe could read them, but never taught me.

You never earned the right, she scolded. *You had so much promise.*

I continued staring at nothing when I heard a shuffling sound from the other side of the door. I hesitantly peeked into the nook, not knowing what I would find when Soren's face appeared inches from mine.

I screamed and threw my fist out, hitting him directly in the nose, and heard a loud crack.

"What the hell!" Soren landed hard on the ground as his hands went up to his face.

"What the fuck are you doing here?" I looked toward the windows and saw that it was still dark. It would be hours until sunrise. "You should have retired to your room hours ago."

He looked at me over the top of his hands that were holding onto his now-injured nose.

"I couldn't sleep, and you never forbade us from the library." He moved his hands which were now covered in blood to look down and found the front of his shirt drenched in the cold, sticky substance. I could see his eyes roll into the back of his head, and he fell back with a thud.

I stared at him, mouth agape, confused at this entire situation. Would he ever stop surprising me? I knelt down and assessed him: his nose was obviously broken, and with the sound his head made when it connected with the ground, I was sure it had some damage.

He started coming to and blinked up at me slowly as I hovered over him.

"Are you an angel?"

"Far from it."

"What happened?"

I didn't respond as I cut my wrist open and held it over his mouth. He was about to say something else, but I used my shadows to enter his mind and assist him in drinking a few mouthfuls. I smiled at him as I grabbed his nose, and before he had time to overthink, I readjusted the bones of his nose back into place.

I stood up, continuing to smile sweetly down at him. The shadows faded from the control on his mind, and as he came to his senses he winced, the pain now apparent.

He breathed through the pain as he looked up at me, still on his back, and said, "You know you are a little sadistic, right?"

I shrugged, dropping the smile.

"So I've been told. I must live up to everyone's high expectations of me, should I not?"

He stood up, now completely healed. He touched his nose and the back of his head, seemingly checking himself for the injuries he thought he had, and asked, "Did you just give me your blood? And did I voluntarily drink it?"

I ignored those questions and instead focused back on the matter at hand.

"I don't care for the reason why you are awake at such an hour. What I care about is that you stay out of places that are of no concern to you."

He threw his hands up, exasperated.

"It's a library! I like to read when I can't sleep." His eyes went wide as he peeked over my shoulder. "Wait! What is that room?" He pushed past me, and his eyes quickly roved over every inch of the room before I could move fast enough to pull him from it.

I could see the excitement in his eyes, hear it in his voice. Another part of the mystery that is the Everhart legacy. A part that I would never allow him to be privy to.

I pushed him back with my magic and shut the door.

"I highly recommend you leave now before I do good on my promise and kill you."

He sighed. "You know, that threat is getting rather old."

"Doesn't make it any less true."

He knew this was a losing battle and walked away, then paused, looking up at the portrait of my family. I readied myself for another fight before he said the one thing that I never thought I would hear uttered on another's lips. A word that was as foreign to me as emotions were. A part of me that was dead.

"Calathea?" He said it while looking at me through his peripheral. Wanting to see my reaction to it. As if he already knew the answer, but just wanted confirmation of his hunch.

I stilled. "How do you know that name?"

"So, it's true? You are Calathea Rose Everhart."

I swallowed. "That girl is dead."

And she was. She died when her human life ended.

"Why aren't you in any of the texts that I have read, but you are in every book that mentions your family in this castle? You have been completely erased from the history of this kingdom. I was shocked when I read that they had another daughter and didn't fathom that it was you." He was getting too excited over this revelation. "I only just now realized it because of this," he said, pointing toward the portrait.

That was part of the curse. I would be forgotten, cursed to be alone. I didn't know how she did it, but she succeeded.

"Scholar, I would recommend that you get away from me right now before I do something neither of us wants."

He swallowed, thankfully realizing that it was not the moment to press the subject. He turned and hurried out of the room without another word.

The audacity of this boy never ceased to amaze me. How had my speech earlier not shaken him enough to leave all this be? What did the past have such control over him? Nearly as much as it did myself?

I leaned against the wall of books and slowly slid to the ground, suddenly exhausted. More than I had been. If I hadn't been so transfixed by what Soren had just said, I could have fallen asleep right there on the ground.

Was he going to tell Bastian my name? Did it even matter?

It doesn't matter what they call you, you are still a monster. La bête.

I needed to know what he planned to do with this information; he looked too excited to not share my name. I lifted my hand, focusing my energy as shadows licked the skin over my hand, creating a ball of swirling violet light. When my father closed off the tunnels under the suspicion they were being used, Circe taught me this trick to spy on the people within the castle.

The moment the ball of light fully formed, Soren burst through Bastian's chamber doors.

Bastian startled awake. "Ren?"

I could see Soren striding toward the window, throwing the curtains open, letting in the natural light from the moon's rays that were able to penetrate the fog.

Bastian rubbed the sleepiness from his eyes, and when he finally looked at his brother, he jumped from the bed. "What happened!"

Bastian hurried over to Soren, grabbed his face between his hands, and moved it around to get a good look at him.

"I am going to kill her," he seethed.

Soren seemed to be annoyed by this as he rolled his eyes and swatted his brother's hands away. He then pulled something from the waistband of his trousers. A book.

I stiffened. That little snake.

He held it up in front of Bastian's face and began his rambling, unable to hide the excitement now that he had someone to share it with.

"Calathea Rose Everhart, born on December 21, 1391. Her parents, King Jean and Queen Angela Everhart, along with ninety-seven percent of the kingdom, were killed due to a mysterious plague. The only ones to have survived were people who were away on holiday, at university or work. Annabelle Paige Everhart died before the plague and had been rumored to be the first to fall ill from it, infecting everyone else. Though others say that she was murdered. Because no one had dared to enter the kingdom for many years after, not even to claim the bodies in fear of contracting the disease, no one can say for certain what is the truth. Not to mention the myth of *la bête*."

Soren looked mad, out of his mind, at all of these new revelations. Overcome with intrigue and filled with even more questions than before. His eyes bulged out of his head as he opened the book and flipped carefully through the worn pages. Even in this erratic state, he knew to be careful with the ancient texts.

He was pacing, unable to keep himself still, running his hands through his hair as he continued, "She has been eradicated from every single text except for the ones in her library. And she has this room—"

"Soren, you need to slow down, I don't understand a word you're saying. And tell me why the fuck you have blood on your face and clothes."

Soren took a breath and snapped, "Let me explain this in a way you'll understand. The queen punched me, broke my nose, and I passed out from looking at the blood. I think I may be hemophobic, but I can test that theory at a later date."

Bastian looked enraged, whether it was at his brother's comment, my actions, or a mixture of both.

"She punched you? I am going to kill her."

Bastian walked past him, but Soren grabbed his arm, forcing him to stop.

"Brother, are you not listening? Yes, she punched me, but that isn't the point. Look, I am fine, she fixed it. Her blood heals!"

He was too wrapped up in the revelation that had his entire attention. A little broken nose was of no significance. I was sure that he would allow me to break his nose a hundred times over if it meant that he could get his hands on more information.

"Now, our very own queen is the missing princess. She isn't technically missing because no one knows she exists."

Soren was too intelligent for his own good.

Leave it to the most annoying scholar in human history to stick his nose in business that didn't concern him. No one had ever looked through my books, so I didn't even think to hide them.

I wasn't annoyed that they knew the truth. I was annoyed because I knew what it meant; the bookworm would stop at nothing to find out the truth of my past. More questions. Just thinking about it made my head pound.

Bastian stared at him briefly before dropping his head and walking back over to his bed.

"If that is all then could you please take your leave before I—"

"Are you serious? Do you know what this means?"

"It means that you have officially gone mad, and I will have to put you out of your misery, but that can wait until the morning."

He brushed past his brother's words and continued, "I was walking around in the library, merely looking around, and I found this." He showed Bastian a book of my family tree, with all the gritty details of my past. "I swear, it's her. I now know why she refused to tell us her name."

Bastian took the book from Soren's outstretched hands, taking a moment to digest everything his brother said, still groggy from sleep.

"And you know this for a fact?"

"I just saw her and called out her name to test the theory and you should have seen the look on her face. She paled, you could almost hear her heartbeat from how fast her chest was rising and falling. If I hadn't left she was going to kill me just to make me stop talking about it."

Bastian's face paled, the same color as my own despite our difference in skin tone, after reading over a certain section of the page and said, in a haunted tone, "If what you are saying is true and this date is correct then that would make her—"

He couldn't even finish the sentence as he gulped.

Soren finished for him with a huge grin on his face, so big that I could see deep dimples forming. "Precisely three hundred and seventy years old." He was giddy.

"You are infatuated with her. Have you fucked her yet? Does she have a magical cunt or something?"

"You're out of line." The grin on Soren's face immediately vanished.

They stared at each other. What they were trying to find I was unsure, but I couldn't look away.

"Nevermind." Bastian turned from Soren and headed toward the closet, grabbed his satchel, and silently threw his belongings into it.

"Bast. Bast." Bastian was ignoring him. "Bast!"

Bastian stopped once he was satisfied and said over his shoulder, "She must still be in the library, so now is the perfect time to go. It'll be hours before dawn and we will be long gone by then."

Soren looked at him confused. "What?"

"We need to get the fuck out!" Bastian hissed, took a few steps to his brother, grabbed his wrist, and yanked him toward the door.

Soren pulled his hand from his brother's grasp and said, "I am not leaving."

"Oh yes, you are."

"You made a deal with her! You—" He pulled his shirt down exposing the scar on his chest. "We—can't escape even if we wanted to, and I am telling you, that is the last thing I want to do."

"We don't need her deals! We escape, tell everyone, and then come back and kill her to ensure that she doesn't come after our family. No more sacrifices. Problem solved."

"If you think I am going to leave after finding out that we are living under the same roof as a woman who has lived for almost four hundred years then you are sorely mistaken." He looked away and mumbled to himself, "Is that why she keeps calling us boys? Because if so then that makes so much sense!"

He removed the quill from behind his ear and scribbled notes down in that damned notebook.

"I am responsible for your well-being, Soren!"

"Since when?" He was now staring at his brother, quill in hand. "You have never cared enough to take any interest in my life before, so why now?"

"What are you talking about?"

"Bast, you didn't even know that my entire academic career has been centered around the three hundred and seventy-year-old woman who is alive and breathing in another room in this very castle."

Alright, he could stop mentioning my age now, I didn't need any more reminders.

"How was I supposed to take interest when you were always stuck in your room reading? Or off somewhere traveling and studying? You took any chance you could get to escape home."

"You were always Father's favorite; there was never any room for me."

"You are an entitled bastard!" He spat. "You never had any pressure, Soren. You were allowed to be exactly who you wanted to be. Don't you see that? The family, the legacy, all the rules, that was on me. Forgive me if I didn't ask whatever the fuck you were drawing in your sketchbook from day to day."

"You sound just like her," he said evenly, and I knew he was referring to me and my lecture to him earlier. "You are right—I have had the privilege and freedom to escape home, but the cost of that was a disappointed father. I was a stain to him, one he couldn't scrub off. Perhaps I do not understand your pressure, but you do not understand what it is like to be nothing to a man who brought you into the world."

My heart hammered in my chest—all the words I threw at him in anger, about him not understanding me or Emilia, all the while he'd been living with his own loneliness and pain.

There was silence between the brothers. They just stood staring at each other until Bastian turned away, running his hands through his hair, unsure of how to proceed.

He whispered to himself, "It wasn't fucking worth it. This is all my fault."

Soren asked, "What wasn't worth it?"

"Not killing her when I had the chance," Bastian seethed.

Soren sighed, seeming to want to put his brother at ease.

"Bast, nothing you did would have stopped me from coming here. I was already planning on coming the moment I got home from university. What is happening to me is not your fault."

"Why do you care about her?"

Soren lifted his round glasses from his face and rubbed the back of his hand across his forehead, taking a minute to gather his thoughts.

"Do you remember my friend, Léna?" When Bastian shook his head, Soren continued, "She was my best friend when I was younger, and then she was one of the chosen when I turned ten."

Bastian lowered his head. "I didn't know. I'm sorry."

"I vowed to save her. I promised her that we would run away together, but Father caught me and hit me, knocked me out, and by the time I had awoken, it was too late to meet her. I followed her path and saw Léna standing before the queen and another woman. Anyway, that's not the point." He chastised himself. "I have been obsessed not just with this castle, but with this queen from the moment that I laid eyes on her. And this is the first time I have had a chance to return, and you will *not* keep me away."

"If you think so highly of her, why hasn't she ended the Reapings? She's had several hundred years to find a way, yet she's sat back and allowed it to continue." Bastian gave Soren a moment to answer but continued when his brother stayed silent. "I'll tell you why, brother. The Reapings protect her. She'll let hundreds of children be torn from their families if it means nobody finds out who—what— she is." Bastian slammed his fist into the bedpost. "All of the fucking sacrifices were pointless, and she knows it. She even kept one for herself! That girl, Emilia. She could have had a new life somewhere with a good family, but instead, she's trapped in these walls so that monster can have another pet. She's sick."

My stomach began to roll because even if I wanted to fight his words, nothing he said was wrong.

"Perhaps we just do not understand her like we think. Maybe there's more to all this. Back then, they were burning witches... The famous War on Magic. Maybe it's all connected to her."

Bastian scoffed. "It doesn't matter what you say. My word is final."

Soren sighed and turned his head, crossing his arms over his chest.

"You sound just like Father." He missed the horrified look on Bastian's face, but I didn't. After seeing what his father was like in the memory, I knew that was a vile comparison.

"Spit your venom, Soren. On this matter, I know I'm right." He walked up to Soren and hit him on the back of his head with a glass bottle of wine, effectively knocking him unconscious.

I frowned. Poor little scholar.

Bastian hoisted him over his shoulder and then set out into the hallway. He was cautious and stuck to the shadows, not wanting to be caught, not wanting to take any chances in case someone was awake in the castle.

I smiled, suddenly excited. The fool had no idea what he just did, what he just awakened in me. My heart rate increased; the smell of fear potent in the air and the wind whipping around my face was all so invigorating. There was something about stalking my prey and then pouncing on them that made my insides molten. My mind flicked to a memory of chasing Callum in the woods and fucking him right where I found him.

I walked through the opening I created with my shadows and was transported to the same spot where I met this foolish hunter not long ago, waiting for the brothers to arrive. I guessed that it took Bastian a while because he wanted to take his time to ensure that he wouldn't be caught.

I was leaning against a tree, using the darkness to hide, as I heard rustling down the path. A moment later Bastian came into sight. He stopped at the gate, readjusted the slipping Soren back on his shoulder, and stepped through it. I smiled to myself as he was forced back by my shadows, waiting for the fury that would come when Bastian found that he couldn't get through.

They were both on the ground as Bastian stood up, clearly confused.

"What the—" He walked to the gate and tried stepping through it again but was thrown back once more.

"How many times are you going to try that before you realize it won't work?" I asked in a bored tone.

He jumped.

"Goddammit, woman!" He paled when he realized that he had been caught. His ingenious plan to flee was over, and they were seconds away from the repercussions of attempting escape. "I wasn't... This wasn't—"

"So, you weren't just trying to escape before dawn?"

He looked toward the gate, at the vine-covered path ahead.

I tapped my hand against my chin.

"Hm, I wonder whose brilliant idea this was." I pondered, looking down at Soren's unconscious body.

He eyed me, furious at his failed attempt.

"Why can't we step foot over the gate, witch?"

"Are we still name-calling? Rather childish, wouldn't you agree?"

"Why can't we leave?"

I walked up to him. "How many times do I need to remind you that your life is no longer yours to do with as you please?"

He pointed to his chest.

"This is keeping us from leaving?"

"No," I said coyly.

"Then why?" He shouted.

"You're no fun... It's just my shadows." I jutted my bottom lip out, pouting. I released my powers and rolled my eyes. "I told you that the mark binds you to these lands, but that was a lie. The truth? You could leave at any moment;

the mark simply brands you as mine. The only one cursed to be here is me. What can I say?" I raised my hands above me and shrugged. "I have a flair for the dramatics."

"Why lie at all?"

"You wouldn't have stayed otherwise if you knew the truth, and I wasn't in the mood to keep watch over you constantly."

"We are leaving."

Bastian reached down to hoist Soren over his shoulder. Just as he was about to take a step over the boundary line, I shot my shadows out and clutched onto Soren's wrist, tugging him out of Bastian's arms once more, and laid him gently in front of me.

Bastian turned and was about to charge at me when I yelled, "Leave! I told you from the moment your brother came that I didn't need you. He will take your place."

I kneeled down next to Soren as Bastian walked over to us.

"Do not touch him."

I cocked my head to the side and gently swiped my finger over Soren's injured head, remnants of his bloody nose still prevalent as well as the new welt from his brother. He needed to be healed soon. I was not a doctor, but even I knew that all of these hits to the head couldn't be good for his health.

I bit into my palm and was about to give him more of my blood when Bastian moved, and grabbed my wrists, pinning them behind me.

My chest pressed against his, back arched.

"Stop." Bastian's hot breath fanned my face. "Please, just stop."

"Oh, the neanderthal knows how to use manners. Who knew?" I paused for a few moments, staring up at him, our faces inches apart.

"What do I need to do for you to grant my brother his freedom?"

"What makes you think he wants to leave? Actually, he has communicated quite clearly with me that he wants nothing more than to get to know me." Rather my history, but that was neither here nor there.

"I don't give a fuck what he thinks he wants with his life. I am the eldest, and I know what is best for him. So, I ask you one more time: What. Do. I. Need. To. Do?"

"If I told you that you had to be on your hands and knees every single day without complaint, would you?"

"Yes," he said without hesitation.

"You would become my whore to save your brother?"

He gripped my hands tighter behind me and leaned down to growl in my ear: "I would lick your pussy until my jaw numbed, from sun up to sun down. I would let you chain me to your bed so that you could have your way with me whenever the fuck you wanted. Whatever twisted, fucked up fantasy was in your mind, I would gladly oblige if you let him go."

I looked up to the sky to ponder; pretending that the growl didn't make my toes curl and then met his eyes once more.

"No."

He hissed. "I will find a way to get out of this hell with my brother."

My lips thinned into a hard line.

"I promise if you ever attempt to escape again, I will make sure that when your sister is sent into the forest she never finds her way out again." He didn't have to know I was bluffing—I just couldn't think of another way to keep him here.

He was staring at me so intently and for so long that I thought he would call my bluff when he roared, "Fuck!"

He was doomed and he knew it. Soren would never leave willingly, and if he took Soren by force, he would only come back on his own. And even if he did leave with a willing Soren, he would never be able to convince his father to abandon his belief and secretly save his daughter. There was no situation in which he came out on top.

Except staying here—with me.

"You are stuck with me, hunter. Now and forever." I taunted, "Tell me who owns you."

I closed the distance between our faces and brushed my tongue lightly against his lips before drawing back enough to catch his reaction.

His eyes narrowed, the words turning over in his mind.

I knew he didn't want to say it, but he surprised me when he answered: "You own me."

The light in his eyes dimmed; the thread of hope that he was holding onto had finally snapped. I couldn't focus on that; the sooner he realized he needed to stop thinking that he could leave, the better off he would be. As much as I didn't want him here either, there was no other choice.

"That's right. I fucking own every inch of you."

We were interrupted by a rustling sound behind us. Soren groaned as he reached up and felt the place where Bastian had hit him.

"Not again." Then he looked around. "Why are we outside?"

"It doesn't matter anymore. I won't be attempting this again."

"No?" Soren questioned and then smiled, knowing that Bastian's grand escape was thwarted.

"Nope. Looks like your mysterious queen is a master manipulator and will be getting exactly what she wants. What the queen wants the queen gets, right?"

I narrowed my eyes at him as Bastian helped his brother stand, and he barked out in protest at all the abuse his body was getting that night. Bastian put an arm around his waist and walked slowly with him back to the castle.

I stood there watching their forms slowly slip away and into the darkness until I let out a breath. Bastian was affecting me the more I was around him. My body reacted to him whenever he came into view or whenever I thought about him. It was starting to become a damned nuisance.

Chapter Fourteen

The next few weeks had gone by smoothly enough. Emilia barely came out of her room, feigning illness. Bastian refused to talk to me, let alone look at me. Callum was beginning to worry not only for Emilia but for Bastian, which was a surprise. Soren was begging me to make another deal with him, but I couldn't dive back into his memories. As much as I wanted to see more, it hurt too much knowing that I would never see them for myself.

I had spent the time reviewing the books on curses just to see if I missed anything. The curse was meticulously worded, and no matter how hard I tried, nothing worked. I spent years doing everything I could until the loneliness and insanity started to weave its way into me. Not just breaking down my will, but beating it out of me.

You'll never rid yourself of me. You would miss me too much. I am your oldest friend, after all.

"I don't have friends. Even if I did, you definitely would not be one of them."

There's no need to be nasty.

I ignored that comment, knowing full well that I could be nastier if I wanted to. It was quiet long enough that I thought she went away when she hummed with pride.

My curse really is a work of art.

"That's one way to put it." I knew that talking to myself always put everyone else in a state of unease, but she was all I had. No matter how much I didn't want to admit it. As much as I hated her, I needed her.

My mind created her, of all people, to not leave me completely lonely in this isolated world that my ancestors created. A tomb of their own making. Deep enough into the Forbidden Forest that one would get lost if they didn't know the path. A labyrinth of trees that would turn you around, the environment killing you before any creatures had a chance to rip you to shreds.

I am your constant.

I didn't know why that comment made me pause because it was true. She would be with me forever, but today, the knowledge broke something within me. I had been walking back into the castle to find Soren in the library, but I hadn't wanted to see him, knowing that he would continue his assault of questions. Instead, I diverted my path to the cellar.

The door to the underground tunnels and rooms was down a long, narrow corridor that led to a dead end, or so it would make you believe. There were heavy drapes at the end and behind that was a secret door with a corridor so long that you couldn't see where it led. There was a torch sitting in its metal hatch to the right of me.

I lit the torch and began my descent. The path curved around various twists and turns at least a few floors down until I finally stepped off the stairs onto soil. No one had ever bothered to bring enough stone to cover the floor. The narrow stairwell opened into a large circular room with even more corridors leading to different parts of the castle. Some went another floor down meant for prisoners who would never see the light of day again.

I took the corridor directly to my right, which led to a wooden door, and opened it to find a large room full of alcohol of all kinds imported from across the world.

We had a wine cellar, but these were the bottles that were used for only the most elite guests. There were so many that even after all the time I had been here, I had yet to go through half of them. Of course, I only used them for special occasions: when my emotions started to become a little too much, and I wasn't ready to use my *venin*.

I slid my fingers over the dusty bottles and sang one of my mother's favorite songs under my breath. As the song ended, I stopped and picked up the bottle my finger landed on. I uncorked it, took a long drink, and hissed at the taste.

Aloxinum. It was so strong that it made me want to spit the contents all over the ground. I had never tasted it without first mixing it with something else.

I took another swig, and it burned some more. Good enough.

I went out of the room, shut the door, and began to ascend the winding steps. I was almost to the top when I heard a roar off in the distance, loud enough to reach me down here. I groaned, not wanting to find out exactly what trouble they had found themselves in now.

I thought it would be fun having them here to play with, but it had become the complete opposite. I reached the door and took a deep breath in. One. Two. Three. Deep breath out. One. Two. Three. Then, I opened the door in time to hear another roar, but this time, I knew exactly who it belonged to.

Callum.

Surprise and intrigue wrapped around me, so I followed the roar. To my surprise, the roaring erupted into laughter at the same moment I found Emilia staring at something in disbelief.

Bastian and Callum were standing in the middle of one of the walkways of the parapet. There was a large piece of wood leaning against the parapet with circles drawn on it. Something for target practice.

They were concentrating so hard that neither one of them saw us. Bastian held a goblet of what I could assume was his desired choice of drink. He held the cup in one hand and his dagger in the other. He bit down on his bottom lip as he swayed slightly, brought his hand back, and sent the dagger flying through the air. They both cheered as the dagger found its mark on the red dot in the middle of the wood. Even in his drunken state, he was an excellent shot.

"What are they doing?" I asked Emilia.

"The hunter called it a fun game only to be played amongst the men." I rolled my eyes at that comment.

"Why are you here?"

"I became curious." She shrugged. "And I am absolutely surprised that Callum could look so exuberant."

I looked back over to them and noticed she was right. Callum looked so young, so carefree. He smiled with me and at times laughed, but this was different. Were all men like this only with each other?

I shook my head of those thoughts. Callum was my consort and nothing else, even if I hated the way he was with Bastian.

The boys were talking, and I could hear Bastian explain how to hold the dagger and then let go at the precise moment. After a little more explanation, he passed the dagger to Callum, taking another swig of his drink as he narrowed his eyes on my consort's form. He assessed Callum, roving his eyes over every inch of his body.

Callum was talking to himself as he went over everything Bastian had just said to him. He bent his knees a few different ways until he settled on one he was comfortable with. Breathed in and out a few times until his body became less tense, and more relaxed. He raised his left hand slightly to steady himself and his right hand up to the side of his face. His full concentration was on the red circle as he moved his arm, but he let go too soon. The dagger went flying way too high and right over the side of the castle.

Callum hung his head as Bastian stepped forward and clamped his hand on Callum's shoulder. "That's alright. I have seen others do worse."

"Oh?"

"Well, they were children..."

Callum laughed at Bastian's jest. He pushed Bastian's shoulder away as he walked over to the side wall and looked down.

"Someone is going to have to go down and get it if you want to keep playing your game."

Bastian walked over to him and whistled as he looked down.

"It doesn't look that far."

Callum looked over at him in disbelief.

"I would beg to differ. Come on, we will go get it together." Callum finally noticed Emilia and I. "Your grace."

He bowed immediately.

"Is this how you've decided to spend your time? Throwing tiny swords?"

Bastian looked up to the night sky as though he were contemplating my question and then looked back at me for the first time in days.

"I can't think of a single thing I would rather be doing."

I wanted to remind him that there was at least one thing he was craving to do, but before I could say anything, he downed the last of his drink and threw it over the side of the parapet. The goblet clanged on the stone as it tumbled down. He braced his hands on the side of the crenel and hoisted himself up until he was crouching.

"Bast! Get down!" Callum's eyes were wide, obviously nervous.

I wasn't convinced. He wouldn't do anything to truly injure himself. He wouldn't leave his brother.

Bastian stood and was about to climb on top of the merlon, but he slipped. His hands shot out quickly, and he barely caught himself before falling over the edge. He chuckled and looked down again, then over his shoulder to us. "That would have been bad."

I rushed forward. He was going to be the death of me.

"Get down now!"

He rolled his eyes. "Uh oh, the witch is angry."

He tried again. This time, he succeeded in hoisting himself up and standing. "I can see for miles up here. Join me, Cal!" He screamed, throwing his arms out wide.

"Bast, come on. I'll go get the dagger, and we can continue the game." Callum had come up beside me and was trying to coax him down.

"If you don't get down right now, I swear—"

"Oh, now what? Do you ever stop wanting to hear yourself speak?" He turned back around and started jumping from ledge to ledge.

I could feel myself growing more and more impatient with him. My shadows drifted around my body, and I could see the faint purple glow of my eyes casting a light hue onto the stone wall.

"He is out of his mind. He isn't thinking straight."

Everything happened in slow motion. I could see Bastian tripping over his foot and swaying toward the empty air. He screamed out while trying to catch his balance.

I pushed Callum aside and lunged toward Bastian, lifting a hand toward his body. His eyes were wide as they connected with mine and he reached out a hand toward me. I lept off the wall after him, not thinking twice about it. I wouldn't make it; our hands reached for each other but were still too far apart by mere inches. Thankfully, Bastian's shirt was untucked and billowing just enough for me to grasp. The moment I connected with his shirt, I transported us to the first place that I could think of.

The library.

We crashed against the floor in a heap as Soren yelled, "What is going on?"

I opened my eyes to find Bastian underneath me, arms wrapped tightly around my narrow waist, eyes boring into mine. My long hair hung around my face, shielding us from Soren's curious gaze. I sat up until I was straddling Bastian, and as he lifted himself up onto his elbows, I reared my hand back and slapped him.

"Ask your idiotic brother. He's the one who almost got himself killed!" I was livid, my heart racing.

"Bast?"

I pushed up from Bastian as he cradled the side of his face in his hand, his face beet red, and began to storm toward the door.

"It's not like I meant to."

I whirled around on him. "Didn't mean to? Didn't mean to!" My voice got higher and higher. "You got up on that merlon alone despite our protests."

"The merlon?" Soren asked, not following our conversation.

Bastian looked to Soren, "Cal and I were just playing a stupid game. And I may have almost fallen off the side of the castle."

"Almost!" It wasn't a question of whether he did or not; it was a fact. "You *did* fall off the side of the fucking castle, you idiotic, *dalcop,* pathetic excuse for the male species!"

"You did what?" Soren was next to his brother, looking down at him. "You could have died."

"*Would* have died if it wasn't for my powers that you loathe." I couldn't help the sarcasm dripping from my mouth.

Bastian cursed to himself and stumbled out of the library without another word to either one of us. I looked at the youngest brother.

"If he dies, do not come blaming me for his moronic decisions."

I stormed into Callum's room, nearly knocking him over with how aggressively I threw myself at him. I ripped his shirt open, accidentally using a bit of my magic, shredding the material.

Callum matched my speed and licked my shoulder, nibbling as he quickly undid the lacing of my dress. My fingers were shaking as I tried but failed to unbutton his trousers. I could hear him chuckle slightly as he took over and freed himself.

He sat on the edge of the bed, grabbed my ass, and pulled me into him. I closed my eyes and tried to get lost in this moment. To revel in the way his grasp always left me breathless. To never want his cock to leave my aching pussy.

My brows knit together as images of Bastian's face when he realized that he would never be able to leave assaulted my mind. No... Not now. I squeezed my eyes shut and crushed Callum into my body, my hands snaking into his hair as I forced his head into my neck, demanding him to suck on the delicate skin.

I felt him smile against my skin and almost smiled until my thoughts went back to Bastian and I felt...empathy? A sadness had overtaken me because I had cursed him just like Circe cursed me.

Callum's hand slid down to my slit and as his fingers penetrated me, it hurt. It only took a moment to realize why; I was dry.

"Stop." I pushed away from Callum and turned until my back was to him. I had *never* not fucked Callum, had never said no. Until now.

What were the brothers doing to me?

I wracked my fingers through my hair as I heard Callum ask, "What did he do?"

My body hummed with rage I hadn't felt since I found Emilia. My entire body was on fire. I couldn't sit still, so I paced.

"What did Bastian do?" Callum asked once more, this time more insistent.

I turned back toward him. "I'm going to kill him, Callum. I am going to fucking kill him."

"You can't kill him. He didn't fit the criteria which is why you kept him in the first place."

"You think I don't fucking know that!" I snarled.

"Is this about what he did on the battlement?" Callum asked. "I promise that I will keep a closer eye on him."

"It's not about that. He can kill himself if he is so inclined."

Once the words left my lips, I knew they weren't true. The thought of him never glaring at me, never calling me witch, or the constant barrage of insults made something within me shatter.

Callum sighed and stepped forward, hands reaching for me again.

I took a step back. "I said not tonight."

He shook his head, giving me a small smile. "I know."

He walked back toward the bed and put his trousers back on. I cocked my head to the side, unsure of what he planned next when he sat down on the edge of the bed and beckoned me.

I narrowed my eyes and slowly walked toward him, and he gave me a small reassuring smile. I stood in front of him.

"Arms up, your grace." Not necessarily a demand, but I obliged him all the same.

I lifted my arms and he slid his shirt over my head and through my arms, the bottom of the shirt stopping at my knees. His smile grew wider as this was the first time he was seeing me wearing his shirt. He spun me around and pushed me down until I was sitting on the edge of the bed between his legs.

Before I could ask any questions, his hands squeezed my shoulders in a way that made me sigh.

"This is called a massage. Please just relax into my touch and let me take your mind off of everything."

I didn't answer him, and I tried to do what he requested, forgetting about Bastian and his stupidity. I closed my eyes to focus on just his hands, and in a matter of moments, I could feel myself relaxing, leaning into his touch. Rested my head against his front as I felt his hot breath against the side of my face.

I don't think I had ever had a moment with Callum that didn't lead to sex. Except for the other night when I found him sitting on the battlement. Or before that when I found him in slumber.

When did I start caring about anyone's needs but my own?

Without opening my eyes I said, "Bastian needs to understand that this is all he has now."

"If I may…"

"Yes?" I answered without opening my eyes.

"His entire life has been turned upside down in more ways than he could have imagined. Emilia and I chose you." He sighed, pausing. "He simply needs time."

"It seems like he and his brother are not on the best of terms. And Emilia won't be near him. You are the only one left he has to turn to."

He nodded. I knew he wanted to say more, but decided to continue massaging my arms.

I sighed. My anger and contempt over what Bastian had done had finally passed and all that was left was worry. What if I hadn't gotten to him in time? He would have died, and it would have been all my fault.

In the end, it was all your fault.

Shit.

I squeezed my eyes shut. "Go away."

I opened them to find Callum's eyes had widened, and then I realized I wasn't, in fact, talking to him. The pity in his eyes angered me as the shadows swirled around me.

"Get out, Callum."

He sat up and tried to take my hands in his as he pleaded. "Don't shut me out. Please, I am here. I want to be here for all of it. The good, but also the bad."

"I don't *need* anyone, Callum. He flinched hearing those words, but I didn't care. "Leave."

He nodded once, looked down, and left without another word.

The moment the doors closed, I felt my lap moving. I looked down and saw that my hands were shaking. I gripped them hard together and realized that Callum saw. He always saw and never said anything, instead he always tried to stay. To take care of me.

Well, I didn't need him.

I went to take a bath and then headed down to the dining hall in time for breakfast.

I was usually the last to arrive, but that wasn't the case this morning. Soren was seated in his chair, no one else in sight.

"Where are the other two?"

Soren shrugged. "Your consort takes his job very seriously. He was at Bastian's door at sunrise and didn't leave his side. Not even when Bast stormed past him, right before I came down here."

At least Callum was with him.

As I neared my chair, Soren stood and pulled it out for me. I was confused by the action, but didn't say anything as I sat down. I gazed down at the empty table and rolled my eyes when I remembered that Bastian was in charge of the meal. I was about to fetch something from the kitchen when Emilia walked up the stairs from the side of the room with a tray full of food.

"Emilia?" I questioned.

Soren stood with me. I could see her slow down when Soren turned toward her. It was obvious that she couldn't stand being in the same room as him, but her eyes landed back on me, and she smiled as she approached the table, setting a small bowl in front of me.

My heart skipped a beat. I opened my mouth to reply, but nothing came out.

"I thought I would make this for you to apologize for my behavior in the last few weeks."

I wanted to say that she didn't need to apologize, but I didn't want the boys seeing me too soft. So instead, I asked, "Are you going to join us this morning or take your meal elsewhere?"

Emilia took one look at him, looked back at me, and nodded. She had started to turn from the table to bring up the rest of the plates when Soren jogged past her, calling out from behind him, not giving Emilia a chance to refuse. "Please sit! I will bring up the rest!"

Emilia's face burned red, and she walked around the table to sit in her designated seat. "Is he always like this in the mornings, your majesty?"

I huffed out a breath, as much of a genuine laugh that I could muster, and replied, "He is rather chipper today, isn't he?"

I knew this had taken a lot out of Emilia. For her to share a table with the brothers after knowing everything couldn't be easy. I commended her for it. I was about to say something else to try and get her mind off of it when Soren was back carrying the rest of the food, carefully balancing everything in his hands.

"Wow, Emilia, this smells amazing! I am sure that it will taste just as good, if not better."

Emilia was staring, not knowing how to respond to him being so kind after her not hiding her apparent hatred toward him and Bastian. Her eyes squinted, and then her hand came up and rubbed at the side of her head to relieve some of the tension that was obviously causing her pain.

"Scholar, how about you eat before the food gets cold."

"What about the others?"

I snapped, "Then their meal will be cold. It is their fault for taking so long."

Soren took the hint and focused on me. "Are you ever going to call me by my name instead of 'scholar'?"

"Why would I do that?" I asked, as I leaned forward and grabbed my cup, sipping its contents.

His lips thinned, and he nodded more to himself, focused on eating his warm porridge.

We sat in silence. No one cared to say anything. I wasn't even paying attention to where I was as my mind wandered, moving my spoon absentmindedly around the bowl, not taking a single bite.

"Why aren't you eating? Do you not like porridge?"

"What?"

He pointed with his spoon. "You haven't touched your breakfast."

"I guess I am not very hungry this morning."

He went back to eating, but his eyes kept looming, wondering. He was thinking—about what, I couldn't say. Silence filled the space once again until I heard yelling on the other side of the doors.

Here we go.

The doors burst open as I heard Callum calling out, "Get back here! Sober up before you go and see her!"

"Ah! Get off me!"

Bastian stumbled through the doors, shouting, "Your grace! Apologies for my tardiness. Uh–oh. I'm in trouble, aren't I?"

"And what would you be in trouble for exactly? Besides not doing the one job that I gave you, forcing Emilia to pick up your slack. Doesn't seem fair, does it?"

He lifted his hands up in the air, irritated. "All you do is nag. You know that?"

He was halfway to the table when my nose scrunched up. He reeked of alcohol. I narrowed my eyes. This was incredibly vexing. I could understand his need for release, but this was starting to become a nuisance for everyone involved. However, I knew that adapting to change took time. As long as he wasn't completely harming himself, then I would allow him this small reprieve.

"And you need to take a shower. Save all of us from your musk. I can smell you all the way over here."

Soren rubbed a hand down his face, cursing under his breath. He got up and walked over to help his brother out of the room, but Bastian pushed him away.

They were speaking in hushed tones that I couldn't quite make out until Bastian grabbed Soren by the collar and asked, words slurred, "What do you want from me? I came down didn—" Bastian had turned around to make his way to the table when he cut himself off by tripping over his feet, landing hard on his face. He laid there, not moving, but groaned as Soren rolled his eyes and bent down to check on him.

Could I have stopped him from slamming that perfectly chiseled face into the solid flooring? Yes.

But did I? No, because the consequences of his actions were of his own making. And possibly because of that comment he made about me nagging him.

"Damn it, Bast."

Soren's hand lifted, and because it was covered in blood, he proceeded to faint at the sight. I walked over and saw that Bastian's nose was broken. Blood gushed down his clothes onto the floor. Teeth stained red as he spit more of the blood onto the ground at my feet.

Both brothers were still on the ground, Bastian fully unaware of what just happened to Soren. I didn't say a word as Soren's eyes fluttered open, disoriented. I stood there waiting for him to come to his senses when Soren sat up and looked at me, complexion pale.

He tried not to pay attention to the blood and said, "I think we both need to lie down. May I please have assistance in taking him to his room?"

Bastian laughed and winced from the movement.

"Now you're reasoning with the beast? Are you fucking her now, as well?"

He had already asked Soren that a few days ago. I wondered why he was so curious if we had or not.

"Enough, Bast!"

"Little brother, don't try to speak to that *thing* as if it were still human. Didn't you hear her? Oh wait, you were unconscious," He spat. "She reminded me that we are supposed to be grateful that she hasn't killed us—be grateful for this *hell*."

"I don't think that I put it in those words exactly." I bent down to him as he tried to back away and grabbed hold of his nose before he had a chance to escape. I slid his nose back in place. He screamed out in pain.

"Can't let that pretty face of yours get disfigured; what good will you be then? Scholar, take your brother and sober him up."

Soren and Callum wrapped Bastian's arms around their shoulders and half carried him out of the dining hall. Bastian must have been heavy if it took both of them.

I thought for a moment about compelling him to forget about his fears and anxiety. Compel him to never drown in his sorrows again. But that wouldn't fix the overall issue— me. It wouldn't fix his disdain for me.

It shouldn't be surprising that he hates you. It seems that everyone that you come into contact with either dies or—

I squeezed my hand and shattered all of the glasses on the table, screaming in frustration. This had to end. I ran my fingers through my hair and stormed out of the room, leaving Emilia to eat by herself.

The garden. I could go to the garden, but she wouldn't be able to find me.

I rushed out to the greenhouse as fast as I could, trying to beat Circe from saying another word.

I wrenched open the doors and practically hauled myself inside, slamming the door closed. My body was overheating, my mind was swimming, and I couldn't seem to catch my breath.

Not again.

I doubled over, wrapping my arms around my knees, and put my head between my legs, taking unsteady breaths.

Deep breath in. One. Two. Three. Deep breath out. One. Two. Three.

I sat in a ball on the wet ground and didn't move until my eyes grew heavy. Was my lack of sleep finally catching up to me?

I blinked slowly as my body relaxed slightly, but I knew I would be accosted by images of all the people who had died because of me. Remembered their faces even after all these years.

I hadn't heard her voice for a while. I think I had effectively cast her far enough away into the recesses of my mind that she wouldn't be able to bother me for the time being.

I left the greenhouse, made my way up the steps, and found a hunched figure peeking through the keyhole of one of the windows, with a head full of blonde hair.

"For a scholar, you aren't very bright."

Finally, it was my turn to scare him because he jumped straight into the air and banged his head against the glass.

"Shit!" He cursed, rubbing his head. "Please, do take care and not sneak up on a trained hunter."

"A trained hunter? You?" I scoffed.

"Just because I would rather have my head in a book doesn't mean that I wasn't trained just as rigorously as Bast."

I raised an eyebrow, skeptical. "What are you doing? You're supposed to be finishing up cleaning."

"I am finished cleaning, and well, I thought this was, uh, this was another—"

"I'm sorry. Do you need a moment to think of a lie?"

He rolled his eyes, and I reached out, grabbing his jaw tightly.

"Do I need to take you up to my chambers and teach you some manners?"

He stared up at me and, without missing a beat, replied, "Will that suffice you enough to answer more of my questions?"

His response made me pause, so I brought his face closer to mine.

"Would you really go that far for me just to answer a bunch of meaningless questions?"

"For knowledge? Always."

I stared at him for a few more moments.

"Want to know what I really want from you? Right now?" I dragged my hand up his chest and then flicked his nose. "I want you to clean."

Which effectively changed the subject.

I was about to walk inside when the sky started to turn gray—a storm was coming.

I stood as Soren opened the door for me and said, "Don't bother me tonight. I won't be down for dinner." Then, I headed back inside, leaving him even more confused.

My breathing started to shorten, sweat beaded my brow, and a rising sense of panic surged through my body. The panic I felt earlier crept its way back in.

I needed space. I had no destination in particular and stopped the moment I heard voices.

Fuck! Was there anywhere in this goddamn castle that I could get a moment's peace?

I was about to confront them when I heard Bastian say, "I can't stand her, Callum. And there's nothing you can do or say to make me change my mind."

I heard Callum reply, "Bastian..." I heard him sigh. "As I have told you, numerous times, your life could be so much better if you gave in."

"If I give in, then I lose myself. And that's the last thing that I have."

Another pause.

Circe was right; I had brought nothing but misery to all who had come into my life.

I pressed my back against the wall and shook. It was too hot. I needed to get away, but there was nowhere to go. Nowhere to run. My castle was still a cage, only with a handful of voices to remind me of all the things Circe often did.

I needed to be outside. I quietly walked away from them and prayed I didn't run into anyone else. Something wet hit my face when I stepped outside the back doors. I looked up to see the clouds had fully rolled in, thick and dark.

I slowly crept back inside.

I had nowhere to go.

CHAPTER FIFTEEN

It was after dinner, and Bastian urged that we all gather in one of the many rooms in the castle, which has a large fireplace and lots of seating. Emilia had joined us for dinner for the sixth night in a row, and Bastian thought that it called for a celebration.

"Come on! Don't be a baby and just answer the question."

Bastian threw his arm over Callum as he teased Soren. Bastian apparently wanted to keep drinking as he had insisted we play a drinking game.

He had been unusually cheerful and drunk from sun up to sun down. I continued to allow his behavior, but was getting annoyed with how brazen he had become. It was something that I was intrigued about at first but I was not not sure if I could allow it to continue.

There was a long couch situated right in front of the roaring fire that Callum had lit and a few more chaise lounges placed around an oak table in the middle. I sat down in my chair that was closest to the fire, not wanting to sit next to any of them, not even Callum.

"I would rather not partake in this particular game. Please skip me," Soren said while settling onto a spot on the floor, not wanting to be next to anyone, it seemed.

Bastian threw himself on the couch, taking Callum with him as he scoffed, "It is a simple game with simple questions. Nothing too rigorous. We wouldn't want you overworking yourself now would we?"

Soren narrowed his eyes on his brother. They had not had a decent conversation since the night that his brute of a brother bashed him over the head and tried to escape. He took a sip of his hot herbal tea and looked toward the fire, not wanting to continue talking.

Emilia had taken up a chair next to me, still not talking to anyone, tense as ever. She was so tense that it was making me tense in trepidation of what she might do.

The silence was beginning to grind on my nerves, so to get the night over with, I decided to play along.

"I'll go. Rules seem simple enough. Answer the question honestly or drink. The last person standing wins."

Bastian indicated it was my turn to be questioned with a head nod in my direction.

"How old exactly are you?"

This again. "You are worse than your brother."

"If you won't answer the question then drink." I rolled my eyes. "It's not like it's a secret. We can't be the only ones to know about your sordid past."

I placated him for no other reason than to get everything out in the open. I was growing tired of living the way we were. It was no longer entertaining me.

"Three hundred and seventy." Bastian whistled.

My turn.

"Are you ever going to pull your head out of your ass and stop making everyone's life miserable?"

He shrugged. "I don't know, are you?"

Callum cursed softly and hit Bastian's arm, saying something under his breath that I couldn't hear while we continued to glare at each other.

Soren tried to cut in, but Bastian spoke over him and asked another question to the group, "How many men have you fucked?"

I rolled my eyes, but Callum was the first to answer. "Three," he offered, smiling at me sheepishly.

They looked at me.

"I never kept track." They didn't know that it was only one before Callum.

"Oh, come on, if you could take a guess. How many dicks have you taken?"

Soren chastised Bastian, "There is no need to be so vulgar."

"Fine, then how about you answer." He raised an eyebrow, a challenge.

I looked at Soren. His face had slightly paled, and he was rather quiet. Was the number high? Or was that reaction because it was low? I forgot all about Bastian, as my focus was on Soren, needing to know his answer. Suddenly, this was my favorite game to play.

"None," he mumbled.

"Speak up, brother." He raised the hand with his drink in it and made a show of the room. "We can't hear you."

"I said 'none'."

Bastian began to laugh hysterically.

"You can't be serious. What about Mary? Lucy? Emmy? You courted them, did you not?"

Soren was cool, but there was a look of contempt on his face.

I cocked my head to the side.

"So, you have never touched a woman?"

He shook his head, avoiding eye contact.

"Male?"

"No. I enjoy females exclusively." He didn't say it in a way that he found offense with the question, but rather simply stating the truth.

"Have they ever touched you?"

He swallowed, looked up at me, and shook his head—all that pent-up energy, just ready to burst. It was somewhat exciting to consider, but I dismissed the feeling with a blink.

"What are you? Twenty?"

"Twenty-four, your majesty."

Callum sat up and tried to change the subject for Soren's benefit. "Where have you been in your travels?"

Soren was about to answer when Bastian stood, swaying enough that he almost tripped on the carpet.

He exclaimed, "This is boring. You're all boring." Then, he set his eyes on me. "You made me a wager, and I lost. Yet, you haven't used me in weeks." He strode toward me until he stood directly in front of my chair, his groin situated at the same level as my face. "Use me, *your grace*. Make good on your promise."

I leaned back as he put an arm on the back of my chair and ran a hand down my face. He was pushing his limit with me, and I was just about ready to show him exactly who was in charge in this relationship.

"Bastian, enough. Sit down before she kills you. She has threatened it enough times that she might follow through if you keep pestering her." Soren tried to reason with him, annoyed with his brother's brazen behavior.

I could see Callum on high alert, ready to come to my aid if I called for him, but I wouldn't. This was between Bastian and I.

"Listen to your brother, hunter. He seems wise for his years, unlike a certain male standing before me."

Bastian laughed. "Relax a little, your majesty, and enjoy the ride." And before I could make a move, Emilia had dropped her goblet on the carpet and screamed.

We were all shocked at her outburst, that such a strangled noise could come out of her.

"You," Emilia said in a strangled voice.

Bastian had straightened and looked around, unsure why Emilia was looking at him like that. "What did I do?"

She tucked her feet under herself on the chair and began to beat the side of her head with her fists. I pushed Bastian back hard enough to make him fall flat on his ass as I rushed to her side and held her hands.

"Emilia, stop!"

Tears streamed down her face as she sobbed, then screamed again. "You did this to me! You and your family made me like this!"

"Get out!" I commanded the room, but no one moved, frozen at the sight of the scene.

"No!" She struggled against me and shot at Bastian, "I live with regret every day of my fucking life because of what *your* father did to me!"

I looked back to find Bastian, still on the ground, eyes widened. He was speechless.

Soren said calmly, not wanting to anger her further, "We know you're one of the chosen. Our sincerest apologies—"

Emilia continued on and pointed to her throat. "I was only thirteen. Do you know what they do to the children who get chosen?" Complete silence. No one moved. "They treat them like kings. But not me... My aunt was given extra gold coins to allow a few of the men to use me because they found my body appealing. I had a very little body, then."

"Oh my god."

I couldn't tell who said it as my attention was completely on Emilia.

Her entire body was shaking as she stood and screamed, "No! Look at me!"

I fell back on my heels as she took a few steps toward Bastian and pointed at him. She put her hand on her throat, doing her best to breathe. Failing, she continued, "The night that I was sacrificed, I was sent down one of the alleys where three men were waiting. I tried to run, but they caught me. They all laughed at me as my aunt sneered, saying that she couldn't afford me anymore, that I was a burden she was happy to be rid of. That I should be thankful that I would be able to help more before being slaughtered."

She looked at Soren, he was kneeling on the ground, horrified.

"I begged. I yelled. I pleaded. But nothing worked. 'Relax and enjoy yourself'. That's what they said to me. I was thirteen fucking years old!"

She began to hyperventilate, but I didn't dare touch her. Not when she was baring her soul out to that man's sons.

"No wonder you hate us," Soren said barely above a whisper.

"I—I don't know what to say." Bastian had moved to sit on his knees. "I am so sorry, Emilia. I am so sorry for what happened to you."

"When they were done, they beat me until they thought they killed me, punching my throat several times." Her hand went to her throat. She looked down, not in shame, but in rage. "And now... I can barely speak for long without having to use my hands because my throat still aches, even after all this time."

Soren stood and walked over to her cautiously. He seemed defeated. I could tell that he wanted to apologize, but no amount of remorse or groveling could undo what had already been done. The damage was irreversible.

"You look just like him. The monster from my nightmares!" She screamed before all hell broke loose. "I can't do this. I can't do this anymore!"

Emilia jumped on Soren so abruptly that they both fell backward. She wrapped her hands around his throat, sinking her nails into his skin.

"Emilia!"

The spell was finally broken, and everyone was up and trying to get them away from each other. Emilia was scratching him, gripping and trying to pull him back to her so that she could keep attacking him.

"How dare you!" She screamed at the top of her lungs.

I took a few steps back and used my shadows to push them apart.

I commanded Bastian, "Take your brother and leave! Callum, make sure they don't come back!"

I waited until they were all gone before looking into Emilia's eyes. She was holding onto the back of the chair that she had vacated and looked ready to go after the brothers.

It wasn't until the doors had closed that I turned back to her.

"Breathe Emilia. I need you to slow down and take deep breaths."

"I–I can't. I want to rip them apart!" Her body was shaking so badly that I had to grip her firmly to try and steady her.

I started to hum a spell that always relaxed her and set her at ease no matter how volatile she became. After a few moments, her body shook less and less until she was limp in my arms. We sank down on the ground, and her head landed in my lap. She was so out of it that she didn't notice and I didn't want to move her, worried that she would start hyperventilating again.

I hesitantly placed my hand on her head and slowly stroked it. I looked down at her frail body. She had lost a considerable amount of weight in the past few weeks. That wouldn't do.

As always. Paying attention to boys when there are others that need your attention. What would Belle say?

I gritted my teeth together.

I told you not to speak her name. You don't have the right, I growled.

Circe laughed. *You will always fail those who depend on you. Best to give up now.*

I breathed through her words and tried my best to focus on Emilia, staring off into the distance. I needed to bring her back to the here and now, not the past.

"If you allow the rage inside you to stay and target two people who had nothing to do with what happened to you, then you will turn into me. You are good. Pure light." I sighed. "You can go."

She blinked a few times before sitting up straight and staring at me.

"What?" She winced in pain.

"I see now that bringing them here is causing you nothing but pain. You barely leave your room. You haven't been eating. I can't watch you suffer anymore."

Her shoulders slumped. In relief? I couldn't tell until she looked back up at me and signed, *Thank you. Thank you so much.* She dropped her hands to her lap and began to cry again.

We sat there in silence for another moment until I helped her up and back to her room.

I tucked her in and said, "I will have Callum take you to the cottage tomorrow."

She nodded and signed, *I am sorry.*

"Don't be." I blew the powder in her face to ensure she got an entire night of rest.

I immediately left Emilia to sleep and went in search of Soren. His injuries weren't life-threatening, but they still needed to be tended to. He wasn't in his room, so I checked the library, the only other place he ever was.

Nothing.

He was known for being in places where he had no business, but I was too flustered to search for him. Not wanting to stall any longer, I conjured my ball of light and thought of him. I scoffed when I saw where he was.

The door creaked open, and I found Soren sitting in the front pew directly under the stained glass window casting beautiful patterns on his body.

He turned around at the noise. "Your majesty?"

I walked to him, our eyes not leaving each other. The closer I got, the easier it was to see that his eyes were red, dried tear streaks ran down the length of his cheeks, and his hair looked like he had run his hands through it for hours. He looked remorseful for a crime that was not his own. But I knew better than anyone that the children can't be blamed for the faults of the father.

I placed a single finger under his chin and rubbed my thumb along his jaw. "You can feel sympathetic to her plight, but not pity and definitely not regret."

"Do I not have anything to be regretful of?"

"Were you in charge of the Reaping? Choosing her? Selling her?"

He dipped his head low, but I gripped his chin between my thumb and forefinger and brought it back up to me, "Were you?"

"No, but—"

"But nothing. It wasn't you. The only one to blame is your father for allowing this to continue," I paused for a moment, and thought of Bast. His words were fresh in my mind. "And mine, for not finding a way to end it long before now. There are things I could have done."

"Not without giving yourself away," he reasoned. "The fear of the castle, the forest...the beast... Well, it all keeps you safe."

"All those children ripped away from their families to keep me safe?" I asked him, wanting him to see fault in me—to hate me. Somehow, still, the fascination and wonder never left his eyes.

"I don't think the truth would have stopped my father. Fear is powerful, and he uses it to control the village. Even if you were dead, he'd find a way to keep the beast alive."

"It sounds like your father is the real problem, then," I countered, waiting for a response—a quip.

Just silence, lingering and heavy between us. I sat next to him and lifted his chin so that I could assess the wounds that Emilia had inflicted. She scratched him all over, down his neck, over the top of his chest. His clothes were ripped and there were deep fingernail grooves marked into his skin. Blood had leaked down from his neck and onto his shirt, but nothing was life-threatening.

I pricked my finger with the tip of my fingernail and brought it to his lips to heal him. He put his hands over mine, stopping me.

"Scholar, don't fight me on this. Not now." He squeezed my hands before letting them fall onto the wooden pew between our bodies.

Neither one of us spoke a word as he wrapped his lips around my bloody finger. I never knew why my blood healed, never understood the layers of Circe's curse. I only knew that I could save a life just as quickly as I could take one.

Once his skin healed, I didn't know what else to say to him. I was never one for small talk and quickly grew uncomfortable with how close we were sitting, all too aware that our knees were millimeters apart and if I moved, we would touch. I looked back at him and found that we were leaning toward each other.

I swallowed at the closeness. My breathing was heavy, and I could feel my core getting wet for him, preparing itself to take him.

"You wish to ask me a question, don't you?"

"Many."

I slumped even further into the pew. "I do not have the patience to deal with your questions tonight." I got up to leave, but he grabbed my hand and pulled me back down.

He pressed my hands against the sides of his head. "Enter my mind again. I'll think of another beautiful place for you to visit."

I pulled my hands out of his grasp. "I don't wish to do that again."

"I will be quite forward with you since you seem to covet that trait. I have so many questions that I am yearning to find out." He moved off the bench and kneeled in front of me.

I was nervous, and I didn't understand why.

"Scholar, what are you doing?"

"That's the first thing I want to end. I have a name. Please, you use Callum's... Use mine."

He hesitantly placed his hands on either side of my ankles and rubbed them up and down, finding courage to do what exactly? But then it hit me.

"Soren..." I breathed. "You don't want me to be your first time. All I know how to do is break everything and everyone around me."

"If you think I was whole to begin with then you would be mistaken. But that's not what I am after right now." He slid his hands up my legs and up to my thighs, lifting my dress in the process. "This isn't about me."

"Then what is this about?" What else could it be about other than him wanting to fuck me? Here. In the chapel. My mind reeled with memories of my mother forcing me to my knees to pray away my uncertainties over my father's war.

"I want some questions answered and I know that you are exhausted." I was about to argue, but he was right; I was too tired to think straight. Especially not when my dress was so close to baring myself to him, his face close enough to feel his hot breath. "Answer five of my questions and I will help you to relax a little."

I laughed in his face.

"I have Callum."

"And yet, your desires have changed since my brother and I arrived, haven't they? I don't hear you two in the middle of the night anymore."

I swallowed, and my face hardened. "My desires are the same."

"They aren't," he said, as if he could see the lie in my eyes.

"What makes you think that you can get the job done when you have never even kissed a girl?"

I knew I was taunting him, but it was ludicrous to think he would be able to pleasure me so thoroughly that I would be able to relax.

"Then what do you have to lose?"

I shrugged, feigning nonchalance, though I felt anything but. I spread my legs a little wider for him. "Do your worst."

The moonlight hit the windows just right so that our bodies were lit up in shattered fragments of light. Broken pieces of a whole. The dust in the air added a sense of fragmentation to the way that Soren was looking at me.

His eyes slowly roved down my body, drinking me in. He leaned his head into my leg and skimmed his nose along the inside of my thigh. Inhaling as his hands pushed the dress as high up on my hips.

"Lift," he quietly commanded, gaining more confidence. I obeyed, lifting my hips so that he could bunch the rest of my dress up around my hips. "Fuck…"

I couldn't help but look down at him and see him staring at my bare pussy. Heat flooded my core, knowing that I was the first woman that he had ever seen and that he would touch. I began to squirm beneath his gaze as he brought his hand over my clit and ran his fingers down until they stopped and spread me.

I couldn't help but gasp. Callum had always worshiped me, but I had never had someone feel as though they were analyzing me—making sure to memorize every noise and movement.

"You are divine." Soren laid me down on the pew and crawled above me, lifting one of my legs above his shoulder and setting one down on the ground.

"Soren…" I saw him dip his head down and run his tongue from my ass all the way up to my clit. "Soren!" His name left my lips as I closed my eyes and moaned, lifting my hips to get closer to him.

I needed more, my mind entering that foggy place.

He kept the pace slow and precise. I would expect nothing less, but I didn't need his analytical side—I needed him to ravish me. I reached down and ran my hands through his hair, shuddering when he stopped at my bundle of nerves and sucked. I opened my eyes to find him staring at me, no–studying me.

He lifted his head as he inserted a finger into me, and I almost came right there, my inner walls clenched around his thick finger, refusing to let go as he slowly pumped into me.

He stopped, brought a finger up and ran it through my slit covered in my cum, and brought it to his full lips. Then he sucked on both of his fingers, eyes rolling into the back of his head.

"You taste so good. Oh my god."

I narrowed my eyes. "*I* am your god."

He smirked at me from lowered lashes, licked his lips, and sucked more at my clit. He was fixated on it, relentless with it.

"Soren!" I screamed out as I came all over his fingers, and he didn't stop until my body had stilled from shaking.

I tried to catch my breath as I taunted, "If you think that was enough to calm me down then—"

"Did I say I was done?" He interrupted.

Words wouldn't come when his tongue was back on my sensitive pussy. I wasn't used to him being so aggressive. No. Aggressive wasn't the right word to use. I didn't even have a word for what Soren was.

It wasn't long before I had my second orgasm with just his tongue. And just when I thought we were done, he inserted two fingers, curved them up, and hit that spot that had me having another orgasm moments after the second one. Or was this the same one? A different one?

I could feel my eyes growing heavy more and more after every orgasm he pulled from me. I almost had to beg him to stop when his breathing on me made my legs tremble, anticipating his own form of torture. No matter how much my body craved his type of depravity.

Maybe he wasn't so different from me.

"Sleep well, your grace." I could barely hear him. He sounded so far away. I tried to open my eyes, but I was thoroughly fucked without the fucking. Then I remembered that I had yet to see all of him and I wanted to. I heard him laugh. "There's time for that later. Sleep."

Did I say that out loud?

More laughter, but it sounded even further away. I was being dragged underwater, and my body was thankful for the exhaustion finally taking over.

"What about your questions?"

"Tonight wasn't about me. I have plenty of time."

I had to shield my eyes from the light flooding onto my face. Strange. Even if I slept with my curtains open, my bed was back far enough that the light would never hit me.

It took another moment before I was sitting straight up. A blanket fell from my lap. I was in the chapel, sleeping on the pew.

Sleeping? I was sleeping!

I slapped a hand to my chest and thought back on last night. Soren promised to relax me and he succeeded. I had never slept through the entire night. And...and...no nightmares.

That wasn't possible.

Right?

There had not been one night that I hadn't had a nightmare. Was it truly possible?

I looked to see if he was around but found an empty chapel.

I scoffed and smirked toward the door as if I could see all the way to his room. He won this round, but the next time I got my hands on him, he would be screaming my name.

His god.

Chapter Sixteen

I wrapped myself with the blanket Soren had used to cover me last night and started walking toward the dining hall.

Wake up. Eat. Garden. Fuck Callum. Eat. Repeat.

Though that was slowly changing wasn't it? Soren and Bastian were turning my world upside down, and even though the past few weeks hadn't been easy, they had been lively. I thought back to last night and thought of another word: transformative.

There was no other word for Soren's feat in getting me to fall into a deep slumber. Even if it was only for a few hours.

I stopped by one of the glass doors leading outside and saw the landscape covered in a blanket of snow. The light that hit the snow made it look like there were millions of stars twinkling amongst the morning haze.

It was so beautiful that it made my heart catch. Winter always did that to me, reminding me of a simpler time.

I opened the door, wanting to feel the bite of the chill air, when something startled me. I gripped the handle of the door and heard two young girls squealing in delight as they rushed past me and jumped, flying through the air and landing in a mountain of snow.

"Slow down! Don't hurt yourself!"

I snapped my eyes to the woman next to me. She was wrapped in her winter coat lined in ermine fur. Her chin was high, hair wrapped into a braided bun atop her head with a crown pinned in.

"Mother," I choked out.

I couldn't move, frozen in place as she rolled her eyes and braved the outdoors for her daughters.

I remembered this day; I was ten and Belle was five. I followed after Mother barefoot, not caring that my feet burned from the cold snow. I would burn in Hell for eternity if that meant I could live in this moment forever.

I saw the younger me surge up through the snow, shivering. Laughing.

Belle surged up, but she had her arms crossed with a scowl on her little face. "Hey! You cheated, sister!"

My hand flew to my mouth, covering it, as I choked back a sob. I hadn't paid close attention to the last memory in Belle's room as I was too shocked by their sudden appearance to take it all in. This time I listened to the nuances in their tones. How high-pitched and sweet Belle sounded even when she was scolding me. She acted just like Mother.

I could see myself sigh. "Please forgive me. I should have let you have a head start since your legs are so little!" She flew forward and grabbed Annabelle's feet, making her squeal some more and wiggle out of her arms.

Belle only made it a few steps before dropping into a crouch and then looking back with a wicked grin right before throwing a snowball directly at my face.

Younger me screamed as it hit her straight on. From the corner of my eye, I could see my mother covering her mouth, holding back her laughter. I stared at her as I could hear more screaming in front of us. She was looking at us with so much love in her heart. I didn't have to decipher what she was feeling; it was clearly visible on her face. I remembered that she always wore her heart on her sleeve.

I looked back over and saw myself gathering snow into a ball. I grinned broadly at Belle as she was pleading, "No, no! I didn't mean it!"

She turned and ran as I threw the ball at her back and hit it square on. Not hard enough to hurt her. I would never hurt her.

"Oh! Now you've done it!" She hurried and rolled a ball of snow, throwing it as hard as her arm could, and I saw myself dodging it right at the last second. Which only enraged Belle further.

Mother stood there watching us with such amusement lining her face and I spent the time watching her. Trying to memorize her face, the color of her eyes, how her hair glowed under the light, how she stood. All of it. Begging her to say something else, anything else.

When she didn't, I walked down the steps onto the landing and walked to where Belle was once again crouched in the snow, getting another snowball ready. I bent down next to her and lightly brought my hand up so I could skim her laughing face lightly.

"I miss you so much."

I bit back a sob as I heard Mother call over my shoulder, "It's time for lessons, girls!"

I turned to look at her, but the image faded before I could get another look. When I turned back, I was once again alone.

Isolated. Forever alone.

I bent my head, wrapped my arms around my body, and screamed in frustration.

"If you are going to show me these images, the least you can do is allow it to last longer than a moment!"

I wasn't sure who I was screaming at or why I was seeing these memories to begin with. Maybe it was the last stage of me completely losing my mind?

I could barely feel my body shaking, getting soaked through to the bone from sitting on the wet ground. I had stopped caring about anything as I sat there staring at nothing in particular. Willing the memory to come back. Or any other memory to present itself to me and take me away from my miserable existence.

"Your majesty!"

I didn't even look as someone came into view.

Soren. A worried Soren, by the crinkle in his forehead.

"Why are you out here?" He was searching all over for injuries and then looked back into my eyes when I didn't respond. What injuries could I possibly get?

He wasted no time in reaching forward and lifting me into his arms. I knew he was strong, but I didn't realize just how strong. I looked up at his face while he barked orders at someone in front of us.

I was brought inside, Soren's face shadowed by the dark halls, and taken back into a room where Callum was stoking a fire. I wanted to tell them I was fine, but when Soren sat me down, I looked at my toes and saw that they were a deep purple.

"I wonder how much longer it would have taken until someone would have had to amputate?" I muttered.

Emilia chastised me, "That isn't funny, your majesty. Please don't jest like that."

I had spoken my thoughts aloud again? I sighed, annoyed that everyone was fussing over nothing.

"You all realize that I can't die. Right?" This time, I was able to find my voice and address them. I looked around to see everyone in here except for Bastian. "What? The hunter is the only one not worried about me?"

"It's not that he doesn't care." Callum tried to come up with an excuse.

"Don't lie."

"He is still brooding."

Of course, he was. I scoffed because I expected nothing less.

The heat helped to thaw my toes enough to be able to move them slightly, getting circulation through my veins. A cup entered my eyesight which was being held out by a worried Emilia.

Why was everyone so worried?

"I am not thirsty."

"It's hot tea. I added a few herbs from the greenhouse to help aid in your recovery," Emilia said softly.

"You know better than anyone that I am a few moments from being healed."

"Humor us, please," Soren pressed.

I lifted my hand through the blanket and took the mug. I sniffed it, peppermint. I took a sip and allowed the scalding tonic to work its magic and fix me because, apparently, my magic wasn't enough.

I stared into the fire, watching the flames as I heard Callum and Soren settle themselves. Emilia stayed kneeling at my side.

I knew there was much to talk about and handle and I didn't want to disappoint her, but the trek to the cottage wouldn't be possible until the snow cleared slightly. It was too dangerous in these conditions. Not admitting, even to myself, that I was relieved she would be delayed.

"Your majesty..." I glanced at her from the side. "I am not going to leave until the snow clears."

I breathed a sigh of relief and then wondered if she had powers and could read minds.

"You're leaving?" Callum asked.

She looked over to him, explaining, "Her Majesty has graciously accepted my offer of being the new go-between for the children."

"But–"

"But nothing, Callum."

"Is this about us?" Soren wasn't asking me. Emilia looked at him and then quickly looked away. "Please don't leave on our account. This is your home. We can stay away from you... We can..." His voice trailed off.

Her head was bowed. "I can't live here with the sons of that man, and you can't leave. It's either you stay or you die."

We were both looking at Soren as he stood and walked over to us, determination set in his features. Emilia tensed the closer he came.

"I am so very sorry, and I know that doesn't make up for what happened, but maybe..." He took a deep breath. "Take my life."

I sat up straighter. What was he doing?

Emilia's mouth opened in shock. "Pardon?"

"I am not my father, but I'm close enough. If that's what it will take for you to receive the justice that you deserve then so be it."

He produced a knife from under his shirt and presented it to her. She stared down at it as he took her hand and placed it into her palm, closing her hand over the handle. Soren then brought it up until the blade lined up with his heart.

No one said anything. Was this actually happening? Soren was going to be a sacrificial lamb for his father's sins? I couldn't allow Soren to die, and I wouldn't allow Emilia to go down my path—allow her heart to be tainted forever.

Before I could stop her, she let go of the knife and leaned into him, her head on his shoulder as she sobbed. My body relaxed while I sat there staring at Soren, who hesitantly placed his hand on her back and stroked it tenderly.

I bundled myself closer to the fire, wanting to give them space to have their moment, healing wounds from a man who deserved to be six feet under. I made a silent promise that the next human I killed would be that man. I didn't know how, but I'd do it. He'd hurt Emilia, and he'd hurt my boys.

Your boys? Circe's voice teased.

I shut my eyes, willing myself not to reply to her.

The hunter loathes you. Every night, he thinks of new ways to kill you. Why would you protect him?

"Because he is my responsibility," I whispered, my voice low and unnoticed. I looked over to find Callum wiping a tear from his face. We both knew what this meant to Emilia.

Emilia's body started to slow. She moved away from Soren's shoulder and tried to talk. I knew her throat was paining her when she massaged it, and then brought her hands up and signed, *I am sorry for attacking you.*

Soren was confused. I realized he didn't know the hand language that Emilia, Callum, and I knew, so I translated.

"No, please. You have nothing to apologize for."

If I don't, then neither do you. Emilia replied, meaning every word.

She gave Soren a half smile. I could tell that she looked at him in a completely different light now. He had proved himself to her. Proved that something good could come from that town. That good could be born from evil.

He nodded and gave her a lopsided grin of his own.

"I'll leave you all to do whatever it is you do at this time of the day."

He stood, and Emilia signed, *You don't need to go.* She had accepted him so quickly into our group, or whatever this was.

He bowed, smiling to himself.

"Thank you for the invitation, but there is a castle that needs cleaning."

"The castle will be here tomorrow. Stay." I didn't necessarily order him, more like offered.

He nodded at me. "Thank you."

He took a seat on the couch next to Callum.

Emilia got up as well and situated herself back in the chair.

Callum clapped his hands together once and said, "Does anyone want to play a game?" We all looked at him, knowing how well the last game went. He rubbed the back of his head and said, "A different game, I promise you will all enjoy it."

They all laughed. I sat back and watched them while Callum went over the rules of his game. The other two were excited to play, finally finding some common ground. They were all laughing, and I absentmindedly brought my hand up and rubbed the side of my mouth. The corners of my mouth had curved slightly, and I could feel my chest wanting to expand into what I could imagine would be laughter, but I refrained.

When was the last time I had laughed? Genuinely laughed?

I wasn't sure that I could even remember how.

Part of me wished that Bastian would come and join, but he wasn't ready yet. He would need a little more time. Or rather, maybe a lot of time. I sighed and rested my head on my knees, smiling while watching them.

This could work. My life could be more than mere existence. So much more. With all of them. These humans—people—knew that part of me and didn't hide. They didn't fear me.

But, that's exactly what they are...humans. You will never be one of them.

Circe.

Have you forgotten what you lost? You know your curse means you will lose it all again. That when they are dead and rotting in the earth, I will be all you have left.

She was right. Fuck. She was always right.

They would die and I would be here, all alone.

Isolated. Unloved. Cursed.

I turned my back to them and stared into the fire.

CHAPTER SEVENTEEN

I spread my legs apart and ran my hands down my stomach, stopping at my pussy. I dipped my fingers in between my slit, and brought my fingers up to my face. I watched how our cum intermingled between my fingers and brought it down to my lips. Tasting us.

"Tell me, Callum, what do I taste like to you?"

I turned to find Callum staring at me and at what I just did.

He focused back on me after being transfixed by my mouth and replied, "I would drink your cum for sustenance if I could. It is the most exquisite taste."

I pondered that.

"I have never tasted your cum before. You taste rather salty."

He looked worried.

"If the taste is not to your liking—"

I lifted my hand, stopping him. "I didn't say that. Just stating a fact."

We laid next to each other in silence. I rarely allowed him to stay, but I didn't mind it at the moment.

Desperate for any contact? I thought you were the big, bad beast who needed no one.

Mind your business, Circe, I replied to her silently.

I heard her scoff in the distance of my mind.

I focused back on Callum. On the here and now. But my mind wandered to Soren.

"I wonder what I taste like to the brothers."

I grew irritated at the look on Callum's face, unable to decipher its meaning.

"Have they tasted you?"

I nodded.

"Does that bother you?"

He took time to think about my question before sighing.

"Honestly, I would be lying if I said that I didn't feel slightly jealous." He sat up and looked down at me. Why was he getting serious all of a sudden? I sat up as he continued, "I meant it when I said that you could have many lovers and it wouldn't diminish my devotion and love for you."

Love. There was that word again.

I looked away from him, suddenly uncomfortable with the way this conversation had gone. He could tell where my thoughts had headed, but before he could say anything more we heard a crash somewhere in the castle.

Now what? I hung my head; I had planned on taking a nice long bath.

Callum jumped up, throwing his night pants on as he rushed from the room to assess the situation. Though I knew who was behind that crash and the next and next. I could hear raised voices and knew that Callum was arguing with Bastian.

What could have been the cause of this outburst?

I lazily got out of bed, threw on the nearest robe, and tied it around my naked body. I ventured into the hallway to determine the source of the sound.

I followed it out of the South Wing, down the stairs, through the halls, up the steps of the East Wing, and right into Bastian's room.

Emilia was against the wall on the other side of the hall, staring at what was going on inside. I didn't spare her another glance as I entered and found Bastian's room torn apart. His furniture was shattered, the curtains were shredded, and his bedpost splintered.

"There she is! The whore of the hour."

I narrowed my eyes at him and cocked my head to the side.

"What is your problem, brother?" Soren asked, exasperated.

"Brother? Is that what we are?" Bastian's eyes were wild as he couldn't steady his breathing.

"What else would we be?"

Bastian turned and punched the wall, bones crunching against the stone, and I knew that his hand was broken.

"Stop it!" Soren rushed forward and tried to subdue him, but Bastian was too fueled by his rage and threw him off.

"You tasted her!" Bastian yelled.

The room went silent and I could see Soren blush.

Ah. Everything became clear. He overheard what Callum and I were talking about. Though why he was making a big deal out of it was beyond my comprehension.

"What does it matter?" He threw his hands up. "Callum fucks her every single day and you haven't had any issue with that."

"How does it feel not being a pathetic virgin anymore?"

I could see that his words stung Soren. I was tired of Bastian's hateful words that were directed at the wrong person.

Soren seemed to be over his brother's antics because he walked right up to him and punched him. Bastian fell over and landed on his broken hand and screamed in pain.

"You fucking asshole. We haven't even fucked yet." Yet. I didn't miss that part. "And even if we did, why do you care?"

"Soren, leave him to wallow in his self-pity."

This was my first time using Soren's name aloud in front of them, and Bastian caught it. Even in this state, he was alert and paid attention to every detail. Maybe he and his brother weren't so different after all.

Bastian looked away and made a show of slowly standing up to face us. The three of us were next to each other, with him on the outside. But he was only like that because he wouldn't pull his head out of his ass and give in. Let go of his hatred of me and live a little.

"I don't care."

There was hurt in his eyes, which was the only reason I walked up to him. He tensed as he watched me, not moving.

"I should let this heal on its own," I stared up at him, "but I wouldn't want it to heal wrong and you need this hand if you are going to jerk yourself off at night when you're listening to me being the whore you say I am."

He growled at me as I used my shadows on him, freezing him in place. I sliced my palm open knowing that he would need more blood than normal to heal his shattered hand. He fought me as hard as he could. I could feel my shadows working harder to keep him under control as I forced him to drink a few mouthfuls of my blood. I saw the bones mending and snapping back into place.

I leaned in and whispered, "We could be having so much fun if you stopped being so stubborn." I leaned back and could see that he still wasn't ready. Though if he kept up this attitude, then I would have to do something about him soon.

Lightning lit up the room, and the hair on my skin rose, anticipating what was to follow. Thunder.

I hurried out of the room as I called over my shoulder, "No one is to bother me tonight."

I loathed the rain.

Not so much the rain, but the thunder that came with it. I hated to admit my shortcomings, but this was something that I couldn't push through. I couldn't sit there and pretend that the noise didn't scare the shit out of me. So when it rained I would instruct everyone to not come near the library.

It had been that way ever since I was a small child. I had been playing outside with one of my father's guards when the sky grew lighter. I marveled at the way the lightning lit up the night sky until I heard the most earth-shattering noise that shook me to my bones. The ground shook and I stood there thinking that the ground would break apart and swallow me whole.

I screamed and screamed while the guard was trying to calm me down, but it was like I couldn't hear him. Not until I was lifted into strong warm arms that wrapped me in a tight embrace.

Father.

The scent of musk and cigar smoke cradled me and I swung my arms around his neck, squeezing my eyes shut, continuing to cry hysterically. I remembered how he slowly stroked my back, waiting for me to stop crying as he brought me back inside. Ever since that moment, I hated storms because no matter how docile the rain seemed to be, the thunder would rear its ugly head. Reminding me of my place in the world.

Before Emilia, I didn't care about destroying the castle when the storms rolled in. I would ravage parts of it, not caring if it finally did me a favor and caved in, crushing me underneath. Emilia's arrival changed everything because with her around, I could no longer be reckless.

Instead, I would go into the library and close myself off until the storm passed, even if it lasted days. I knew it wasn't the smartest choice to stay in a room with wall-to-wall windows, but it was where I felt the safest. The one place I was still able to enter that held precious memories without feeling fully debilitated by them.

I wasted no time barricading myself in the library. I shut the door and took a few deep breaths trying to ground myself into the here and now. Deep breath in. One. Two. Three. Deep breath out. One. Two. Three. It no longer held the same musky scent that encompassed my father or the sound of little Annabelle learning to read with Mother.

I shook my head of the memory, not wanting to relive it, and pulled out the blanket Annabelle always used while she read. And as I went to head toward the corner that I always sat in, shaking until the storm passed, I heard a piercing laugh ring throughout the room.

No. It couldn't be.

I looked up to see another memory playing itself out in front of me.

The fireplace was ablaze as if it had been lit for hours, and a woman said, "Belle! Where do you think you are going?"

My mother was tickling Belle as she screamed and laughed at the top of her lungs, squirming around.

This couldn't be happening. Not again. Not so soon. I didn't want to watch. Didn't want to see them all. It hurt too much.

"Mother! Stop!" Though I knew she never wanted it to stop. She loved Mother with all of her heart.

They were so alike. Gentle. Kind. Good.

I loved Mother, as well, but I was more like my father and would do anything to be just like him. I was standing over by the bookshelf nearest Father's desk, trying to glimpse the parchment. I was determined to help him in any way that I could.

I could see myself jump and go right back to pretending to read when Father walked in. He headed over to my little sister, who had escaped Mother's arms and ran into his. He picked her up and kissed the top of her head, then walked over to Mother. He bent down to capture her lips in a long and vomit-inducing kiss.

I looked over to see myself pretending to throw up at their blatant display of affection to make Belle laugh.

We were all giggling when Mother asked Father, "How was the hunt? Did you catch anything?

Father gave Belle back to her before approaching me and kissing the top of my head. He replied in a huff once he sat down. ,

"Nothing to boast about. I am hoping for something better tomorrow."

I ran up to him and leaned over the desk to watch him work. I loved it. He looked so serious when going over documents, and the veins in his forehead always twitched.

He laughed heartily and glanced at me. "Yes, my sweet girl?"

"I want to go hunting with you! I can be of some help."

He cut me off before I could finish my pre-written speech.

"You are just nine years old; besides that, you are a girl. Girls are not meant to hunt."

He saw that I was clearly disappointed so he sighed and said, "I love you so much that if anything were to happen to you, I don't know what I would do with myself."

Not wanting to cause him any further stress, I decided to placate him and replied, "Of course, Father."

I kissed his cheek and returned to pretending to read the same page I had been reading for over an hour, watching him work.

I knew I was crying from how wet my face felt, but I couldn't stop. His voice was so deep—commanding, yet so soft when he wished.

"I am so sorry that I did this to you."

I knelt down next to his chair to watch the scene, taking it all in the younger me had sat down in the chair next to the desk, both of which were beside one of the large, stained windows. A huge grumble interrupted the painful memory by shaking the room.I squeezed my eyes shut, gasping, knowing what I just did. I opened my eyes again, and my fears were recognized; they were gone. As my chest constricted tightly, I grabbed the blanket and leaned against a sidewall that wasn't in view of one of the windows.

I curled into a ball and wrapped my hands around my legs, my head resting on my bent knees, wishing for the storm to pass quickly. I wasn't sure how long I stayed like that until I felt someone grab my shoulder. I reached for their hand and threw them against the wall where I was seated, knocking the air out of their lungs. I straddled them, lifted my hand, made a shadow blade, and held it to their throat. All in a matter of seconds.

The figure was shrouded in darkness, and tears blurred my vision further.

We were both panting when his voice finally registered, his hands raised in surrender as he said, "Your grace, it's me... Soren."

I blinked, wiping the tears away, finally seeing him when I shuddered out a breath that I didn't know I was holding. The blade disappeared into thin air, and I slammed my fist against the wall next to his head. He didn't move an inch. I rested my head against the crook of his neck, needing a moment to calm my erratic heart.

"What are you doing here?" I commanded.

What did he hear? What did he see? I was paranoid to say the least. Our faces were mere inches away from each other. I could smell him, like fresh soap and rosemary. It was oddly refreshing.

"I always went into our library when there was a storm. My library at home was the best place to hear it. Always calmed my nerves, especially since my mother died."

"That is no longer your home." His words struck something inside me that I didn't like.

He didn't say anything. I was tired of the conversation anyway, and made my way off him when a loud crack of thunder sounded. I instinctively reached my arms around his neck, pulling my legs up around his waist, and squeezed like my life depended on it. Like he was my anchor to this world.

The thunder cracked for longer than normal, which made the windows rattle so hard that I thought they would surely break. I didn't realize I was shaking until I heard Soren whispering a soothing lullaby, one hand behind my head and the other on my back holding me tightly.

I flew my magic out, pinning his hands above his head, and gritted out, "Do not touch me."

He was panting, concern marred his beautiful face, and said, "You were scared, and I—"

"I was not scared!"

Of course, the thunder had to choose that moment to come back louder than ever. The magic disappeared, and it took a moment before I felt hands on me again. He continued the song as if I hadn't interrupted him.

I wanted to scold him for disobeying a direct order, but another clap of thunder exploded and it went on and on and on. And as much as I didn't want to admit it, Soren's presence helped me not to be as scared of the thunder as before.

I would never admit this to him, but his embrace was comforting. It felt so good. We stayed like that for the entire night, not saying a word, besides Soren's soft voice singing to me.

His voice was so soothing that I hadn't realized I had fallen asleep. I felt sturdy arms carrying me for a while before I was placed gently on a fluffy cloud, my tense body melting into it.

I heard him whisper, "You are a complicated creature," and felt pressure on my forehead.

Then, complete darkness.

I jerked awake, feeling like my body was on fire. Burning. Circe rushed into the room, the sound of my screams still bouncing off the walls. She tightened the maroon robe around her body and sat on the bed beside me, reaching for my face.

"Wake, child, it's only a dream."

I leaned into her hands, breathless, soothed. I still felt like my skin was burning.

"The same one again?"

I nodded faintly.

"Tell me about it."

I hesitated a moment, but found comfort in her face—so warm, eager to help me.

"I'm burning," I finally told her. "I'm burning at the stake."

She surveyed my face, and looked deep into my eyes. "Have you seen one of the burnings?"

I nodded meekly.

"Your father took you?"

"No, he didn't know I was watching. I was too curious. It was horrifying." My chest hurt thinking about it. "And I've read some of his books, the crimes that he's burning those women for. He told me he just knows magic when he sees it, but how can that be true?" I knew I was speaking too freely of her, that my words were treasonous. "I'm sorry, please don't tell anyone I said that. It's just the dream getting to me."

Circe gathered my hands. "You need not hide your feelings from me. I am at your service, Princess. I, too, have had my reservations about the burnings. The king is much too fast to cry, witch."

Her words felt so wrong to hear, and yet, so comforting.

"Sometimes I think he'd burn anyone he suspected, even if he loved them."

Warning bells rang inside my head—I was talking too much, letting myself speak too freely.

"He will not burn you, dear girl," she assured me. "Your dreams are not always warnings, but fears. You think if he finds out your secret, he will—"

"Don't say it," I cut her off.

"You are ashamed, but you shouldn't be."

"I live in shame!" I cried to her. "I have something inside me that my father hates. How do you live with it?"

"My family loved me," she said warmly. "My magic did not scare them."

I couldn't fathom it, but was envious at the thought. "What happened to them?"

A moment of silence passed between us, where I wished I could read her mind. "Most died and the rest... They left, ran far away. They were too scared to stay."

"But you stayed?"

"I am good at hiding who I am, and there's only so long we can run. At some point, we just have to learn to live amongst the rest—to pretend. Over time, your magic will understand that it must pretend, too. It will feel less chaotic, and eventually, you will have trouble using it. It will bury itself. You just need to give it time."

I wanted to believe her; needed to believe her.

"But you must learn not to fear it," she advised. "Fear is only going to make it stronger...more unpredictable. If you start to trust it, it will start to trust you."

I snapped my eyes open, it was just a dream, only a dream. More like a memory. I looked up and found someone directly above me, pressing something cold against my neck.

Bastian.

I tried to move my hand, but he pressed the cold metal further into my throat.

"Ah ah. I wouldn't do that if I were you. I will kill you before you have a chance to move your hands."

I took a deep breath.

"What is this going to accomplish? You kill me, and then what?"

He loosened his grip on the blade for a split second before securing it back and spat out, "You are a vile creature and I would be doing the world a favor in killing you."

"Oh?"

"You'll never be able to harm another person again."

"And who is it that you think I am hurting?"

"Where to begin? Innocent lives. Anyone who steps foot onto your land."

"Your brother?" I teased, knowing that would get a reaction out of him.

He ground his teeth together. "For starters."

"Want to know exactly what he did to me? How he had me screaming his name?"

I squirmed under him and would have been able to move around more if he wasn't pinning me down, his thick thighs holding me securely in place... Now all I could think about were those thighs and the damage they could do to my body if he chose to squeeze tighter. I wanted to continue teasing him just to feel the muscles of his thighs constrict more.

"Enough. Leave him alone."

"Let me ask you something instead. In your drunken stupor, you decided to break into my chambers and try to threaten me with a mortal blade. I suggest you go back to bed before you force me to punish you."

"Shut up."

"What? Are you afraid of your desires?"

He hesitated again, and I took the opportunity to my advantage, used some of my power to flip us, straddled him, and pinned his hands down.

"Get off of me."

I looked down into his eyes, hooded and heavy with lust. He wanted me. No matter how much he tried to deny it, he wanted me.

"I don't know how much longer we can keep up this charade of ours."

Once I had him under me and sleep had officially faded away, I could finally get a good look at him. He was shirtless with just a pair of trousers on. His breath reeked of alcohol, but he looked as though he would be sober in an hour or so. As if he drank just enough to gain some liquid courage to attempt murder. I couldn't help but stare at his rippling pectorals moving as he struggled to get out of my grasp.

I leaned down, unable to stop myself, and licked from his stomach up to his breast, lingering on one of his nipples, biting it roughly. He hissed, and I could tell that he was aroused by the bulge that began to form. I couldn't help but grind on him.

With nothing but my thin silk chemise on, there wasn't anything in the way of making both of our desires come to life. Something we could both pretend we didn't want, but definitely did.

He caught me off guard as he flipped us back over, legs straddling my stomach once more. He flew his hand out until it was securely wrapped around my throat. I waited, curious to see what he would do next as he dragged the blade down my body, goosebumps rising along my skin as his eyes stayed on mine. I held still and my breath grew more rapid as I thought that this was *finally* happening.

He lifted the knife and stabbed it into the pillow next to my head, close enough that I felt a little prick at my ear. He released my neck and ran his hand down my chest, gripped the edge of my nightgown, and ripped it open to free my breasts.

I could see his throat bob as he hungrily eyed my hardened nipples. Without wasting another moment, he bent down and took them between his teeth. I threw my head back at the sensation and arched my back into his chest.

He licked and nipped and when he felt satisfied, he moved on to the other. His hand slipped underneath my silk chemise and rubbed my clit in slow circles, just like that first time in the forest.

He sat back on his heels, bunched up the fabric, and pressed his thumb even further onto my clit. He used his other hand to release his throbbing cock and then rub himself up and down. He roved his eyes down to my pulsing pussy and spit on it. I curled my toes and squirmed beneath him, almost begging him to take me and put both of us out of our misery.

He leaned forward and slapped my pussy with his dick. "You want my cock, don't you?"

I gasped. Words escaped me, and before I could try to find them, he slapped my pussy again.

"Be a good girl and use your words."

I closed my eyes and lost myself to him, ready to let go and feel him entering me when I felt him rubbing his tip through our juices that had seeped out.

I waited and waited, but nothing. He had stilled, his tip at my entrance. If I moved even an inch down, he would be inside of me. I looked down to find him staring at my pussy hungrily. He didn't move. He seemed to be warring with himself.

I didn't know what made me say it, other than almost being at my breaking point.

"Bastian..." He snapped his eyes to mine, having said his name for the first time. "Tell me to stop."

"What?" The fog in his eyes seemed to be clearing. He was coming back to his senses and he tensed on top of me.

"If you don't tell me to stop right now then I will fuck you, and I won't care how you feel about it in the morning."

"I—I—"

I knew with everything in me that he wanted this—wanted me—but he would hate himself. He truly believed that giving in to his desires made him less than.

I stilled. I didn't want to take him like this. Not when he was half drunk and especially not when he wouldn't admit that he wanted this.

I pushed off of him and started walking to the bathroom as he called out, "What are you doing?"

"You hesitated." I barely turned my head, not fully wanting to look at him. "Go to bed, hunter."

He left a few moments later and I soaked in the tub, watching the bleak sunrise.

Chapter Eighteen

"**Y**ou need to talk to him, your grace."

"Pardon?"

I leaned back in my chair, held up, and stared at the beautifully crafted design of my cup, as Callum was standing next to my chair at the dining table. He looked just as tired as I felt. They all did.

Days had turned into weeks, and at this rate, none of us would survive another moment in this chaos. Of Bastian's chaos.

"It has been this way for the past month and I don't know what else to do. I have tried helping him. I have tried listening to him ranting about his hatred for you. I have tried beating him senseless because he seems to love fighting. But nothing, and I mean *nothing* has worked. If anything, everything I have tried has just kept pushing him over the edge of the cliff and soon he is going to fall off," Callum finished as he ran a hand through his hair.

"You think I don't know that?" I snapped, draining the full glass of wine in one go.

"I would never insinuate that I know more than you. I am merely stating that you won't have a pet to play with any longer if he continues down this path."

No, I wouldn't, but it took me over three hundred years to get a grip on my reality. If I was being honest with myself, it had only gotten 'better' when Emilia arrived because I was terrified that I would harm her. I looked away and thrummed my fingers against the table, contemplating what to do. How to get him to fall in line and stop drinking?

"Ah, my elder brother, the drunk." Soren lowered his eyes, and I could see that he was just as worried. Shit. I needed to do something. "I'll be honest; I am at a complete loss."

I stood suddenly and asked both of them, "Where is he?"

They both looked over to the entrance of the kitchen and right at that moment, we all heard the clanging of pots and incoherent shouting.

I walked to the door and called over my shoulder, "Leave us. I don't want anyone interrupting."

I continued without waiting for a response and followed the steps down to the lower level. If I didn't know my way around, then I could have just followed Bastian's grunts and words of profanity. I stalled at the entryway, not wanting him to see me just yet. He was bent over the sink and threw the piece of cloth he was holding as hard as he could into it, splashing water everywhere. His body was so tense that veins were popping up along his arms and neck. His curly black hair was damp from the sweat and tangled from running his hands through it.

He slammed a fist onto the counter and cursed, "Why God! Why would you do this to us! Have I not done everything that was asked of me? I was the perfect son—I—"

I rolled my eyes and made myself known.

"Do you really think that your god listens to your pleas? Or do you think that you are already in Hell with the Devil herself?"

He turned around so swiftly that he lost his footing and nearly fell over, but caught himself just in time. He narrowed his eyes at me, watching my every move as I leaned against the doorframe.

"Must you constantly glare at me?"

"Then you do not wish for me to gaze upon you at all."

I scoffed and pushed off the doorframe, walking around the kitchen, casually looking at the ingredients laid out on the table in the middle of the room.

"Your brother is worried about you. Callum, as well. All that time alone must have softened him up. I was asked to come and check on you and plead to your higher sensibilities. Though I'm not entirely sure you have much going on up here," I said, pointing to my head.

He flipped the knife casually, catching it by the hilt.

"Nothing going on?" He scoffed. "I think I have enough brains to know that I want to kill every last cell of it so I can enjoy the rest of my life. Here. With *you*."

As if to add insult to injury, he reached over to grab a bottle of something and took a swig, keeping his eyes on me the whole time.

"You can't continue drinking."

"You drink all the time and no one stops you."

"I'm immortal. Drinking is all I have."

"And now it's all I have."

"That's not true. You have your brother here."

"Then it can be argued that you have Callum and Emilia."

I thought for a moment about what he said and what it meant. After all this time, was I that easy to read? Yes, Emilia and Callum were here in my castle, not because they wanted to be but because they had nowhere else to go.

"What I have are two people who depend upon me to keep them alive, another who is infatuated with me, scientifically speaking, and his brother can't stand to be in the same room as me. I don't have anyone, not like you. So stop wasting your fucking time drinking and—"

"And what!" He lifted his hands in the air. "What else am I supposed to do?"

"Me."

"Stop talking nonsense and get out."

"You stop." I moved around the table and stood directly in front of him. "I am tired, Bastian. I am tired of fighting."

His eyes widened at hearing me say his name again. He grabbed my hips and spun me around until my back bit into the edge of the counter. His hands rested on either side of my body as we stared at each other, not moving an inch. Something in his eyes spoke to a deep part of my being.

I breathed.

"I want to forget." Forgoing all pretenses that I knew what the fuck I was doing, only able to focus solely on those large, calloused hands that were barely brushing my sides. "Would you want my lips wrapped around your cock?

Licking... *Sucking*..." I stretched out each word, making no move to touch him. I looked down and smiled. He had grown and was strained against his pants. "Beg, hunter."

"Shut. Up." I knew he loved our little fights as much as I did.

I clamped my mouth closed as he reached forward and grabbed a knife from the counter, nodding toward it. "That is getting old."

"Shut. The. Fuck. Up."

I held still as he brought the knife up, grabbed the top of my dress, and felt the material between his fingertips. He grazed the tip of the knife across my breasts. My nipples hardened at the cold sensation. I gasped when I felt him moving the tip up to my neck, lightly cutting my skin. I didn't so much as flinch, almost daring him to cause more damage, our eyes making a wager that neither one of us wanted to admit aloud.

He gripped the handle harder and sliced the knife through the dress, tearing the fabric to shreds. The clothing dropped in a heap at my feet.

"Like what you see?"

I smirked until I saw his eyes darken and the way a muscle in his jaw ticked. My throat bobbed at that look in his eyes.

"Fuck it."

He bent down and wrapped his arms around my thighs, lifting me up, locking my legs around his waist. His tongue was on my breasts, teasing my nipples and biting down, sending a jolt of electricity down my spine. I ran my hand through his hair and pulled until he was forced to look at me.

We stared at each other for a moment. The look in his eyes was so intense, piercing right through my soul. His head leaned in toward mine. Oh god. Was he going to kiss me!

I blurted, "Take me. Now."

He stopped. I think he realized what he was about to do and said, "So fucking bossy. But I know exactly how to shut you up."

He turned and swiped the counter clear of the food he was preparing and slammed me onto the surface. I gasped at how rough he was being. Not treating me like a porcelain doll that would crack. *Fuck.* It was hot.

He was palming my breast as he shoved two fingers into my mouth.

"Suck," he commanded.

I obliged. Wiggling my hips, desperate for friction. His fingers were out of my mouth a moment later and then I felt the intrusion. My eyes almost rolled to the back of my head, not realizing how much I missed those thick fingers. I loudly moaned, not caring who heard. A hand clamped over my mouth as he pounded those fingers inside me.

I could feel the rising ache deep inside me. My walls clamped around his fingers and just as I was about to feel that delicious rush, he stopped.

I stared at him wide-eyed, confused about what was happening, until I saw that smirk. That fucking bastard.

Shadows began to swirl around me as he said with lethal clarity, "Use your magic on me and this stops."

The shadows lingered for a moment, to see if he was bluffing, but he wasn't. That look in his eyes told me that if I used it, for whatever purpose, then he would stop, no matter how much we both wanted this. I let the magic dampen and fully extinguish as I glared at him.

He said mockingly, "Must you constantly glare at me?"

I stared into his eyes and could see that mine were still glowing purple. Maybe it hadn't been fully extinguished, though I had never seen them look like this without the shadows that followed. Yet, he didn't shy away.

"Now what?"

"Now, you will suck my cock, like the good slut you are."

"I will not get on my knees for you."

"Who said you had to get on your knees?"

He unbuckled his trousers and lowered them, revealing a thick cock that was waiting to devour me. He fisted it in his hand, staring at me the entire time while stroking it. I was still resting my forearms on the table as he climbed on top of it, pushing me down once again. He lifted his leg and swung it over me, straddling my chest. His hardened length rested between my breasts.

My eyes became hooded. I should not have found this as hot as I did and he fucking knew it.

"That's a good girl. Look at you. Needy for my cock, aren't you?"

I swallowed and knew that he caught that movement, as well. He was more astute than I had previously realized. He grabbed my chin with his thumb and forefinger, opening my mouth as far as it could go. He grabbed his length and brought it to my lips. I couldn't help but flick my tongue against the bottom of him.

He hissed, "I am warning you, I am not gentle. I will not make love to you like your precious, little bird. I will fuck you. Hard. So fucking hard that you'll regret ever keeping me."

Before I could answer, he turned so that he was squatting over me, tipping my head back and shoving his cock down my throat. I gasped at the force behind what he was doing to me. Never in my life had I been in this position, completely helpless to the assault against my throat. I tried to move my hands up, to grab something to hang onto, but he held down both my hands. I almost used my magic and then remembered his warning.

I was completely at his mercy. And...it was *liberating*.

He pounded into me and then only as I choked from lack of oxygen did he give me a reprieve. Then he shoved his cock back in before I had barely taken a full breath. On and on we went like this. Pressure built within me again, and I tried to move my hand toward my pussy to do something to help the ache. Though he just clamped down harder on my wrists. It was unbearable, borderline painful.

I thought that I would have to stop him, use my magic because I couldn't take much more, before I felt his mouth on my cunt, licking so fast that I was shaking from the rush. From everything. And just as I was about to release, he stopped and pulled his cock out of my mouth, sitting up. No longer touching me.

"What. The. *Fuck*."

One moment I was turning toward him to give him a piece of my mind and the next I was on the ground with him leaning over me. He grabbed my shoulders hard and thrust into me, no warning. The scream that came from my mouth was a noise that I hadn't made before. It was pain and pleasure and surprise and everything in between. I could almost cry out from the pain as he was so thick and gave me no time to get used to him. I couldn't even move to help with the pace as he held me in place by my shoulders and rammed into me.

"Fuck. *Fuck*. Look at you taking my cock like a good girl."

I couldn't form one coherent thought as I was soaring higher and higher. Doing my best not to react, giving him time to pull out of me. I held my breath as I was almost there, my fingers reached up and closed around his bulky arms. I leaned forward and bit into his shoulder and he roared at the pain. Loving it.

His breathing turned ragged, the movements jerky, and I knew he was close. I smiled as I felt a wave wash over me, finally. He ground his teeth as a scream tore through him and his movement stilled.

His arms were shaking, as were my legs. I didn't think my legs could work well after what just happened, so I was grateful when he pulled out and laid down next to me.

We laid there, on the ground, panting and attempting to catch our breaths, when I remembered the challenge. The challenge was that the other would beg if they wanted to fuck. We whispered at the same time.

"I won."

We took a moment to catch our breaths, coming down from the high of a thorough fucking. It felt liberating, but I couldn't push past a small feeling of doubt. That he didn't want this and was just placating me. I couldn't handle where my thoughts were heading.

"I loathe you."

I turned to look at him as he continued staring at the ceiling. "I know you hate me. I know you want nothing more than to kill me." I took a deep breath. "But I also know there is a part of you that wants nothing more than to let go. A part of you that wants the depravity and fun that comes along with being with a creature as wicked as myself."

I could see him knit his brows together, working through it in his mind. Part of me was fearful of his response because it would change nothing...or it could change everything.

He finally looked at me. "I loathe you," he repeated. I looked away from him. I felt crushed, I wouldn't let him see me affected by his words and was about to get up before he continued, "But...you may be right."

I whipped my head back to him, not sure if I heard him correctly. This was the first time he had admitted to having any feelings for me other than hatred.

"I was raised to obey. If my father believed that I was straying from the path he had chosen for me then I was disciplined accordingly. I learned early on that if I didn't cause him trouble then everything would be fine." He sat up and I followed. "I pushed every desire and craving down to be the perfect son. I withdrew into myself and soon even I started to believe my father's narrative: to live a sedentary life with a wife and children."

I hesitantly raised my hand to do something to bring him comfort—I could hear his voice hitch and thought he could be close to tears—but I didn't want him to flinch from me or stop talking, so I placed my hand next to his, instead.

"Then I met you and you challenged me. Made me want to give in to every desire that I had and...it terrified me." He finally looked at me, our faces inches apart. "It still does."

This man was prideful, arrogant, passionate, obsessive, and ruthless when it came to those that he loved. But all of those traits and more were what drew me to him. It made me care for him. My heart skipped a beat when I realized that I cared... I cared more than I wanted to admit.

But I couldn't tell him that...at least not yet. So I brought my hand up to his face, caressed his cheek, and slowly moved my thumb back and forth in a motion that I hoped would be soothing.

"Thank you."

"For?"

"Sharing a part of yourself with me."

He stared at me, as if seeing me for the first time, and nodded.

Chapter Nineteen

I sat restless in the library, still feeling like Bastian was between my legs. I fought images of us in the kitchen—how he felt, the anger in his eyes, the passion we couldn't deny. And I felt giddy from our talk afterward. He was coming around! My heart was still pounding.

I held the quill in my hand, ready to write to Belle. But what would I tell her? My mind felt foggy, my thoughts a strange mess. I could tell her the truth; that I was becoming attached to my prisoners, but then it would be too real. And I was already feeling so close to Bastian. It was probably best that things would progress slowly from now on; give both of us time to adjust.

I pushed up from the small desk in the hidden room in the library, pinching the bridge of my nose. I blew out the candles and left. I was tired and craved another full night's sleep. It was shameful to seek him out after having just been with his brother, but I needed him. The virgin had become useful to me, in ways I couldn't have ever predicted.

I went to Soren's room and pushed open the door. Mischief twinkled in my eyes, but he wasn't there. Strange. I conjured the ball of light and thought of Soren. He appeared to be in the chapel, bending over a stack of books. I sighed. I should have known he would be in there; it seemed like it was his new favorite room.

*I wonder why...*I thought to myself coyly.

I let the ball fade as I gleefully walked over there and saw that Emilia was scolding Soren.

"What's going on?" All thoughts of lust went away when I saw Emilia tense and on guard. I thought they were past this.

She looked at me, then took a deep breath. "He is getting into things that do not pertain to him."

I followed her finger and found multiple books open with a notebook next to them, having been just written in.

"Soren? What is this?" I was too stunned to fully understand why Emilia would be in such a rage with him when he constantly had his head in a book.

"Your grace—let me explain."

I ignored him and scanned my eyes over the words and what I saw had me holding my breath. I slowly turned to him and asked, "Where did you get these?"

"I—"

"Do not lie to me!"

"I found it in your secret room."

He had out a stack of my books—my *private* books—that I recognized from the room in the library. All the books were about witchcraft and my history, including the book he had shown to Bastian.

"You went in there after I explicitly told you—no—ordered you not to?"

"Just listen to me. I am learning so much from these texts, and I know that if I have more time with them I *will* find something." He was trying to plead his case, but the room was starting to spin. He needed to be punished.

"You had no right!"

Violence. Always your go-to when emotions run too high. I taught you well.

"Shut up!" I needed to get away from him, but I was curious how Emilia knew about what it was he was looking at. "Emilia, what did you mean just now?"

"What do you mean?" She looked shocked that I would ask.

"You said that he is getting into things that he has business getting into. How do you know what he is getting into?"

"Well, these are obviously your books, and I didn't think that you would want him snooping in your private rooms." Her words sounded off, too proper.

I opened my mouth to question her further, but Soren pleaded again, "I think I'm getting closer to understanding how curses, in general, work. Specifically, the rules."

Emilia and I whipped our faces over to him as he stood, head lifted, as if he were declaring something ordinary like the weather.

"I don't remember asking for your assistance."

He looked exhausted and it dawned on me that this had been consuming him—this research. Me.

"I can read some of the books in that room that are in other languages, even some of the dead ones." He walked over to the table. "I have studied over thirteen different languages and thank god I did because I can be of use to you."

"I don't need your help," I repeated, quieter. I was mildly curious, but feared letting that curiosity turn to hope.

"I know you don't want to be stuck here for the rest of your life."

"I don't have a life, Soren. I exist. That's it."

"You could be so much more. Have so much more."

Don't let him get your hopes up.

Go away! Go away! Go away!

My heart beat grew erratically, I felt it beating in my chest, shaking my rib cage. "There is no way around the curse, and if you think that helping me break it will free you and your brother then you are mistaken."

"That's not why I'm doing this." He clenched his hands together, frustrated that his words weren't coming out the way they were intended. He obviously wanted to do more research before bringing his findings to me. "From all of the research that I have gathered, even from a few fairytales, curses can be broken. It is merely finding out the true meaning of the phrase that was used. What exactly did the witch say?"

I had heard enough.

I walked up to him as he backed up and hit his back against the wall. "Go into that room again without my permission and I will torture you until an inch of your life, heal you, and do it all over again. I'll even make your brother watch."

"Just think about what I said." He was still trying to plead his case—Gods, he was relentless when he set his mind to something.

"Why should I?"

"You want out. I know you do. Or else you wouldn't have looked into my memories, specifically the ones about my travels. I know that you once planned to travel the world with your sister."

The blood drained from my face. "You read my diary?"

It only took him a moment to realize his mistake. A moment to know that he had ruined anything that could have ever been between us.

"No—wait."

I felt betrayed. Violated. If I didn't leave now, I would kill him. I tried to walk past him, but he blocked my path.

"Soren, what are you doing? Get out of her way," Emilia hissed. "She needs space."

"Get out of my way, scholar," I sneered. "All I want to do is hurt you."

"Because someone hurt you," he reminded me, his voice cold. "You are right—I am a second son with privileges, and those privileges have granted me knowledge. The kind of knowledge that is going to help you. I shouldn't have read your diary, but I needed to understand the horrors you have faced... I needed to understand everything. Now, I do."

"You don't understand anything," I ground out in defense. I wanted him to shut up, to stop speaking the truth. "You're just a child."

"I'm not a child," he said. "You were cursed younger than me. You were a child then," his voice lowered. "You are still one in so many ways."

I lifted my hand, my bottom lip quivering. I imagined squeezing his throat, fingers crushing his windpipe. I resisted, holding my hand in mid-air. "I want you to shut your fucking mouth, Soren."

"The temper of a child," he mocked. "The selfishness of a child. You'd only been with one man before Callum, that stable boy. Does Callum know? Does he know that you're all talk? That beneath the magic is just a sad, scared, girl, wanting to be loved and saved, but too afraid to ever admit it?"

Emilia gasped, covering her mouth with her hand.

I gripped his throat and shoved him down, his body thumping against the hard floor. He groaned when the back of his head made contact, then gasped, clawing at my hand. I leaned down, my hair dripping to his face, covering us both. I felt the words slip out of my mouth through gritted teeth. "All you had to do was obey the rules. Why couldn't you stop? Why couldn't you just listen to me?"

"I don't know how," he croaked out. "I don't know how to stop when I want something."

"What do you want, Soren?" I begged him, eyes watering.

"I want to," he pried my fingers off his throat, "show you the ocean."

Time felt still, the air around us thick with tension. I battled for control, desperate not to hurt him, but my body longed to. I didn't want to hear him speak again—I didn't want someone to know my darkest secrets.

Kill him, Circe mocked. *Get rid of him.*

"Get out of my head," I shouted. I jerked off him and stood, backing away from him.

He knows too much. Kill him.

"Is that her?" Soren's eyes widened as he sat up, his throat raw. "You wrote about her in your journal. The witch, Circe. Is she talking to you right now?"

I pounded my fist against my head, trying to silence her, and Soren. Emilia walked closer, reaching out for me. I shuddered away from her. "Please, don't touch me. I don't want to hurt you."

I stood, moved through the chapel door, and took off into the night. I ran down the steps on the side of the castle until my feet hit the green grass and pumped my arms as fast as they could go. Needing the wind in my face, the bite from the chill air. I passed the greenhouse, the castle walls, and the rose garden, and then my feet took me over the bridge. I could hardly register the pain of the gravel cutting into my bare feet as I pushed my body faster and faster.

Then I saw the broken main gate appear ahead and I pushed my body as hard as I have ever pushed it. And ran straight into the invisible barrier. The pain that radiated through my body was something that I had never experienced. The air was knocked from my lungs and I was thrown back with such force that when my body hit the ground it bounced a few times.

I ground my teeth together and roared. I pushed my body up and wiped the dirt off of my face and it stung. I looked at the back of my hand and found blood.

I snapped my head up at the barrier, called my shadows to me, and sent a blast of energy straight at the barrier.

Blast after blast after another fucking blast of energy.

Nothing.

I strode up to the barrier and punched the wall. "I am done! I am so fucking done! Fuck you, Circe for doing this to me!" Punch. "Is this what you wanted?"

I expected her to answer me, but she wasn't saying a word.

"Shy now are we? Figures!" I threw my entire body into punching the wall. After a while the bones in my hands began to ache, my muscles atrophied from not using them like that in so long. Not even my healing abilities were healing me fast enough before I was injuring it all over again.

I collapsed, trying to catch my breath, and sobbed. "You made me into this. Bloodthirsty. Reveling in the pain of others." I hung my head. "A monster."

"A monster indeed."

I whipped my head up and found an older man standing just on the other side of the gate. Did he just see everything? I needed to kill him before he could get away and tell others about me, but panic delayed me. "Who are you?"

He said nothing.

My thoughts ran rampant, spiraling down scenarios that had yet to happen when I finally took him in and realized that I knew him.

He had graying hair that was pulled back by a strand of leather, and his clothing looked to be finely made, with not one hole in sight. Even in his later years, he looked fit and deadly. And his face. The mirror image of Soren.

Oh gods.

"Father?"

We both turned to find Soren and Callum standing a few feet away from me. All the color from Soren's face drained and Callum kept looking between their father and myself. Concern was etched on his face as he took a step in my direction, but Soren's hand flew to his chest, effectively stopping him.

"Son...what trouble have you gotten yourself into this time?"

Soren didn't take his eyes off of his father as he commanded Callum, "Get Bastian." Callum was staring at Soren, clearly irritated that he dared to keep him away from me. But, before he could argue, Soren pushed him back toward the castle and pleaded, "Hurry. Get Bast."

Whatever look Soren gave him was desperate enough that he looked at me one last time before sprinting off in search of the elder brother.

Soren walked up to me and bent down, but he didn't dare touch me. "Are you alright? Did he hurt you?"

I narrowed my eyes at Soren as their father scoffed, "You haven't seen me in months and you don't even greet me properly? I taught you better."

Soren gritted his teeth together. "*You* didn't teach me a damn thing. You sent me away!" He scoffed. "But that isn't even the fucking point. What are you doing here?"

"Would you believe me if I told you that I was here to see you?" The man smiled.

"I would sooner believe that you grew two heads than the lie that you just spat out of your mouth."

I looked around, if he was there then there's a high possibility that he wasn't alone. My worst fear was coming true. "Are there others?"

He didn't even glance at me while he continued to stare at his youngest son, the same inquisitive look that Soren always got when trying to figure out a problem. "Yes, I can't have my people knowing that my sons were bewitched by the beast. How would that make our family look?"

"Of course, the only thing you are worried about is your image."

"So, you know?" I arched a brow and stood up, not caring to wipe away the dust and grime on me.

"I've known for years, dear girl. This land is rich with the history of the witches that used to roam. I always knew there was no beast; we would have seen it after centuries, but I never imagined it could be someone as delicate-looking as you." He smirked. "When you sent back those butchered men to warn my people of the beast in the forest, you did me a great favor."

His voice robbed me of all my courage. There was nothing more terrifying than a man who could rally forces against me. Burn me like all the others—like my father. I was a covenless witch.

"You created a fear that would allow me to hold power, real power. Power that perhaps, is even stronger than what grows inside you."

When I said nothing in response, he grinned widely and said, "Hysteria."

I blinked slowly, thinking about what hysteria did to my father, all the women and children he burned. All those lives taken out of fear.

"You have no idea of the power inside me," I threatened.

"Your grace, do not humor him," Soren warned.

"I stay on this side of the line, I am safe." He motioned at the barrier.

"Safe? I am sure that a mere female would be no match for someone like yourself." I tried to taunt him, pull him closer with words.

"I haven't lived this long without a strong sense of self-preservation and good judgment. And something tells me to not underestimate you."

I sauntered over to the line, and Soren flinched the closer I got. "How about you come over here and find out?"

I was baiting him. He just needed to walk over that line and I could kill him. Bring justice to Emilia. To Soren. To Bastian. To every child that he sent out into my woods to be slaughtered.

He huffed a laugh and walked up to me until only an invisible line kept us apart. "Why would I do that?" He slid his booted foot forward until it was millimeters from the line and pressed a straight line across it. "You are the beast. I need the beast to live."

He was arrogant, but incredibly observant.

I wanted to laugh because that was exactly who Bastian and Soren were. One was passionate to a fault and the other too intelligent for his own good.

I heard approaching footsteps and knew that Bastian and Callum had arrived. I didn't dare take my eyes off the man—biding my time to attack him.

"Father?" Bastian was shocked, but recovered faster than his brother and stood a little straighter. After everything he learned about his father, he still sought his approval.

"Good. Now that you are here, we can go." Their father called them over, pointing to me as if I were a stray animal. "Say your goodbyes, boys. You will return to the village infamous, survivors of the beast. They will crown us." He thought long and hard, tapping his chin. "But do I need the beast to live?"

No one moved.

Soren swallowed audibly. "Father."

"Perhaps not—we could slay the beast, stop the Reapings. What a legacy we'd hold. With her death, we can move into this very castle." He played with the idea, staring past me. "We could crown ourselves."

Callum got too close, pulling a weapon free—a blade.

"Don't!" I took my eyes off the man for a moment to push Callum away from me, when I felt a searing pain in my side, I turned my attention back to their father before hearing shouting from behind me.

I looked down to find a calloused hand gripped around the hilt of a deformed blade protruding from my stomach. I slowly looked up at the man and found him staring down at me, eyes wild and determined.

I brought my hand up to use my magic, but nothing. Not even a drip of power came to my aid when I needed it most.

"Not so powerful now, are you?" He laughed a bit, and I felt powerless. Helpless. My legs gave out, having no strength to keep me up, when he wrapped both hands around me and held me to him. "Beautiful, though, isn't she?" And he shook me, causing the blade still in my side to move and jerk. More pain seared through me and I couldn't help the cry that escaped my lips.

Callum yelled, "Let her go!" Spit formed around his mouth. Callum took a step in our direction when the man's hand wrapped around the blade and warned, "Tsk tsk. I wouldn't do that if I were you. Step back."

He crushed me even harder against him, so hard that I could almost feel my bones snapping under the pressure.

"Enough, Father." Soren stepped forward. "You have made your point."

"Oh, I don't think I have. It doesn't look like she is going to give up easily." A chill ran down my spine as his nose grazed my neck and he inhaled. I could feel my body betraying me as it grew weak, my limbs not obeying the order to attack him. My arms wouldn't even raise, and I could feel myself sinking into his hold.

What was happening? This shouldn't be happening.

You are finally learning your lesson.

Circe?

Everything started to slow. My mind was hazy, though I could feel his hands roaming over my stomach and took a few steps over the line he drew in the dirt.

"Did you fuck her?" I wasn't sure which brother he was asking, but I could see both of their cheeks flushed at the question.

He laughed. "Both of you? I don't blame either one of you for being enticed by this witch." The word was poison on his tongue, not having the same effect as when Bastian said it.

"Do not speak of her like that," Callum hissed, taking another step forward, but Bastian stopped him.

"Any of you get closer, I'll stab her in her heart and end it!"

Callum shook, I could see him. My eyes pleaded with them. "Just do what he says," I told Callum, my voice weak. "Don't hurt him," my voice begged, and that seemed to delight him.

The man looked me up and squeezed my body hungrily. His hand had roamed up, pulling at the fabric of my dress to expose my breasts. He scooped up one of my nipples into his mouth and bit down—I cried out. Tears began to form in my eyes.

"I wonder if she would like to fuck me, too? Wouldn't want her to miss out on having a taste of the entire family."

Soren lunged forward to grab me, but Bastian released Callum to go after him. With one swift hit to his face, a punch that sounded as if it cracked his precious cheekbones, he fell to the earth.

Callum took the freedom to move around Bastian. He was going to try and save me, and he was going to die if he did. "Don't," I said again, harder. "Don't you fucking move, Callum."

He froze mid-step, nostrils flared, eyes watering.

"You like my boys, don't you?" He freed my other breast from the fabric, toying with it. "Have they grown on you?"

"Yes," I said weekly, feeling my body start to go numb.

Bastian merely stared at the scene, warring with himself on what to do.

You can't blame the boy. He has been searching for a way out of here ever since he arrived.

I swallowed hard. I knew that he hated me, but I hadn't realized that it went this deep.

You forced him and his brother to stay here forever. You can't blame him for jumping on this opportunity.

I knew I didn't have any reason to feel this way, but his betrayal hurt. Why did it hurt? My vision started to blur, and I felt his hand snake up my neck. "I think I'll fuck her, then leave her dead on the earth where her ancestors burned."

"Get your filthy hands off of her!"

My head bobbed up and down until I found enough strength to see that Emilia was standing next to Callum, holding up a small knife of her own. Shaking from head to toe.

There was a pause, and then the man said, "Another beauty hiding away in that castle?" From the tone in his voice, I could hear him appraising her, but he didn't recognize her. Had there been more after Emilia? So many little girls he'd hurt that he couldn't even remember their faces?

I gritted my teeth together, finding my voice. "You will not touch her."

I screamed out in pain as he twisted the knife further into my abdomen. "Enough out of you."

"What is that blade laced with?" Bastian asked.

His father chuckled. "Soren never told you that this specific metal and belladonna is a weakness to magic folk? All that history and lore he's consumed over the years...you didn't use it to your advantage? Have I taught you nothing?"

"He didn't tell me," Bastian said.

Soren knew how to kill me? All this time?

"I always said if I could combine the two of you into one man, I'd have my heir—my real legacy."

I couldn't even think straight. The pain was unbearable, it felt as though acid was traveling throughout my body.

The man pulled the blade from my side and pushed me down into the dirt. I pushed my hand into my side to try and staunch the bleeding, but it was coming out too quickly.

I looked up at Bastian, my eyes pleading. I thought I had nothing in this world to live for, but I did. "Please, protect them."

"Women speak when they are spoken to." Their father wrenched my head back painfully by grabbing a chunk of my hair and hissed in my ear. He then threw his blade to Bastian.

"Go on, son. Kill her and let's go home." I could see the grin on his father's face out of my peripheral. "Prove to me you are ready."

I looked over to find Bastian staring down at me with a sadness there that I couldn't pinpoint.

Just go to sleep, Callie. This is what you have been praying for.

"Not yet," I mumbled—the poison was doing its job, coursing through my veins. It took everything in me to stay present.

"What was that?" The man asked. "Bastian, is she talking to herself?"

Bastian didn't answer him, still staring down at me.

This was happening. My powers were locked far away from me, and who knew how long it would take for them to come back. I needed to fight.

"Do it! Get it over with!" His father urged.

"Yes, do it, Bastian," Callum said. His eyes were cold—locked in. He was holding Emilia so tightly that her arms were likely bruised. "Because that is what you were bred to do. You are whoever your father makes you. You can never be anything more."

Bastian shook his head, looking between us three.

Callum didn't relent. "Kill her, and kill that part of yourself with her."

His breathing quickened. He looked to his father, his voice desperate when he asked, "What about the Reaping? Joséphine?"

Their father laughed. "Did you really think that I would allow my own flesh and blood to be sacrificed to the beast? No. I was going to switch her out with a girl that looked similar. No one would be able to tell the difference from a distance."

Evil incarnate. That's what this man was.

"What are you going to do with them?" He pointed to Callum and Emilia. Was he stalling? Or did he truly care about their fates?

"They will die, of course."

I snarled at him.

"It's a small price to pay for his silence; can't have him coming to the town and spilling all of our secrets."

Bastian kept staring at him, and then Emilia. Their eyes locked for a long few moments before he asked the question I'd known the answer to the moment we'd met. "She was one of the children. Her name is Emilia. She said she was raped before she was thrown into the forest. She was thirteen, the same age as Joséphine. Did you...?"

His father scoffed, not even sparing Emilia a glance. "Did I *what*, son?"

"Did you partake in it?"

"I don't fancy little girls," he said simply, but Bastian looked like he was going to be sick. Something about the response told him everything.

"You're lying," he said.

He breathed deeply, growing frustrated with the delay.

"You're a monster."

His father pointed at me. "No, she is a monster...and if you don't kill her, I will."

Before I knew what was happening, Bastian had run toward us and rammed his body into his father, knocking me over. Then, they were nothing but a blur of grunts, fists, and kicks. I sucked in a shallow breath when it felt like hot pokers stabbing me everywhere. I wasn't going to make it. Fuck.

I felt the blood pool in my mouth until I was coughing it up. Gods wait! Don't take me yet. I needed to make sure he died. That Emilia got the revenge she rightfully deserved.

The man got Bastian under his feet and kicked him off his body. I looked over to find Bastian had been cut a few times. The poison would work its way through his body much faster than mine.

I dove into the well of my power to find even a flicker, but nothing still. Fine. I would fight him until my last breath. He was looking at his son when I pulled myself up and lunged at his side, catching him off guard.

I dug my nails into him wherever I could grip. I would rip him apart with my bare hands if I had to. I couldn't fight him properly from the belladonna and loss of blood. Useless body.

His hands gripped my shoulders as he kneed my stomach and I doubled over, coughing up more blood. I looked up at their father as he reared back his fist and slammed it into the side of my face.

I could hear screaming around me as my body twisted and I landed on my side. I didn't even have enough strength to move my head to see who was screaming my name.

Would they mourn?

They will all be dead soon enough.

I opened my eyes to find the man had straddled my stomach, put his hand around my throat, and raised his other hand high in the air that held the blade laced with belladonna.

This was it.

I could see my family.

I closed my eyes, welcoming the darkness, but I felt nothing happen. Was it over? Then I felt something drop onto my face. I barely opened my eyes to find Emilia was on the man's back and was driving her blade into his neck over and over again. She was so quick that not even he could swing her off of him in time to save himself. His blood poured out of him, bathing me, intermingling in the dirt around us.

I couldn't stop staring at her as she screamed things that I couldn't hear. Letting all of her aggression, pain and suffering go with each strike of the blade. I felt a stinging in my eyes as his blood dropped down the side of my face.

No. Emilia. I didn't want this for you. I was supposed to take on this burden. Not you.

His body slowed, and the damned blade dropped from his hand as she gripped her tighter and drove it straight through the side of his head.

She stood and pushed him off of me. Spitting on his corpse.

"Your grace?" I could feel hands touching me again and a distant voice screamed as darkness overtook me. "Your grace!"

CHAPTER TWENTY

I sucked in a deep breath as I opened my eyes and looked around wildly. Where was I? What happened? I squeezed my eyes shut and focused on my breathing. I couldn't do anything until I gained control of my body.

Deep breath in. One. Two. Three. Deep breath out. One. Two. Three.

I did that a few more times until I wasn't gasping for air and could think more rationally. I tried to think back to what had happened when a rush of memories flooded my mind.

Soren read my diary.

Their father arrived.

Bastian... Bastian was ready to kill me to leave. The wind knocked out of me at the realization.

I knew the father was dead. Emilia stabbed him multiple times, there is no way that he was able to survive that. But, I needed to see them all for myself. Needed reassurance.

I struggled to sit up as the pain radiated through my body. I gathered my strength, calling upon my powers, and could barely feel the slightest flicker. So they still weren't back yet. Fine. At least it didn't permanently erase them.

What was the blade? I shook my head. Something to worry about for later.

I swung my legs off the bed and sat there, exhausted. I looked up to the ceiling as I pushed off the bed and almost collapsed, my legs were so shaky that I could hardly stand straight. I strained as I caught myself by gripping the side table and then walking to the wall.

If this is how I would have to walk, then so be it. I slowly made my way out of my room by using the wall as support until I reached the door. I took a few deep breaths before glancing down the long hallway that led to the staircase.

Breathe. You can do this.

I pushed myself down the hall and threw myself against the stair railing. I wouldn't have the energy to search for them and couldn't use my powers to conjure my ball. I would have to call for them. Soren and Callum would come running, but I didn't want Bastian anywhere near me.

What did mother say about a woman's scorn?

"Your grace!" I looked down to find Callum racing up the stairs to get to me. "You shouldn't be up. Your wounds aren't healed!"

"Emilia?" I said her name with a groan.

"She hasn't left her chambers since last night." So, it has only been a full day since I have been asleep? My next question must have been written all over my face because he said, "I have checked in on her every hour." I nodded. I would need to check on her myself right after I took care of one problem.

I narrowed my eyes and glanced down the steps. "Where are they?"

"Outside at the back of the castle."

"Why?" Silence. I looked at him in a way that promised he would be next on my list of punishments if he didn't speak up.

Still bowed, he answered, "Burying their father."

"On my soil?" He nodded and I blanched. They dare to bury him on my lands.

I rushed down the steps but tripped over the nightdress that someone put me in and would have fallen down the stairs if Callum hadn't caught me.

"Get your hands off of me!" I pushed him back weakly. I wasn't even strong enough to have him move even a single inch.

He took a step back as he followed me down the stairs using the railing until I reached the main floor. Then I used the walls until I had finally made it to the back doors that were already open. I was sweating. My entire body was hot. And I could feel something sticky dripping down my body and I knew that my wound was reopened. But I couldn't focus on any of that.

No.

I couldn't stop staring off into the distance at the two men digging a hole into the ground. *My* ground. *My* soil. *Mine.*

"Stop!" I ordered.

They stopped digging and turned to me. I couldn't see their facial expressions from where they were, but I could see one of them drop the shovel and run toward me.

A head of bright blonde hair. The scholar.

He took the steps two at a time as he stood an inch before me, looking me over. "You shouldn't be up. I just finished your sutures." He looked toward my abdomen and went to touch it when I smacked his hand away. "Your wound reopened. I need to stitch you again. You've lost too much blood."

"Enough." I observed him more closely, the swelling of his cheek. I reached for him, touched the skin, and looked behind him at Bastian. He stood behind his brother, his head low. Raged filled me.

"I'm fine," said Soren, in a sudden panic. "You know how many times Bast has punched me?"

"Shut up," I spat, taking him by the chin, tears filling my eyes. I urged them to stay within my eyelids. "I told you not to move...to stay put. You never listen."

"Perhaps I could still use some lessons on obedience? Should you still like to teach me?" I couldn't smile, my body hurt too much. I pulled his chin forward, pressed my forehead to his, and rested there a moment. A silent thank you. Then, the fleeting moment escaped us when I heard the shuffling of dirt again.

"Did I give you permission to bury that monster on my lands?"

Bastian sucked in a breath. "No, but—"

I raised my hand, silencing him.

"You're a coward. You couldn't even muster up the strength to kill me when that's all you have talked about day in and day out."

"I am sorry." His eyes stayed low.

"You still can't look at me!"

He flinched.

I gathered enough energy to slap him. My hand stung from the contact and I fell forward, slamming into his body. His arms wrapped around me. I hated that my skin still heated under the contact, it felt like my body betrayed me as I wanted more than anything for him to say that it was all a bad dream.

I pushed off him and fell to the ground. "I never want to see you again. You were going to let me die." My voice broke.

Bastian finally looked at me with a pained expression. "You stopped a monster, but this monster..." I pointed to my chest. "...this monster meant nothing to you. I wasn't enough." A sob broke through me, tearing my soul apart. "I. Wasn't. Enough."

He shook his head and tried to reach out to me, but thought better of it. "You don't understand—"

"Stop," I shouted, lifting my hands up. "Your father is dead. The head of the council is dead. Go back home and make it right. Rid the town of the Reaping. Fuck and marry whomever you wish. I don't *care*." Those last three words caught in my throat.

I told you to trust no one and look where it got you again.

I was so broken that I started hysterically laughing until the pain brought me back to the present.

"I want you gone by the time I wake tomorrow." I could feel the pull of sleep calling to me. My head felt light, and knew it must be the blood loss.

"I am not leaving."

"Then I will kill you," I seethed. I needed to hurry; my mind was slipping away. I looked at their father, rolled up tightly in cloth. "Take that body with you. Or else I will leave him in the woods for the animals to devour." My vision started to blur and I could feel my body drifting down to the ground until someone caught me just in time. I was weightless in someone's arms, drifting back inside.

"Her fever is back. Shit." I heard the sound of rustling and my nightgown ripping and then pain. Soren must be sewing my body back together. My mind wandered as he gave commands to various people in the room.

Then, I could hear quiet sobs.

Emilia? Her voice brought me back to reality, and I tried my best to open my eyes and see her pained expression above me. She was sitting on the bed, crying.

Oh, Emilia.

I tried to talk, but it hurt. My throat was so scratchy. She leaned over to the small table and raised a rag above me, dripping some water into my mouth.

I swallowed and then asked, "Are you alright?"

She shook her head. "Me? I'm not the one who was stabbed and—" She bit her tongue and lowered her head.

I knew what she was thinking about, but I had done my best to not think about it. I couldn't think about how his calloused hands felt against my skin, his hot breath wanting to make me vomit. I wanted to forget that it ever happened, but I couldn't. Not when I looked into Emilia's eyes and saw the pain that she was going through by seeing him again and knowing what taking his life meant for her.

I pushed past my own feelings and said, "Emilia, please don't mourn for killing that monster. He deserved it for everything he did to you. I am just sorry you were the one to do it. That I didn't have the strength to fight him."

"And what about you?" She was near hysterics, staring at me with wide eyes.

"What?" My heart began to beat irregularly.

"Stop being strong for us. You were assaulted, too." I tensed at the word. She must have seen this reaction as she lowered her voice. "You are always putting others before yourself, even after everything."

"I just wanted to protect you." My voice trembled, barely above a whisper.

"You did," she urged. "You have protected me for twenty years. *Always* taking care of me when I had my spells, my tantrums, giving me food when we were running low... I remember everything."

I wanted nothing more than to shield her from all the horrors of the world, and if I had the means, I would resurrect him just to make him suffer more for the rest of eternity.

When I turned my head, she continued, "You act as though you are so tough, invincible, but you aren't. You care so much. We can all see it."

I opened my mouth to protest, but nothing she said was wrong.

"You push us away and keep us at arms-length to protect your heart." She grabbed my hands and brought them to her chest, willing me to hear her. "Why do you think Callum and I have stayed by your side? We *love* you."

I shook my head, pulled my hands out of her grasp, and winced from the sudden movement. "Please stop..." I dug my fingernails into my palms and bit back the sob that threatened to escape. "Loving you will destroy me."

Her shoulders slumped at hearing my words—my truth. I know she seemed to believe her words, but I heard nothing but lies. There was no plausible reason why she would love me. The only reasonable answer was that she wanted to keep me alive. I didn't tell her any of this as I knew she would insist on her sincerity.

Without another thought, she grabbed my shoulders and embraced me. I tensed as her shoulders shook, and she cried on my shoulder. It only took a few moments before my body began to shake uncontrollably as the weight of what that monster did to me and what he could have done began to settle into my bones.

I allowed myself this one moment of weakness, and I clutched her even closer to me, digging my fingers into her back as we used each other to mourn.

Hours passed and as tired as I was, I couldn't fall asleep. I sent Emilia away under the pretense that I needed rest, but really I couldn't look into her eyes any longer. Our conversation took more out of me than I cared to admit.

"Just let me in to see her!" Someone shouted.

Silence, then another voice saying, "You betrayed her in the worst way possible. You need to leave before she wakes up and finds you still here." More silence and then that same voice said a little more delicately. "Just let her rest Bastian, her body needs it, as well as her mind."

Callum and the hunter.

I didn't hear anything else until someone opened the door. I looked over to find Callum carrying a bowl in his hands. "You're awake."

I continued staring at him as he walked over and set the bowl down on the side table.

"Where is it? The blade?" I didn't want to hear any more lies. Not from him.

"How about you worry about it when you've rested?" I didn't like his answer, but I was too exhausted to fight with him.

He grabbed the spoon that was in the bowl, scooped a small amount, and brought it to my lips. I closed my mouth. I didn't have an appetite.

"Your grace, you must eat if you want to heal." He sighed, and I could hear him standing there. "Just please eat something when you feel up to it."

I closed my eyes and curled up into a ball slow enough that my sutures wouldn't rupture, I didn't want to see anyone else.

I heard the door close and tears lined my eyes. I tucked my chin to my chest and begged them not to come, but they didn't listen, and my body shook from the resistance. I was so tired of crying. So tired of trying to be someone that everyone wanted me to be. Whom I would never be.

I sat there in silence until her voice made another appearance. It was just us. Again.

No one loves you.

"Emilia said she did. Even Callum... Maybe..." I gave myself a single moment to hope before shutting my heart down once more.

No one loves you.

"No one loves me." I parroted Circe.

Everyone hates you.

"Everyone hates me."

You hurt everyone who loves you.

"I hurt everyone who loves me."

I fell asleep to her repeating over and over again.

Chapter Twenty-One

The clouds above were dark as the wind whipped around me, I shielded my eyes from the onslaught of the rain beating down. I wiped a drop from my cheek and brought it up to my face, it wasn't rain. It was blood.

I looked down and found that I was dressed in a white nightgown, the picture of innocence as I looked out and found a battle waging before my eyes. Faceless men and women ran around in front of the castle, fighting each other, and murdering each other. I tried to move, but it was as if my feet were rooted to the stone steps. My body paralyzed with fear.

"It is all your fault. How could you do this to us?"

I looked up and saw my father standing in front of me, a look of pure contempt written clearly across his features. "Father! Please!"

"Look! Look around at the carnage that you have left in your wake!" His voice boomed over the roar of the battle.

I screamed as a head rolled to my feet... Mother was staring right up at me.

No no no no! I fell backward and crawled away. This can't be happening. Tears ran down my face as I looked up to find everyone on the battlefield standing and staring at me, all of their eyes the milky white color of death. They were horrified of me, of the monster I had become.

I looked to my right and found Annabelle's body slumped against a stone wall. I rushed to her, and fell to my knees, screaming at the top of my lungs. Her eyes were open–lifeless. This can't be real. I hugged her to me, rocking back and forth. "This isn't real. This isn't real. This isn't real."

This wasn't supposed to happen. This didn't happen!

Father tore me away from my tormented thoughts when he yelled, "Enough!"

He grabbed my shoulder and shook me vigorously. I tried to push him away, clinging to Annabelle, when my hands went through her body. I looked around for her, but my surroundings had changed.

We were in the tower. The windows were knocked out, the wind whipped my face, the chill biting into my skin.

I ignored the cold as I pleaded with Father, begging him to listen to me. He gripped me so hard that his hands were leaving bruises on my skin.

He suddenly stopped, hands still on me, his face slowly contorted into something inhuman. Animal. It was utterly terrifying. I tried hard to pull myself away from him, but his grip was too strong, and overpowering.

He brought his face so close to mine that our noses were touching, I could feel his staunch breath, as he said with deadly accuracy, "You should have died, witch. Not them."

And he pushed me out of the tower window.

I sat straight up in bed, screaming at the top of my lungs. Sweat dripped off of every inch of my body, the sheets sticking to my skin, the pain in my stomach secondary to the nightmare.

"Your grace... Your grace!" I was still screaming and thrashing about when I heard, "Calathea!"

I stilled.

My name.

Breathing rapidly, I looked up into the eyes of the hunter, and in this light, they were too similar to my father. His hands were placed on my shoulders, and his face was inches from mine. Callum was standing by the door, looking between the two of us. I looked back into the hunter's eyes as my breathing started to slow when it finally clicked that he was here, witnessing whatever *this* was.

"Traitor!" I pushed his hands away and yelled, "Get the fuck off me! Get out!"

Tears appeared again, I was so fucking tired of crying, but I couldn't stop them. I remembered the dream again and doubled over on the bed, screaming from the pain of the nightmare. It felt so real that it was nauseating. I had never felt a nightmare as real as that one.

I couldn't breathe.

The room felt like it was closing in on me. I started clawing at myself, if I could just rip open my chest that would help bring air into my lungs. I was in a frenzy. I couldn't focus on anything that was going on. The only thing I felt was hands all over me, and it burned.

"Breathe, your grace. Come on. There you go. Breathe." Callum was next to me, rubbing

my back in what he thought were soothing strokes.

"What is wrong with her?" I heard another voice ask Callum.

"I don't know. She has never done this before." Then addressed me. "I am here. I have you. You are safe."

They were treating me like a fragile doll. A glass vase ready to shatter at any moment. I was not that girl. Their touches were burning a hole through my skin. The same skin that Father just bruised, I tried to look at my shoulders to see if he had left a mark. It was too dark, but the pain was still there, still sore.

I grabbed one of the hands and tore it away from my body, scrambled off the bed and as far away from them as I could. I finally got a good look at the room. It was in total shambles. My magic was swirling around the room, destroying everything in its path.

Had I done this? Was my magic back?

I planted my body firmly against the wall as Soren and Emilia came into view. "I told you to get out," I said with deadly calm. The same calm as Father had before he pushed me out the window. A sob broke past my lips before I could stop it at the thought of his face. "Get out!" I waved my hand, threw them from the room, and slammed the door behind them.

I could faintly hear their shouts of protest, but I couldn't have them around me. Too many emotions were wreaking havoc on my mind, body and soul. I clutched my stomach as I fell to the ground, expelling all the emotions that I felt in that nightmare.

Anger swept through me. Rage so potent that it was almost palpable in the air. Thick and heavy. I threw the closest thing to me against the wall. Shredded the sheets. Shattered the table. Broke every single glass surface until I was numb.

I stepped back until my back hit the corner of my room next to my bed and I slumped down. I was breathing heavily, looked around at the carnage that I had just inflicted upon my room, and knew in my heart that this was how I was supposed to live. A life of loneliness. Scaring off every person who ever tried to care for me. Never deserving of anything good and pure.

I couldn't trust myself around anyone.

I climbed onto my bed, in the torn sheets, and stared up at the feathers floating above me, slowly descending, with no care in the world.

And just laid there.

Empty.

Cold.

Alone.

I sat at the dining table, waiting for my pets to arrive. I had not even bothered to change out of my wine-stained dress, straps falling off my shoulders, hair in disarray. What a vision I must have looked like when they finally entered.

I raised my bottle to them as all three of them entered and I laughed, widening my arms to the side of me. "Oh, you're all still here? Didn't I send you two away? And Emilia, didn't you promise to leave as well?" I brought the bottle back up to my lips, took a swig, and waved my hand in their direction. "Nevermind all that nonsense. Sit. Dine with me." They all stopped and gaped at me, none daring to say a word. I then laughed some more at the horror and confusion mixed on their faces, which made me laugh even harder, that I almost fell out of my chair.

Callum moved forward to help balance me, the wine splashing all over the ground and on our clothes.

"Your grace... Are you alright?"

I brushed him off and leaned against the table for support. "Of course, little bird. Does it not look like I am the vision of perfection?" I used my hands to scan down my body, as if that made my entire point.

Soren had moved to the table and Bastian had disappeared off to the kitchens. He returned with a bowl full of soup and set it down in front of me.

He said, "You missed a few meals. You must be starving. I have made you a vegetable soup as I am not sure your stomach could handle much more than this."

I grabbed his chin between my fingers and drawled out, "Oh, Bastian darling. You have no idea what I can handle." I touched his face, licked his lips, and said, "Feed me."

He sucked in a breath and dipped the spoon in the soup and brought it to my lips. It tasted heavenly. He was right... I was starving. We all sat there in silence as he fed me every last drop. When it was finished, I got up, brought my bottle of venin to my lips, and drank deeply.

I could see Soren out of the corner of my eyes as he stared at the bottle. I walked over to him and sat on his lap. Running my hand through his hair and the other brought the bottle up to his face. "No no Soren. You can't have any of this." I then whispered in his ear, "It will kill you and I can't have that, can I? Your brother might try to kill me again."

I took another swig from the bottle. Laughing when a little more fell down my chin, licking the juice from my fingers. He was staring at me, so I asked, "What's wrong with you?" When he still didn't say anything, I pouted. "You're no fun."

I set my eyes on Callum and he sat up a little straighter, ready for whatever I was going to throw at him. "My little bird. Always there for me. Always ready to please." I slipped my dress down my shoulder until my breast was out, making a show of it. I always loved the way he looked at me. Like I was the main course and he would never tire of me. Just like he was now, roaming his eyes up and down the length of me, slightly moving forward, his cock straining in his pants. "After all these years Callum and yet you still are so ready for me when I haven't even touched you."

"Your grace, I will want you until my last dying breath. Nothing you could do or say would change that." He always knew what to say.

"So smooth."

I stood up, sat on the side of the table, and ate a few grapes, my stomach recoiling from it, having not had anything of substance for quite a long time, and spit it back onto the platter.

"How about you hand me that glass so I can feed you more soup." I looked over to see Bastian reaching his hand out, ready to take away my cup.

I narrowed my eyes on him. "If you think I haven't forgotten your treachery, then you would be sorely mistaken."

"Your grace..." He stopped moving for a moment before resuming unfaltering, "I am sorry, truly. I wasn't in my right mind."

"And you think that I care. You know what? Nevermind! I don't feel like talking about that right now." He was sullying my joyous mood!

"Your joyous mood?" Callum asked.

"Oops, did I say that aloud?" I looked around and every single face was scrunched in worry, concern, or a mix of both. "Enough. You are all stifling."

I left the room without another word.

I needed the fresh air licking and caressing my bare skin. I wholly enjoyed being naked, reveled in the feeling it gave me. Especially under the rays of the moon, though the moon wasn't currently out. I guess the fog would have to do.

I stumbled out of the back doors, and stopped only to take a swig out of the bottle, but found it empty. I tossed the bottle down, shattering at my feet. I looked down at the beautiful broken pieces of the glass glistening. Without thinking I brought my foot down on top of the pieces.

Nothing.

I stretched my arms high above my head, giggling at the tingling sensation the poison gave me. I had never had this much in my system before, maybe, it would finally do its job and kill me.

I wriggled my feet, laughed at the shards shredding the bottom of my feet, and took off, running around to the side of the castle. I passed by the greenhouse, past the treeline, and into the woods. I didn't have to walk long before I saw the archway made naturally by the forest over a millenia. Flowers lined the arch, and the petals would fall during the spring, casting a soft pink on the floor bed. Like something out of a dream.

I slowed my pace and walked through the arch leading to my paradise. The sounds of the waterfall lapping at the water below it, causing a constant rippling effect along the top of the water. The pond was large enough that it would take a few minutes of swimming to reach the other side of it. The water had an ethereal color to it; a beautiful blue-green hue. There were large boulders surrounding parts of it around the cliff.

I could never reach the top or get a glimpse of what was beyond my confinement. It was part of the border of my lands.

I cast those thoughts away and focused back on my paradise. My skin had bumps running along it from the cold, frigid air; the fog made it seem even colder. I was still high from venin's effects, my head spinning, my skin singing.

I climbed up one of the boulders and looked down. I stretched my arms out and fell.

I hit the surface of the water hard and the wind was knocked from me. I closed my mouth and opened my eyes. Stared down into its depths, wondering exactly how far down it went. I had never tried.

No matter, I could stay here forever. I started running out of air and swam up, taking a deep breath when I reached the surface. I laid back and floated, loving the way the water felt against my skin. I could always depend on my little pond to stay at the perfect temperature year-round, having spelled it years ago.

The floating feeling is what I can only imagine what death is like. Maybe that is why I loved coming out here. It was the closest thing that I could get to actual death. The elusive minx. How much had I screamed for the release of ending it? How many times had I been on my knees crying out and *praying* to a false god? Because if he were real, he wouldn't allow me to suffer as I had. I was a devoted follower and *if* he were real then he wouldn't do this to me.

They say he only puts his children through the worst of it if they are the strongest and it was just a bunch of bullshit. My last time talking to him was also the last time that I would get on my knees for a man.

I am now my own god.

I shut my eyes and cast all those thoughts out of my mind, and Venin was still doing her job of getting rid of anything that displeased me. I watched as flowers floated above me, dancing in the soft breeze. Flowers? I laughed at the absurdity, but didn't want to move and have them go away.

I moved my arms back and forth in slow rhythmic movements until I could make out the moon. How long have I been out here? Did I go down for breakfast or was it dinner? Oh well...

Part of me knew I should get out, but I didn't want to. My thoughts led me to staying in this pond. I didn't need any possessions. I would sleep in the waters' warm embrace, forgetting about everyone and everything.

Would they even notice I wasn't there any longer? Would they care? Or just miss what I gave them?

I moved until I was treading water, reached around, and grabbed the blade that was tucked tightly in a holster cinched at my thigh.

Whoever had brought this to me must have heard my prayers. Maybe there was a merciful god after all. I couldn't remember the amount of times I have tried to end it. And every single attempt failed. But, this time it would work.

I brought the blade up to my face. I was so tired. So very tired. The thought brought a little bit of peace to me, I looked at my other hand, still swaying, water flowing through my fingers keeping me afloat.

If I—If I ran out of air...

I don't know if it was the effects of la venin or if I was just done. Done with living this way. Being this way. Living in a waking nightmare. I couldn't do it anymore...

You win, Circe.

I expelled all the air from my lungs, slipping under the surface of the water. Down down down down down.

I took the knife and, stabbed it into my stomach and floated there for a few moments before a burning sensation spread throughout my chest. The need to take a breath was overpowering, so I did. My body spasmed at the air that was unable to enter my body. Then there was nothing.

I felt at peace.

This is it. I was going home.

I will see you soon, little sister.

Sleep. *Successful.*

CHAPTER TWENTY-TWO

"Your grace! Your grace! Take a breath!"

Belle? Why did she sound so scared?

"Calathea!"

I felt my head being lifted back slightly, fingers pinching my nose, and then a mouth covered mine, breathing into me. Something pounded on my chest. Hands moved back to my nose, a mouth on mine, and the process repeated until I opened my eyes and expelled water. The burning sensation was back in full force as water was being purged from my body.

I turned on my side and coughed until I started to dry heave. Wait. That was Belle's voice. I turned back around wildly and stared into Soren's face.

No no no. She was here! I heard her! I whipped my head around, looking for her. The desperation burned me. I couldn't have imagined her. She was right here.

Soren pulled my face back to his, frantically searching for something, and when he was satisfied, he slumped back onto the ground, tugging at his hair.

Then someone else was in front of me, anger glistening in those piercing light green eyes. "What the *fuck* were you thinking!"

I sat there still trying to collect my thoughts before realizing they pulled me from the water.

"Why would you save me?" I said, barely above a whisper. I was still in shock that I was alive and not dead.

My mind was racing. I took a shuddering breath, and something stabbed me. I fell over from the pain, face-first in the mud, hand pressed into my side. That's right. I had stabbed myself. I brought my hand back up to my face, bloody.

It didn't work.

How asinine for me to think that even if I had finally found a way out I could succeed.

I screamed once more, pounding the mud next to my face. "Why did you save me!"

"Stop!" Hands encircled mine as they tried to stop me.

"Get off!" I looked over and saw the blade. I must have held onto it when I was in the water.

"You're hurt! Stop!" Callum pleaded.

I kneed him in the balls and pushed him off of me, making a beeline for the blade that I saw out of the corner of my eye. Ignoring the pain from my side, I lunged for it, but someone grabbed my leg just before I could get to it. I turned to find Soren pulling me back. I reared up and kicked him in the face, and he let go immediately, cursing. I paid him no mind as I bounded for the blade again.

I gripped it between my hands, lining it up to my heart, and pressed it in. I gritted my teeth together as the blade broke skin, but I was thwarted again when someone's entire body pummeled me to the ground. So many hands were trying to get me to let go of the blade, but I hung onto it for as long as I could. I was so close to ending it.

Then someone ripped it from my hands. I looked up to find Bastian tossing it into the middle of the pond.

"NO!" My voice sounded so primal, like an animal.

I tried to use my magic on him, but it wouldn't come forth. Callum's entire body was still on top of me, and I fought with everything in me. I used what little strength I had left until Callum was pushed off of me, and Bastian replaced him. He straddled me and pinned my hands wherever they landed next to me.

"I said stop," Bastian growled with enough force that I stopped my desperate attempt to get away.

We glared at each other briefly before I said, "Are you wanting an audience this time? I don't think the scholar will appreciate seeing that."

He ignored my taunt. "You just tried to kill yourself."

I didn't respond. We both know what I had tried and failed to do. I didn't need to confirm it.

He tried again. "Why did you try to kill yourself?"

"You just tossed away the *only* thing that can kill me."

"Because we won't allow you to harm yourself."

I stared into his eyes and decided on a different tactic. "Think about it, hunter. If you had let me succeed, then you could walk out those front gates as we speak. That's what you want, right? I promise you that it will work this time. It will still take a while before the effects fade, like last time, but there is still time. Use your hands, and tighten them around my neck. Just do it."

"Bast..." Callum's tone was on edge, warning him not to make the wrong decision.

I didn't pay him any mind and continued staring at Bastian, willing him to listen to me. "Come on, you know you want to. Kill the beast."

He leaned down until our faces were close. "You wanted me... Now you have me, now and forever." A mix of sweat and water dripped onto my face; he was soaked.

"Excuse me?"

He leaned back, still pinning my body to the ground. "You heard me. I'm staying."

I barked out a humorless laugh. "You can't do that."

"Yes, I can."

"No, you can't."

"Yes, I can."

"No, you can't." He was about to reiterate that he, in fact, can change his mind when I said instead, "There is no way for you to have suddenly, out of the blue, changed your mind and decided to stay out of your own free will. What is it? Do you want me to beg? Fine. Let me up, and I'll do just that. I want to die. Don't you hear me? I want to die!"

His eyes softened, and some emotion I couldn't quite read crossed his features. "I would have once loved to see that, but not now. Not after everything." He narrowed his eyes. "You are not going to succeed. I will not allow it."

"I ordered you to leave these lands! That I would kill you if I ever saw you again—"

"And yet I am still here!" He yelled, cutting me off.

"Because you *had* to be! Because I had not allowed you to leave until now, so go!"

His expression turned pained. "It may not have seemed like a long time to you, but I have regretted my choice ever since I watched my father ram that blade through you. And now..." He swallowed hard. "Pulling your lifeless body..."

I heard it—the emotion, the shift in his feelings and thoughts, but I just wanted things to end. I was done fighting.

"You only made that decision *after* you found out what a monster he was. Not because of me. Save your lies."

He squeezed my wrists even tighter, the pain biting hard enough to make me flinch.

But Soren interrupted us. "Bast, let up, you're hurting her."

The moment Soren said that he let go immediately, sitting up. He cursed under his breath as he ran a hand through his hair and whispered, "Fuck it."

He reached down, pulling me to him, and kissed me. It was desperate and messy. I was so in shock that it took me a moment to wrap my mind around what was happening. I didn't know if I was too exhausted to fight it, but I hesitantly opened my mouth, then ran my hands up his muscular arms, gripping them like my life depended on it as if I could hang onto this moment.

As if he would help me change my mind.

I melted into his body, reveling in the way our mouths fit perfectly, as much as I didn't want to admit it. He let me go, still cradling my head in his hands as he leaned back to look at me.

I was at a loss for a moment, but I knew his intention and motive. He was trying to distract me.

"You won't stop me from ending it."

"Yes, I will. If you think that I will let you out of my sight for even a moment, you are sorely mistaken."

"Stop pretending that you care for me." He was about to say something else when I tried to push him off again and couldn't help wincing from the wound in my stomach.

Soren said with more conviction, "Off her, Bast. Now. She isn't going anywhere."

He reluctantly got up, and I looked around. Soren was sitting on the ground, still holding his nose. Bastian was standing above me, and Callum was nearby, with silent tears running down his face. I heard a noise near the archway and found Emilia standing there with her hand over her mouth, crying.

Finally, the horror settled into me. I tuned out everyone except Emilia, watching her body heave from how heavily she was sobbing. I had almost left her. I promised never to leave her and I'd almost left her.

"Emilia," I said her name. Tears welled in my eyes until I could no longer see her before me.

She turned and left the scene in a rush.

My skin heated from the concern written over all of their faces. I knew that Bastian would keep his word and wouldn't leave me, even for a moment. I tried standing to walk back, wanting to chase her down.

Before I could move an inch, as if he read my mind, Bastian scooped me up and into his arms and walked back toward the castle.

I was about to demand he put me down when he cursed and said, "Callum, she's shivering. Give me your cloak."

A moment later, I was wrapped in a thick cloak, teeth chattering so hard that I could have chipped a tooth. I had forgotten about the cold.

I choked back the tears, instead needing to focus on Bastian and try one more time. Make them understand that it would be better for everyone if they just let me go.

I looked up at Bastian, ready to plead my case, but what came out instead was, "Emilia saw everything?" I sounded pathetic, but that's what desperate creatures were.

"Don't think about it."

I leaned into his warmth, resting my head on his chest.

We made it back to my chambers in no time, and I saw everyone running around the place. Emilia went to my wardrobe to grab a fresh nightgown, Callum moved swiftly to the bathroom, and Soren walked away to grab the medical kit from another room.

Bastian walked into the bathroom and set me gently on the ground next to the tub. He started peeling off my dress, but I smacked his hand away in protest. I winced again; any movement was intolerable.

"Stop. We need to clean you up so that Soren can tend to your wound. Do you need me to remind you that you currently have no powers? You won't win."

He was right, I looked off to the side and hung my hands limply at my sides, allowing him to continue taking off the dress. It wasn't anything that he hadn't seen before. He lifted me with ease and sat me in the tub. Emilia came into view as I stared out the window. She added an assortment of salts and liquids to the bath, which immediately seeped into my skin and eased the pain.

She came to the side of the tub and I watched her dip a cup into the water, using it to wet my hair. Her movements were light, ensuring that none of it got in my eyes. She didn't talk to me, and I didn't try to make conversation.

Why was she still here?

I could see her lathering a liquid in her hands, and then she massaged it into my head. The action was so relaxing and calming that it reminded me of when Mother used to do that to me as a little girl. She would insist that she be the one to do it, even at the handmaid's protests. The memory was so sudden that I began to sob again. For what, I wasn't sure.

The tears had stopped by the time she had finished with my hair and washed the dirt from my skin. Numb once again, I did my best to separate myself from my body to no avail.

Once she deemed me clean, she looked up to someone and moved out of the way. I could hear someone trying to talk to me, but I was still trying to dissociate from life and ignored the person. Then hands were once again on me, lifting me from the bath and wrapping something around my body. I looked down to see that Emilia was drying me.

She nodded to whoever was holding me up, and then I was being carried into my bedroom fully clothed. When did that happen? I looked up to find that Callum had laid me on my bed. Then Soren came into view, tending to my wounds. I would wince every once in a while when whatever he was doing caused enough pain that I couldn't stay silent, crying out.

I could barely hear him order, "Callum, hold her shoulders. This is going to hurt."

Before I could brace myself, he had poured something over my stomach that had me convulsing.

When the pain finally subsided, my head was being lifted as a vial was placed up to my lips.

Callum begged, "Please drink it, your grace."

I parted my chapped lips and forced the vile liquid down my throat, swallowing all of it. Before I could ask, my eyes started growing heavy, my body relaxing.

I could feel someone press their lips to the top of my head, and I allowed sleep to claim me once again.

I awoke to a searing pain in my side and some of my muscles spasming. I began to panic because I couldn't remember what happened. Why was I in pain? I searched through my memories, but everything was shrouded in a dense fog.

Everything felt as though it would take immense effort, like I had run for miles on end. I tried to take deep breaths, but every time my chest expanded, the pain followed.

"Calathea?"

Wait. Is that who I think it is? I willed my eyes to open and when I did I had to blink a few times before I could see clearly. I sucked in a fast breath, and it took a moment to fight through the blinding pain. I stifled a sob.

"Father. Mother." I croaked out. Then when her beautiful little face peeked behind Mother, I sobbed. "Annabelle..."

She was the most beautiful creature that I had ever laid my eyes on. Long auburn hair cascaded down the middle of her back, wild. Her tanned skin was glowing as she sat down next to me, holding my hand.

Father came forward and cupped my cheek gently, cooing, "My dear daughter, you gave us quite a fright. I am so happy to see that you're awake." I looked over at Mother, who was silently crying, holding onto Father's arm.

"I have missed you all so much."

"We have missed you too, darling," Mother said. "You have changed so much, yet not at all."

Belle's eyes widened. "Tell me, sister, do you still play in the snow?"

I shook my head, my stomach twisted with longing. "Not since you."

"What about me? Have you missed me as well?"

I glanced over at the voice. "Circe?"

"Hello, Callie." Circe walked around to the other side of the bed that Father just vacated to make room. She sat down, bent over, and kissed me softly on the forehead just like she did whenever I was ill.

My vision began to blur from tears dripping down my cheek.

I reached up and sobbed, "I am so sorry... Please forgive me."

Circe looked so confused, her features twisting, and replied in a voice that wasn't her own, "No, your majesty. It's Emilia. Bastian, Soren, and Callum are here, too. We are here."

I ignored her strange words. "Please tell me how to fix it. How do I earn your forgiveness? I will do anything."

She looked so worried about me. Hope filled my chest as she said, "You did nothing wrong, your grace. It's Emilia."

"Emilia?" My head was clearing slightly, but not enough to register what she was saying. "Circe, don't be silly. I don't want you upset with me any longer. I am sorry." Tears continued to stream down my face. "I was just scared. Don't leave me." The last three words came out in a sob.

Circe smiled down at me and replied, "I would never leave you. Please, stop crying." She patted my hand gently. "Get some rest."

"Yes, you're right."

I settled back down as I looked around the room at all of their faces. Everyone I loved was in this room. I tried to stay awake for as long as possible—I never wanted to leave.

But, my eyes grew heavy, and I allowed sleep to take me once more.

I could barely hear someone say, "Emilia said that part of the symptoms of belladonna poisoning is hallucinations. Let's take our leave."

There was nothing.

Pure silence.

The same silence that wrapped its barbed blanket around me since that day. I couldn't show Annabelle how broken I had become, and prayed that she couldn't see me from Heaven. I was meant to protect and shield her from the cruelty of the world, but I failed.

The anger was instant. Enveloping me in a burning rage that never truly burned out, no matter how hard I tried. My only constant, besides Circe. For centuries, I allowed the pain to control me. And when the pain became too unbearable, I would destroy all that was in my path. Do my best to breathe through the pain of losing my parents, people, sister—my entire world.

Though Belle's death hit me differently. When she died, I felt as if I had died right alongside her. Nothing was left of me besides pure, undiluted rage. Rage toward Circe. I remember screaming into the world all of the despair I felt at losing such a pure soul. It wasn't fair that she died, and I was cursed to live in a place that would be a constant reminder of what I allowed to happen. I was so close to her moments ago, that I just wanted it back.

My mind tricked me again, sending me plunging into another memory.

Emilia was young, sitting around the table in the library. I had been reading to her every night to get her to sleep. It always worked in the beginning. She'd slumber for hours and then wake up screaming. Tonight, she couldn't be swayed back to sleep.

"What is this?" Her voice was hoarse, a breathy gasping thing. She stared down at the tea, steaming and warm in her small hands. She'd only been with me for a month now, and was still hesitant over my orders. It was strange trying to care for her. She was stubborn and small, and so very burdened by the haunting things that happened to her—how she ended up nearly dead in the woods. I shuddered at the image, still burned into my mind. I reached for her hand to steady it, but she retracted it and placed it in her lap.

"I will not touch you," I told her warmly. "Nobody will touch you again. The tea is lavender...it will calm you. I added some honey."

A moment of silence passed between us, where she still hesitated, then finally took a small sip. Then another, and another.

"The nightmares will get worse before they get better," I said, watching her eyes drop to the tea, staring at the honey along the edge of the cup. "The days will get better first. You will feel comfort in the skies, trees, and earth. Nature is very healing."

Her eyes blinked slowly, and though she said nothing, I knew she was taking it in. "Eventually, you will look forward to the days that the nights will be quicker, less painful."

"How long will you..." her voice broke a moment. "Keep me?"

My heart ached at the words. "You are free to leave when you wish...should you wish it."

"I don't want to," she mouthed.

"I do not have much," I reasoned with her. "I cannot give you what your family gave you."

She shook her head at the mention of it. "No family, not anymore."

I swallowed and urged her to drink more of the tea. "I don't have one either. We're better off without them. If we don't have anyone to love, we do not have anyone to lose. You see?"

She nodded in understanding.

"I will teach you how to use your hands to communicate with me. I have many books on how, and we shall learn together."

Another nod.

"When you are strong and ready, you can leave...but not a moment too soon."

She finished her tea over the next few minutes, and I walked her back to bed, but she stopped me halfway and directed me back to the library. There, on a chaise, she asked to sleep with my father's worn and tattered blanket. I waited with her, long into the night. She opened her eyes often to check I hadn't left.

"Sleep, child," I'd tell her, and she'd drift away again.

I opened my eyes. It was bright enough that I could make out my room. It took all of my energy to turn my head and hiss as I saw Bastian cutting my arm with the same blade that he threw into the pond. My eyes went to his face, but he wasn't even looking at me, concentrating on his task.

Good. Then he wouldn't see the pain coming. I dug deep into my body, calling for my powers, but the well was empty. I blanched at the realization, dug deeper trying to find a scrap of it, and came up empty again.

"I told them all to go bathe and change. That was a while ago, so I am sure that they will be back any moment."

"And you?"

"And me what?"

"Are you going to bathe?" I made a show of sniffing him. "You smell foul."

He scoffed. "That tongue is as sharp as ever."

"My wit is the least of your worries."

He was silent for another few moments before asking, "Still thinking about killing yourself." He said it more like a statement, already aware of my answer. I loathed how well he knew me.

I narrowed my eyes. "When my powers come back, I will kill you."

"As you have already declared, but thankfully, you aren't healed yet. Thus, the murdering and torture will have to wait, and from my calculations, we have about twenty-four hours until that happens." Then he smirked and waved the blade in front of my face. "Unless I cut you with this blade." He sighed. "You have no idea how long I had to hold my breath to get it." He threw the blade up in the air and caught it.

This was all a joke to him.

I gritted my teeth. "I *hate* you."

He just widened his mouth and gave me a smile that only Soren had given me so far. "Say it again. I rather missed your voice."

If only I could move... I would end him in the most unique of ways.

"Why are you still here?"

He adjusted the blade into a sheath that he situated along his hip and then looked back at me. The easygoing smile was gone, replaced by his usual serious expression; only now, instead of hatred lining his features, he simply looked sad. No, 'devastated' would be a better word.

"You had a dream."

I raised an eyebrow at him, curious why the sudden change of topic. "A dream?"

Bast nodded. "You woke up and were speaking to your family and—" He paused as if uncomfortable saying the next part. "Circe. You called Emilia 'Circe'."

I stilled. "What exactly was said?"

He cleared his throat and said, "You told your parents and sister that you missed them. Then you started talking to Circe and telling her that you were sorry and that you would do anything to change what had happened. And then—"

"Enough," I whispered, feeling the pain return to my chest.

They all bore witness. All saw me in such a state, and watched me beg *her* to forgive me! That was the most absurd part.

"Emilia did say that Belladonna poisoning can cause hallucinations. You haven't been harmed by the blade in almost a week, so it should be completely out of your system by now. You can rest easy."

My head throbbed, and my breath came out in rapid succession.

Awe. You dreamed about me, Callie? I'm touched.

I stilled. Circe always reappeared, yet I couldn't help getting my hopes up each time she was gone for an extended period of time.

"Get out!" I screamed.

I didn't need Circe's opinions, and I definitely didn't need Bastian to stay true to his word and never leave my side again.

I felt like I was, once again, going insane.

We both know that you went insane after the death of your sister.

Don't talk about her! I screamed, attempting to get my point across.

Touchy touchy.

I didn't respond to her. She was just a figment of my imagination, after all.

Should we talk about it?

Bastian grasped me by the shoulders and said sternly, "I will not leave. I will never leave you."

There is a way to die. The hunter brought it to our front door wrapped in a beautiful green package.

Their voices overwhelmed me. I couldn't focus on both of them at the same time. I needed my *venin*, but I couldn't use magic, and I knew he would never give it to me in my current state.

I stared at him as I answered her, *That doesn't matter anymore.*

Doesn't it?

I was hesitant to respond, remembering the peace that washed over me at the thought of everything ending. The pain, grief, fear—everything.

There it is. That flicker of hopelessness and despair. Hold onto that. It's all you have left.

Bastian and I were staring at each other, not saying a word, but his eyes said everything.

I have people that need my protection, I said.

They don't need you. You need them. If you went away, then they would all be able to lead normal lives.

Circe quieted down when Bastian took a deep breath, gaining a bit of courage before saying, "I have thought about what I would say to you because I feel as though 'I am sorry' isn't going to be enough."

He stood up so suddenly that the chair almost flipped back from the force. He then paced to the side of the bed searching for something to say, I suppose. His face was contorting, showcasing how angry he was getting with himself.

I laid there and waited to see what vile lies would spew from his lips while I waited until I gathered enough strength to attack him. The well was still empty.

He stopped the annoying pacing and turned to face me once more. When I focused back on him, I was taken aback by the tears in his eyes. His breathing was ragged, and his hands were balled into fists at his sides.

"Hunter—"

I wasn't even sure what I was going to say when he pointed a finger at me and commanded, "That word will never cross your lips again!"

"I would be happy to never have that word cross my lips ever again if you would just *leave*." My voice was rising, matching his own.

He ran a hand down his face. "This was not how I wanted this conversation to go."

I ignored him as I strained myself to sit up. I groaned from the pain searing through my body, grasping my side in an attempt to stifle it, when I felt a warm hand helping me. I looked up at him. His face was so close to mine that if I shifted forward, even slightly, our lips would graze.

My cheeks heated when I was suddenly accosted with the memory of him kissing me. I squeezed my eyes shut and pushed him back. I could hardly focus with him so close to me, but bit down the bile that rose up my throat at the sudden movement.

I raised my hand to stop him from coming closer as I caught my breath. "You no longer have a right to put your hands on me."

He reached his hand out, wishing to comfort me, then thought better of it. Instead, he kneeled low on the floor, rested his hands on his knees with his palms up, and looked me straight in the eyes. "I have regretted my choice since my father came and tried to kill you."

I shook my head. "Do *not* try to deceive me with more lies. I remember everything. He may have been the one to stab me, but that pain was nothing compared to that look in your eyes when you held that blade in your hand."

"You're right. There are no excuses. I wanted you dead. I wanted to kill you so that my brother and I could go home and put all of this behind us. Put *you* behind us and move on." He swallowed, taking a moment. "But, when I saw him *touch* you. When he talked about—about—" a muscle in his jaw ticked, his eyes darkening. "I wanted to rip him to pieces."

I remained silent, stubbornly so. I didn't want to hear it—didn't believe it. Nobody ever chose me except Circe. And only because I was weak, and begging to be loved. She knew she could twist me around her finger and break me.

"I choose you," he said.

"It's too late."

He shook his head. "I don't just choose you. I *love* you."

I tensed. My jaw slackened as I stared into his eyes to find another lie, but I couldn't. I was a master at sensing deception, and there was none on his face. I turned away from him, the tears threatening to come back full force and overtake me. I didn't need him seeing me like this. He couldn't have picked a worse time to fall in love with me. All I wanted to do was die.

"Go away."

"Please don't hide from me."

Anger pierced me, and I whipped my head back toward him. "All I have done for the past four hundred years is hide. Hide from my pain, from the truth that everything that has happened in my life is *my* fault, and there is nothing I can do to fix it." I looked up to the ceiling in an attempt to stop the tears that were now flowing freely down my face. "Do you even comprehend how I have lived my life? The fucking *agony* of living in this castle all alone!"

"I—" His skin looked pale at everything I was saying to him.

"I am cursed to be alone for all eternity. I lost every single person that ever mattered to me. First, my sister, then my family, and lastly, my entire kingdom in a matter of a few days! Thousands of people who counted on me. *Trusted* me." I knew I was saying too much, but I couldn't stop the words from flowing. "I have not trusted anyone in so long. How could I when the last person I trusted took everything from me? And in the moment when you were wrestling with whether to kill me or not, I realized that I wanted to. I wanted to trust you. I wanted it to be you."

"It still can be." He leaned forward.

I shook my head. "You proved to me again that being by myself is the best option. If I never hope for more then I won't be disappointed when it doesn't end up working out. And truthfully, it never would have. You are a human, and I am not. You will die one day, and I will not."

"I don't care about any of that... If all I have are a few decades left, I want those moments with you."

"Why can't you get it through your thick head? You can't love me. I want you to leave. Just go."

He got up from the ground, determination now set in his features, and sat down in the chair, pulling it closer to the bed. "My vow to you is to never leave your side ever again. Even in death, I will come back for you. I am yours. Always."

I rolled onto my side, my back facing him, and tried to process everything he said. Even though I wanted to cast him out, and keep him away, I couldn't help how those words warmed something in my frozen heart.

Chapter Twenty-Three

"**Y**ou are both insufferable."

Bastian and Callum had not left my side for one moment. Bastian was the one who carried my salvation with him, who cut me like clockwork every time the chime first sounded at midnight, who kept me weak to keep me alive.

They were talking amongst themselves near the fire, the roar keeping me from hearing their conversation. It wasn't until they turned and Bastian spoke to Callum that I understood the reason for the secrecy.

"I don't care what she says or how much she tries to seduce you. You do not give her what she wants. She is on bedrest until she comes to her senses."

Callum rolled his eyes. "I think you forget that I have been here taking care of her for years."

"And have spoiled her."

"I am not going to give her a chance to kill herself," he insisted, now seemingly annoyed.

He walked over to me, looked me up and down, then settled his gaze back on my face. "I will be right back. *Don't* try anything."

I turned my face away from his, and he left. The moment he was gone, Callum replaced him by sitting on the side of my bed. "I don't approve of what he did to you, but he has been working hard at trying to earn your forgiveness."

"I don't remember asking for it."

"Just give him a chance."

"Since when did the two of you become the best of friends?" I glowered.

"Since he was the reason we went to check on you in the first place."

That caught my attention. "What?"

"He had a gut feeling that something was wrong not long after you left, so we followed the path of blood to the pond where you slipped under. He was the first one in, swimming out to you like his life depended on it. He has been by your side ever since. If it wasn't for his instincts, you would be dead." His eyes softened at the thought. "I am forever in his debt."

I rolled my eyes, tired of hearing how amazing Bastian was. I wanted Callum to focus on more important matters, like fucking me. If I could distract him just long enough...

I pulled the blanket from my body. "Enough about him." I ran my hand up my thigh, pulling the nightdress with it until I was completely exposed. I saw his eyes darken at the invitation, but he held back per his new master's orders.

I cupped myself, delicately running my fingers through the slit between my legs up and down. "Come on, little bird," I brought my fingers up to his face covered in me, "have a taste. It has been so long."

I knew I almost had him as he leaned his mouth toward my fingers, but pulled back at the last second. "I will not be the reason you die."

I huffed, exasperated, and tried to reason with him, "Callum, I still have needs. No matter the reason. Are you going to deny me the pleasure? Or your-self, for that matter?"

His gaze ignited the desire within me, and I needed the release that only a thorough fucking could give me. His eyes flicked from my face to my fingers a few times before closing his eyes in an attempt to fight through his own longing. He knew I was right; it had been too long.

He leaned forward and wrapped his lips around my fingers, sucking and lick-ing. He moaned at the taste and was moving forward when we heard someone yell, "I can't leave you alone with her for even a moment?"

Callum jumped backward, almost falling over from the sudden noise. I turned to find Bastian standing at the door with a steaming bowl of soup in one hand and a glass of something in the other. I looked down to find the blade still strapped to his hip.

Callum moved away from the bed, cursing himself under his breath.

Bastian replaced him and tsked, "You are a sly minx, aren't you?"

I crossed my arms over my chest. "As I have told my consort, I still have needs." I was still exposed as I didn't care about covering myself, hoping that Callum would come back and finish what he started. Bastian looked down and, without another word, covered me with the blanket.

"Now is not the time."

I wasn't sure if he was saying that because he cared or was just jealous and didn't want anyone else touching me. Not that it was his choice at all in who I chose to share a bed with.

"Then when is it going to be the right time? Because sex isn't something that I can be denied."

"When you aren't a danger to yourself or others."

"I am always a danger to others and just recently myself." Then I saw my opening and teased. "How about this? Watch us."

"I don't think so."

"Well, that's the closest that you will get to ever touching me like that again, so you may as well watch since you can't trust us alone long enough for me to have a proper orgasm."

He tensed, and I knew that I had him. Unfortunately, the thought of Bastian watching us sent heat coursing through me. I chastised myself for even fantasizing about him in the first place.

I could have teased him about his brother having already had a taste, but I wanted to save that for later when I was truly desperate. That memory made me think about Soren, who hadn't come by to see me at all since I sent everyone out. He knew I was no longer furious with him about the journals, but I couldn't imagine what kept him away now. I would have much rather preferred him over his oaf of a brother.

Bastian worked through whatever torment was happening in his head and sat on the bed. He dipped the spoon into the bowl and brought the food up to my lips. I turned my head away from him and laid down, pulling the sheets up and over my body.

If they weren't going to give me what I wanted, then I would ignore them, knowing full well that it was petty and childish. But I didn't care. I am the queen.

Childish indeed, Callie.

I sighed. *You're still around?*

I told you. I am the only one who has stood by you after all these years and will continue to be here long after they are gone.

I wanted to shut her out, but they wouldn't give me the poison. So I just rested, listening to Callum and Bastian talking again, but Circe's words haunted my mind. Doomed to be together forever... How romantic.

I was grateful that they didn't try to feed me any more of the food. My appetite was completely gone after Circe reappeared. She had left on her own volition, and I had lain in bed, taking in everything that had happened in the last few days.

It had been about a week since I had almost succeeded in taking my own life and just like Soren, Emilia was staying far away. Emilia had tried to come in and see me, but I pushed her away. I was doing my best to push everyone away so that I could finally put an end to all of this madness. Then there would be nothing else forcing them to stay here. After a few days of Callum insisting that I needed rest, she stayed away.

I couldn't tell if I was thankful that she had given up or terrified that I succeeded. When the worry fully reached me, I asked Callum what she had been preoccupying herself with. He had told me that she locked herself in her room and refused to come out. I knew then that I needed to go check on her. My plan to push them all away wasn't working.

I sat up in bed to find Callum and Bastian sitting on the couch, talking about something I had no interest in. I found that the pain in my side was still prevalent, but I wasn't doubling over in agony with every breath. Though I would have healed much faster if it wasn't for Bastian keeping to his word and injuring me every night.

I pushed the blankets off of me and stood, the pain strong enough that I groaned as my feet hit the ground. I rolled my eyes, knowing they were seconds away from rushing to me.

I opened my eyes, and sure enough, Callum was in front of me. "Your grace, do you need help using the washroom?"

"No! I don't remember the last time my feet touched the ground." I could see Callum moving to lift me, and I warned, "Little bird, if you so much as try to help me in any way, I will refuse to fuck you for the rest of your life."

I could see the color drain from his face; he knew I meant every word. I was bluffing, but he didn't need to know that.

"We are only trying to help you heal," Bastian said, clearly irritated.

"Again...I didn't ask."

"You know, you would get your strength back sooner if you would eat something," Bastian prodded.

"I would get my strength back if you would stop slicing my arm open with that blade," I snapped.

Callum pleaded, "Please just eat a little bit more." "Please," Callum pleaded, "just eat a little bit more."

"I do eat. If I didn't, then I would already be dead."

"You eat one bite a day and only because Callum holds your mouth open as I feed you," Bastian chided. "You're acting like a child."

"Shut up!" I put my hands up, tired of this entire conversation. I was already exhausted and ready to go back to sleep, but I couldn't. I took a step forward and swayed. My body was weak from not being used, and hands grabbed onto me.

I growled, and Bastian growled back.

"I need to see Emilia," I announced.

Callum straightened. "Let me go and get her, your grace. You are in no position to move about."

"I am going to her, and you will not stop me."

Bastian stepped in front of me. "Fine. You can go, but let one of us carry you."

"No."

He held out his arm. "Then lean on me as you walk."

"No." I was adamant about walking over there on my own and I was sure as hell not going to lean on him.

He seemed to understand this and stepped to the side, sweeping his hand in front of him. "Fine."

I held my head up high and continued toward the door. It was a little difficult, but not as painful as I thought it would be. And it felt nice to stretch my limbs and walk on my own. I made it past the door before I saw two shadows overtaking my frame. I turned to find both Callum and Bastian a few feet behind me.

"What do you think you are doing?"

"I made a vow that you would never leave my sight again," Bastian stated matter of factly.

I had hoped he would grow bored, but his resolve had only strengthened. Was this what my life would be? I huffed, making sure they saw the annoyance on my face before turning back around. I made my way down the hall and around the corner to Emilia's chambers.

I was thankful that she was in a room not terribly far from mine. Her door loomed in the distance, and I could feel my strides slowing.

What's wrong? Afraid that she will leave just like the rest of them?

Yes. Knowing that there would be no use in lying to her. She already knew everything, and I was tired of lying to myself.

You should be. She will leave just like everyone else.

"Mercy, Circe, mercy." I stopped, squeezing my eyes shut.

"Your grace?" Callum asked.

I opened my eyes to find that I was standing directly in front of Emilia's door. I didn't turn toward them as I knew that Callum was most likely aware of what my actions meant. Knew that I was talking to myself but was too kind to say anything. I focused back on the door.

I lifted my hand and knocked hard three times. I don't remember the last time I announced my presence. Someone either did it for me, or I would simply burst into any room.

I waited for her to open it, then waited a little longer.

My nerves were getting the best of me when Callum stepped forward and said through the door, "Miss Emilia, her grace is here to see you." He took a step behind me and whispered, "Maybe she is sleeping and didn't hear you."

Ever the mother hen, attempting to smooth over any conflict between family. I ignored him and didn't have to wait another moment before one of the doors opened, and Emilia stuck her head shyly around the door.

I couldn't say anything as I took in her appearance. She looked ghastly; she clearly hadn't eaten, her hair was in disarray, dark circles lined her eyes, and her cheeks were sunken in. Just how I felt, as I hadn't looked at myself in a mirror in so long.

We were both wasting away, but I couldn't understand how she had changed so drastically. Our last conversation was good. Or so I thought.

Her head was bowed. I gathered my strength and asked, "Are you going to allow me in?"

I could see her face flush as she stepped aside and bowed even further. "Of course, your majesty."

I started to move forward and stopped, knowing full well that they both were about to follow, but I did not want either of them to be privy to this conversation. "You will wait out here until we are done."

"But—" Bastian started to protest.

"I am still the queen and if you want my cooperation in the future, you will listen to me and stay outside."

I could feel him wrestling with himself, then finally conceding as he stepped back and closed the door.

We were shrouded in darkness until I opened the blinds to her room. It was light enough that we didn't need to light any candles to see each other. I turned around to find her hands wrapped around her waist, eyes darting around the room as if she were looking for someone. My eyes roved around but found nothing.

The silence was deafening as I stared at her terrified form. Was she still worried about their father? Still scared of the past?

"Let's sit." I began to move toward the fireplace, where there were two chairs situated in front of it and a small round table in between. I slowly sank into the chair, but Emilia stayed where she was, fidgeting with her hands.

I couldn't wait any longer and asked, "What's wrong?"

She tensed and looked away. I wanted to comfort her, but it seemed as though she didn't want me to.

"Emilia…" My voice was pained as I pleaded with her.

She finally looked at me with tears in her eyes, not even bothering to wipe them away. "There's something wrong with me."

My heart sank. "What do you mean?"

"Something doesn't feel right."

I stood back up at her admission and found her body shaking heavily.

"Are you sick?" I placed the back of my hand on her forehead and felt that she was burning up. "Why didn't you come to me sooner? I would have given you my blood."

I bit into my palm and held my hand up to her as she tensed, pushing me away from her. "You aren't listening!"

My body froze. Every instinct was on high alert. She had never raised her voice so much at me. I could feel the anxiety seeping out of every pore of my body.

"My body no longer feels like my own. I have tried to fight it, but I don't know if I can anymore. And the voices…the voices are getting louder." She looked at me and pointed at her head. Her lip quivered. "Make it stop."

"I can't help you if I don't know what's wrong. Let me help you," I pleaded with her. "When did this start?"

"Ever since I came here."

"When you were little?" I asked, stunned. How could I have not noticed?

She nodded her head erratically, her blonde hair moving wildly around her face. "I never told you because I never wanted you to send me away."

"I would *never* send you away. You are my everything. The reason I get up each day."

She bared her teeth. "If you care *so* much for me then, why? Why did you try to kill yourself!" She said that word with so much disgust and hatred that it felt like a punch to the face.

She couldn't hate me. Not her. *Anyone* but her.

I could feel my heart beating wildly in my chest. "I am tired and done and want all of this to be over. That had nothing to do with you."

"But you were still going to leave me! Alone! All I have ever known is *you*. All the kindness that you offered means nothing if you were going to give it up so easily as if I meant nothing."

You deserve this hatred.

I was about to respond to her when Emilia slammed her fist into the table and screamed, "Get out of my head!"

I rushed to her side, fear ran rampant through my body. What was going on with her? She sounded like me, talking to a voice in her head. She'd never done this before, not even during her worst days.

"Emilia, you need to calm down. Okay? Everything is going to be fine."

I reached out toward her to assess the damage when she ripped it away from mine and slammed the heel of her hand into the side of her head. "I need space!"

"Let me help you! Please, Emilia, I'm sorry."

She raised bloodshot eyes toward me and said in a low, strained voice, "How many times do I need to say it? I want to be left alone."

I stood firm, unyielding.

"Leave!"

I flinched. All I could do was stand there, I didn't know what to do.

I heard the door open behind me, and I knew our conversation for the time being was done. I couldn't get through to her...not right now. I could hear one of them ask a question, but I was too focused on Emilia to understand it.

I walked up to her and said with as much conviction as I could muster, "I will leave for now, but I'll be back soon."

"No," she snapped. She finally turned to look at me and whispered, "I just need a little time."

I wanted to reach out and beg her, but she deserved to have her wishes respected. I wrapped my hands behind my back and dug my fingernails wherever they landed. I had to do something to help me focus on keeping myself grounded in the here and now.

She is fine. She has to be fine.

She just needs time to adjust to everything.

I can do that. I can give her that time.

I kept repeating this to myself as I willed myself to believe it because it was glaringly obvious that nothing about Emilia was fine.

"Take as long as you need, but you must promise me to eat whatever Callum brings you. You need to keep up your strength. And keep the curtains open for some fresh air."

She nodded.

I left.

My body felt numb, but I had given her my word that I wouldn't bother her until she was ready.

I could hear Bastian next to me, grumbling something that I had effectively tuned out, but it was only causing him to be louder. I rolled my eyes and splashed him with the bath water. I didn't even spare him a second glance as I continued staring straight ahead, not focusing on anything in particular.

"Was that truly necessary?"

"Are you annoyed?"

"Yes."

"Then it worked." I tried to flick more water toward him, but he was quicker than I was at the moment and caught my hand in midair.

I slid my eyes to him and saw only compassion in his eyes. "I don't know what Emilia said to you, but she will come around."

I tried to rip my hand out of his grasp, but he simply tightened his hold. "She loves you. She just needs to be alone."

"I should be there for her," I persisted. "I've been what she's needed for years, the only person she has trusted." I paused. "You should have seen the way she looked at me."

He let go of my wrist and dangled his arm along the edge of the tub, his fingers barely dipping into the milky water, and shrugged. "We're all allowed anger from time to time."

I sighed and brought my knees up to my chest, closing my eyes. I willed Callum to hurry and come back from whatever errand Bastian had sent him on. I thought Callum was a mother hen; no, Bastian was much worse.

"Speaking of anger, you're suffocating me."

Water splashed on me, and I screamed as Bastian said, "Good try, but that won't work. I told you I am not leaving you alone again, and I meant it."

I growled, and he flicked my nose, reveling in this power switch. "Now come, you need rest." He grabbed a towel and lifted it, demanding without words that it was time for me to get out.

"I will kill you."

He smirked. "I love it when you flirt with me."

I seethed but stood, or else I knew he would lift me out.

I waited while he wrapped the towel around my body and helped me out of the tub, much to my protest. Everything was a battle of wills with him.

Circe had quieted down since I left Emilia. My mind was momentarily clear, and I was ready to sleep, even if the nightmares came. My eyes felt so heavy.

I walked into my boudoir and let the towel fall to the ground. Callum was there waiting, hands holding a nightgown. I raised my arms and winced from the movement. He bunched it up and lifted it over my head. I gently moved my arms to put through the holes. He placed a hand on my lower back and led me out of the room.

I looked up to find Bastian leaning against the doorframe, arms, and feet crossed with a dark look in his eyes. I couldn't focus on anything other than getting back into bed.

"Callum, she needs to *wear* something with short sleeves." To slice into the wound on my arm. At this point, if I didn't get my powers back, it would scar. Did it even matter?

I huffed as I passed him, reached up, and tore the sleeve right off. I didn't say a word as I threw the ripped sleeve to the ground and stalked to my bed. Callum ran past me, lifted the blanket, and held his hand out for me to grasp if I needed any assistance.

I wanted this to end. All I felt was either pity or anger. The notion that they would all be better without me was still prevalent in my mind.

Out of spite, I crawled into bed and fell face-first into the pillows as my arms gave out. Callum helped me to turn over and swiped the hair out of my face as Bastian chuckled behind him.

"What a view."

He was doing anything to get a reaction out of me, but I wouldn't give him the satisfaction of letting him see that he was getting under my skin.

I pulled the covers up to my chin and closed my eyes. "You can leave now."

Although I knew they wouldn't leave, I didn't expect what happened next. I felt my bed dip. My eyes sprang open as I turned to find a smiling Bastian lying on his side with his head resting in his hand.

"Get off."

"Why would I do that?" He stretched and laid on his back with a hand resting behind his head. "This is more comfortable than that blasted couch."

"Then go back to your chambers."

Bastian continued to lie there. I looked up to find Callum's arm wrapped around his waist, his elbow resting atop the arm, and his fingers pinching the bridge of his nose. He was clearly exasperated by this entire conversation.

"Callum," I whined. I *fucking* whined.

He looked at me, clearly distraught. He didn't want to disobey me, but knew that Bastian wasn't going to leave. There was nothing he could do.

"Come on, Cal, get in," He said without opening his eyes.

He gave me a small shrug and got under the covers on the other side of me. "Sorry your grace, but I am not leaving either, and," he looked at me sheepishly, "your bed is a lot comfier than the chaise."

"Then bring in another bed." I was trying everything to get them away from me.

"Why would we do that when there is plenty of space in this one?" Bastian questioned flippantly.

I turned my head toward him as much as my weak body allowed. "So what? I won't allow you back inside of me, so the next best thing is to get blue balls by sleeping next to me?"

He opened one eye, turned his head just enough to look at me, and shrugged. "I'll take what I can get." Then, he closed his eyes.

Fine. Two can play his game.

I turned my back to him and sidled up next to Callum.

He was shocked when I lifted the covers to intertwine my legs around his, my stomach attached to his side, and an arm snuggly wrapped around his middle. He lifted his arm so I could get even closer to him, my head resting perfectly in the crook of his shoulder.

"Enjoy your night, hunter, all alone over there."

He scoffed but didn't say anything after that.

I smiled and snuggled into Callum's side, my head lifting each time he breathed, lulling me into a deep sleep.

I was roused from sleep when I felt a pinch and then hissed as the pain radiated down the length of my arm. I looked up to see Bastian kneeling next to me, my arm in his rough hand, the knife in the other. Callum was snoring lightly next to me.

He took a cloth, wrapped it around my arm, and pressed down to stop the bleeding. The wound was never deep, and the bleeding always stopped within a few minutes.

He bent his head and whispered, "It hurts me every time I have to do this."

"Then stop."

He looked back at me. "The moment I stop, you will cease to exist."

"Is that the worst thing that could happen?"

Bastian looked toward a sleeping Callum and sighed. "To Callum? Yes. He would follow you into the afterlife the moment your heart stopped beating. To Soren? Yes. He would not stop talking about the woman in the woods as kids. If you die, he would never forgive himself for what happened to you. Emilia might be angry with you...look at you like she hates you, but it's the opposite. She would go to the ends of the earth for you."

I stared at him as he was still bent over me, my arm still wrapped in the cloth. The look that crossed his features had me lifting myself up, my good arm supporting my weight. I sighed. "I am tired, Bastian."

His gaze went back and forth between my eyes and lips as he grappled with what to say.

He begged, "Please, say it again. I need my name on your lips."

I didn't give him what he wanted and instead said, "I am tired of the lies."

"If you died," he reached up and gently stroked the side of my face before laying his palm against my cheek, brushing his thumb up and down as he swallowed hard, "I would fear for the world for what I would become without you."

I couldn't move—too shocked by the admission.

"I would be a shell again, fearful of the things I want, the feelings I deny. I would never recover. Don't you see that? Emilia wasn't the only one you saved."

I lightly pulled my head out of his calloused hand and laid down next to Callum who sleepily welcomed me back into his arms. I considered his words long and hard and denied them until the pain felt real again. Until I hated myself again. They couldn't be true. I knew it just like the witch knew it—I couldn't save anyone and wasn't worth anything.

I told him I was done with the lies.

CHAPTER TWENTY-FOUR

I t had been days, and Emilia had yet to come out of her room. She would only allow Callum to leave food at her door but completely refused my company. Unless I wanted to force her to be around me, I would just have to respect her space and wait.

I loathed waiting.

And then there was Soren. The scholar who went on and on and on and *fucking* on about being obsessed with me, and now when I almost died, he was nowhere to be found. The least he could do was check on me, but nothing. Callum and Bastian had made excuses for him, but I didn't want to hear it. I wouldn't beg for his attention.

As much as I hated Bastian, at least he was trying.

My thoughts must have summoned Soren because he was standing next to his seat at the table awaiting my arrival.

"Your grace." He gave me a small smile as he pulled out my chair. I walked over and sat down, ignoring him completely. I began to thrum my fingers against the arm of the chair while Bastian set down platters of food.

"Your grace?" Soren asked.

Something appeared in front of my eyes, and as I focused on it, I could see that it was a spoon filled with potatoes and meat from the stew Bastian made.

I narrowed my eyes at Bastian, and he rolled his. "Please give me the honor of feeding you."

"I'm not particularly hungry."

He cocked his head. "Then indulge me."

He brought the spoon to my lips, and I swatted it away. "I am not in the mood to eat."

"You are skin and bones."

"I have never had anyone complain about that," I spat out. "Your brother seemed delighted when I let him lick me from the inside."

He blanched. "What did you just say?"

I raised an eyebrow, toying with his emotions, knowing full well that Soren wouldn't have told him the naughty details about our night in the chapel. Bastian turned to Soren, who had straightened up at the admission.

"It was only the one time you already know about it," Soren stated, matter of fact. "So, this shouldn't be a surprise."

A muscle feathered in his jaw. "Eat." He grabbed his spoon, dipped it back in the soup, and brought it to my mouth more forcefully.

"No."

"I won't sit around while you waste away. Not after everything."

"I'm not eating."

"You're stubborn," he spat.

"You're relentless and exhausting."

Callum sighed. "Bastian, let her be. It's been a long couple of weeks. Everyone is stressed."

"Which is exactly why she needs to eat. She needs to keep her strength up so that she doesn't die!"

"I told you that I am not hungry!" I turned my head away from the spoon. "I have gone longer without food or water."

"Because of the curse, but now it's different."

I shrugged. It's not that I didn't want to eat, but I truly wasn't hungry. Every time I thought of Emilia, my hunger dissipated.

"Fine. Then at least drink this." He poured me something and held it out, wanting to help me, but I didn't need *his* help. No matter how much it seemed as though he was trying to stick by his word to me. I smacked the cup away, spraying whatever was in it all over the ground and on him.

I could see Callum staring at the both of us, looking haggard and exhausted. For days, they had slaved over my every need. But it was Bastian's fault; he kept me weak and I was so exhausted from everything that had happened that I simply stopped caring. I prayed that I would wither away to nothing, and that I would be past the point of no return.

Not even knowing that it would cause irreparable damage to Emilia could stop the thoughts from coming on.

Bastian and I stared each other down, and I waited for him to tire of me and leave. I saw his chest rapidly moving up and down as he fought through every retort I knew was on the tip of his tongue. But he didn't say anything.

Instead, he drank whatever was left in the cup, grabbed a fistful of my hair, and yanked my head back. I began to protest, but the moment my mouth opened, he descended upon me, covered my mouth with his, and spit the drink into my mouth. I tried to fight him off, but he held strong and pinched my nose, forcing me to swallow.

The moment the liquid ran down my throat, I stood up and pushed him as hard as I could, but he didn't move an inch.

Some of the liquid dripped down my chin as I seethed, "What do you think you are doing?"

"You're right, I am relentless," he ground out. "And you're human again...at least for the moment. If you don't eat and drink, I will make you."

The tables had turned on me, and the vulnerability left me heated. "I will fucking kill you."

"And cue the threats." He raised his arms in the air. "You are becoming rather predictable."

"Can you both please stop? I have something to say." Soren raised his voice loud enough to cut through our bickering. We all turned to him. "That night, you never gave me a chance to explain that it was all a misunderstanding."

A misunderstanding? Is that why he kept his distance? Because he thought I was still upset with him?

Soren was looking only at me. "Yes, I read some of your journal, but I stopped the moment I realized that it belonged to you. I only read that one passage, I swear it. I want to hear your story from you, not from this." He slid the journal to me—a peace offering. I didn't know what to think of it, and after another few moments of silence, he said, "I knew the only useful thing I could do for you was research. That's all I was trying to do."

I flicked my eyes from the journal to him and sat back down. Bastian nodded to his brother to continue.

I sat up a little straighter. Was he about to tell me what I thought he was about to tell me?

"I was in the chapel reading." I wondered why he read in there and not the library, when his cheeks reddened. I scoffed as he continued, "I stood and began to pace when I felt one of the floorboards give way, and when I lifted it, there was a book."

He reached down onto the chair next to him and lifted an old leather-bound book in his hands. I paled at the familiar-looking book I hadn't seen since I confronted Circe about her plans.

He flipped through a few pages before stopping on one and read, "Calathea is coming into her own. I have successfully ostracized her from her family, and she is ready to come with me. To her people. At times, I lose my conviction. She is a marvel, this girl, and knowing that I can free her from her father's wrath and give her life where she can be truly herself...it's all worth it." He gently shut the book.

I shuddered at her words, feeling like I could hear her voice again, standing in front of me.

"I think it's time we heard the truth. Your story."

I looked around to find that they all wanted to hear it. But I wasn't ready. "Who are you to order me?"

He sighed. "I am not ordering you to tell us, but if you want out of this curse, then I am your best bet."

"I don't want your help."

That's it. Push them away. You don't need them. I couldn't help hearing a slight inflection in her tone, as if she were worried.

"Yes, you do. I have been slaving away reading these texts to try and help you, but I can't do anything unless I know the whole truth. Please..."

His tone was calm, his shoulders relaxed, and he gave me a smile that begged me to trust him.

He is only treating you this way so that you don't explode again. He thinks you are fragile. You are anything but.

"I am not made of glass, Soren!"

"I wasn't implying anything of the sort. You are anything but fragile, your grace." Suddenly he was sounding too much like her...too smart for his own good. I looked around, and their faces changed. They weren't my men anymore, but my mother, father, and Belle. My family stared me down, wondering how I could have betrayed them.

"Stop acting like you care for me—like you know me!" I screamed.

"Then tell us," Soren begged.

"I can't trust any of you. I can't trust anyone."

"Did you trust her?" Soren pointed to the book. "Is that why you think you can't trust anyone? Because she made you believe in her, in whatever promises she made, and then she—"

He was getting too close. "Stop."

"What did she do? Does she have something to do with the curse? Who is she to you?"

Too many questions. My head was starting to throb, the room spinning. "You will stop this research right now."

He walked around the table until he was standing over me. "I have spent every moment that I could in the chapel reading through all of the books and documents at my disposal. I haven't gotten through them all yet, and I haven't found much of anything that could be of use, but some things might make more sense if I knew everything that happened."

Tell him everything? I had never shared what happened all those years ago with anyone, and I wasn't about to start.

"Your grace, I beg you to tell us what happened. Maybe there are clues in those memories that can help us break the curse," Soren pleaded, his eyes urging me to not shut him down again.

As much as I didn't want to admit it, he was right. There could be something within those memories that could help. And I wanted out. I didn't want to die, I just wanted my torment to come to an end.

"I don't know what I could tell you that could possibly help. I've been through it all a thousand times. Don't you think I would have found something? Or do you think your intellect is superior to mine?"

"Well…" he reasoned, and Bast coughed. Soren took the hint and instead said, "I have found that a fresh pair of eyes and ears can make a tremendous difference. Just humor me."

I rested my head in my hand and leaned against the side of the chair. I was calming down, my heart returning to a steady pace.

"It is a rather boring story." Maybe it was time to tell them, get it all out in the open. "Once upon a time, there lived a princess who was loved by all who met her. She was the perfect daughter, perfect sister, perfect princess. Perfect, perfect, perfect. Though, what they didn't know was that she held a dark secret. A secret that would get her killed if anyone were to find out."

I looked around, and everyone was leaning in, waiting to hear more. "She was born with magic. It didn't begin to manifest until she was at the young age of seven. She was scared and didn't understand what was happening to her. She was aware that magic once flourished, but was hunted to near extinction over the last few hundred years. She was also taught that having magic flow through your veins meant you were evil. Tainted. So, even though she was young, she knew that she needed to keep it a secret."

Soren's eyes brightened. "The purges," he said to Bast. "The one's mother talked about. Kings all over the realm banded together to purge their kingdoms of magic. Thousands died. Your father, he was one of those kings."

I continued on, "The princess had successfully kept her powers a secret until she hit puberty, and that, coupled with her hormones, was almost too much to bear. She had many governesses come in and out of her life, and she made their lives miserable because she thought that she would be found out. That was until she met Circe. Circe changed everything."

I reached forward and grabbed Bastian's cup, brought it to my lips, and drank the entire thing. I lifted the cup toward him, and he refilled it. His features softened, obviously relieved that I was finally drinking something.

"Circe became her lifeline in a world where she felt like she was drowning. She was the only one who understood her because she, too, was born with magic." I gripped the cup hard. "They spent years together. She taught the princess how to control her magic and fight, and..." I looked up at Soren, "as you have read, ostracized the princess from everyone she loved. She took the position to kill the king, but when Circe found that the princess was like her, her plans changed. Circe wished to make the girl a queen who would save her people."

I took a breath, changing the narrative. "My people. What I didn't know was that it would be at the expense of their killers—my father, my family."

Soren sank down into his seat, the story weighing on him.

"I wanted it for a moment," I told them, my vision grew cloudy. "After seeing all the people...the women and children he murdered, I wanted him dead. Circe told me he'd burn me with all the others if he knew, and to this day, I still think there might have been truth to that."

I felt a hand being placed on mine. Callum. My rock. He nodded, showing me that he was here, they all were. That I could take all the time in the world if I needed it.

I held his stare. "But I always suspected she had a hand in killing my sister, and now she was going to kill my father, so I told my mother. I told her of Circe's plan, knowing it was going to be a death sentence."

I pulled my hand from Callum's and wiped away the tears that had collected, but had yet to escape.

How did it feel betraying me, Callie? Did it feel good to finally enact your revenge?

I yelled, "You got exactly what you deserved."

As did you!

Before anyone could ask me what was wrong, our setting changed. We were no longer in the dining hall, but at the town square, outside the boundaries that I had been contained in. I was turning around in circles, looking at everything. A visual memory had never been this vast before.

"What is this?" Bastian whispered. "Where are we?"

I spun around to him. "You can see this?"

They all nodded, wide-eyed.

"The execution of the enchantress Circe will commence for the crimes against the kingdom!"

We all turned to where Circe was tied to a wooden pole, standing on a pile of large pieces of wood. She was struggling against the ropes that held her, biting harshly into her skin. Her eyes were full of rage.

My breathing turned erratic. No.

Now everyone will know the truth about you.

"No!"

But there was no stopping the memory.

I saw my father and mother seated off to the side so everyone could view her. The entire kingdom gathered around the raised platform for miles. Some were even hanging out of windows to get a good view of the spectacle.

Father stood and raised his hands in the air, and a hush fell over the crowd. "The enchantress has been accused of being born with magic. But worse, she has committed a crime like no other...she lied to gain our trust and acquire knowledge to bring down this kingdom! She aided in my daughter's teachings, and we treated her like family." A roar erupted, and my father spoke above the ever-growing mob. "Had she succeeded, she'd have murdered the entire royal family, and for that, she will pay."

Cheers were heard all around. Food and rocks were thrown at Circe. The chaos was a blurry mess, a looming mist in the background encroaching upon us.

She held her head up high and stared straight ahead as Father asked her, "Do you have anything to say?"

She snarled, "You murdered my entire clan...but worse, you've murdered innocent people who had not one drop of magic in them! Just because they were different."

Her eyes found mine as I sat next to Mother, and a wicked smile spread across her lips. I could see myself shaking my head in quick, deliberate movements. *Don't say it, don't tell him.*

Father's face twisted to that of disgust. "Your ancestors all deserved to die for their treasonous actions!"

"You killed children!" She screeched. "You would kill your own if they were like me."

I could see myself straightening in my chair, attempting to put on a brave face in front of her, knowing what she was telling me. My father would kill me if he knew. I'd burn with her if he knew. My entire body began to shake under her hardened gaze.

I could see myself standing. "Father, we can end this now... All the death and bloodshed. We can end it."

"Silence," he roared, and I sucked in a fast breath. He turned just enough so I could hear him, his voice a spiteful whisper. "How long did you know, Callie? How long did you know she was a witch and kept it from me?"

I looked to my mother for comfort, but she looked down at her lap.

"I will deal with you later," Father said with so much venom that I flinched under his heated gaze.

Further words and pleas died in my throat as I raised my eyes to Circe who was staring right back at me. Her gaze held a sense of longing, a desperate plea, one last attempt to make me see what I should have always known—the truth behind everything she tried to teach me, the sincerity of her tries to save me. To save me from my own father. Maybe I should have done the same for her—maybe I should have tried harder to stop him, to make him see reason, to do something. But I didn't. I couldn't.

I sank down back in my seat.

Circe's eyes darkened, and with it, the fog grew closer. "How does it feel, my king, hunting down magic borns, killing witches, all the while you have sired one?"

The blood in Father's face drained when Circe's words sunk in. He hesitated and turned to look at me. His eyes took me in, and for the first time in my life, he didn't see me as someone he loved, but as an enemy.

The crowd went silent before my mother stood, and ordered, "Burn her now!"

Whispers erupted among the crowd as they wondered if Circe's words held any truth, as the executioner held the torch to the stake until it slowly caught on fire. The flames slowly made their way to Circe, who had the biggest smile on her face despite her body being claimed by the flames.

"You have chosen your fate. Remember that, when everyone you love is gone. This was your choice. Your blood took everything from me, and now I will leave it with nothing," Circe said as she glared at my broken form next to my mother.

The fire raged around her, trying to consume her, and her voice—distorted and horrifying—chanted the words that would come to haunt me. "All you know will fade like mist. As you have shown the heart of a beast, so shall you live as one. Silence your prison, loneliness your true companion. Isolated. Unloved. Cursed. Only when our tangled thread unbinds, can you reclaim what was lost." As the curse ended, the fog closed in.

Watching myself clutching my chest and crumbling to the ground, was a physical reminder of the pain I felt that night. I covered my ears as I couldn't stand to listen to my scream from so long ago; remembering how it felt as though molten lava was being poured into me. The pain was worse than anything that I had ever felt before. I could see Mother kneeling beside me, doing her best to help me, but nothing lessened my torment.

I was on the ground, writhing in pain, but my eyes were on Circe, who looked at me with pure disgust in her eyes. No—not just disgust, but something deeper.

She taunted, "Let's see how you fare alone with not one person who loves you."

I looked up to see my mother gasping for air, and then my father followed suit. It was excruciating watching this, reliving it after all these years. The fog was killing them. I didn't know it at the time, but now knowing what was about to happen did nothing to ease the grief I felt.

Bodies began to drop. Screams filled the air as the people ran, trying to outrun their fate. Women and children weren't spared as they dropped, their eyes not even having time to close.

I watched myself screaming for everything to stop. Pleading with Circe to take it all back. To take me instead, but it was too late.

I dropped to the floor. My legs could no longer hold me up as I watched myself reach for my mother with trembling hands, holding her close to me as her vacant eyes stared straight ahead. Mother was dead. Father had collapsed in front of Circe, his sword in his outstretched hand as he ceased to move. Circe laughed hysterically, knowing she had won.

When the only noise that was left was the crackling of the fire as it engulfed Circe, I finally looked back toward the raised platform and found that Circe wasn't looking toward a broken, newly cursed Calathea, but at me...in the crowd.

A chill ran down my spine. I didn't remember this.

Her mouth continued to rise, her eyes widening as she opened her mouth and screamed.

The image faded, and we were back in the dining hall. I didn't look at their faces; I couldn't. I felt something drop onto my arm. My hand shook as I reached up and wiped away tears. I was crying. I stood up abruptly and felt my head swim from lack of food and drink. Soren stepped forward and lifted me into his arms.

My arms felt heavy, and my head fell against Soren's chest. I guess that took more out of me than I thought. I closed my eyes because everything was spinning, and if I kept them open any longer, I would expel everything that I had just consumed.

I could hear Bastian order to Soren, "Give her to me."

Soren's chest rumbled as he replied, "You aren't the only one who cares for her, Bast. Now get out of the way."

Bastian growled, but he must have listened because Soren was moving.

I could feel Soren's mouth close to my ear as he whispered, "Thank you for telling me." He kissed the top of my head, and I let him, because, for the moment, I was that scared girl clutching her dead mother's body.

I felt my body being laid on the bed and ointment being applied to the sides of my head. It smelled of lavender and something else familiar, but I couldn't place it. Not long after, the pain began to subside, and I opened my eyes.

Soren was sitting in Bastian's chair, writing in his journal. Bastian was pacing behind his brother, and Callum was on the edge of the bed, massaging my feet.

I laid there just watching them all, as I took a moment to gather myself. I couldn't stop shaking after what everyone just witnessed. I wasn't sure if I felt embarrassed or relieved that it was all out in the open. What I was sure of was that it felt as though a small weight was lifted from my shoulders.

I still didn't understand how the memories manifested; it didn't matter at this point. I wanted to forget it ever happened. Wanted to do my best to erase the look of disgust my father gave me before he died.

And I knew just how to do that.

I moaned, which caught all of their attention, and they looked at me with lust in their eyes.

I sat up in bed slowly, not wanting to feel dizzy again when each one of them lurched forward to help me, fighting amongst themselves as I leaned back against the pillows. It would have been comical if I wasn't annoyed and exhausted.

I looked up to the ceiling and closed my eyes, knowing what to do. I opened my eyes and looked at Bastian.

"Hunter," he narrowed his eyes at the name, and I pressed on, "I will make another deal with you. Stop cutting my arm with that knife. Let me heal fully, and I promise to allow Soren to find a way to break the curse."

"Why now?" He was skeptical, understandably.

"Because I don't know how much longer I can go without having sex." I tried to say as nonchalantly as possible, as I looked at Callum and smirked, his cheeks reddening.

"How can you jest after everything we just saw?" Bastian asked incredulously, gaining my attention once more. "So you want your powers back and are willing to allow us to find a way to break the curse, just so you can have sex?"

"You won't break my curse," I told him, certain of it. I shrugged. "What do I have to lose? We all have our vices, and Callum is mine."

I could see the look of disappointment on both of their faces because I didn't include them.

"You need to also promise that you won't use your magic to find the blade and try to kill yourself again."

I rolled my eyes. "Fine."

He looked at his brother, who nodded and then looked back at me. "Deal."

CHAPTER TWENTY-FIVE

Bastian would not allow me to heal until after a few days of eating and drinking consistently. He took his role as my caretaker seriously, and only when I kept my food down did he re-offer me the deal and stop cutting me.

Soren had set up an area in the chapel to read over the books, but would come in to check on me throughout the day. He stated that keeping away from me all those days before was unbearable, and he would never subject himself to that kind of torture again.

I would never tell him this, but every time he said it, a part of me would melt at the dramatics of it all. And when I thought of one brother, the other wasn't far behind. I found myself often fantasizing about the brothers' lips. Soren's attention to detail and Bastian's passionate abandon.

I absentmindedly touched my lips as I thought back to that kiss with Bastian. It was everything I had dreamed about but would never have given away voluntarily. Yet he took it, which seemed to be a theme throughout his life. He simply took what he wanted, and what he now wanted was me. If he was to be believed.

He wouldn't stop telling me everything he loved about me, including my sharp wit. As much as I wanted to believe him, I couldn't. Not yet.

We were all in the library because Soren had come in the night before to tell us that he needed help going through the enormous stack of texts and documents. I stretched, feeling my magic humming beneath my skin as if it were telling me that it was happy to be back and connected with me.

I looked out the window and wondered when Emilia was going to make an appearance. I was content in giving her space, but it was proving to be quite a challenge as the days dragged on. I would often sit outside her room and wait for her. Sometimes, her nightmares woke her from sleep, and it would take everything in me not to burst through her door.

I blew out a breath and told myself that if she didn't come out today, then I would drag her out just as Bastian did to me.

I heard books slam against the table that Bastian and Callum brought in. I snapped, "Be careful with the books. They are far older than even myself, and I don't need idiotic boys ruining them."

"Can you please drop the 'boy' thing? Having fucked you and then being called 'boy' is rather absurd," said Bastian.

I could see Soren stiffen as Bastian said that so callously. I knew he only said that to get a reaction out of his brother. It was childish, but fun to watch.

They pulled all the books that Soren gathered from the chapel and brought them in, but there were hundreds more in my secret room. I walked over to the portrait, hesitant to share another part of me, but knowing that I had promised to give them a shot at breaking the curse. I took a breath, lifted my hand to the book, and pulled.

The hidden door opened, and Callum exclaimed. "Woah! I had no idea this was back here."

"That was the point, little bird."

Bastian looked to Soren to share in this moment of surprise and found that Soren was smiling wide. I wanted to roll my eyes, knowing that he loved to be in on this little secret with me.

"You knew, didn't you," Bastian asked incredulously. "How could you keep something like this from me?"

Soren looked at his older brother and said, "Don't be jealous brother, it is not a good look on you." He patted Bastian's back as he walked into the small room.

Bastian and Callum shuffled in after Soren to get a good look at the space. "And remember pets, set them *gently* on the table."

Soren stuck his head out of the doorway and raised an eyebrow. "You think calling us 'pets' is better than 'boys'?"

I lifted a shoulder. "It's one or the other. I wouldn't want you to think that I like any of you."

I could hear Bastian scoff. "You seemed to like me the other day."

Soren shot his brother a glare, knowing that Bastian was taunting him.

Callum groaned, and stepped inside the room. "As much as I love imagining her grace naked, can we please get to the task at hand?"

Ever the peacekeeper. Seconds later, he walked out with a stack of books in his hands. It didn't take long before all of the books were set up along the table, everyone taking a seat.

Soren walked over to sit next to me, much to his brother's protests, and said, "I have read through all of these." He pointed to a stack of books at the far end of the table. "I found some relevant information, but even after hearing and..." he continued hesitantly, "seeing her grace's past, I am no closer to breaking it. Though I have some theories."

The stack of books that he hadn't read was far larger than what he had read, and I knew that this wasn't going to be fast or easy. This would take time, something that I had an abundance of.

But they don't. I wonder if they will die before they get through half that stack of books.

I ignored her taunts as I leaned back in my chair, curious about what he found that I didn't. He looked at the three of us. His features were set, and determined, and he was in full research mode.

"There are way too many books for us to thoroughly go through each one, so skim over each sentence looking for anything related to curses, magic borns, or the surname 'Morahan'." Soren paused and looked at me, knowing that Circe's surname might cause a negative reaction. He hurried along, "Poetry and storybooks should also be skimmed through as you never know where the answer lies." He then turned to me, a crease forming between his brows, and said, "Remind me of her exact words that she said when she cursed you."

I could recite the words in my sleep, even if I hadn't seen the vision a few days ago:

All you know will fade like mist.
As you have shown the heart of a beast, so shall you live as
one.
Silence your prison; loneliness your true companion.
Isolated.
Unloved.
Cursed.
Only when our tangled thread unbinds, can you reclaim what
was lost.

Soren was scratching his chin, deep in thought. "Word choice is vital when placing a curse upon another. The mist makes sense because that is what eviscerated thousands of people."

"Soren," Bastian hissed.

Soren winced at the tone, realizing what he said. He cleared his throat, not wanting to bring more attention to the massacre of my kingdom, and continued, "Circe, obviously, had an immense amount of resentment toward you if she believes you have shown the heart of a beast."

"Simply because you did the right thing and told your mother about Circe's ill intentions," Bastian scoffed.

Callum intervened, "Back to the topic at hand." Then, he turned his attention toward Soren. "Is there anything else we should be looking at when going through the texts?"

"I suppose anything related to the War on Witches." He shrugged. "Other than that, take notes of anything that jumps out to you."

We all seemed to nod as Soren mumbled to himself, "'Our tangled threads unbind.' What could she have meant by that?" He sat down in his chair and pulled his journal out.

I grabbed a book and could see Bastian out of the corner of my eye as he stared at the endless pile, dread crossed over his features. Callum, I could see, was doing his best not to stare at Bastian. It was a look I couldn't quite place, but now wasn't the time.

I turned away from them and back to the pile of books. As much as I hated to admit it, Soren was right. I needed help and a fresh pair of eyes. Hopefully, they would find something that I couldn't.

We all turned when we heard someone enter and found Emilia walking toward us with a smile and a large platter of food. Callum hurried over to her and lifted the tray out of her hands and onto the table.

My back stiffened, and I shot up.

"Callum told me that you were fully healed and that you were all re-searching. I thought you all might be a little peckish."

Hope blossomed in my chest at how relaxed she seemed to be.

She looked down, suddenly nervous, and my stomach dropped. It was another moment before she barely looked into my eyes and asked, "May I speak with you...alone?"

I nodded and followed her out of the library.

We walked down the hall far enough away so we wouldn't be overheard. We stood awkwardly as she mustered up the courage to say whatever she had been thinking about. She twirled a strand of hair between her fingers.

I had thought long and hard about what she could be worried about, what could be making her slowly lose her mind. The only reason I could fathom was her desire to still want to move on with her life.

"If this is about you leaving, just know you have my blessing. I will give you plenty of money so that you won't need to worry about your needs." She looked up at me, tears welling in her eyes. "You can come back anytime you want. Long ago, I told you you could leave when you were strong enough. I've known for years you were ready, I just couldn't let you go."

"You made me strong," she said softly.

I shook my head. "No. You persevered against all odds. I had nothing to do with it." I paused for a moment. "You changed me; turned my entire world upside down, and helped me see past the darkness that had overtaken my life. You are my light."

She lunged for me then, wrapping her arms around me as her body shook, the side of her head resting on my shoulder. I stood there in shock, my hands limp at my sides.

Her hug was tight, and I wasn't sure if this was goodbye. Before I could overthink it, I slowly raised my arms. I leaned into her touch and hugged her just as tightly.

I could feel something wet on my shoulder, and I knew she was crying, though not a sound was coming from her. We had been through so much together. Her body was still shaking, but then I felt a hand slowly circling my back and realized that I was the one who was crying. Tears cascaded down my face as I let go and leaned fully into her embrace.

The sobs slowed as my breathing returned to a normal rhythm, and I pulled back to look her in the face. She wiped at the tears that I let flow freely down my face as she said, "I am so sorry. I should not have yelled at you the way I did before. I was just—"

I grabbed her by the shoulders. "I am sorry that I forced you to be around them, that I thought I knew what was best for you."

She shook her head. "No. I was wrong about them, about so many things. I would like to start over if they will allow me. And what I really wanted to say was that I am not leaving you. You are my home, the only one I've ever known. How can I let that go?"

Her sudden change of heart was startling, to say the least. Part of me didn't want to believe her because she seemed so sure of herself not too long ago. What could have happened to change her mind? But I mentally shook my head.

No. She was here, and she said she wouldn't leave me. She was staying, and I wasn't going to ruin the news by questioning it. I was going to try to live in this moment.

Everyone was staying because they *wanted* to and not because I forced them. They were *choosing* me.

Part of me was still upset with Bastian, not because I was truly upset but because anger was as much of a lifeline to me as Emilia and Callum were. I depended on that emotion to keep me grounded in the present, but maybe… Maybe I no longer had to hide behind those feelings.

My breath hitched, and I straightened my back, willing the tears to stop because we had more pressing matters at hand. And I was sure the rest of them were dying to know what we were talking about. Best not to wait any longer.

I turned to leave when she piped up, "Your majesty, if I may…" I turned back around. "Bastian is a good man. He made a mistake, and I feel as though he has suffered enough. It is not my place, but I wanted you to know that I do not blame him—either one of them—for what happened with their father. If I can forgive him, why can't you?"

She was already speaking so calmly about their father that it sent a chill down my spine. I could barely talk about it without wanting to burn down the forest.

I pushed the thought away, not wanting to press her. "I don't know if I'm ready."

She gave me a small smile. "We have limited time to be here with you. One day, we will die, and I am afraid that it will break you. Don't let your anger cloud your time here with them."

I watched her walk away, giving me a moment to contemplate everything she said. She wasn't leaving. She didn't blame them. So I shouldn't? Yes, Bastian had tried to kill me. But did he? Or was he so afraid of his father that he thought he should strike me down to save his brother? Would I have not done the exact same if it were Belle?

I knew the answer immediately.

I took a deep breath before following her back into the library. I entered just as she grabbed a book and made herself comfortable on the lounge chair. She looked up and said, "No time to waste." As if nothing happened.

I could tell the brothers wanted to say more to her, feeling as though they didn't get to apologize the way they wanted. Especially Bastian.

Emilia looked into each one of their eyes, smiled at Soren, and then landed on Bastian's. She said, "Your stew smells delicious."

She was being brave, and so would I.

I walked over to Callum, who was silently watching everyone and smiling to himself. I sat on his lap, placed my hands on either side of his face, and brought his lips to mine. It took him one single moment of shock before he wrapped his hands around my lower back and deepened the kiss.

I was tired of living life in fear and hiding behind anger. They'd spend years trying to break my curse and never succeed, and maybe I selfishly didn't mind that. At least they'd be here. I'd have them to myself.

I licked the seam of his lips, ordering him to give me entrance, and he happily obliged. Our lips moved in sync, and I chastised myself for denying me this pleasure. Tingles shot down to my core, heating as I heard someone cough.

I pulled back just enough so that I could smile against his soft lips. I sunk my teeth into his bottom lip and pulled. He hissed as I bit down on him, then pulled back fully and slapped his face just hard enough to jolt him. His length hardened beneath me.

I got up without any sort of explanation, picked up the book in front of me, went over to the couch to get more comfortable, and began to read. I could feel their questioning gaze on me, but I ignored them as the light from the large stained glass window beamed onto my back, illuminating the book in broken shards of light.

The book was from the early twelfth century, and its pages were worn from time. Dust had collected over the pages, and it made me think about all the books in the library that were probably close to falling apart. I should have taken better care of them. I could worry about that a different day when the pressure of breaking the curse wasn't looming above us.

A few hours had gone by, and I had barely made a dent in the book with well over five hundred pages left. I stood up and stretched my arms above my head. I had chosen to wear something with more coverage than I was used to, but still cut low enough to leave nothing to the imagination. I heard someone's breath hitch and found everyone staring at me.

"Seriously? All I did was stretch," I teased.

"In our defense, you are stunning," Bastian said, leaning forward, resting his head on top of one of the books, eyes darkening.

I scoffed, rolled my eyes, and sat back down. "Keep dreaming, hunter."

I leaned back onto the cushion of the chaise and began to read again when he said, "Oh, I do. Often."

My eyes snapped to him over the top of the book, thinking about the words left hanging in the room. I knew exactly what he was insinuating, what he was offering.

"Blatantly flirting with me?" I said, my attention back on the book, flipping through the pages. Not wanting to look directly into his eyes because I knew I would have him take me right there, but I wasn't ready.

"How else are you going to get it through that thick skull of yours that I am yours?"

"When you stop with whatever it is you think is going to get you back in my good graces." Then I laughed, the sound strained. "It's rather funny if you think I am going to let you fuck me again."

He closed his book and slowly leaned forward, resting his arms on his knees. "You don't have to like me to fuck me, your grace. I think you rather enjoy how rough it can get after one of our arguments. So…is this foreplay?"

Soren cleared his throat. "I would rather not be privy to whatever game this is. Some of us would like to help find a way to break the curse."

I rolled my eyes and ignored his comment. He hadn't touched me in weeks, but I knew he was thinking about our time just as much as I was. I could tell from the longing looks he would give me when he thought I wasn't looking.

We all went back to reading, and when there wasn't enough light for us to continue reading, I recommended that we all get some sleep and start fresh in the morning. I set my almost finished book on the end table next to my chair and looked toward Callum, my smile turning wicked. It had been too long since I had him balls deep inside me.

I spared a glance at Bastian and found him staring at me from under his lashes. The look he was giving Callum and I promised punishment. His eyes had darkened, a deep green so dark that they appeared black in the light.

He strode out without another word, and Soren went with him, stopping in front of me to say, "You're playing a losing game with him. Once he has set his eyes on something, he gets it."

"I think you forget who the beast is."

He slowly shook his head as he passed us.

Sometimes, I wondered what they thought about me, knowing that they each wanted me badly. That thought led to other salacious thoughts about the both of them in my bed. I groaned at the mental image that assaulted me, and I opened my eyes, focusing on Callum. I needed release.

I stood and saw that Emilia hadn't moved. She'd lit a small candle beside her.

"Emilia?"

She looked up and nodded, bidding me goodnight.

I grabbed Callum by the front of his shirt and pulled him from the room.

Chapter Twenty-Six

W e were back bright and early the next day. I felt insanely relaxed after Callum thoroughly fucked me. He took his time with me until I was a wriggling mess and came all over his face.

I sighed in pleasure at the memory, smiling to myself as I ignored the rest of them, knowing they had heard me, and knew who put a smile on my face.

More hours passed as I finished the book and started a newer, shorter one. I finished it by the time the light faded from the room. I conjured balls of light for each of us so that we could continue reading into the night.

After two full days, nothing had been accomplished besides a dip in morale, not to my surprise. I had warned them that this wouldn't be as easy as they thought. I think Soren only suggested it to keep my mind clear of darker thoughts.

He would be horrified to find out just how dark my thoughts already were.

I got up and walked to the window, needing a reprieve from the monotony of reading. I carefully crossed my arms and leaned against the windowsill, staring out at the garden below.

My beloved rose garden. I planted the garden a few years after everyone died in front of the castle so that I could see it every day. I don't know why I did it as I was still so full of a raging anger that I suppose I just needed to focus on something good. Something that helped me to not forget the past.

Roses were Belle's favorite flowers. She used to tell me that they were her favorite because it was part of my name, part of me. Having the garden reminded me that I needed to be strong for her. That I wouldn't allow Circe to break me. I never realized that I had been broken long before Circe arrived.

My thoughts wandered back to the humans behind me. My thoughts always went back to them, wanting to focus on happier memories. Of cocks buried inside of me. Of soft lips caressing mine. Being held. Desires that ignited whenever they were in a room. Of friendships created out of despair and mutual understanding. It was more than I had ever been given.

Even when I was human, I was never close to anyone my age, having always felt a disconnect between myself and others. I never let anyone in besides my family, Belle and...Circe.

So, just thinking of letting them in terrified me.

But could it be that simple?

Could I trust them? Could I truly let go?

Could I simply decide to change? Wake up and decide to be someone different? Someone loving, caring, *trusting*? I suppose that was what being human was all about—choosing to be someone different despite your past mistakes. To wake up and choose to be better.

The idea was absurd and confusing.

Soren sat across from me, mirroring my movements. "It has been weeks since you last answered a question of mine."

I looked at him and chuckled. It was a small laugh, but it was genuine. Not forced. It felt good. "Was my story a few days ago not enough to keep you reeling for years to come?"

"I don't believe I have ever heard you laugh," Soren said as wonder sparked in those ocean-blue eyes.

"You may be shocked at this revelation, but I used to do quite a bit of it."

"You don't say." Soren looked outside and then back at me, like he was taking a moment to ponder. "Nope. Don't believe you. Do it again; I think I imagined it."

I couldn't help but laugh again and playfully push his shoulder. He was being playful, and I couldn't help but notice how his eyes lightened. He had the sleeves of his white undershirt pushed up taut against his lean arms. I wouldn't say they were slender. No, he was muscular, but not bulky. I wanted to run my hands up his arms and feel just how tight the sleeves were against him, but I refrained.

Instead, I looked at his face. He was wearing his glasses, which made him look sophisticated and boyish at the same time. And when he bowed his head down, his golden hair fell into his eyes.

I had to tear my eyes away.

"Your grace, how about we retire for the night? Hearing you laugh has me hard for you." Callum was at my side, hands racking over my body. He had become more emboldened ever since I kissed him, touching and kissing me any chance he could.

"No need to worry, little bird. Soren doesn't wish to fuck me; he only wants my mind."

Callum looked at Soren. "Then he's a fool." He lifted my hand and kissed the back of it.

I reached up and patted his face hard enough to make him gasp. "On the other hand, Bastian, you may have to worry about."

I bit my lip as I gazed at Bastian from under my lashes, and the look he gave me was feral. As much as I willed my body to not react, a pulse shot through me, remembering the delicious way he had choked me against the tree.

"Your grace?"

Callum pulled me from my thoughts, and I stilled when I felt my hand absentmindedly skim my neck, remembering how Bastian's hand had felt. I forced it down and looked quickly away from Bastian. Smiling wickedly back up at Callum, I said, "Let's go break a bed, shall we?"

We had barely entered my chambers when Callum was on me, mouth skimming my neck, hands squeezing my ass to his already hardened length. My nipples pebbled at the change in pace. He missed this—us—together, multiple times a day. He was making up for lost time.

I pulled his hair back, and ran my tongue up his neck, tasting him, needing to drink him in.

"Fuck," he hissed.

I smiled against his neck and turned around, giving him my back. He leaned down and kissed up my shoulder, then nibbled the lobe of my ear while unlacing my dress, letting it drop to the ground. Layer after layer until I was just in my stockings.

I raised a knee and placed it on the bed, leaning over to show him exactly what I wanted him to focus on. I heard him whimper behind me as he got on his knees, lifted my foot, and licked the sole, sucking on each and every toe, taking his time.

He splayed his hands on my thighs, rubbing them up and down as his nose skimmed my inner thigh before spreading my ass and pressing his face against me, inhaling deeply. I had to hold onto the sheets for support, my legs suddenly going weak. The material of my *culotte* was thin enough for me to feel his hot breath and the lap of his tongue.

He pulled them down over my waist, down my legs, and threw them aside. I turned my head, our eyes landed on each other, and he leaned in to run his tongue from my clit all the way up to my ass. His tongue swirled around my back entrance, making my insides melt.

"Callum." His name came out in a whisper, unable to speak louder. I reached behind me and grabbed his hair, pushing him closer. His movements turned frenzied, my movements started jerking and I knew I was close. He reached his hand between my legs and circled my clit with his fingers. I couldn't hold it in any longer and screamed out his name.

We were both breathing hard as he kissed each cheek before standing behind me and grabbing onto my hips. I lifted myself, grabbed his arm, and tugged him until he stood between me and the bed.

I pushed him back hard enough that he bounced a few times when he fell. I swayed my hips, gliding my hands from my hips up to my chest and up to my hair. He slid up onto his forearms and watched me, enjoying the show.

I closed my eyes and lifted my head as I fully let go and allowed myself to be in this moment with him. I opened my eyes and looked down at him, fisting himself, getting ready for me. It was a beautiful sight to behold. I removed his hand and replaced it with my own. I had never done this, never cared to, but tonight felt different. I felt more connected to Callum than I had ever before.

He raised his hand, palming one breast, tongue flicking the other. He bit my nipple and I arched into him. It was delectable.

I gripped him harder, not taking my eyes off him to gauge his reaction, seeing how much he could handle. He hissed through his teeth as I stroked him harder, and I kneeled in front of him.

"Fuck. Just like that." His body jerked as he felt my hands over him. He tried to keep his eyes open, but couldn't help but hang his head back and enjoy the pleasure that I was finally bestowing upon him.

Sparks erupted all over my body. I couldn't handle this anymore.

I pushed him until he was lying on his back and straddled his waist. His cock was hard against my ass. He fisted his hands in the sheets, needing to grip something as I moved my hips in slow circles, tormenting him. I reached up and pinched my nipples between my fingers, threw my head back, and moaned loud enough that Callum bucked under me.

"Please, your grace. I've been a good boy, right?" He was begging. Fuck, I loved it when he begged. "Please..."

I reached behind me, fisted him in my hand, lifted myself up, and slowly sank down on him until he was balls deep inside my pussy. I didn't want to rush, wanting to feel every stroke.

I looked over at the open balcony. The moon was prevalent and shone brightly in the sky, even through the fog. A full moon. Full of wonder and, in this case, lust. Then, I felt a presence behind us.

As we kept a slow and steady tempo, I threw my head back, calling out Callum's name. I ignored the figure at the door, wanting him to see exactly what he was missing out on. I made him wait for a few more moments before I said without stopping, "If you are going to watch, then you may as well get a better view."

Callum stopped and was about to ask when the door opened, but Bastian stood there, panting.

I smirked at him. "Did you go for a run?"

He didn't answer but didn't step into the room either.

Well, if he wasn't going to answer then... Callum draped his head back, moaning, as I painfully slowed the pace. Now that we had an audience, I wanted to take my time. I leaned against Callum's chest, arching my back as much as I could, and lifted myself off of Callum, all the way to the tip, then slowly sat back down, ensuring Bastian saw everything.

Saw how swollen my lips were.

I swore I heard Bastian's heart beating hard in his chest. I jumped when there was a loud noise at the door. I turned around and saw that his fist was above his head. Had he just hit the doorframe?

I eased off of Callum, my pussy begging to have someone inside once more, and walked to Bastian, who looked wild, eyes crazed like he was going to attack me at any sudden movement.

Like he was the beast, and I was the prey.

I licked my lips, wondering what was going to happen next. I felt lighter ever since I talked to Emilia. She was right; life was too short. And as much as I didn't want to admit it, I wanted his mouth back on mine.

"Tell me something. What exactly would you do to touch me again?"

He swallowed and continued staring down at me, not moving a muscle.

I scoffed—he was not ready—and half turned to head back to Callum when I saw movement out of the corner of my eye.

I stilled.

Bastian had knelt on his knees in front of me, staring up at me.

"What do you think you're doing?"

"You asked me what I would do to touch you again. This."

"You're serious."

"I told you I wanted you. I have regretted that night with my father ever since. And hearing you fucking him for the past couple of nights had me wanting to charge into this room and—"

"And what?" I asked, holding my breath. "And what, hunter?"

"My name is Bastian." He gritted his teeth. "Use it when I am fucking you tonight."

He was so confident that I would allow him back in my bed. I cocked my head and gave him a sly smile. "It seems as though your eyes aren't working." I half-turned back toward Callum and said, "I am currently in the middle of something."

He didn't say anything, so I looked down at him from the corner of my eye and found him staring, not at me, but at Callum. His eyes scanned Callum's naked and erect form sitting on the bed.

I knew it.

I looked back at Callum whose eyes were just as hooded as Bastian's, and I smiled wickedly. I said nothing as I had him stand and hooked a finger through the top of his trousers, leading him to the bed.

He didn't resist, but I could feel his body tense with each step we took until we were a foot away.

No one said anything. I had never experienced this before, but I was more than ready. Looking up into Bastian's eyes, the hesitation was clearly evident, though not surprising. I knew the type of upbringing he came from. I saw it in his mind when he first arrived here. Traditional gender roles, the pressure of producing an heir, and giving up everything one was in order to ascertain these goals. I was all too familiar with it. Enjoying the company of the same sex was highly frowned upon and if such relations were to happen, then it was kept in secret. Something to be ashamed of.

But not here.

I ran my hands up his hairy chest, standing between the two, grabbed his face between my hands, and forced Bastian to look at me. The way he looked down upon me was worrisome; he was no longer arrogant or proud, but rather timid like a small child—scared and nervous.

Shame passed across those moss-green eyes.

That wouldn't do.

"Bastian." He tried to move away, but I pulled him back. "You may leave if you like, and neither one of us will say a word. But..." I paused, making sure to get my point across, "Just know there are no judgments here. Don't be ashamed to be exactly who you are with us. You said it, didn't you? That I made you feel like you finally knew yourself?"

My breath caught in my throat when another look passed his features—love. He looked like a man in love.

I couldn't handle that look any longer and asked Callum, "You're interested too, aren't you?"

He answered me by getting up and standing in front of Bastian. Bastian became tense, warring with himself, if he wanted this, if he was finally ready to give in.

I stood next to them. "You can leave right now. Everything we do here is by choice, and no, I won't get mad if you leave." He didn't move a muscle, so I continued, "Don't think. Just do what feels right. You can be yourself here."

Callum wrapped his hands around the nape of Bastian's neck, and pulled him closer until their mouths met. It took one last tense moment before Bastian finally let go and kissed him back.

I had no idea that watching two men kissing each other would turn me on as much as it did. The passion in the kiss, the way Bastian's mouth moved, was as if he had wanted to do this his entire life. As if he had been deprived of oxygen and only now was getting the reprieve he desired.

After a moment, Callum pulled away and started undoing his belt and all of our breaths went ragged. I walked behind Bastian and reached around, pulling off his shirt until he was bare in front of us.

He began to crawl on the bed when I stopped him and turned him so that he was sitting on the edge of the bed. I looked at Callum, who smiled and got on his knees and started rubbing Bastian's cock up and down. Then he took him in his mouth and went slow.

Bastian threw his head back and moaned. I seated myself behind him, pushing his hair out of the way, and licked from his collarbone all the way up his neck. I nibbled on his ear, clawing my hands down his chest as he hissed.

Once Callum was satisfied, he brought Bastian's face down to his, letting Bastian taste himself. The need to have them both was overwhelming, and I couldn't wait any longer.

I pulled Bastian back onto the bed until his back rested against the headboard, and I straddled him. I kissed down his chest, nipping him as I went along. I could feel his cock throb beneath me. He loved pain just as much as Callum and I.

Callum moved to his side, on his knees next to Bastian. Bastian took no time in grabbing his hard cock and licked his tip tentatively as Callum gripped the headboard for support. Callum gripped Bastian's head and guided him to take him in his mouth, but waited until I was seated on Bastian's tip. At the same time, Bastian took Callum in his mouth, I slid down Bastian's cock.

Fuck. I missed this.

Bastian's cock curved a little bit up, hitting that perfect bundle of nerves inside of me. I leaned back, bracing my hands on his thighs, and rode him without abandon. I couldn't handle the looks of ecstasy on both of their faces; I had to throw my head back, screaming, calling out their names.

We were a mess of moans as the sound of our bodies slapped against each other—my new favorite sound.

Callum's body jerked as he came inside Bastian's mouth. Bastian bucked his hips, which hit a deeper part of me. "Bastian! Yes!"

I don't know how it happened, but I became even wetter seeing him pull away from Callum's cock, cum running down his chin, and said to Callum, "I think it's time we give our queen a little royal attention."

They both looked at me as Callum moved behind me, and I could have almost squealed with excitement. Bastian leaned me forward while I was still inside him as Callum settled behind me, spreading my ass. I kept staring into Bastian's eyes as I heard Callum spit and then felt him position himself, rubbing me with his tip, getting me ready.

I have had Callum fuck my ass before, but I had never had two men at once. I was a bit nervous and Bastian could read it on my face. I could have sworn he grinned a little. He brought my lips to him as Callum slowly pushed himself into me. Inch by fucking inch. So slow. Letting me get used to the sensation of how full I was.

I couldn't breathe.

Bastian bit my lip, and I opened my mouth, needing him to explore me, distracting my mind.

I made a pained noise, and Callum stopped and began to slide out of me, but I insisted, "Do not pull out. Just give me a moment." I took a few deep breaths, my head resting on Bastian's shoulder, tears stinging my eyes from how intense it all felt. They weren't moving, so I slowly sat back on Callum, going at my own pace until they were both fully inside.

Even though it was painful, it was also riveting.

After a few moments, there was another feeling working its way through me. My body was begging me for more friction, and I gave her exactly what she asked for. I commanded, "Fuck me."

They both took their duty seriously and got into a rhythm that had my legs shaking and all I could do was hang on and moan in Bastian's ear as their punishing movements were relentless.

I could feel my walls squeezing around them, and they became feral—that was my undoing. I called out Bastian's name first, followed by Callum as I felt each of their releases.

Callum pulled out of me until the tip and then rammed back into me, making my legs fully give out and I landed on Bastian's chest.

We laid there for who knows how long. Time had never been relevant, but I swear that time stopped. I was getting wet all over again at the feel of their throbbing cocks.

That was new.

Callum had never been inside of me long enough after to feel the pulsing sensation that had my toes curling. I pushed back against Callum, and he pulled out of me, laying on one side of Bastian and I pulled out, laying on his other side.

No one said a word. No one moved.

The cum between my legs hadn't subsided, and I knew that what we had just done wasn't enough. I was riding a high that the poison had never once given me.

I almost started crying when I choked it back as I thought... If this is what it means to stay here. In choosing to live. Then maybe this was enough.

I pushed the thoughts away, turned on my side, and slid my hands over Bast's chest in lazy circles.

I gave them both a wicked smile and asked, "Ready to go again?"

CHAPTER TWENTY-SEVEN

We spent endless hours in the library researching with little to no progress. My patience was starting to thin. The hope I was holding onto slowly slipped through my fingers, and I could tell everyone was feeling defeated.

We needed a break.

I snapped my book closed and set it on the side table.

"I say that we all take the afternoon away from the library and away from these books." I could see Bastian and Callum smirking at each other from across the table, and I knew exactly what they were thinking, but I also needed a break from them. Needed to clear my head.

"Emilia, let's have tea in the sunroom. Bastian, prepare my favorite snacks for us." It was far too cold for us to take the tea outside.

His shoulders visibly slumped, and then he nodded his head, "Of course."

I stood. "We will reconvene after dinner tonight."

They all nodded. I got up and pulled Emilia's arm with me, walking out of the room with my hand in the crook of her elbow. The walk over was quiet as we simply enjoyed each other's company, never needing to fill the silence.

We rounded the corner, and I couldn't help but smile at the decadent room that still had the tables set up as though there were ladies and members of royalty on their way to have high tea. I hadn't been this far in the castle in ages, not wanting to take a chance in accidentally destroying this room.

The sun room was one of the more unique rooms located at the back of the castle as the walls were pure glass. This room was everyone's favorite for no reason other than the view. My parents made sure that nothing was obstructing the mountains beyond.

I sat at the table with an unobstructed view of the landscape and Emilia slid into the chair opposite me. We both sat there staring off as far as the fog would allow.

I took a breath and was about to say something when Bastian entered with a tray full of miniature sandwiches and fruits. There was a steaming pot of tea and two cups from the finest china that we had. I smiled when I saw that he had unknowingly chosen the set that Belle and I would always use when having tea parties in one of our rooms.

"Is there anything else you need?" Bastian asked.

"No, that will be all." He nodded and left. I ignored the longing in his gaze as we had just fucked a few hours ago and focused on the snacks he served.

I reached over, picked up one of the small sandwiches, and took a bite. I groaned, "That man has many talents, but I think cooking is where he shines."

Emilia made a small sound, which interrupted my savoring.

She smiled behind her hand, cheeks growing red. "I can't speak on his skillset behind closed doors, but if this is better than that, then I can't begin to imagine."

While she spoke, I took a sip of my tea and then spit it out in my surprised amusement. Liquid ran down my chin as I stared at her. We looked at each other and burst out laughing. We were laughing so hard that I had to hold my stomach to try and get control of myself. But it wouldn't end, turning incredibly painful. Every time we quieted down and thought it was over, we would glance at each other and be thrown into another fit of hysteria.

I could feel eyes on our backs and could only imagine what we looked like. Finally, the laughter gradually died down.

"Thank you for inviting me to tea."

I waved her off. "I shouldn't have waited this long to invite you." This is the way that it always should have been.

I devoured the rest of the sandwich and tea, and asked, "Will you tell me about your life before?" I had never asked her, but I had always been curious about the family she left behind.

She looked over at me mid-sip. She took the sip, pondering, and set it back down with a tiny clink. "I don't remember much of my life before arriving here. Now I know that it was my mind simply protecting me from the horrors that I faced at such a young age. But one thing I do remember is that my aunt used to bake me honeyed bread on special occasions. Similar to the cake Bastian made the other day. It was the last thing I ate before—" she stopped.

"It's good to know that she wasn't always cruel."

She gave me a sad smile and slowly shook her head. "No, she wasn't. She was kind until the taxes were raised, and she took to drinking more often and would invite random men to our home. I didn't know it at the time, but that was how we survived until I was chosen for the Reaping."

"I can't say that I understand what it means to suffer and starve. I won't pretend to. But I do know what it feels like to be desperate enough to make decisions that I otherwise wouldn't have made."

She huffed a laugh. "My aunt would set me on our table as she kneaded the dough, and I would sit there, listening to her tell me stories about my parents and her life."

"You don't remember anything about them?"

She looked away before she set her eyes back on me. "My mother died in childbirth, and my father drank himself to death after. My aunt is the only other family I am aware of."

I let the silence settle between us, not wishing to push her any more than I already was.

"Which brother is your favorite?" She asked, clearly ready to change the subject.

This question took me by surprise; she was getting rather bold. I looked toward the ceiling, taking a moment to think about it. "I don't think that I can answer that. I enjoy both of their company equally, but for different reasons." I thought about their arrival. "Bastian was so passionate and determined to get away from me, but every time he disobeyed me, a thrill shot through me. No one had ever disobeyed me before, which helped with the monotony that had become my life over the years."

I sighed, blissfully reminiscing. "Then my scholar arrived. I was stunned when he practically proclaimed his devotion to me the moment he came. His intellect drew me to him. He was a breath of fresh air."

"And you most definitely are Callum's world."

We both giggled at that.

"Ah, my little bird. There has not been one moment with him where I felt as though he judged me and my level of depravity. He has always been right by my side, holding my favorite pair of blades to carve up the prisoners. I could completely let go and give in to my darkest desires. For that, I am grateful.

"And what about you?" I inquired.

"What about me?"

"Do you ever dream of a life with a family? A partner? Just... More?"

"I have allowed what happened to me to affect my life for too long. I want to move past it. I would be lying if I said that I didn't sometimes wonder what it would be like to have a family of my own. Though, I don't believe that is likely to happen. I don't think I deserve to have those things."

"Why would you say that?"

She swallowed and sat up a little straighter, and began to fiddle with the napkin in her lap. "I don't know what it means to be a mother. A loving wife. What right do I have to possibly bring another soul into this world?"

I took a moment and let her words sink in.

I lifted the kettle and filled her empty cup. She looked over out of the corner of her eye. "Have you not taken care of me? Have you not cried over me when you saw me injured?" I sighed and set my lips in a thin line. "It seems like we have both allowed fear to rule our lives."

Such a cowardly thing to do, she signed and bent her head down and took another sip of tea.

I leaned across the table, placed my hand atop hers, and squeezed hard enough to get her attention. "We are *not* cowards. We have both lived through unspeakable atrocities that were out of our control."

She nodded her head, but I wasn't sure if she believed me. After a moment, she asked, "Do you mind if I ask you a question?"

I set my teacup down and gave her my full attention.

"Please tell me if I am out of line, but," she turned until she looked directly at me, "I came out of my room the day you told the three of them about your past." She hesitated. "I saw everything. I didn't mean to intrude, but I didn't know how to get out of it."

I raised my brows and nodded for her to continue. "I was wondering how you found out about the witch. What made you so sure that it was her?"

I cocked my head to the side, wondering what prompted this. She saw my confused look and rushed out, "I am only asking because there might be something in that part of your history that could help us figure out how to break the curse."

I contemplated her question. I could see her unease, but instead of answering her with words I lifted my right hand and conjured a ball of shadows. I concentrated my memories on it until an image appeared.

I could hear Emilia gasp, "Is that you?"

"Yes."

I could see her focusing back on the ball of shadows and light as the image became clear.

I said to Emilia, "I didn't want to believe it, but I couldn't deny what I saw the day Belle died, her words...everything about her felt different that day. I knew I had to get to the bottom of it before it ripped me apart."

We watched my younger self walking through the halls, talking to herself, making her way to the servant's quarters to confront her, hesitate, and then slip into an alcove along the hallway.

I saw Emilia sitting up a little straighter.

At the end of the hallway, we could see Circe passing by, cloaked. We watched as my younger self pulled up her hood and followed after her.

She kept to the shadows and stayed back far enough to not raise suspicions. They curved around the edges of the castle and into the treeline of the forest. She stopped and hid behind a tree when she saw Circe stop in a cluster of trees under the arch leading to the pond. She didn't have to wait long until another cloaked figure emerged from the darkness.

"You're late." The voice sounded like a female.

"It couldn't be helped, Audra." Circe took off the hood and placed her hands behind her back.

The woman, Audra, uncloaked herself and placed a fisted hand over her heart. "Merry meet, high priestess."

Ausra had long strawberry blonde hair that reached well past her hips and would have probably been longer if her hair wasn't in braids. She had scars all over her body and was missing an eye.

Circe placed a fisted hand over her heart. "Merry meet, sister." Circe looked around and kept her voice down. "I have news."

"So, is it true? Did you kill her?"

Circe lifted her chin and nodded. "Yes, it couldn't be helped. She found out about Princess Calathea's powers, and I am certain she had plans to tell her father."

Emilia gasped beside me.

Audra nodded slowly. "A shame, but good riddance. One less Everhart in the world, murdering our people. Our plans are still in motion?"

Circe took a deep breath. "Yes, but the plans have changed."

Audra's eyes narrowed. "What?"

"I believe if the princess is to take the crown, she will bring peace to our people. Peace that will last. She will stop this war."

"You've grown attached." The words came out sharp, and Circe's face hardened. "Even if she can take her father's crown, how keen will she be on murdering him to get it?"

Circe opened her mouth to reply, but Audra cut her off with a hiss. "And if she were willing to kill her own blood, what makes you think every kingdom around us will not turn on her the second they find out she is one of us? Don't you understand, Circe? There's no peace. There's no world where we can coexist. They have made it so."

They were silent for a moment before Circe continued, "That child is more powerful than the entire coven combined. She has powers she hasn't even begun to tap into yet." She pondered to herself. "How that blasted king became blessed with a witch of such magnitude is a cruel joke. But perhaps, she is our savior."

Audra shook her head firmly. "We are at war, Circe. Kill the royal family... That is the mission. Spare none of them. I will tell the others to be in position when the moon has peaked at its highest. We will be ready."

I dropped my hand and the ball of light, my memory, with it. When I was young, her plan felt like a stab in the heart, but in the memory, she looked vulnerable—desperate. At the very least, she believed in me and tried to fight for my safety.

I looked over to see Emilia crying, her hand shaking as she dried the tears with her napkin.

"How? How did you not rip her apart?"

"I hated her, and...I loved her in some ways. I had a family, but they didn't understand me. Not like Circe. Finding out her plan broke my heart. I couldn't feel rage, not in the moment." Truthfully, I still couldn't sort through the mess of emotions I felt when it came to that witch.

I reached across the table, took another sandwich from the plate, and ate it in a few bites. I didn't know what else to say. Quite frankly, I was growing rather exhausted from all the talking and was about to excuse myself when Emilia asked an intriguing question.

"Could you ever forgive her?"

"No," I said without thinking, and my heart felt the pain all over again. Though, I wasn't sure if my answer was the truth. Before Callum, before Emilia, she was all I had in these lonely castle walls.

Emilia's gaze was solemn in response. "Do you think they'll find a way to break your curse?"

I gave her a small smile. "Gods no, but it's keeping them busy, isn't it?"

A grin pulled at her lips.

When she smiled, I was about to say something else—perhaps how beautiful she looked, but then doubled over in pain. Her hands shot out to apply pressure to her lower abdomen. She fell backward.

"Emilia? Emilia!"

"Your majesty, I need to tell you something!" Her eyes were wide with fear. Where was this coming from?

"Tell me?" I grabbed her shoulders tightly.

"It hurts…"

She clenched her teeth and bowed her head to bear through the pain. I took the knife from the table, cut myself, and was seconds away from putting it to her lips when she pulled away.

"Emilia?"

Her breathing was hard as she took a moment to catch her breath and then looked up at me. "I highly apologize. I must be tired from all the research that we have been doing lately. I think I will take my leave and lie down for a while."

"Do you need me to help you? Please, let me help you."

"No! No, please, I will be fine. I haven't slept in days…I'm just not myself." She bowed her head. "Thank you for sharing your story with me. I am honored." And then left.

"Emilia, stop!"

I watched her as she rounded the corner back to her chambers. I started to follow them all when a familiar voice called to me.

She is hiding something from you, Callie. Perhaps we are not so different.

I stopped and commanded. "No more Circe. She is nothing like you. She is good."

I was good.

"You wanted blood for blood! You used me," I hissed, ensuring that my mind understood that I was done listening to her nonsense. "I have to let you go. You are my guilt, and you have lived inside me for centuries. I have to let you go."

You can't. I am a part of you.

"Not anymore."

I took a moment, shut my eyes, and willed myself with everything I had, placing mental barriers around my mind—fortifying it and then reinforcing the walls.

Callie!

Then it was over.

My mind was cleared from the fog that had plagued me since the day I was cursed. The silence wasn't unbearable. It was comforting, normal—human, even.

I laughed and then cried and then broke down, clutching my stomach. Was that all it took? All these years and all I needed to do was let her go?

I wiped the tears away and nearly skipped to the door.

Clear! My mind was clear, and my body was as light as air. One gust of wind and I would be swept away.

I wanted to laugh. I wanted to cry. I wanted to punch someone. I wanted to fuck. I wanted... I wanted to walk out those doors and through those gates.

I wanted to *leave*.

But...did I?

Did I truly want to lift the curse? I knew they wouldn't break it, that it was a wasted effort, but now I was considering it. Where would I go? Who would I be? Who was I without my guilt, without Circe plaguing my thoughts...without my memories haunting me.

I rubbed my temple with my fingers, adding enough pressure to relieve some of the pain. Deep breath in. One. Two. Three. Deep breath out. One. Two. Three.

I moved to my balcony.

When I thought back to being a child and what my dreams were, I came up empty. I knew that I wanted to travel the world. I knew that would never be a reality since I was the eldest and thus, the next in line for the throne. My fate was sealed.

I slammed the doors open, the wind whipping around my face, and stepped forward until I could lean over the railing. There was always a third option floating in the back of my mind, but I wouldn't consider it. At least not for now.

They had all given me a taste of what it felt like to be loved if only I gave myself over to it. I wrapped my arms around myself, unable to stop a chill from running up my spine.

CHAPTER TWENTY-EIGHT

"What are you thinking about, witch?"

I blushed at the nickname as Bastian's arms grabbed my hips and gently pushed inside of me, Callum's lips sucking on my nipples.

We had all just finished fucking on the couch in my chambers next to the fireplace when I was thrown from my thoughts by Bastian's cock, a happy surprise.

I ran my hands through Callum's hair, holding him tightly to me.

"Do either of you ever tire?"

"With you? Never." I could barely make out the words as Callum murmured them around my breast. The vibrations sent sparks across my body.

Bastian reached around to rub small circles on my clit and had my legs shaking once again in a matter of minutes.

We were all panting hard when I pried myself out of their reach and said over my shoulder as I put my dress back on, "Go clean up before dinner."

I could hear them snickering behind me as I walked into my bathing chamber.

It didn't take long to clean up before I walked into the dining hall. I had not eaten here in so long. I made it to my chair as Bastian walked in with a large platter of food in his hands.

"You're here early. Very unlike you."

"I aim to please, hunter."

"Oh?" He set the platter on the table and walked over to lean his body against the table. "Now is that any way to greet me?"

"And how should I greet you?"

"I could think of a few things." He looked up, and rubbed his chin, considering it for a few moments before he said, "Have you say my god-given name, preferably as you are screaming and trembling beneath me."

My lips pulled into a grin. He was so playful; it was refreshing.

We both turned when we heard a noise and found Soren standing in the doorway, watching our flirtatious exchange. I glanced at Bastian and saw him smirking at his younger brother.

"Now, now, Bastian, we don't want to make the scholar jealous." I waved him off as Soren rolled his eyes and sat down in his seat. Bastian went back to the kitchen.

"Do I need to let them in on our little secret?" Soren whispered, placing his chin on his hand.

"What secret would that be?" I asked, intrigued.

He leaned in close. "That even though they warm your bed at night, you can't stop thinking about our time in the chapel."

I placed my chin in my hand, copying him. "If you are jealous then just say so."

His mouth opened then closed, straightening as Bastian brought out the last of the dinner platters with Callum in tow. The two of them were laughing at something Callum had said as Emilia strode into the dining hall and took a seat.

She sniffed the air. "This all smells delicious, Bastian."

He sat down in his chair and replied, "Thank you, Emilia. I remembered that you once said that you loved poached truffles, but didn't eat them often. I had Callum grab some, as it is a special occasion, and thought this was as good a time as any to cook it."

"Well, thank you for thinking of me. I am honored."

My mind wandered as everyone eased into easy, small talk.

It had been an entire day since I cast Circe from my mind, and so far, she hadn't been able to invade any part of my life. It was like she vanished. And I definitely was not complaining.

"Thea."

I looked up. "What did you just call me?"

Bastian shrugged. "I am just trying out a different name. See how it feels on my tongue."

"And how does it feel?" I circled the rim of the cup with my forefinger.

He chuckled. "Rather nice. I think I will use it later tonight."

"You are incorrigible!" I laughed. I loved it. I loved this. It was all so easy.

"Now, Thea, do I need to feed you again in order for you to eat something?"

I was so used to not eating that I sometimes forgot to do it. Thankfully for me, Bastian was there to remind me and ensure I ate enough to not look like 'skin and bones'. His words.

Apparently, women who look half-dead weren't as compelling as I had once thought.

I rolled my eyes, picked up the thigh of the pheasant, and bit into it. "Happy?"

He gave me a satisfied smile and returned to eating his meal.

Callum moved to put his hand over Bastian's, and at the last moment, Bastian froze, slipped his hand under the table, and continued eating. Callum gave us all a strained smile and moved on as best he could despite Bastian's rejection by cutting the meat.

Emilia didn't seem to notice the tension; if she did, she didn't let up on it. I knew that Bastian must not have told his brother about the three of us, even though it was blatantly obvious what we were doing and with whom.

Bastian had never told us not to tell his brother, but neither of us thought it was our place to say anything. Bastian would bring it up when he was ready, and until then, we would pretend that nothing was going on between Callum and Bastian.

For which they were failing miserably, in my opinion, but maybe to everyone else, they merely seemed like close friends.

I sighed as I sat back and sipped wine.

I heard Soren clear his throat, and we all looked at him. He was looking at Bastian with so much love and understanding that it took my breath away.

"Brother, you no longer have to keep it a secret. In fact, it was never really a secret."

Bastian's eyes widened. "What?"

"You don't have to hide who you are. Not with me. *Never* with me."

Bastian averted his gaze from Soren and looked toward Emilia, who gave him a wide smile. Bastian squirmed in his chair, visibly nervous...or relieved, I couldn't tell.

Callum smiled widely, placed his hand back over Bastian's, and looked directly at Soren. "Thank you."

Bastian reciprocated Callum's hand squeeze, and I could tell he was getting emotional, as this had been weighing on him for his entire life. The relief washed over his features as he lifted a hand to clasp his brothers' shoulder and nodded, not saying anything.

His demeanor immediately changed, and he appeared more relaxed throughout the rest of the meal.

The rest of dinner went by without any fuss. No one was trying to murder anyone. No one was being stabbed. No one was playing dangerous games that in turn would get themselves killed. No one was drinking themselves into oblivion.

What more could I ask for? It almost seemed too good to be true.

After taking a stroll around the castle after dinner, I returned to my chambers to find Callum and Bast kneeling naked on the ground in the middle of the room. My nipples immediately hardened, looking at their submission, my pets patiently waiting for their queen.

I slowly walked over to them, watching their muscles move from the anticipation of what I had in mind, when an idea struck.

"Bast, help me out of my corset." His eyes met mine, and he was already breathing hard. Callum hadn't moved an inch.

I turned around, and I could feel his calloused hands working at the strings as he roughly pulled me into his body, nibbling at the exposed skin.

I laughed breathily. "Nuh uh, tonight I want to watch."

I stripped off the rest of my clothing and sat in a chair facing the bed. I could tell that they were both a little nervous until Callum grabbed Bastian's face between his hands and kissed him. It was slow and sensual. Lost in their own little world, as if they were memorizing each other's bodies.

Bastian's hands roamed all over Calum's body. Callum turned him around so that Bastian's front was facing me. Callum kissed every spot his lips could touch, his hand reaching around to grip Bastian's cock.

Bast let his head fall back against Callum's chest, and he reached his hands behind him, squeezing Callum's ass. Earning a moan from Callum.

Fuck. This was hot.

I brought my hand down to my core and started slowly rubbing my clit in slow circles.

They both looked over at me as I moaned loudly, and something changed in the air. Callum pushed Bast to his knees. I wasn't sure how Bastian was going to handle this more confident side to Callum, but he just smiled and grabbed Callum's cock and stroked him up and down, never taking his eyes off of Callum's.

He brought his lips to Callum's cock and ran his tongue over the tip, causing Callum to hiss. Callum was ready; there was already cum dripping out. Bast smiled and licked the cum, swallowing it, moaning at the taste.

He was definitely enjoying this.

Without warning, he took Callum fully in his mouth and started pumping fast. Callum gripped his hair and helped keep up the pace.

I was in shock at how much this was making me wet. I stuck a finger inside of myself and pumped it in and out at the same pace they were going.

Callum brought Bast up and kissed him, wanting to taste himself. They were both panting when Callum turned him around and bent him over the bed. Bast knew what was coming and he was nervous, but also excited.

Callum kneeled and spread his cheeks and spit on his ass. Callum rubbed it in, lubricating Bastin's tight ass. Preparing him for what was about to come.

Bastian breathed. "Callum..."

Callum smiled. "Don't worry, Bast. I promise to go easy on you."

Callum moved his hand to wrap around Bast's cock and started moving up and down, squeezing tightly. Callum moved his eyes to mine and, without warning, stuck his thumb in Bast's ass. He jerked forward, trying to get away from Callum, but to no avail. Callum wouldn't back down.

He let Bastian get used to the intrusion before he pushed his thumb in further while stroking Bast's cock faster, trying to get his mind off the uncomfortable feeling.

Callum removed his thumb and stood up, shoving his fingers into Bastian's mouth, forcing him to suck. Once he was satisfied, Callum positioned himself on the side of Bast and leaned forward, biting Bast's ass.

He started pumping fast and inserted two fingers into Bast's ass, filling him up. I then inserted two of my fingers into me and started pumping.

He stopped just as Bast was about to cum and stood up. "You ready?" All Bast did was nod, his head bent.

He positioned himself in front of Bast's ass and slowly pushed himself in. Bast gripped the bed so hard that his knuckles turned white.

I knew it was hurting him; Callum's cock was thick. Callum stilled, allowing him to adjust to his size. He was about to start moving, but I commanded, "Stop."

They both looked at me. Both had sweat beading down their faces and bodies.

I walked over to the bed, climbed on, spread my legs in front of Bast, and said, "Don't think of the pain. Focus on me. Focus on how good I taste. Lose yourself in us."

He was trying to breathe, his face a mixture of pain and desire. He nodded and attacked my pussy. His hands were clutching my upper thighs as I nodded to Callum.

He kept a slow and steady pace, still allowing Bastian to get used to his size. Bast lifted his head, squeezing his eyes shut as tears flowed down his face.

I lifted his head to look at me, my eyes saying everything that needed to be said. He shook his head in answer. He didn't want Callum to stop. So I put his head back between my legs and ordered Callum to go faster. Bast gripped my thighs so hard I could feel bruises forming, and I couldn't care less.

Watching Callum fuck Bast while he was eating me out was nothing short of a revelation. We were all just a mix of sounds, from Callum's balls slapping Bastian's ass to the moaning coming from Bastian to my screams of pleasure.

We were all working in tandem. Callum fucking Bastian's ass while stroking his cock, Bast eating my pussy, and me squeezing his head tightly with my thighs. I started rubbing my clit, almost reaching my climax as I screamed Bastian's name. I came so hard that I squirted on Bastian's face. I had never done that before, and he made sure to lick everything up.

Callum dug in and thrust so fast that Bastian was screaming out as he came, followed by Callum. Callum collapsed on top of Bast, who then collapsed between my legs. They couldn't hold themselves up any longer.

Yes, yes, yes.

I fell back against the bed, just as exhausted as they were. Bastian pushed up with all his strength and looked at Callum, saying, "I want a turn."

Callum's eyes went wide, having assumed that our night was probably over, when he smiled and nodded. He moved so that he was bent over the bed. His chest hit the side, and he grabbed the sheets, saying breathlessly, "Don't hold back."

Callum looked back up at me and grabbed my ankles, pulling me down to the edge of the bed. I squealed as he said, "Your grace, I wouldn't want you to miss out." Without any warning, he drove into me and stilled, and I knew exactly what he had in mind.

There was nothing sweet about what was about to happen. Callum wanted to be taken aggressively, and I would be taken just as hard.

Bast moved behind him, stroking himself to get ready, and grabbed Callum's hips, lining up his cock at Callum's ass, allowing his cum to coat it. And without warning, he shoved his cock in all the way into the base.

Callum screamed out in ecstasy and demanded, "Faster, Bast!"

It felt so good!

Bastian was panting hard as he drove over and over and over again into Callum relentlessly as Callum drove into me. The feeling was unlike anything

I had ever felt before. The sounds that were coming out of our mouths were completely primal.

I looked at Bastian as his back was hunched over, moving his hands around to get a better grip on Callum as our bodies were slick with sweat. I could tell from the look of ecstasy on his face that he was reveling in the feeling of being inside Callum. Callum leaned forward on my body, his tongue biting and sucking on my breasts.

This is why Callum and I got along so well. He loved pain just as much as I loved inflicting it.

Callum groaned around my breast, "Fuck Bast, this feels so fucking good. Harder."

Bastian gave him exactly what he was asking for. He grabbed onto his shoulders to use as a brace and moved his hips as fast as he could. Bastian was thrusting so hard into Callum that Callum's cock was hitting the back of my pussy.

It wasn't long before Bastian and Callum screamed as they orgasmed and at the sight of seeing them cum, it was my turn. Stars exploded in my vision. The orgasm sent me over the edge so far that my eyes rolled into the back of my head, overly sensitive. I could feel my body shaking from the pressure of it all.

They both collapsed on the bed on top of me and each other, all of our bodies coated in sweat and the room filling with the scent of sex. My favorite scent.

We laid there trying to catch our breaths before Bast got up and laid on the bed beside me. Callum followed after and collapsed on my other side.

After a few moments of nothing but our breathing filling the quiet room, I got up on wobbly legs, went to the bathroom, and shut the door.

Their cum was running down my legs, and as much as I loved the feeling, I needed a bath. I sat there, too exhausted by what happened to think about anything in particular.

I got out and opened the bathroom door, smiling to myself, to find my two men passed out on my bed. Their naked bodies were tangled around each other in a mess of hair and limbs. They did well tonight.

I walked toward them. They looked so peaceful that I didn't want to disturb them, but they couldn't stay in my bed.

Or could they?

I crawled on the bed before I could think too hard about it and wiggled my way in between them. Without waking up, Callum moved over enough for me to fit perfectly between them. Bastian moved until he securely wrapped me in his arms with a hand around my throat and Callum's hand resting on my hip.

I smiled to myself as I welcomed sleep for the first time in my life.

Wake up. Eat. Garden. Eat. Fuck Callum. Sleep.

Every day for ten years, this was the only thing that kept me sane. Those two humans were my reason for putting even the smallest bit of effort into my existence. I wouldn't even consider it a life. At least not a life well-lived.

After I tried to kill myself, I never picked my routine back up because everything seemed pointless. And then I became so engrossed in research that I realized I no longer needed a routine to keep me grounded. Each day had been full of surprises, and I reveled in it.

This morning, I had woken up in their arms, and they were so shocked that I allowed them that each of them worshipped my body for hours as a thank you.

I had to nearly rip myself away from them to get anything done, and I wanted to do something other than research. I wanted to get my hands dirty in the soil of my plants. It had been far too long.

When I walked into the greenhouse, I expected plants to be rotting, bugs flying around, and general chaos. I was shocked to find that everything was in order, and Emilia was toward the back on her hands and knees, repotting one of the oleander plants.

"Emilia?"

She turned around, bowed while still on the ground, and said, "I wanted your sanctuary to look nice when you came back."

I walked over to my *euphorbia milii* and lightly rubbed her petals. Emilia could have been the royal herbalist if she had been alive back then. I smiled at the thought. We both settled into our comfortable silence as we trimmed the leaves, repotted two trees, and replaced soil in quite a few pots.

After a few hours, I left the greenhouse and went back inside, suddenly ravenous, when I rounded the corner and stilled. Bastian had Callum pinned against the wall, skimming his nose along Callum's neck.

"Are you happy that Soren finally knows about us?" Callum asked breathlessly.

Bastian rested his head against Callum's shoulder and smiled. "It feels like a weight has been lifted off of my chest. I have had these feelings for as long as I can remember, and I knew I would never be able to act on them. For the longest time, I thought it was evil for me to have these inclinations and would bury myself into every cunt I could find, praying to God that He would cleanse me."

Callum turned his head to stare into Bastian's eyes. "Do you still feel that way?"

"No," Bastian said with not a hint of hesitation.

"I care for you, Bast. I—I love you. And I am selfish enough to say that everything that has happened to you has led you to this castle—to her. For *us* to happen.

Bastian sucked in a breath. "You love me?"

"I think I fell in love with you the moment I saw you strapped to that chair in the tower."

Bastian laughed and lightly pushed his shoulder. Then, he grabbed it and slammed his lips against Callum's. I could see Bastian lick the seam between Callum's lips, and Callum happily obliged.

Bastian ran his hands through Callum's hair and, staring into his eyes, said, "I love you, too."

I retreated to the shadows, not wanting to disrupt their moment. I took a deep breath and searched for the appropriate reaction to what I just saw. I was greedy, there was no denying that, and I was jealous that they said that to each other without me there. I wanted to share this moment with them, but I was happy.

Truly *happy*.

But, still being me, I was a tad bit envious. Though happiness trumped any other feeling that tried to creep its way inside. Another bright light shutting the darkness that did its best to claw into my heart. I wouldn't let it, not anymore.

I pushed off the wall and turned to find Soren staring at me. I wondered how much he heard from their not-so-private conversation. I lifted my head high, blushing from being caught spying, and approached him. I was about to say something to him, but he put a finger to his lips and extended his arm.

I sighed and linked my arm with his as he led me away from them and toward the library.

We were silent as we padded through the hallways until we reached the library doors and he said, "I am happy for my brother."

"You knew." It wasn't a question, more of a statement. I saw no surprise in his eyes when Bastian told him, rather relief.

He nodded, still staring straight ahead as he walked us over to the table with the books. "I have known ever since we were kids. I would catch him staring at some of the boys we grew up with in a way that I would look at some of the girls. I knew it was different, but I never said anything. It wasn't my place."

It was silent for a couple more minutes before he asked, "Does it bother you?"

"About?" Trying to avoid the question.

"Don't be coy. About what they said to each other."

"Callum tells me practically every day that he loves me." I shrugged and looked away. "To be honest, I am happy that they have each other."

"Why do you say it like that?" I sadly looked back up at him. He missed nothing. "You don't expect the curse to be broken, do you?"

I sighed. "I have lived for centuries. I have scoured the library and every nook and cranny of these lands, not just the castle. I have looked for any weakness within the barrier and nothing. It is not that I have given up...completely... I just don't understand how you think you can find something when I haven't been able to."

"I have dedicated my entire life to understanding your history, *your* truth. I will."

"And if you can't?"

His shoulders slumped and he gave me a small, crooked smile. "Then we will live here forever. I don't think there is one person in this castle who would willingly part from you. Not in this life or the next."

I pushed away from him, crossed my arms, and walked toward the window. "Don't jest, Soren. I don't particularly find this form of humor amusing."

I didn't like that he was promising to stay with me forever when there was a better life for all of them outside of these walls, apart from me. The thought of never seeing them again always sent me into a state of paralyzing stupor.

I tightened the hold on my arms as I felt him approach. He stood so close that I could feel the grooves of his muscles against my back. The heat radiating from his body was so intense, it could keep me warm all winter, but right now, it was too much. We stood there wordlessly, our heavy breathing breaking the oppressive silence that settled between us.

He brought his hand up to skim my bare arm as he dipped his head to graze his nose behind my ear.

What was he doing? I could feel my body wanting to lean into his, but didn't want to ruin what we had created over the last few weeks. How easy being with him was. I didn't want to ruin it like I ruined everything else.

He doesn't want you, I thought. Take a deep breath. *He doesn't want you. He just wants your mind, your history. He's obsessed with that, not you.* I kept reminding myself of that fact and willed my heart to slow.

As if he could read my thoughts, he said in a low, gravelly voice, "You were wrong earlier. You told Callum I just wanted you for your mind...and that isn't true."

I stiffened.

"Continue using me. For whatever you may need. *Use* me." He rested his forehead on the back of my head, inhaling deeply. "I don't care that you are fucking Bast and Callum. I don't care that I have to put a pillow over my head to try and drown out your moans of pleasure because one day, I know you will give in and also choose me. I don't know what's stopping you now from taking what you want from me."

"I would destroy you, Soren," I breathed.

"Then destroy me."

My chest heaved when I thought... *fuck it.*

I spun around, wrapped my arms around his neck as he gripped my hips and crushed me to him. I stood on my toes as I brought my face up to his and kissed him lightly, savoring his soft lips on mine. He moved his hands up my sides, skimming the sides of my breasts and up until he was cupping my face and deepened the kiss.

Last time, he ensured I felt all the pleasure, but this time...it was his turn.

I dropped to my knees in front of him as his eyes widened, surprised, as I unstrapped his trousers.

"What are you doing?" He asked, voice labored.

"It is your turn to relax, scholar."

I slowly slid his trousers down his lean legs until his cock was thrust out of its containment. It bounced until it settled straight up, and my mouth watered at the sight.

He was *massive.*

Soren's cock was heavy in my hands, long and just thick enough for me to barely be able to wrap my hand around. He hissed at the sensation of my hands sliding up and down his length, our eyes never leaving each other. I leaned forward as I stuck out my tongue and licked him from base to tip, just like he did to me.

I repeated the movement a few more times before I lifted his dick up and gently sucked on his balls, swirling my tongue around. Soren threw his head back and moaned loudly, reveling in this moment. My tongue moved up his shaft as I licked his tip. His eyes found mine as he jerked at the sensation. I took him into my mouth devastatingly slowly.

He lifted his hands, wanting to do something with them, but not knowing what to do, and finally slammed them against the glass window. I smiled around his dick as I lifted my hand to his and placed it in my hair. I wanted him to take control and show me exactly how he wanted it.

I had never been on my knees for anyone, and it made me so wet that I was dripping profusely down my leg.

Relinquishing control once more.

He grasped my hair and thrust deep into my throat. I choked from the intrusion but welcomed it, and moaned at the feeling of being filled by him, causing him to jerk even further into me.

He pulled all the way out and then sank back into me. I hollowed out my cheeks as his movements became faster.

"You are beautiful, my queen." My eyes rolled into the back of my head as I reached down and inserted a finger into my pussy, needing the friction. "Fuck. Me."

He pulled out of me and pulled me from my knees until I was being lifted into his arms, my legs straddling his waist. I waited for him to take me right then before he leaned in to kiss me, turned us around, and walked to a wall lined with bookshelves.

He leaned me against them for support as he pulled away enough to look into my eyes. His hands were idly running up and down my thighs, squeezing as he went.

We couldn't catch our breath and were more than ready to give each other what we both desired. But I couldn't help but ask, "Are you sure you don't want your first time to be on a bed?"

He smiled against my lips and answered my question by reaching between us, grasping his hardened length, and guiding it to my aching pussy. He rubbed it against me, soaking up the cum that was dripping out of me, coating himself. "I want to fuck you on the very things that made me feel close to you for all those years." He looked down as he pressed inside of me, agonizingly slow.

His was girthier than his brother's dick, and it stretched me until I could hardly breathe. He still wasn't even in all the way.

"Take my cock like a good girl." His deep tone sent chills along my spine. I whimpered and nodded. "That's it." He leaned forward and captured my breast in his mouth. He sucked and licked, and it made me pool around him even more.

The feeling of the books pressed into my back helped me focus and not completely lose myself. I wanted to remember every stroke, kiss, and touch. I moved my hands over his chest, running down through the hardened lines of his stomach, needing to hold onto something as he pulled out of me. My pussy tried to grip him, begging him to stay.

I leaned my forehead against his. "I can't wait any longer. Fuck me, Soren. Now," I demanded.

He didn't hold back as he pulled out of me and thrust all the way to the hilt. He stilled until I groaned, "Soren, you feel so good." He smiled and leaned in, kissing my neck while slowly pulling out and pushing back in, getting into a rhythm.

Soon, our rhythm got faster, and the sound of his balls slapping me filled the library. He was gripping my hips, digging his fingers in, and hitting the back of my pussy, causing little bursts of pain. But the pleasure overrode any other sensation.

He pressed his body against mine, our sweat intermingling. He shifted us, lifting my legs one at a time until my legs were above his shoulders, and rammed into me. I couldn't hold back the screams of pleasure that erupted as he fucked me so hard books were falling onto the ground.

"Don't fucking stop, Soren!"

I could hear him laughing to himself and sinking back into me hard, and I gasped. My eyes were closed, too lost in him. "Yes, *my* goddess. My Rose." He quickened his pace, and I was so close to exploding that when he growled, "Be a good girl and come for me."

I was done.

A violent orgasm erupted from me. My legs shook as my pussy milked him, and then one more thrust had him exploding in me. We were both panting as the high of him being inside of me was starting to wane. He rested his forehead against the crook of my neck, eyes closed, trying to catch his breath, and we stayed there in silence with him still inside me.

I loved the feeling of a throbbing cock inside me after finishing—the pulse matching the erratic thrumming of my heart.

I reached up to caress his face as tears started to form in my eyes. What we just shared was so beautiful that I was overwhelmed with all of the emotions running through me. I still was uncomfortable having other people witness my vulnerability; hiding had always been my first instinct. But not anymore. I let him see everything without turning from him.

He opened his eyes and cocked his head to the side, eyebrows pinched together. He said nothing as he lowered my legs to wrap around his waist again without pulling out of me and carried me to the chaise lounge.

The movements had the walls gripping him even tighter to me, the sensations overwhelming.

He sat down with me, still straddling him, and wiped away the tears as he waited silently for me to decide if I wanted to share whatever was going on in my head. I broke down, wrapped my arms around his neck, and cried.

I held onto him tightly as the fear of them dying one day, leaving me to be alone once again, started to take hold. Before the panic could set in, Soren began to hum the song that he used to calm me during that night in the library.

I never wanted to let them go. I felt like I was starting to feel like myself again—my old self.

My breathing calmed, and I said teasingly into his neck, "You know…usually after fucking, the man pulls out of the woman."

My body moved with his chuckle. "Why would I when this is my new favorite place to be?"

I leaned back so that we were looking at each other.

"Thank you," He whispered.

Our breaths were intermingled. He had such an alluring scent. It was one I could get drunk on for the rest of my existence.

I laughed lightly at him, moved the hair away from his face, and asked, "Whatever for?"

"For not dying. For choosing us."

I stopped laughing at that, and I stared at him. "Sometimes I think you were made for me…the old me."

He stared, considering the words deeply.

"That girl, that princess, needed someone like you to tell her the world was vast. That she could escape it all if she were brave enough, that life wouldn't end if her family didn't accept her."

He tucked a strand of hair behind my ear.

"I've been afraid of you," I admitted. "Afraid of what I'd feel if I let you in."

"I know," he said. "I can read you just about as well as I can read my brother."

I looked down, my instincts still trying to get me to flee from how overwhelmed I was. He took me by the chin, making me level my eyes with his.

"You are still that girl, afraid of not being accepted. But you have been accepted, and when I break your curse, you will see that the world is still vast. You will get every experience you lost."

The life he painted for me was almost cruel. It had been so long since I'd considered life beyond my curse—traveling, seeing the world. The longing filled my stomach. "And if you can't break it?"

He grinned. "I am persistent."

We both shared a laugh.

"I love you," he whispered, staring into my eyes, ensuring I knew he meant what he said.

He smiled at me, knowing full well I wouldn't say it back, but said it anyway. I wanted to tell him how I truly felt, but I couldn't. All I could do was kiss him. It was a kiss that had me screaming for air, but it didn't matter. I ran my fingers through his hair, pulling him even tighter to me.

He finally pulled back, and I chased his lips with mine, fully prepared to die by suffocation. He gave me a hearty laugh from deep in his chest and my insides lit up at the sound.

"You look like an angel." My hair was wild, skin flushed. My whole body was exposed to him.

"I can promise you that I am no angel."

He gave me a smile that didn't reach his eyes. A smile that told me that he was up to something. "No? The Devil herself, then? Do us both a favor a fuck me like one of your whores, Rose."

I perked up at his words. I loved to see this new side of him. "Scholar, aren't you tired after your first time?"

He leaned back and said, "No, I don't think I will ever tire of you."

That was all it took. I slid up and slammed down on his length. We went at each other like rabid animals and didn't relent until we were both so exhausted from fucking that we could barely move.

I was lying on his stomach as I looked into his eyes and said, "And I am not *that* loud."

He just chuckled and took me again on the couch.

CHAPTER TWENTY-NINE

We had cleaned up in my chambers and headed down to the dining hall together, arm in arm. The moment we entered through the double wooden doors, we heard someone say in a loud, exaggerated voice, "Well, well, well... Look who decided to grace us with their presence, Em."

I stared at Bastian incredulously, "Em?" And then to Emilia, who raised her shoulders in a shrug. She looked a little worried.

"Short for Emilia." He lifted his nose in the air. "A nickname I gave her, which you would have known if you were there."

This man. This man was actually pouting, with his lip puckered and everything.

"What are you going on about, brother?"

Callum put his hand on Bastian's arm and rubbed it, "He is just a little sour about..." Callum scrunched up his face as though he were thinking carefully about how to word the rest of his sentence.

Bastian finished for him. "We heard you fucking."

I raised my eyebrows and looked up to see Soren smiling. He wasn't fazed at all. He wrapped a hand around my waist and tightened his grip as we approached the table.

Soren looked down at me and smiled wide. "I told you so."

He leaned down to kiss my forehead and pulled out my chair.

"And now they have inside jokes." Bastian rolled his eyes, waved a hand in the air, and looked at Callum. "Is this how you felt when I fucked her?"

"I have told her majesty that it doesn't matter to me how many people she has sex with. I will love her always."

"Now, now, Bast. Jealousy is not a good look on you," Soren said playfully.

He was jealous? I slapped my hand over my mouth as a fit of laughter bubbled its way out of me. My body shook as I tried to stop, but that only made me laugh even harder, especially when I looked around the table at their stunned faces.

"And what, pray tell, is so funny?" Bastian asked.

"I didn't realize that my darling Bastian could be so jealous when he tried to kill me not too long ago," I said between the gaps in my laughter. Tears lined my eyes, I tried to blink them back to no avail.

I wiped the tears away to focus back on Bastian as he said, "It's a little too soon to be joking about that, don't you think?"

I shrugged and reached forward, taking a sip of wine.

He crossed his arms and sat back, cutting his eyes toward his brother. "I am *not* jealous. Especially not of Soren."

Emilia spoke up finally after this little heated exchange. "Your actions are in direct conflict with what you're trying to convey."

When Bastian lifted his brows, Callum simplified, "Your temper tantrum shows everyone that you're jealous."

Bastian stood and announced, "I'm going to go get the food that I slaved over all afternoon."

When we heard his retreating footsteps, I leaned forward and asked, "What in the world was that all about?"

Callum answered, "Well, we were in the hallway," heat enveloped his neck, face, and ears, and I knew exactly why, but kept the smile hidden as he continued, "headed back to the library, but heard noises and when we looked in we saw how he," Callum pointed toward Soren, "was taking you."

So they saw everything... Interesting.

Just then, Bastian walked up the stairs with two large platters full of roasted pork, swiss chard, steamed potatoes, glazed carrots, fresh blueberries, goat cheese, and bread. He set down the platters mumbling something nobody could hear and began cutting into it aggressively.

I sighed, stood, and walked behind his back as he split up the portions of meat he cut and wrapped my arms around his stomach. It felt so good to be this casual with them all. Allowing them to see my affectionate side. I never realized how draining it was to always be on guard.

Bastian finished slicing the pieces, set the cutting utensils aside, and wiped his hands on the damp towel hanging from his left shoulder. He threw the towel down, clasped a hand over my own that was sliding up his chest, and pulled me until I was in front of him. He lifted me in his arms, just as his brother had a few hours ago, and held me to him by grabbing my ass while his other hand grabbed the nape of my neck and crushed his lips to mine.

He squeezed as he pulled back and breathed huskily, "I just missed you today, is all. And seeing you with my little brother, well, okay, yeah, it made me a little jealous."

I smirked, thinking about the perfect way to mess with him. I slid my hands over his shoulders and down his stomach and back up as I leaned in until our lips were almost touching, drinking him in, and whispered, "Did you imagine me bent over the chaise as your brother fucked me from behind, wishing it was you who was buried so deep inside of me that it was *all* I could think about?"

I nipped his bottom lip, took advantage of him being too stunned to react to hop off of him, and sat back down, eating a large bite of pork.

He asked me incredulously, "Are you going to say all of that and pretend as though nothing happened? My balls are aching now!"

Soren couldn't contain his laughter any longer, and it was contagious because everyone had joined in—even Bastian.

"I suppose we should talk about what this means," Soren suggested. We all looked at him, waiting for him to elaborate. "We all want her. So what does loving the same woman mean for us?"

He wasn't asking anyone else, but his brother. Were we going to talk about this now?

"And if I tell you to back off?" Bastian raised a brow.

"That's not something I can agree with."

I interjected, "Would anyone like to know what I think?"

They ripped their eyes from each other and looked at me expectantly. Did they want me to choose? "I don't think I need to remind everyone that I am my own woman who can choose who she wants to mount her."

Someone choked on their drink as I continued, "There is nothing to do or decide. I want you both and I will not choose. If that is a problem for anyone, then you are more than welcome to stay away from my chambers."

It was my turn to cross my arms and stare them down.

The brothers looked back at each other, and Bastian rubbed the nape of his neck as he said, "We both love her, it seems. And she has made it abundantly clear that we either agree or she will cut us off."

"Neither one of us wants that option." They both shook their heads.

"Just know that in any other situation, I would fight you for the right to be with her. And honestly, as long as I get to be with her, I don't mind sharing her with one more person."

"Well, that was poetic." Soren ran a hand through his hair as I smiled at Bastian, appreciating what he said. "It is rather unconventional, but I have waited my whole life to be with her, and I am not going to let something superficial get in the way of that."

I clapped my hands together and popped a blueberry into my mouth. "I am happy we are all on the same page because it would have been rather difficult for me to keep my hands off of any of you. Well, except for Emilia."

She snickered. "Yes, I would rather be kept out of this foursome of yours. Respectfully speaking, of course."

"Speaking of happy occasions. Were you ever going to tell us that your birthday is in a few days?" Emilia asked.

I lifted my brows, stunned they even knew about it. My eyes slid over to Soren's, who looked at me sheepishly and said, "Don't be cross, but I read it when I found that book about your family history."

I smiled as I rolled my eyes and shook my head. "I am not upset, but I didn't see a reason to bring it up. Which is why I didn't."

"Well, how are we to celebrate if we don't know?" Emilia asked.

"I don't see a point." I huffed. "I am—"

"Three hundred and seventy years old. Yes, yes, we get it." Bastian waved his hand.

"I think after everything that has happened, we all need something to celebrate, don't you think?" Callum said matter of factly.

I looked to Emilia to help me out, to agree with me, but she shrugged and said, "I think they have a point. A party is a good way to let loose a little and have some fun."

Traitor.

I sighed and pinched the bridge of my nose. "Is this really what everyone wants?" They all nodded their heads.

"And you don't have to do anything. Just don't go into the ballroom until we bring you in," Emilia added.

I smiled, slowly getting excited over the idea as Callum laughed to himself. "Let's eat before this delicious meal gets cold."

We all dug into our food and had a strange sense of unshakable peace. I was smiling so much that my cheeks were in pain. All I had ever wanted was a family that welcomed me—saw me for who I was, flaws and all, and loved me. I thought I had found it in Circe, all those years ago. Never did I imagine I'd find it here, all this time later.

A sense of dread began to wash over me. I had what I wanted, and I was cursed to be alone. I'd watch them all die and wither like the forest around me, only they wouldn't grow again in the spring. They'd be gone, forever.

I swallowed, and Callum cleared his throat, as if trying to pull me from my dark thoughts. "Are you happy, your grace?"

I suppressed my fear. "Very much so."

"Good. It warms my heart seeing you so..."

"Affectionate?"

"Happy. Just happy."

I smiled some more.

Dinner had died down and we were all chatting away happily. None of us were in a hurry to rush off when I asked, "Can I show you all something?"

No one asked where we were headed, though I could feel their curiosity. I didn't know why I thought this was a good idea, but I had already let them in, and it felt like the next step was for them to see this part of me—my human side. The very part that I hoped I would be able to give them one day.

I stopped at the bottom of the stairs and stared at the top shrouded in darkness. I stepped forward and ran my hand along the banister coated in dust.

"Thea, what are we doing here?" Bastian asked.

"You don't have to do this, Rose. If it's too soon or too hard, then let's go back and enjoy a stroll around the—"

I took a deep breath, and said into the abyss, "I want to share this side of me. I think it's time you see me, just like I see all of you. I have to face it and I would rather have my family here when I do."

I turned to find Callum wiping at something on his cheek and Emilia patting his back, smiling at him. The brothers straightened their shoulders and looked proud of themselves, like they accomplished the impossible.

With that, I started climbing and my family followed behind. Each step felt like a brick being placed upon my chest. I was so very afraid to finally face my past, but I would do it. I would be afraid no longer.

It was a long hallway that had only a few doors down it. Annabelle's room was the first on the right, my parents' room was down at the end of the corridor, and my room was between both of theirs on the left. All the doors were identical, with intricate detailing painted in different golden hues.

I stopped directly in front of it. The door was moving—no, I was. I was shaking so terribly that Soren and Bast both held onto a part of my body, lending me their strength. I slowly reached for the door handle and grabbed it gently so as not to frighten it away—more like making a sudden movement that would frighten me away. I remembered the memory that happened last time I was in the West Wing and didn't want a similar one to manifest.

"Breathe, Thea."

I had not realized I had been holding my breath. I let it out and turned the knob, pushing it open.

I stood there for what felt like eons before saying quietly, "This was my room when I was eighteen. Well, technically I am still eighteen, but…you get it." I was rambling, running short of breath once more. I hadn't been here in so long that everything was covered in dust and cobwebs. But it was all how I had left it.

I had a tall, four-poster bed that took up the majority of the space on one side of the wall. The balcony was straight ahead and looked over the back of the castle where I could see the panoramic view. I loved looking at the scenery so much that I had my bed placed on a side of the wall where I could lay in bed and stare straight out the balcony doors.

There were paintings of my family that I had placed intricately around my room. Some were paintings that Belle and I would do together—we were not professionals by any means—and they were the ones I most cherished.

My new family was behind me, waiting to see what I wanted to do, but I was stuck at the door frame.

Deep breath in. One. Two. Three. Deep breath out. One. Two. Three.

I opened my eyes and took a shaky step forward through the doorway. I wrapped my arms around my stomach as I slowly made my way around, not touching a single item, too afraid my touch would taint it.

I could feel doubt and regret filtering through me as I felt someone thread their arm through mine. I looked over to see Emilia giving me an encouraging smile. I nodded. I would not allow the past to control me.

Callum stopped in front of my dresser and stared at all the trinkets, using his finger to wipe a smudge of the thick dust off. He picked up a small stuffed animal as I walked beside him. I watched him as he was turning it over in his hands.

"It's still soft after all this time."

"My father gave it to me when I was a little girl. I wanted to play outside with all the other children, but when he finally let me, I got hurt. So he gave me this doll to make everything better. He said that I should hold her tight whenever I felt sad and everything would be better."

He gave me a small smile.

He held it for another moment before setting it back on the dresser. "This was Belle's favorite toy of mine when she was a small child. I would often find her sleeping with it at night, holding it close."

I felt hands caressing my arms, sliding up and down as Bastian whispered in my ear, "Can you show us any good memories of Annabelle?"

I nodded, but before I could play the scene in the ball of light, Belle and I materialized before our eyes. Soren stood next to us, lacing his fingers through mine and brought them to his lips as we watched the scene play out before us.

"Belle, please! Stop it!"

"You may stop me anytime, Sister. You are stronger than I."

We were both on my bed with Annabelle on top of me, tickling my stomach. She was right; I was far stronger than she was, but I never wanted this to end. I loved her with all of my heart. Her laughter was my favorite melody.

"You are, dare I say, evil, little sister! What crime have I committed that you would torture me so?"

She stopped for a moment and pondered the question, before accusing, "You ate the very last piece of my blackberry pie."

"I did not!"

"Did so!"

We stared at each other, willing the other to break eye contact and admit defeat. I never would—well, that was a lie. I always would for my Belle.

My beautiful little sister.

I broke eye contact first, and she raised her arms in victory. I took the distraction and launched my assault, throwing her back on the bed and started tickling her.

Her hands and feet were clawing at me to stop, screaming at the top of her lungs as I didn't let up. Tears started stinging her eyes when our parents burst through my doors with a few guards in tow, nightgowns and all.

We all stopped and looked at each other. Time paused until both my parents were sighing with relief at the sight.

My mother put her hand to her heaving chest and my father laid his hand upon Thesius, our head guard, as if to catch his breath, chest moving just as fast as mother's.

"My girls, why are you still up?" Mother chided.

We both looked at each other, waiting for our punishment when Father said, "Move over, my darlings." He took Mother's hand and strolled over to the bed, getting in.

"Thank you, Thesius. You may leave." Thesius nodded and exited swiftly with a smile.

We all snuggled under the covers when Annabelle asked, "Tell us a story, Father."

He groaned and we all laughed and started begging—even Mother had joined in. He could never say no to her.

"Alright. But then bed." We both nodded our heads enthusiastically, getting comfortable.

"I was twenty-three years of age. I had been a soldier in my very first war, which went on for nearly six years. But we had won because I had gone out in the middle of the night to scope out where our enemy slept, seeing if I could overhear any of their plans. I had been lucky that night because where I was perched in a tree, a couple of their generals had come over to the base of my tree to pis—" Mother gave him a look, and he corrected himself, "--to use nature's bathroom, and I heard the plans for their attack the next day."

We were all on the edge of our seats, not knowing how it ended even though it ended with him alive as the king with us.

Father continued, "After they left, I hopped down and went directly to our generals and told them everything I had heard. I was reprimanded by my father, who was angry at my violation of his direct order to not engage, but I knew he was proud of me. So we won the war on my intel, and my father knew I was ready to become king. This is when I had my very own coronation ball and met the love of my life...your mother."

They leaned toward each other, effectively smooshing us in between their bodies as they kissed and we protested, squirming.

They laughed as they pulled away, and Mother said, "I wasn't even after your father that night."

We all looked at her with surprise and asked an array of questions, to which she replied, "I wasn't of high status, and I wouldn't have been a good match for your father. I came from a bloodline that married courtiers and dukes—not a king. I was dancing with Sir Claes when I looked over to your father and our eyes met. I was smitten. Though I made no move to approach him, he had other plans, and now I have the two most wonderful little girls a mother could hope for."

They kissed each of our temples. "Now off to bed."

"Goodnight, darlings, and have the sweetest of dreams."

My family faded away until nothing was left to indicate they were ever here. I stared at my bed and willed the memory to come back, but it didn't. I wanted to see them again. The last few years of their lives were spent with me hating them for what they did. I hated them for so long I had forgotten this memory.

"Your parents seemed like wonderful people. I know why you miss them dearly," Callum whispered into the silence.

My chest was still heaving at the guilt I felt for what they went through because of me. My father was so loving, so understanding, until he wasn't. I swore to Circe he'd accept me, but in that final moment, I knew otherwise. His hatred for magic would always overpower his love for me.

No matter what they did, they were still my family.

My legs wouldn't keep me up any longer, and I crumbled to the ground and cried. I didn't look up to see their reaction to me falling apart, but I could feel them sitting next to me. They didn't make a move to touch me as I sat there and cried, but they were just present, lending me their strength when I was quickly losing my own.

CHAPTER THIRTY

I woke up feeling refreshed.

I hadn't felt like being with any of them after I had cried in my old chambers for hours, purging all of the water from my body. I bathed alone for what seemed like forever, and while I felt like a part of me was missing, I knew I needed to take the night for myself.

I sat in my bathtub, arms wrapped around my shins, head resting on my knees as I gazed down at the rose garden slowly swaying in the wind. I felt free and shaken all at once, still considering this new family of mine and what it would feel like to lose them. The thought was almost debilitating. I'd escaped Circe's voice in my head, but the feelings of doubt she left behind lingered.

I had decided to take a long walk to get a bit of fresh air before anyone woke up, needing the chill bite of the air on my exposed flesh. I put on a beautiful gown that I had taken from my old wardrobe. It was a dark, royal blue with yellow beading and white lace accents. The sleeves were long—perfect for this weather—but it was still cold enough that I had the sense to grab my favorite muff and a fur-lined cape.

I lifted my head to the sky and closed my eyes, listening to the sound of the flowers rustling together. I leaned forward to sniff one of the roses and inhaled it deeply.

"Don't tell the others, but you're my favorite," I whispered to it.

I continued walking through the rows when I had to shield my eyes from a bright light. What the—

I squinted, trying to see what was blinding me, when my eyes widened, and I gasped.

A sliver of light pierced through the fog. A SLIVER OF LIGHT PIERCED THROUGH THE FOG!

"Soren!" I yelled. "Soren!" I screamed at the top of my lungs. I was walking in circles, my head searching the sky for more light, but there was none.

I rushed back over to the original sliver of light, stood directly under it, opened my eyes, and stared directly into it. After a few moments, my eyes began to burn, but it felt so fucking *good*.

"What happened!"

I could hear multiple people screaming at me, but I couldn't be bothered as I closed my eyes, reveling in the warmth of the light with arms outstretched. Warm. It was *warm*! How could I have forgotten about that? Even in Soren and Bastian's memories, I couldn't feel the sun's warmth.

I had only known cold for so long that I wanted to bathe in the tiny piece of light forever. I could feel the damp cold seeping into my clothing on my knees and looked down to find that I had fallen to my knees. I didn't even remember that happening. I knew there were people around, but I couldn't care less as long as the light didn't go away.

I felt a hand on my shoulder, but I didn't dare look away from the light. Whoever it was reached out and brushed a tear that had fallen down my cheek.

I was still too stunned to speak, but I didn't have to as Soren put a hand over his mouth. "Rose?" When I didn't respond or look at him, he bent in front of me and placed a hand on my leg. "Rose, has the sun ever shone through the fog?"

I shook my head.

"What could this mean?" Bastian asked from behind me.

Soren looked behind my shoulder and answered, "I don't know how it happened, but something has caused the curse to wane, or else this," he waved into the ray of light, "wouldn't be happening."

Those words brought me out of my stupor and I asked, "I haven't performed any spells recently. We haven't found anything of use over our weeks of research. I haven't done anything different."

"Except almost die."

I rolled my eyes at Bastian's comment.

"And starve yourself," Bastian went on.

Where was he going with this?

"The bouts of anger. Don't forget the torture. Did I forget to mention that you gave me blue balls." He held up two fingers. "Twice."

I slapped his arm, and he laughed, rubbing it.

I looked around at the rest of them, Callum had stood and was rubbing Bastian's back, laughing at Bastian for his nonsense. Soren had his leatherbound journal and quill and was writing in it with fervor. His glasses had slipped down his nose slightly, his hair bouncing with each stroke of the quill.

He looked back up at us and said, "There was a book that I read at the beginning of my research that solidified my theory after getting all the information from Rose's memory. Each curse is uniquely worded in a way that only the one casting the curse knows exactly how to break it. There is no universal way to break all curses, and Circe did a splendid job concealing all evidence that would have helped us break your curse." He took a breath. "But my current theory... Love."

My mouth fell open at the word, once again left speechless by my scholar.

"Love?" Emilia asked.

"Well, there are a variety of variables, but the bottom line is that there is a change happening within Rose at a fundamental level. Not as a monster that she has come to deem herself as, but a girl."

"You're sure?" Bastian asked.

"It is only a theory, but it is the only thing that makes sense at this moment." Soren pointed at the shard of light. "There is light shining through the fog for the first time in three hundred and fifty-two years. That has to mean something."

"Soren's right; it has to mean something," Callum said, beaming.

Bastian groaned, "Yes! I was growing tired of reading through those boring texts all day. I am just happy we are finally making some progress."

I left them to talk more about the curse and what the light could mean. I was still in shock over everything that it was taking longer to process our new discoveries. I looked over to Emilia who hadn't said a single word. The expression that was on her face was slightly concerning. Her brows were furrowed, her breathing irregular, and she was fidgeting with her skirts.

I stood and walked over to her. "Are you alright?"

Her eyes slid to mine, but she swallowed as if not knowing exactly how to answer me. I embraced her, not knowing how else to set her mind at ease as I whispered, "This is the first step in breaking the curse. If we can do this, then there is nothing to fear, Emilia. You won't be alone."

She pulled back until she was looking at me. "What?"

I gave her a small smile and brushed a stray hair out of her face. "Well, aren't you worried about what this means for you—for us?"

I cocked my head to the side as she slowly nodded her head. She was about to say something, but then she touched her throat and opted to sign. *Of course, your majesty. This is just surprising, is all.*

Yes, it was surprising. It was nothing short of a miracle.

I brought her back into my arms and laughed at the stupidity of crying over a tiny fragment of light, but to me, it was everything.

Hope.

That feeling was warm within my body, casting out any harboring doubt that that couldn't be a possibility. But that light. That light was timid proof that everything I had gone through over the last few centuries would be over soon.

I pulled away from her, and as I turned around to talk to my men, I was squealing as someone hoisted me over their shoulder and roared, "I think this is cause for a celebration!" I yelled as Bastian slapped my ass hard enough to cause a sting and then bit into it.

"Bastian!" I wanted to scold him, but I could feel the apex of my thighs clench together to try to stop how wet I was becoming from his actions.

I looked up through my hair falling in front of my face and found Callum smirking at the two of us. Soren was stealing fast glances our way as he hurried to finish whatever last thought was going on in his mind.

"Bast, wait!"

Bastian was carrying me through the rose garden and up the steps as he slapped my ass hard again, and I groaned at the sting pulsing straight to my core.

What had gotten into him?

I could see that Callum was next to Bast, smiling widely. Soren had finished writing, tucked the journal back into his trousers, and put the quill behind his ear as he jogged over to catch up with us. But Emilia didn't even give us a second thought; she continued to stare at the shard of light with crossed arms.

"Follow me, boys!" Bastian boomed, then moved through the front doors, down the halls, up the staircase, and into my chambers. He threw me down on the bed and stood back as Callum came up to one side and Soren on the other.

I narrowed my eyes at them. "What is this about?"

"We talked this morning, and all came to an agreement," Bastian said.

"An agreement?"

"Yes. We all needed to set up some ground rules," Soren chimed in.

Ground rules?

"We all made it clear that each one of us loves you more than our own lives and what that means moving forward," Callum added.

They looked at each other and smirked, and I couldn't help but ask, "So...that means?"

Soren leaned down first and pulled me off the bed and into his arms, taking my face between his hands and kissing me. His tongue caressed the crease of my lips, and I happily obliged, parting them, allowing him in. He deepened the kiss and I felt lips kissing slowly up my shoulder. We broke the kiss long enough for me to see lust-filled eyes and a smirking Bastian.

Callum said beside us, "We all want a piece of you. While we would still be able to have you individually, we all decided to share you this first time."

Share me? All of them? At once? My heart began to race.

Fuck yes.

I closed my eyes as I swallowed and asked, "And the brothers agreed to take me together?"

Bastian bit into my shoulder, causing me to whimper. I pushed my back into him, begging for more of his torture, when Soren suddenly leaned forward and kissed the spot his brother bit into.

The conflicting movements had my legs almost giving out, and the only thing that kept me up were the brothers' hands around me, caressing me, squeezing me.

Callum took a step forward, and Soren happily turned my head to Callum, who captured my mouth on his. I could feel hands unclasping the beading on my dress. It slipped down my body and fell to the floor with a soft thud.

"Fuck... How could I have ever lived without this?" Soren breathed as he took me in.

"I don't know. I am almost furious with myself that I never believed she existed. We could have been fucking her for years."

"It was all well worth the wait."

I continued giving my attention to Callum while the brothers talked as if we weren't there. I didn't care as long as they put their hands back on me.

I almost pulled away from Callum to demand they do what they were just talking about when I felt a hand grasping my thighs and pulling me forward. I gasped and looked down. Soren parted my pussy and sucked on my bundle of nerves. He continued his lazy assault as I felt Bastian spread my ass and spit. I tried to look behind me as Callum brought my face back to his, smiling, and kissed me deeply while Bastian focused on my ass, licking my ass.

I couldn't help the noises that came out of me. It was almost too much. The sensations sent liquid fire through my veins.

"Please..." I said when Callum finally let me come up for air.

I could hear Bastian chuckle behind me. "Has our queen forgotten how to speak?"

Our queen.

"Be a good girl and use your words." Soren's hot breath against me as he spoke was almost my undoing as I tried to rub my thighs together for the friction my body was begging for.

I could hear Bastian tsking. "Use your words."

"Please, fuck me. Please." I panted. I wasn't above begging for exactly what they were offering me.

The brothers stood up, and I had never felt so small as I looked up at their faces.

Bastian smirked as he said, "On your knees."

His words shocked me and I didn't move, not yet used to being ordered around.

"You know I don't like to repeat myself." Bastian's eyes darkened, promising delicious punishment as he repeated. "On. Your. Knees. *Thea.*"

Thea. That name again.

I couldn't have gotten on my knees faster.

"Look at our good girl," Bastian said.

"Yeah. She's such a good listener. Who knew?" Soren laughed.

I didn't know who was going to use me first when they all started undressing.

Fuck, this was happening. I would often daydream of this exact scenario, but I never thought that it would ever become a reality. I reached between my legs and rubbed myself, feeling exactly how wet I was—it was running down my legs. I was a mess. Their mess.

All of theirs.

"Now, don't get hasty," Soren mused as he discarded his trousers last by the side of the bed and fisted himself. This was a side to Soren I never knew existed, and it was alluring.

I was about to lean toward him when I could feel my head being pulled away toward Callum.

"It's only fair that you suck your little bird's cock first. He has waited long enough to see you on your knees for him," Bastian said.

I looked up from beneath my lashes to find Callum's face flushed. This was new to us. Our dynamic was always the opposite, but Bastian was right. He deserved to go first, and I planned on giving him everything he had been denied for so many years.

I wrapped my hands around Callum's cock and gently kissed it. He hissed and held onto Bastian's shoulder for support. It was my turn to smirk at him as

I licked the seam of his tip. Cum was already protruding out of it, and I made a show of swallowing it.

He rolled his eyes into the back of his head and groaned. I leaned forward and wrapped my lips around his long cock, working my way up and down as I grasped his balls and lightly squeezed.

"That's right. Take my cock, your grace. Fuck." It wasn't necessarily a demand, but he sounded more like Bastian in the bedroom, and I rewarded him by taking him to the back of my throat, moaning. He jerked into me, going down my throat as I coughed, drool sliding down the sides of my face as tears formed from the sudden intrusion.

"Why is this so hot?" Soren asked, as he continued slowly stroking himself. I loved that he was learning more about himself sexually.

Bastian knelt and kissed me, tasting Callum on my lips before standing and shoving his hardened length into my mouth. "My turn."

He was rough. He tightened his grip on the back of my head and thrust his hips against my mouth. I kept my mouth open and just sat back as he took what he wanted from me. His grunts egged me on and I reached up, grasping both Soren's and Callum's cock in my hands, stroking them. Bastian's hips jerked even faster.

"That's it, Thea." I could feel he was close, but he stopped himself just as Callum had. I didn't have time to think about it before Soren pushed his brother out of the way.

"My turn."

My throat burned, but I would never stop. I wanted to give them every part of me. I opened my mouth wide and stuck my tongue out, ready for him. He chuckled, stuck his thumb in my mouth, and pulled down, opening me even wider. I had to hollow out my cheeks even more just to fit him inside as he slowly slipped out and then back in.

He was the complete opposite of his brother. Bastian loved the pain with passion, but Soren preferred to take it slow, each movement deliberate and precise.

He rolled his hips into my mouth and worked up a steady rhythm as I brought my hands up and squeezed his ass, my nails biting into his skin. He hissed.

Then he did something that surprised me; he rammed into the back of my throat and held my head there until the air had been completely sucked out of me, and I felt lightheaded.

He finally released me, and I put my hand to my throat as I coughed and stared up at him.

"Goddamn, brother. Who knew that was in you."

Soren simply shrugged.

Maybe I was wrong. Maybe he was also a glutton for punishment.

But I realized that none of them had finished. They must have seen I was confused because Callum said, "Our cum belongs in one place, your grace."

Soren then lifted me as the others walked off. Were they all done? I was almost disappointed because I wanted exactly what was promised. He set me on the end of the bed.

He spread my legs wide and hissed as he looked down at my swollen pussy. He said over his shoulder, "Do you think this is far enough?"

Bastian answered him, "That's perfect."

The elder brother came into view with pieces of leather in his hands. What was that for?

Leather. *Oh gods.*

"Do you trust us?"

"Yes," I said immediately. I had never trusted three people more fully in my life.

Bastian handed his brother a piece and began to secure the leather around my thighs to the frame of the bed. Bastian moved around the other side, and I watched him secure a long piece of leather around the banister of the bed. He then reached his hand out, palm up.

I placed my hand in his, and he wrapped the leather around my wrist tight enough that I couldn't move it an inch. Soren did the same to my other wrist.

I could only move my head, and swiveled in time to see Callum hand something over to Bastian, who was grinning like a madman.

The collar from the tower.

He clamped it around my neck with the leash attached. Fuck. What game did they have planned for me?

Callum came up behind Bastian, and held up a thick piece of silk. "We are going to play a little game. You'll be blindfolded and each one of us will have a turn."

"Then you will guess which one of us was inside of you," Bastian continued.

"Guess all three correctly, and you'll win a prize," Callum said excitedly.

"What's my prize?" I asked breathlessly.

Bastian said, "You are going to take us all."

"One for every hole," Soren finished for him.

I blanched and looked at the swinging length between each of their legs. I felt so exposed with my legs bound wide open for them, but welcomed it. Loved it.

"And if I don't guess right?"

"Then we edge you," Bastian spoke. "All night long."

I was confident that I could guess them all correctly. I nodded as Callum secured the silk over my eyes until all I could see was darkness. This would have terrified me at one time, but now only a thrill of anticipation soared through me.

I could hear them moving around until I jerked at a single touch at the apex of my thighs.

"She is so ready for us."

"What a sight."

Their voices mingled together. I couldn't concentrate hard enough to figure out who was talking because my only focus was the fingers rubbing my core. I tried to buck into those callused fingers, but he retreated, and I nearly cried from the loss of that touch.

Another hand replaced his, or maybe it was the same hand? He gripped my hips and slammed into me as I cried out and pulled at the restraints to touch the man inside of me, to give me some type of reprieve from the intrusion. This man was thick. His cock was stretching me and filling me, and I moaned from the pleasure that it elicited.

He pulled out and rammed back into me all the way to the base. I couldn't hold back the tears as he continued his torturous, slow pace. He thrusted, only to still until that intense feeling subsided, and then continued on and on and fucking on!

I gritted my teeth together. "I thought the edging wouldn't come until later!"

None of them said a word. Not wanting to give me any hints on who it might be. He must have taken pity on my cunt because he proceeded to roll his hips into me. He kept a pace that quickly brought me to the precipice of yet another oncoming orgasm. I prayed that he wouldn't stop as he gripped my hips and squeezed, trying his best to keep his grunts to himself.

They wanted to fuck me at the same time as much as I wanted them to as well.

His movements became shorter, and I knew that he was almost ready to explode, and I wouldn't be denied again.

I knew from the moment he entered me who it was, but I kept my mouth shut until I saw stars as the orgasm finally ripped through me, and I called out, "Soren!"

I could hear him groan as his movements jerked and he came inside of me. He leaned forward, kissed my lips, and eased out of me.

"Who's next?" Soren asked.

I could feel his cum leaking out of me when another hand was placed over my pussy and smeared the cum around, and then pushed it back inside of me with a finger.

I gasped as his thick finger was inside of my sensitive walls. He pulled out, and I could feel him lining himself up to me and then easing his way in. I clenched my walls around him, sucking him inside of me, never wanting to let him go.

Realization dawned on me, and I smiled. I knew that cock even more than my own body.

He pulled my hips down a little further, and I could feel his body leaning over mine, a hand on either side of my stomach. He rolled his hips until he was seated all the way inside of me and then moved quickly as he leaned down and bit on a nipple. I cried out as his balls slapped against my ass. The heat crept into me at his steady pace, and his attack on my breasts was enough to undo me.

When I could feel him swell inside of me, I screamed out, "Yes, Callum!" As a wave of pleasure rushed over my body, my legs shook violently at being denied movement. Callum leaned forward and kissed my forehead as he spilled inside of me. Only when our breathing had calmed down did he finally pull out.

I didn't know how much more my body could take. I'd only had three orgasms in one night, but they were promising me far more than that, and I was already seeing stars.

I knew who was last, and I knew he wasn't going to go easy on me. He proved this by swiping a finger through Soren's and Callum's cum, mixing them together, and forcing his finger in my mouth, giving me no choice but to taste them.

It was salty, but I welcomed the taste. It was heaven.

"That's it. Swallow." Bastian broke the silence.

I sucked on his fingers. My body had yet to stop shaking, but I only said, "Do your worst, hunter."

"That fucking name." He grabbed my leash and pulled me up until I couldn't go any further and lined his head to my entrance. He gripped my shoulder and, just as his brother had done, rammed into me. I screamed out, and he leaned forward and licked the tears that had escaped.

Bastian was not soft in bed. He took what he wanted and left me a mess afterward, but that was exactly what I wanted from him; I didn't want him to hold back.

Bastian pinched my breasts, and just when I thought that another orgasm wouldn't be possible, one rushed through me that caught me completely by surprise. I made an incoherent noise, and I might have been embarrassed if I hadn't heard Bastian whisper in my ear, "That's our good girl."

I was completely limp. My arms and legs were utterly useless as all three men worked to unbind me. Someone took off the blindfold. I blinked up at them as they were massaging and caressing my body, whispering about how well I took them all. I purred at the praise.

I closed my eyes, welcoming sleep to take me as I heard each of them laugh and one of them said, "Not yet, your grace. Give us one more, and then you can go to sleep."

I couldn't keep my eyes open as someone lifted me into their arms and scooted until my back was resting against their chest, his legs on either side of my waist. My head laid against his broad chest as he wiped the sweaty hair out of my face, my breathing short.

I could feel him lifting me up slightly and rubbed himself against my ass and then eased inside of me. My eyes flew open as it felt like someone was tearing me in two. I looked up to find Soren breathing heavily behind me as he stared into my eyes.

"How does she feel, brother?"

"She's so fucking tight," Soren responded without looking away from me and then said to me. "That's it, my Rose. Take all of me."

I arched my back into him, trying to breathe through the pain, knowing that soon it would subside and it would feel so good. I couldn't talk. Words eluded me as I nodded my head. I saw through hooded eyes Callum leaning over me and lining up his cock to my entrance.

My eyes widened. "What the fuck are you doing?"

"What we promised, Thea. You'll take all of us if you want all of us."

"Your grace, everything is going to be fine. We'll take it slow." Callum tried to offer me some comfort.

"Speak for yourself," Bastian scoffed.

Callum scolded Bastian, "She is exhausted. You'll go easy on her."

"I love it when you take control." Bastian leaned down to bite Callum's bottom lip playfully.

"Can you guys focus, please?" Soren said, his mouth next to my ear as he finally seated himself fully into me.

Callum had to do some maneuvering as he pushed into me slowly, stretching me to such lengths that my body was protesting. This wasn't going to be possible. I kept shaking my head as pain washed over me.

"Look at you taking us so well."

"What a greedy girl."

"Such a beautiful queen. So full of us."

I felt so full. Full of love as they showered me with kisses and praises.

I was panting at this point. They were doing the impossible. Thank god Callum had a longer dick so that he didn't need to be as close to me. The moment they were both inside me, I felt something wet against my lips and turned to find Bastian fisting his cock, smearing his cum across my lips.

"Open wide."

I obeyed. Bastian grabbed a fistful of my hair and used my mouth as Callum and Soren began to move. It took a moment before everyone found a steady rhythm. The feeling was almost too much to bear, but I could do nothing but give myself over to them. I was overly sensitive, but having them all inside of me at the same time stirred another wave of euphoria in me when I didn't think I had anything left.

Soren rested on his forearms and reached over to rub my clit as they moved in unison.

My eyes were heavy as my body convulsed around them. My walls constricted, begging them to stay inside me forever as I completely shattered around all three of them.

I was broken, but I had never felt so full. They each pulled out of me and collapsed on the bed. I couldn't keep my eyes open any longer. Soren placed a hand around my stomach and held me tightly to him as my body refused to function. I couldn't move even if I wanted to.

"Brother, we need to clean her up."

I was in and out of consciousness. Hands lifted me. There was water. Hands scrubbing over my body. More lifting. Then soft blankets covered my body.

"We are so proud of you."

"Yes, you did so good."

I hummed at the praise.

Someone kissed me on the side of the head, and the last thing I remember was him whispering, "*Joyeux anniversaire*, Rose."

Chapter Thirty-One

I opened my eyes to a darkened room. The balcony doors were open, and the only sounds were the soft snoring of the brothers who held me protectively in their arms and the sounds of the forest outside.

My back was against Soren's front, who had his legs wrapped around mine with a hand around my waist, a hand splayed on my stomach. My front was facing Bastian who was on his side with an arm under his head and the free hand wrapped firmly around my throat, slowly stroking his thumb back and forth lovingly. I barely lifted my head to see a mess of dark brown hair settled in the crook of Bastian's neck, cuddled behind him.

We were all under the covers, but I could tell we were all still naked as Soren's massive cock was resting against my back and his balls nestled against my ass.

My lovers. My men.

My life.

I smiled to myself because the nightmares didn't come to plague me; I slept soundly throughout the whole night. I clenched my thighs together and almost groaned at how deliciously sore I was. My body was completely relaxed, and I reveled in the phantom touches that felt as though hands were still caressing me, their cocks pulsing inside of me.

I knew they each wanted to have their time alone with me, but after last night, I was not sure how I could ever go back. Though I didn't think it would take much convincing, I knew they all had as much fun as I did.

I laid in their arms, completely content with my life. But after a while, my legs began to cramp and I needed to walk off the soreness that seemed to be radiating through my entire body. I maneuvered myself carefully out of their arms as I didn't want to wake them. As close as I felt to them, I did need a little bit of space away, as well.

I crawled out of bed and watched Soren mumbling at my absence, laughing to myself as I put on my robe. I grabbed my journal from the top drawer of my vanity before heading out. The halls were silent. Silence used to torment me, a constant reminder of all I had lost, but now it just felt peaceful. No anxiety followed. No fear. I almost skipped to the library because of how light I felt.

I hurried over to the small room that was now kept open for anyone to research whenever they wished. I had removed my journal as I didn't want anyone reading my innermost thoughts, especially not the ones from when I was first abandoned. Not even I ventured that far back into my past.

I sat in the same chair I always did, producing a floating ball of shadowy light that was just bright enough to help me grab the quill and ink Soren kept on the desk. I opened my journal to the next available page.

December 21, 1761

My sweetest sister,

So much has changed since I last wrote to you. I'll admit that not all of it was good. I tried to kill myself, and I almost succeeded. I wanted to succeed—yearned for it.
But...everything has changed. They saved me. And for a while I was so angry with them because they ruined my one chance to finally be reunited with you. Now, I'm thankful they did. The way that each one of them makes me want to be a better woman. I never knew that I could feel this way, especially after all these years. All I know is that I feel like a new woman. A happier woman.
Human.

I saw something drop onto the page and wiped at a stray tear I didn't know I had shed. I took a deep breath and knew what I had to do.

> *Belle, I am so sorry I couldn't protect you while there was still breath in your lungs. I would have done anything to save you, would have given up my own life for yours. But in order to give them a chance at happiness…I have to let my past go.*

> *I love you with all of my heart.*
> *Goodbye.*

I shut the book and bound it. I set the quill down and stood, suddenly tired again, ready to go lay back in the arms of my loved ones. I exited the small room and walked by my painting but stopped to look up at the portrait of my family and me from so long ago.

I used my magic to pull the chaise lounge to me, walked over to grab a blanket, and situated myself in front of them.

I stared at each of their faces and wondered what they would think of their daughter now.

I didn't know how long I stared at the portrait when I heard a noise behind me. I turned to find a clothed Callum standing in the middle of the room.

"Your grace, I didn't mean to disturb you. I—"

I gave him a small smile, called him over with a flick of my finger, and patted the spot next to me. He sat down, and I cuddled into him. He wrapped an arm around my shoulder and pressed me into him as I rested my head against his side. I shared the blanket with him and we sat in comfortable silence for a while longer.

I moved my nose into his shirt and inhaled deeply, enjoying the moment between us. It had been so long since we had been alone.

"What were they like?"

I took a deep breath and considered the question.

"My father was so kind and loving when it came to his family and his people. He would often walk through the streets of the village and talk with them whenever he could. He was also incredibly fierce. If any threats came onto our lands, he would stop at nothing until they weren't just dead, but eradicated. My mother was wise beyond her years. While my father was the king, he did nothing without consulting my mother first. They were equals in every way, and I prayed that I would find someone who loved me as fiercely as they loved each other."

"And his love for you?"

"He loved me, but he hated magic more."

"You think he would have killed you the same way he did to Circe?"

The truth pained me. "I think so."

My eyes slid to Annabelle, who was about ten years of age. "Then there's my Belle. She was full of life and so incredibly intelligent that if she were born a man she would have dominated the world. I could sit and listen to her talk about anything and everything for the rest of eternity." I giggled, thinking about a memory.

He turned to stare right at me.

My laugh died out immediately, and he begged, "Please don't stop. I love it when you laugh."

I hummed and cuddled into his side more.

The silence passed between us for an unknown amount of time before I said, without turning to him, "I am the same age as the girl in the painting, but I am completely different from her," voicing my thoughts from earlier.

"How so?"

I looked at him, bewildered. "Callum, I am centuries older than her."

"Sure. You have more defined facial features, and technically, you are older than her. But I think that adds to your stature. The way you are right now saved me that night. The way you are right now saved Emilia's life. The way you are right now is nothing compared to that girl in the portrait. I think you are perfect in every way possible. The way you are now is what made me fall madly in love with you."

"Do you believe that?" I knew he did, but I just wanted to hear it again.

"That I love you?" I nodded. "From the moment that you slit their throats. Blood splattered all over your body, eyes glowing—right then I knew. I knew that my life was yours."

I leaned my head toward him and captured his lips with mine. Slow. Sensual.

I moved my hands down to his face and curled my fingers on the nape of his neck, deepening the kiss. It took a moment before he wrapped his arms around me and kissed me like it was the last thing that he would ever do in life.

His lips were so soft. He moaned at the taste of me, the utter bliss of this moment. I smiled and bit his lip. We explored each other as the fog lightened, and we heard noises coming from down the hall.

We laughed, our breaths intermingling as Callum asked, "Will I ever get you fully to myself again?"

I shook my head. "Does that upset you?"

He shook his head. He was content, and so was I.

Today was my three hundred and seventy-first birthday.

I told them I hadn't been counting, but I had been. I'd been carving a tick into an old piece of wood I kept under my bed. I stared down at the newest mark on it; it could be the last one as an immortal being, but then again, I didn't really believe it. Soren's theory was just that—a theory.

Did I want it to be true? Yes. More than anything. I wanted a *life* with them, but I had come to learn a hard truth about the world. We didn't always get what we wanted. And I was cursed to never dream for more.

I could feel my throat close, my palms slick, as I thought about what it would mean when they realized my curse would never be broken. That they would choose to stay with me, never stepping another foot off these lands and die. Die without marrying... Having children...

Deep breath in. One. Two. Three. Deep breath out. One. Two. Three.

I closed my eyes as images of Callum and Bastian holding each other on a couch, watching Soren drone on and on about his next research obsession, crossed my mind. Emilia would be huddled off to the side, holding a book and reading while trying not to laugh at all of us.

A family.

My family.

I had just gotten out of the bath when I entered my chambers to find Emilia staring at the dress I had made for her. The floor-length gown was more conservative than I was used to wearing, made of deep honeyed silk that matched her maple-colored eyes. White lace embroidery was stitched along the neck and cuffs of the long sleeves with ribbons throughout.

I had altered all the clothing for the evening, items that I already had, because it was such short notice and it was the only thing they would allow me to do.

Emilia ran her hands over the soft material, and as I approached her, she turned to me, tears brimming her eyes.

Thank you. Thank you so much, she signed.

We embraced each other and stood there for a few moments until she moved toward the vanity. She grabbed the brush and waited until I sat down for her to brush through my hair.

As she combed through my knots, I asked, "Were you sent in here to keep me busy?"

She blushed and nodded. Thought so.

Everyone had been doing everything in their power to keep me away from the ballroom so I wouldn't spoil the surprise. How grand could it be with three grown men and Emilia planning a ball when none of them had ever attended one?

Of course, it didn't matter to me. They could put out a small spread of food and drink and I would be happy.

I kept quiet as Emilia worked my hair into an intricate pattern of braids and then sinched them with various pins. She picked up a small container filled with a red paste and placed some on my lips and cheek, rubbing them in until they brought some life to my face. I never wore rouge, but what she did only seemed to enhance my beauty.

I stood up, stripped my robe off, and went over to my dress. The gown was an off-the-shoulder, floor-length dress that dipped low in the front, exposing my breasts just enough to see the tops of them. In the light, the crystals I added made the dress sparkle in a way that I had only ever seen snow glitter in the sun.

Emilia helped me put it on, and I had never felt so beautiful. I looked at myself in the mirror and couldn't stop staring. I looked at her when she came up behind me through the mirror.

I signed, *You are stunning. We will be the talk of the ball.*

She laughed and signed, *There are only three men.*

Am I wrong? I asked, smirking at her.

Never, your majesty.

There was a knock at the door, and Emilia went to answer it.

"Miss Emilia, you look stunning."

She blushed and turned away from him as Callum's eyes slid over to me. I could see him reflected in the mirror as he placed a hand over his heart and whispered, "You...You are a vision."

I smiled and turned to him as he strode into the room, stopping a couple of inches from me. His chest was heaving, and his lips parted as if he wished to say something. We stood there as I looked him over. He was so handsome that it took the breath from my lungs. He had on a dark gray, tailored coat with matching trousers and the same colored undershirt. The coat had thousands of sewn-in beads of white, gray, and black to give it more dimension, as was the style from my time.

He looked away and blushed. "Your grace, if you keep looking at me like that, we won't ever make it to the ball."

"If you keep wearing things like that, then I won't complain about never leaving my chambers ever again."

I pulled my attention away from him as I saw Emilia quietly attempting to escape to give us some privacy. I hurried over to her, clasped her hand, and pulled her back toward us. I had been wanting to do that for a while now. Everything started with them and no matter what happened with my curse they needed to know.

"Is everything alright, your majesty?" Emilia asked, suddenly worried.

I kept holding one of her hands as I clasped one of Callum's, squeezing tightly. There was so much that I wished to say, but the words kept getting stuck in my throat.

As always, I deflected. "Who knew we three would be standing here today and all because of two brothers?"

Callum dropped his head, blushing. "Life before them was perfect, but I am forever grateful for how they have changed all of us just with their presence."

Emilia squeezed my hand back, garnering my attention. "Without them, I wouldn't have gotten the closure I craved. I am forever indebted to them."

"Don't forget Bast's games."

We all laughed because Bastian's idea of fun vastly differed from the rest of us. But if it wasn't for his truth or drink game, then I would have never been inclined to know more about Soren and his sexual inexperience.

They were right. Everything changed the moment Bastian struck me with his blade.

I let go of their hands, excitement flowed through me as I hadn't attended a ball in so long. It felt almost normal.

I lifted a finger in the air and quipped, "We must not inform them of this conversation. We wouldn't want their egos to get any larger."

Callum took a step back, bowed, and raised his arm. "May I escort you both to the ball?"

I placed my hand in the crook of his arm, Emilia on his other side, and replied, "You may, little bird."

We reached the doors, and Emilia asked, "Are you ready to see your surprise?"

"Is it a surprise if I already know what it is?"

They laughed, and Callum opened the doors. I started to walk in when my hands flew to my mouth, utterly speechless.

Hundreds, if not thousands, of candles were scattered around the room, casting a soft glow on the walls. Off to the side was the dining table that had an assortment of my favorite foods; soup du jour, hot hor d'oeuvres, beef ragout, cheese souffle, *tarte bourdaloue*, pudding en flambé, and gray stuff that I had forgotten the name of, to name a few.

My eyes swept over the space and landed on Bastian and Soren standing on the other side of the room. They were so dashing in their suits. Bastian and Soren wore colors that matched the emerald and cerulean brilliance of their eyes. Bastian donned a moss-green colored, printed-patterned waistcoat with a cream-colored undershirt. Meanwhile, Soren's waistcoat was damask-patterned with bright blue and gold thread.

They looked delectable.

I finally looked Bastian in the eye, who was smirking at me as if he knew exactly what I was thinking.

I stood tall as they both made their way over to me and bowed.

Bastian grabbed my hand, and kissed the back of it. "Your grace, you are radiant. Of course, I expected nothing less."

Then Soren stepped forward, scooting his brother out of the way to kiss the back of my hand as well. "Happy birthday, Rose."

"Thank you."

Soren clasped his brother's shoulder and slapped his chest, "Do my ears deceive me, Brother, or did Her Majesty just thank us?"

Bastian laughed and mirrored Soren. "Is this Heaven, Brother?"

I rolled my eyes at their jest and walked back toward Callum with Emilia standing beside him, snickering.

"Come now; I am starving."

The dinner went by quickly. Bastian, ever the conversationalist, started almost immediately. Everyone joined in as I sat back and listened to everyone. He would have made a great head of the house; he was a natural.

"Bast, this is the best food you have ever made," Callum praised.

Bastian laughed. "Well, only the best for our queen."

"Funny how you waited all these months to give her the best, Brother. You wouldn't be lacking in certain areas, would you?"

I laughed as Bastian taunted, "I think the sounds she makes with me tells you everything you need to know."

Before I could respond to their brotherly feud, Callum stood, offered his hand, and asked, "Would you do me the honor of giving me the first dance?"

I looked up at him in surprise. "I didn't know you knew how to dance."

"I didn't." Then he looked over at Bastian.

"You taught him?"

"Just a small gift for you." Bastian smiled.

I stood and followed Callum to the middle of the room, and just as I was about to conjure some music for us to listen to, Soren began to sing.

I whipped my head over to look at him, and he smiled at me as he continued to sing one of the most beautiful songs I had ever heard. The tempo was slow, and Callum twirled me around the dance floor with ease and grace.

It was more than I could handle, and I was almost brought to tears by the thoughtfulness of them all. As Soren ended the song, Callum dipped me slightly, and then I was swept into Bastian's arms.

"My turn, birthday girl."

"My bold, brazen hunter."

Soren started another song that was a little faster-paced. Bastian's skills on the dance floor were astounding. I didn't know the dance moves, but it was easy enough to follow him. He swept me off my feet, a natural-born leader. He surprised me even further by spinning me a few times out and then back into his arms. I had forgotten how fun it was to be whisked around a dance floor.

As the song ended, Bastian pulled me tightly into him. My arms were covered in goosebumps, and kissed me on the cheek before stepping back, bowing. He walked over to Emilia and held out his hand, asking for a dance, which she shyly accepted.

"May I have the next dance?"

I turned and found Soren waiting patiently behind me, his hand stretched out.

"If I didn't know any better, I would say that you are just as charming as your brother."

He placed his hand around my waist and said, "I can be rather charming when I need to be." He leaned in to whisper into my ear. "Watch this." And began to sing.

He swept me around the room as he sang to me, not missing a beat. It was rather impressive as I lost myself in his arms. I could see my dress casting bright lights all around the room, as if it were snowing inside.

We spent several hours switching partners and dancing until our feet ached so bad we had no choice but to head back over to the table. All of us except for Bastian immediately collapsed into chairs, while my darling Bastian sat on the table and ate idly from the scraps on the platters.

He grabbed a scoop of the gray stuff and moaned as he plopped it into his mouth. "This may be the most delicious thing that I have ever had in my mouth."

Callum clicked his tongue and asked, "The most delicious thing you have ever had in your mouth? Are you sure about that?"

Bastian threw his head back and laughed so hard that he almost fell off the table. His laughter was so deep that it vibrated throughout my body, igniting flames inside me.

Bastian dipped a finger into one of the desserts and brought it to my lips. "A little preview for tonight?"

I smirked at him and wrapped my lips around his finger, sucking as he hissed.

"Alright, save that for when Emilia isn't in the room," Soren lightly scolded.

I leaned back and blushed. Everyone, including myself, was having such a wonderful time that I never wanted it to end.

Soren handed each of us a drink, raised it, and said, "Cheers to the most beautiful woman I have ever seen in my entire life. You are not only beautiful, but you are brilliant in your passion and wit."

I was about to drink when Bastian stood after him and raised his goblet. "I would like to add that I am happy you knocked me out with your magic and sent me to the tower. Every day is a surprise with you, and I am happy I get to be part of all your chaos."

I glared at Bastian. "I am not that chaotic." They all looked at each other, not knowing how to break the news to me. I scoffed, "Fine, I can agree that I am just a *little* chaotic."

Everyone laughed as Callum stood and grabbed my hand, pulling me with him over to a corner of the room. I finally saw a cloth-draped object leaning against the wall, and wondered how it had skipped my notice until now. Everyone followed as Callum said nervously, "I hope you like the gift. It's a small token of my appreciation."

"Shit, he is going to outdo us, isn't he?" Bastian asked Soren as they followed.

"Speak for yourself; Rose was practically in tears when I sang." He crossed his arms over his chest, looking rather smug and proud of himself.

"Close your eyes, your grace."

I obeyed. Excited for whatever he was about to give me. I heard the rustling of the material.

"Oh wow, Cal, that's incredible."

"Callum, you did this yourself?" Emilia said.

"I'm speechless." Soren breathed.

Now, I was restless.

"Ok, open."

I opened them to find a portrait in front of me. I couldn't move. Couldn't do anything except stand there and stare at the image with my mouth wide open. Callum had painted a family portrait of all of us. I was standing in the middle of the frame with Emilia beside me and my men behind us. Callum perfectly captured each of their personalities.

I looked up at him, my words coming out strained, "Thank you."

He nodded. "Where would you like to hang it up?"

I was about to say that I would like to put it next to the one of my family in the library when Soren intervened. "I may have a suggestion. How about we take it with us?"

We all turned to him, and he handed me something out of his coat jacket pocket. The color drained from my face as I immediately recognized the small black leather-bound notebook with silver engraving on the front.

My hands shook as he held it out to me to take. "Where did you find it?"

"In one of the floorboards in the chapel." It was Circe's grimoire. I had looked for it for centuries. I thought it burned with her.

Panic began to seep through me, and that feeling of dread I'd been trying to bury for days returned. "When?"

"A few days ago. Once I realized who it belonged to, I didn't want to give it to you until I had gone over it and..." He smiled at me. "I know how to break the curse."

I almost dropped the book and asked in a small voice. "You do?"

He nodded. "My birthday gift to you is your freedom."

"You don't know what this is. You shouldn't have touched it." My voice shook. "You shouldn't have read it. Return it to where you found it. Return it now!"

Soren stared with confusion and a drop of horror.

"Return it!" I screamed, and then my vision became blurry, my body numbed. If it wasn't for Bastian, I would have fallen to the floor. Everything felt like it was going in slow motion. One moment, I was yelling at Soren, and the next, there was screaming and a blur of bodies.

"Emilia, no!" I heard Callum's voice screech.

I looked over Soren's shoulder to see Emilia's face twisted in a rage I had never seen before, her eyes glowing a bright gold with her arm raised, holding a blade aimed right at Soren's back.

And Callum. My sweet, little bird, threw his body in between them.

There was a thud, and then Callum's body was on the ground motionless, blood seeping from his mouth and somewhere on his body.

I looked down at him and in a small voice, asked, "Callum?"

Chapter Thirty-Two

There was a ringing in the back of my head. One moment, I was standing, and the next, I was bent down next to Callum with his eyes open, a vacant stare. I shook his shoulder, demanding he wake up. He was supposed to grow old and die. I was supposed to get years with him, decades.

I could barely register someone trying to talk to me; my entire focus was on my sweet little bird. Blood oozed out of him. My shadows called to him, begging him to smile at me and tell me that this was all some elaborate prank. That he was fine. He was fine. He had to be fine!

My throat ached; from what, I didn't know. I could feel my body rocking back and forth, cradling his head in my arms. A noise rose from me, a sound so guttural that I knew something was breaking inside me.

"Rose!"

The name snapped me out of my trance and I looked over to see Bastian had a knife drawn, facing toward a smiling Emilia, and Soren kneeling on the other side of Callum, trying to talk to me.

"Rose, come back!"

I blinked at him a few times, his face blurring every time I opened my eyes. I was crying. I tried to do as he asked, but the words wouldn't form. It was as if all the air had been sucked out of me. I couldn't breathe.

Breathe, dammit!

I could barely see Soren's eyes widen. He leaned over Callum's body and shook me violently.

"Rose! Stay with me." Soren reached down and touched Callum's throat. His shoulders drooped, and I couldn't understand the sadness in his eyes.

Callum's hurt. I need to heal him. Right. I can do that.

I bit into my hand, opened his mouth, and pleaded, "Drink, Callum. Come on, drink." I kept thinking that over and over and over.

When his mouth filled with my blood and he wasn't swallowing, fear shot through me. No. This had to work. My thoughts turned into a desperate plea. He had to wake up. I *needed* him to wake up. I could fix him. I could fix anything with my magic.

"We need to move."

I couldn't focus on Soren. Not when I didn't understand what was happening and couldn't comprehend why Emilia hurt him. It didn't matter. I needed to save him.

Shadows began to surround us, creating a barrier that whipped around the four of us—protecting us. My emotions were so heightened that I had created a tunnel of wind, hair flying everywhere. All noise drowned out except for the one line flying through my mind. Everything would be fine.

Everything *had* to be fine.

I was pulled back and away from Callum. I tried to fight them off, using my powers to send them away, when someone grabbed my face, forcing me to look at them.

Soren's eyes were looking at me with pity, and I said as my voice cracked, "Why won't you let me help him? You will see... He will wake up."

"No, he won't. He's gone, Rose." Soren's words were so soft.

I pushed him away from me, unable to control the energy flowing through my body. I felt hot all over. I looked back down at Callum's cloudy, vacant eyes. My sweet little bird.

Bastian collapsed next to us, body shaking as he grabbed Callum's shoulders and crushed himself against the lifeless body, arms hanging limp by his side. At the sight, all of my anger, regret, sadness, hope, and love left me. I couldn't feel...anything. The shadows dispersed, and all I could hear was clapping.

My eyes slowly roved over to Emilia and focused on her. I was too out of it to notice before, but I froze. This all had to be a nightmare. Another one of my more vivid nightmares. Her eyes were a bright, golden color, alight with mischief and violence. She was laughing to herself, holding a blade dripping with blood and clapping her hands hard enough to permeate the silent ballroom.

"I forgot how powerful you were. You are a wonder."

I knew that voice, knew that laugh. I hadn't silenced her; she'd found a new host.

"Goddammit, Emilia! Why would you do this?" Bastian's voice cracked, spit flying from his mouth as he screamed.

"Bastian, that's not Emilia." I still didn't want to believe it; I needed her to say it. Say what I knew to be true.

Soren stiffened next to me. "What do you mean?"

I swallowed. "Circe?"

She gave me a knowing smile.

All the color drained from my face. "How... How is this possible?"

"Are you truly this dense?" Emilia's voice was no longer her own. It was stronger, more confident.

"Circe?" Soren looked confused and then immediately tried to stand in front of me. "That can't be possible," he said more to himself, working through how this could happen.

I ignored him and bared my teeth. "Then spell it out for me."

She ignored him, not seeing him as a threat, and talked directly to me over his shoulder. "Do you not remember the promise I made to you?"

I remembered every word. How could I not? It had haunted me in every nightmare.

Her smile slowly got bigger and bigger as I recited her words from so long ago. "All you know will fade like mist. As you have shown the heart of a beast, so shall you live as one. Silence your prison, loneliness your true companion. Isolated. Unloved. Cursed. Only when our tangled thread unbinds, can you reclaim what was lost."

"Poetic, is it not?"

Just hearing her voice made me want to strangle her, but I couldn't, not when she had latched onto Emilia. How did that even happen? Or a better question, *when* did that happen?

"Get out of her!"

"Why would I do that? She already permitted me entry into her body." Circe said nonchalantly. "I would have rather had you, Callie. I bound myself to you all those years ago, believing I could return one day. I've tried to break you. Consume you. You were supposed to be my vessel... But Emilia... She was so easy, especially when your attention turned to the maggots."

That couldn't be true. "Stop lying!"

"It is no lie." Circe played with Emilia's hair for a moment and then looked down at her hands. "You only took her in to replace Annabelle, and she knew it. She knew she was just a little doll for you to care for."

Did Emilia feel that way? My heart skipped a beat thinking about all the horrible thoughts Circe had implanted inside her mind. "You will leave her body alone. You will depart from the castle and leave forever."

She barked a laugh. "I will do no such thing."

Soren was still in front of me, and I saw out of my peripheral sight that Bastian had come up on the other side of me, ready to fight. Each was poised and ready to attack.

Circe looked at both of them and laughed. "You think you can take me on? How foolish of you to presume it would be so easy."

"Emilia! Are you still in there?" Bastian called. "Fight her!"

Circe rolled her glowing golden eyes and flicked her fingers. Both of the brothers were flung backward and slid along the polished floor.

I gasped and turned to find Bastian had collided with the table, breaking a piece of the leg off. He made a small sound, and staggered to get up. Soren had flown over the table, knocking into a chair and slamming into the floor.

My shadows roared to my lifted palm, ready to defend them and fight Circe to ensure that no one else got harmed by her hand. I flung my shadows toward Circe, but she sighed, not worried in the slightest. I wasn't sure when she erected a barrier, but my shadows hit something and swirled around her body, unable to strike her.

"Are you done with your tantrum?"

I ground my teeth together, and called upon every shred of power I possessed. My body was overheating, and my head was pounding under the pressure my power was exerting.

I was almost brought to my knees as I pushed every ounce of my energy at Circe, willing her barrier to break. Her smirk waned slightly. She put her hands up in front of her and chanted something under her breath as cuts began to show up along her pale skin. I smiled wickedly; I could see she was almost brought down to her knees. She fisted her hands, and the shadows evaporated into nothing.

Blood leaked from Circe's nose. She wiped it off with the back of her hand and said, "Now now, Callie, you don't want to hurt your precious Emilia, do you?"

My shadows immediately dispersed. I focused back on Circe and remembered that it was Emilia's face that was staring right back. How could I have forgotten that?

I could sense Bastian and Soren getting back up, ready to fight right alongside me, but I couldn't allow them to get in the way. I couldn't allow them to be hurt. Before I could do anything, they both collapsed where they stood. Not moving.

"Bastian! Soren!" I almost ran to them, but didn't want to turn my back on Circe. "What did you do?"

"They are just resting for a moment while the women speak."

I wanted to give Circe a chance to do the right thing, so I pleaded to her, "Atone for your sins, Circe. Depart from this world doing something good for a change."

"Good?" She played around with the word, as if tasting it on her tongue. "Good? What a callous word it is. It could mean many things to different people. To me, I was doing something good for my people. I broke all the rules because I believed in you."

"I know you did," I uttered, desperately trying to appeal to the softer side of her. The very side that had wanted to spare me so long ago. "I made a mistake. I was young and scared. You were trying to save me from my father." My vision grew cloudy. "I am sorry, Circe. I am so sorry. But, please... Please spare Emilia."

"I begged your father to spare my people... You know what he did?"

I didn't answer her.

"Nothing."

I couldn't hold it in any longer. I propelled my shadows to her once more and just as they were about to strike, she deflected them and shot a blast of energy my way. I wasn't expecting it and was hit in the head, and knocked over. My wrist bent back at an ungodly angle, and I screamed at the pain.

I moved to stand quickly, getting my bearings, cradling my wrist into my chest as the healing process took effect, but not as quickly as before.

What was happening?

Before I could call my shadows again, Circe flicked her wrist to the right, and my head whipped with her movement. She flicked her hand to the left and my head followed the direction. She squeezed her hand, staring at my leg, and I could feel the bones crunching together as if an invisible hand were squeezing it.

The pain surged through me like a relentless tide, each wave threatening to pull me under. I could feel the familiar darkness closing in; if it didn't stop, I knew I'd slip into oblivion. Desperate for a lifeline, I clung to the fading echoes of my loved ones—their laughter, their warmth, despite everything that had transpired between us. But as the shooting pain intensified, one face rose above the rest, sharp and clear amid the chaos—*Annabelle*. I clung to her memory in the darkness, using it as my anchor to climb out of the pit Circe had tried to keep me in, driving me forward with an unyielding force. I refused to allow Circe to win; I would fight through this torment, fueled by the ghost of Annabelle's presence.

I shrieked, "You murdered Annabelle!" The words that I knew to be true. "I know you did; I heard you. You were going to kill my entire family."

Her lip pulled back, baring her teeth at me. "I was going to save you. I was going to give you a home! A family that understood you, that was like you. One who loved you, not in spite of, but because of what you are."

"You never asked me if that's what I wanted." I could feel my bones healing itself, but slowly. I needed a little more time.

"Your ancestors killed thousands of my people, but even worse, many of your own people. Hysteria has killed for centuries. Even now, it rules in that little village who sacrifices children to the beast. I wanted to end it and thought you had the nerve to do it with me. But you don't. You never had courage. Emilia, on the other hand? She yearned for revenge. She wanted the same thing I did, and I felt her pain when you denied her. When you kept her hidden in these walls instead of giving her the strength she needed to fight her demons."

My vision grew hazy, and through the pain, I felt longing. "I was trying to protect her."

"You wanted to keep her to yourself. You couldn't let her go." Her voice cracked. "I felt the same about you... I didn't want to let you go. I had grown to care for you. I swore to my coven you were different from your father. That you would save us. But you betrayed me, and you betrayed Emilia."

I pulled my power to me, discreetly gathering as much as I could. "I love Emilia."

"You loved that she was a cure for your loneliness."

She sent out a blast of power toward me, pushing me back. My body lifted from the ground and slammed into one of the pillars, knocking the breath from my lungs. I heard something snap as an agonizing pain shot up through my left leg. I crashed to the ground, and tried to stand but collapsed.

She kept going, never easing. Sending her power at me, and where it made contact, I was bruised, cut, and beaten. I could hardly breathe; my lungs wouldn't expand fully. I couldn't take much more of this. If I died, they would be next. I couldn't die and leave them here with Circe.

She was walking toward me, and for the first time since that fateful day, I felt frightened. "Circe! No, Circe!" True, undiluted fear quickly ran through my veins at her quick approach. She was far stronger than I was. I wasn't going to win. I was about to lose everything.

She raised her hands, and I quickly shouted, "I will be your tool. I will be your slave. This I vow."

She bent down, and grabbed me by the throat. "I can't trust you."

"You were the only reason I didn't completely lose my mind. You have been by my side since I was a child. Why? Why would you stay with me? Was it just to torment me?"

"I was trying to break you," she reminded me.

"I don't believe you," I said.

She pondered a moment, fingers digging into my throat. "Let's make a deal. I will let Emilia go if you freely invite me in."

The idea panicked me, but I didn't have to think about it long. "Fine, but then what?"

"Give up your life for theirs."

"How many people will you hurt if I do?"

"That is not for you to decide."

I must not have answered Circe quickly enough and she brought the blade up to Emilia's neck.

"Stop! I give myself freely over to you, Circe, as long as you make a vow to not harm them. Don't harm my family."

She smiled wickedly at me. She'd won.

I looked over at their slumped forms. I would miss them. All of them. *Please forgive me.*

"Deal. I will spare them."

I nodded, bared my teeth, and pushed myself from the floor. If I was going to give myself over, then I would do it with dignity. My wounds had somewhat healed, the pain lessened, but the limp in my foot was still present. I slowly made my way over to her.

"No! Don't give her what she wants!" I tensed hearing Soren's voice. They must have woken up. I blocked him out, knowing that I needed to focus on what came next. I couldn't have any distractions. I could see him waking Bastian out of the corner of my eye, sending my shadows over toward them to hold them on the ground.

"Thea! We can figure this out! Just stop!" Bastian hands were under him, using all his strength to get up. I sighed at his tenacity; I prayed he'd never change.

Circe placed the bloody knife in the belt of her dress and put both her hands around my face. "We are going to do wondrous things together. Wicked things against those who would hunt us. Our people will rise once again because of you."

I stared at her. My mind cleared, waiting for the intrusion—for the moment I would no longer be myself. I wonder if it would be any different from how it currently was. Would I still be conscious of what she was going to do? Would I have to witness all of the atrocities I allowed to happen because I refused to consent to the murder of my family? Were their lives more important than the lives of millions?

I closed my eyes and felt a burning sensation start at my face where her hands were and then spread throughout my body. My lungs felt like I had breathed in too much smoke. I knew whatever power Circe had stored within her was nothing short of spectacular. She had centuries worth of others' powers within her, fighting each other for dominance. It made my blood boil.

I could tell that I was screaming, pleading with Circe to hurry up and put me out of this misery. I couldn't tell if she had so much raw power that it was taking a while to transfer all of it to me, or if she was doing this as punishment.

I wasn't sure how long the process was, but the pain ceased, the burning extinguished and I could hear her in my head.

"Ah. It feels so good to be powerful again."

No. That wasn't in my head. She had control, but I was still present. I was still present!

I could hear her laughter growing louder and louder, but I didn't focus on that. No. All I could focus on was Emilia's terrified eyes as they changed back to her honeyed eye color.

Her hands were still on my face. She tried to talk, but I simply gave her a wide smile. What must I look like to terrify Emilia? I used the rest of my energy to force Circe to the side of my mind. I could feel her confusion and panic as I grabbed the blade from Emilia's side and lined it up to my heart.

"She was wrong," I said to her, voice shaky and low. "I never meant to replace Annabelle. I never meant to keep you. You are not a doll. I loved you the moment I saw you. *I* have been afraid to let you go."

"I know," she said weakly. "I know."

"I am so sorry, Emilia. I should have been paying more attention. I should have seen what was coming."

Emilia's voice was a whimper when she said, "I should have told you she was in my head...but I was scared. I didn't know what was happening to me."

"I'm going to fix this."

I clenched my teeth together. Circe knew what I was about to do; she was erratic, trying her best to claw back up to take control of my body. Once she did, there would be no going back. It was now or never.

I looked back into Emilia's eyes and said in a strained voice, "Please take care of yourselves."

I didn't hesitate as I plunged the dagger straight into the middle of my chest. I felt a pulsing energy burst out of me. I could feel blood flowing out of my mouth, my hands turning slick, and I fell backward onto the ground.

Circe's screams of rage grew softer until they were no more. A calm washed over me—enveloping me in a warm blanket.

As I started to close my eyes, I suddenly became overwhelmingly sleepy. I saw the brothers and Emilia bent over me, tears cascading down their horror-stricken faces, begging and pleading with me to not leave them. I wanted to reply to them, but words wouldn't form. It was probably better that way. I might ruin their last moment of me.

My last thought... *Goodbye.*

I opened my eyes and squinted at how bright the sun was shining down on me. I sat up and looked down to find Callum lying on his back, hands above his head, beside me.

"Callum?" My voice wavered.

He turned his head and smiled brightly at me. There was not a hint of blood on him; he wasn't in pain, no visible injuries. He seemed to be blissful and happy.

"Your grace…"

"Yes, Callum?"

"If you weren't a human, what would you be?"

I stared down at him, blinked a few times, unsure if I heard him right, and then looked around again. We were in a memory. This happened sometime last year. Is this what death was like? Living within a memory of your choosing?

I slid next to him, wrapped my arms around his middle, and rested my head on his chest. He didn't hesitate or say anything as he leaned his head on mine, and wrapped his arms around my shoulders.

I still didn't have the words to answer him, and he continued on, "If I wasn't a human, I would want to be a crow."

A sob almost broke out of me. I wish I would have treated him better, cherished him when I had the chance. I remembered thinking he was a silly little human. Why on earth would he want to be a crow of all animals?

I found my voice and asked, "A crow?"

His chest rumbled. "Yes. They are intelligent, like me. Can build basic tools, like me. And they have an excellent memory, also like me."

I lifted my head to see his face when he said the next part. "I would be able to spread my wings and fly wherever I wanted. Feel the air beneath my wings. Freedom."

I remembered feeling vexed by his admission, thinking that he wanted to leave me, chastising myself for a moment over keeping him. Even once believing that humans would always disappoint in the end.

I swallowed. He traced my face lightly with his finger, his eyes searching mine. For what, I wasn't sure, but it didn't matter. I was content.

"And every night, I would come back here to gaze upon your beauty. To never know what it meant to hold you, but be so very blessed to just be near you."

I lifted my head. There was so much that I wanted to tell him, so much to apologize for. I felt something wet on my face and knew that I was crying again.

I pulled away from him and sat up, looking away. Not wanting him to see me cry.

I wiped the tears from my face, and collected myself.

When my breathing evened and the pounding in my head eased, I was about to cuddle back with Callum, but froze when he said, "You don't belong here, Calathea."

I whipped my head around to him, confused. "What?"

I thought this was the afterlife, forever lying in the grass of eternity. I was content with that. I didn't want to leave the others, but I knew that my sacrifice would keep them safe.

He just smiled at me.

"I—I don't want to leave you. Please don't—"

"Hey, hey, Calathea, look at me." My lips thinned to keep the sob from escaping. I shook my head; I didn't want to listen to him.

"It isn't your time yet."

"But—"

"Emilia, Soren, and—" his voice hitched and cracked when he said, "Bast needs you. They all need you."

I reached out and wrapped my hands around the nape of his neck. "*I* need you. I have always needed you." I was desperate.

He grabbed my shoulders and pulled away slightly to stare into my eyes, "I will always be with you. There will never be a moment when I am not looking over you."

My lip quivered. I hugged him with all of my strength and whispered, "I love you."

He wrapped his hands once more around me. "And I love you. I always have."

CHAPTER THIRTY-THREE

"Thea! Come on, fight, dammit!" I felt someone pressing hard on my chest and then someone breathing air into my lungs. "You are so fucking stubborn, and *now* you decide to just give up?"

I sucked in a huge gulp of air as my eyes looked around wildly. My body ached all over, and I tried to sit up, but pain radiated through me. Every small movement caused me to wince.

"Pick her up! We need to move!" I heard Soren command.

I didn't have time to ask why we had to move. How long was I gone for? Where was Emilia? Was everyone alright?

The questions caught in my throat as I looked around at the crumbling castle walls, debris falling through the air, a huge block of stone not far from where I was laying. My world was literally falling apart.

"I'm so sorry! I didn't know. I am so sorry." Emilia was bent over the side of me, sobbing, fisting her hand and circling it around the middle of her chest over and over again. She looked to where Callum's body was and back at me, sobbing even harder.

Bastian lifted me in his arms and ran toward a shattered window. "Emilia! Run ahead of me! Be careful!"

She continued crying, but did as she was told. I couldn't focus on anything she was saying right now.

I looked behind Bastian and saw Soren hesitate.

"Soren?" Bastian stopped right at the window. What was he doing? "Soren!"

"Go! I'll be right there!" Then he took off back through the room. He disappeared into the smoke and debris, it was so bad that I couldn't see him.

"Ren!" Bastian called, cursed under his breath, and hurried out the window. "I am going to beat his ass if he gets himself killed."

Emilia and Bastian ran as far away as they could from the castle, all the way to the treeline. Bastian set me down. I sat in shock as I watched the top of the tower fall over and come crashing to the ground. Bastian moved his body over the top of Emilia and me as a gust of wind from the impact shot toward us.

I tried to look past Bastian to see where Soren was, but there was too much smoke to move through, let alone see through.

Then there was silence. Bastian kept his arms around us for a few more moments, then stood and looked around. Emilia stayed and sat next to me, but we were both waving our hands in front of us, coughing, trying to get the dust out of our faces to see.

"Ren!" Panic laced his voice.

I tried to stand, to run back into the castle and search for him, but my legs gave out.

Emilia turned to me and whispered, her voice strained, "Don't move, your majesty."

I ignored her and tried to stand again, and this time, my legs held. I lifted my hands and pulled for my magic, but there was nothing there. That wasn't right. I pulled for it again, and there was nothing.

"The blade," Emilia interjected.

I wasn't sure if my powers were gone because of the blade or if they…were just gone. I growled at how irritated I was for not being able to search for Soren.

I coughed and cupped my hands around my mouth, "Soren!"

I started to move forward when Bastian stopped me. "Wait here. I'll go find him."

I pushed his hand away and took slow steps forward, calling his name. I could hear Bastian curse under his breath, and then he ordered Emilia to stay by me as he ran toward the castle. Emilia wrapped an arm around my shoulders to help stabilize me when I almost tripped over a piece of stone.

We walked back toward the ballroom to see if he was trapped somewhere or unconscious. At that thought, I hurried my steps and continued calling out for him. Emilia even tried to yell as loudly as she could.

We heard someone coughing over to our left near the greenhouse, and out came Soren, holding something in his hands.

"Soren!" I screamed. "Bastian, Soren's here!" I broke free from Emilia, and ran toward him, tripping over my feet as I tried to sprint. He sighed a breath of relief as he set down whatever was in his hands and spread his arms wide for me. I jumped onto him, flinging my arms around his neck. He tightened his embrace around me, one hand around the back of my head and the other around my lower back.

After a moment, he pulled me back at arm's length and looked over every inch of me. "I'm fine."

"No, you're not. There is no scientifically sound reason on how you could be alive right now."

"Everything is alright." I tried my best to reassure him.

"You *died*!" He said incredulously, and I flinched at the truth in his words. He was right; I had died.

I didn't have time to think more about it when Bastian came running from wherever he was and barreled into Soren, knocking them both to the ground. "What the hell were you thinking?"

The breath was knocked out of him, so he pointed behind him to the item on the ground. I walked over to get a better look and saw what he carefully placed on the ground. I gasped, as the realization of everything that had transpired tonight seeped in. It was all real.

My portrait from Callum. Soren risked his life to save this.

I was kneeling next to it, too nervous to touch it. I looked over to Soren sitting on the grass next to Bastian. He ran a hand through his hair, "I tried to save him. I tried to get Callum out, but..." A hollow look entered his eyes. "I was too late. I was about to leave, but then that caught my eye, and I thought—I just thought you would want something to remember him."

I blinked back the tears and nodded.

The weight of all that happened had finally broken the piece of me that had been holding everything together. And I, like my home, crumbled. I sat on the ground and wailed into the night. Crying for the loss of such a sweet soul. Crying for the loss of my home. Crying for my past. Crying for a future without Callum.

Mourning my loved ones and the people of my kingdom. To be the sacrifice to spark my curse—the torment and loneliness that I had endured over the past centuries. I let it all out. I didn't care that they were watching. I knew they were grieving just as hard as I was.

When the tears had dried and my body had stopped shaking, Emilia said, "It is all my fault. I didn't know. I just—I didn't know."

I looked up at her and saw that her eyes were rimmed in red, and she was shaking, her arms wrapped around her middle. Her head was bowed, hair falling in front of her face. She was filled with shame, that much was evident.

I stood up, walked to Emilia, and fell to my knees, wrapping my arms around her in a tight embrace. She was shaking her head back and forth and trying to pull away from me. I just held her tighter.

"You did *nothing* wrong. Do. You. Hear. Me. You did nothing wrong."

We were both deceived by Circe, and it almost destroyed us. I wouldn't allow Circe to tear us apart any longer.

When her tears had subsided, I took a breath and sat back, needing to know what happened. Nothing made sense. Soren was right; I shouldn't be here right now.

"Tell me everything." I looked at all of them expectantly.

They all looked at each other, and I waited for them to collect their thoughts.

Soren sighed and said, "You stabbed yourself, and a blast of energy shot out of you. It was powerful and threw everyone across the room. You fell to the ground and...died." He looked away as if he were collecting himself. "I did everything I could think of to revive you, but...you stabbed yourself in the chest!" Soren's voice kept getting louder the more he talked.

Bastian snapped, "Ren."

"Right." Soren paused. "Not a minute after you died, the castle started falling apart. Maybe it was attached to the curse, and when that broke, it brought down the castle. Or that blast of energy that shot out of you caused the very foundation to quake, becoming unstable. Either way, I was wrong."

I looked at him, confused.

"I thought the key to breaking the curse was love, but I mistranslated it. I mean, in a way it was a type of love. A love for others that went beyond your innate desire to survive. The both of you were connected through the curse, so when you stabbed yourself it killed her."

It looked as though Soren was going to continue when Bastian slapped his back and shook his head.

I sat there, allowing everything to sink in. My voice cracked as I asked, "Did I really break it?"

"There's only one way to find out."

Bastian stood and reached his hand out for me to take. I placed my hand in his as he gently helped me up, despite my body protesting the movement. I turned back to the only home I had ever known. Where Callum's body would forever be. It was hard seeing it in this state. I tried to imagine the grandeur that it once possessed.

Now, it was rubble.

I couldn't find it in myself to cry any more tears, but the sadness was so strong I had to rub my chest to try and take the pain away. I wondered if it would ever end, but now wasn't the time to worry about that.

They all gave me the space I needed, and then I turned around and walked away from my home for the last time. I vowed to never come back. To only look ahead from now on. So long as the curse was broken.

We walked around the side of the castle, past the rose garden, over the bridge, and past the overgrown lined trees. My steps slowed once the front gates came into view, and then I stopped completely when I was only a few feet from it. They had all stepped on the other side and turned to me.

"Come on, Rose."

I shook my head at them, and I took a step backward. This was all happening so fast, I wasn't ready. I thought I was, but...

I looked back toward the crumbled castle. Maybe I could stay a little longer and work myself up to this.

"Thea," Bastian said, grabbing my attention once more. He gave me a small smile. "It's time to go."

"The world is so different, Bastian. What if it's too different? What if I cannot fit in?" I couldn't help but share my worries with them.

"This is what we have worked so hard for. Your freedom." Soren pleaded.

Bastian instead asked, "Would you care to make a wager?"

My eyes found Bastian's. "What would we wager?"

He crossed his broad arms over his chest. "Walk through the barrier. If it is still up, we will all stay with you and make this a home. But..."

He left the word hanging, and Soren finished, "...if the curse is broken, then you come with us. Make a life with us. *Live*."

My breathing increased rapidly, and I took a couple of hesitant steps forward until I was directly in front of the barrier.

Deep breath in. One. Two. Three. Deep breath out. One. Two. Three.

I held my breath and took a step, tensing as I waited for the barrier to shoot me back, but nothing happened. I was panting as I opened my eyes and saw everyone smiling at me.

The curse was broken. I could hardly believe it. The night had begun to lighten, specks of light peaked through the trees. I had never felt this light before, this free. Anything and everything was possible.

"What now?" I asked, breathless, uncertain.

"Where do you want to go?" Emilia asked.

I turned and gave Soren a small smile. "The ocean."

He nodded at me. "What the queen wants, the queen gets."

I stopped them. "No. No more titles, no more bowing, no more anything. I am just a girl, traveling with her family."

They all smiled at me, and I smiled at them. Now was the time to begin my life. My human life.

I wrapped my hands in the crook of Emilia's arm. With Bastian to my right and Soren to my left, we began to walk forward. I had little idea what was next, but now that I had such little time—I couldn't possibly waste a moment of it.

Epilogue

I awoke to the sounds of crashing waves and soft snoring, one hand wrapped around my waist and the other around my throat. I always smiled when I woke like this. Warm. Safe. Loved. I had to force myself out of the cocoon we had created as I needed to stretch my limbs, sore from the night before, and the night before that.

I walked to the portrait Callum had painted, hanging just above a small table and chair I liked to use for reminiscing. I pulled a piece of parchment from the table before walking out onto the terrace, where the sun barely peaked over the horizon. This time of the day was my favorite as I loved to greet the sun. There was a serene stillness of the morning that called to me. I sat down at the small table with my quill, ink, and parchment.

Dearest Emilia,

We arrived in Italy just last night and I never want to leave. I know I said that about Western Ireland, Northern Scotland, Germany, and, truthfully, every single place we have visited for the past seven years. But this may be my favorite place. The Amalfi Coast of Eastern Italy has the bluest waters I have ever seen in my life. You can see the seafloor miles away from land.

How is little Joséphine? Her birthday is coming up soon and we want to visit and bring her all the gifts we have collected over the past six months. Be sure to tell her that her elder brothers think

about her daily and love her very much. Tell Père that the moment
he steps out of line I will

Someone wrapped their arms around me, kissed the back of my head, and chuckled. "Will you ever not resort to violence?"

I raised my brows and turned to find Soren smiling down at me. I feigned shock, placing my hand over my heart, and said, "I would never."

He cocked his head to the side and gave me a look. I rolled my eyes and huffed, lifting my shoulders as I turned back around. "I just want to make sure that Père is treating our Emilia well."

He set a cup of tea next to the ink bottle and sat down on the daybed to my left. He leaned back on the pillows with a blanket wrapped around the lower part of his body as there was still a slight chill in the air despite it being summer.

He closed his eyes and responded, "You wouldn't be the woman I fell in love with if you weren't fiercely loyal."

I smiled at that and lifted the quill once more.

Soren caught me. He informed me that I shouldn't resort quickly
to violence, but how else can I be sure that Père is treating you well?
I digress...
I miss you dearly and am excited to meet your youngest, Philippe.
Expect our arrival in a fortnight.

With love,
Calathea

I set the quill down, picked up the parchment, and folded it into thirds. I pulled my shadows forth and thought of Emilia and her home in the South of France on a little patch of land of rolling hills in a quaint meadow. I flicked the paper through the small hole that had formed in front of me and knew it would float to sit neatly on their kitchen table.

My power wasn't as strong as it was before Circe's dark promise, but it was still with me. Soren's theory was that it didn't disappear because this was the power I was born with. I was thankful when the effects of the blade subsided; it felt like I had lost another part of myself and I cried in relief when some powers returned.

I walked over to the daybed, staring down at Soren. He opened one eye and laughed as he lifted the blanket so that I could crawl in and join him. I situated myself between his legs, resting my back against his front. I closed my eyes as he skimmed his fingers softly over my arms and began humming the same song we danced to on that dreaded birthday.

I wanted him to sing it to me every morning. Even though it reminded me of what happened, I wasn't as sad as I was before. I wouldn't allow Circe to ruin yet another memory that I wanted to hold dear to me.

My shadows sang and licked his skin; his chest rumbled from laughter. "Have I told you recently that I love when your shadows dance for me?"

I craned my neck back to look at him. "They adore you, as do I."

He leaned down and kissed me deeply, our tongues gliding across each other. I almost deepened it further until we felt the bed dip. We broke the kiss to find Bastian lounging at the end of the bed eating a piece of dried pear and brie cheese.

"Good morning, witch." Bastian loved using the nickname when he was in a playful mood. He smiled, hair messy over his face. His hair had grown over the years and he could now pull it back in a leather strap.

He held out a piece of the cheese to me. I leaned forward as he fed it to me and then licked a piece of crumb from his thumb. "Why do you both insist on waking up so early? It should be a crime to wake before the sun."

"No need to pout, Brother."

Bastian smacked his brother in the side of the leg and then laid back with his arm over his face. He hated waking up early, but I knew he only did so because he disliked being too far away from me.

I settled back against Soren as he resumed skimming my arms and sang my song. We settled into a comfortable silence, listening to Soren humming to the tune of the waves. My mind wandered and I ended up thinking about their town and how long it had been since I had made an appearance.

"I think we should stop by and pay a visit to D'Arque before heading to see Emilia and Joséphine."

"I wonder what Jo will think about the present I got for her. A dagger with an assortment of rubies, emeralds and other gems." I scoffed at Bastian's idea of a perfect gift for his twelve-year-old sister.

Soren reminded me, "And Père."

I waved him off. Bastian and I both grumbled, "Yes, yes, *and* him."

It wasn't that I didn't like Père; simply put, I was extremely protective over Emilia, and I couldn't see anyone being good enough for her. We had settled Emilia in her home in the meadow with Joséphine after we paid a visit to their town to handle the Reapings once and for all. While I was threatening the new head of the council on the new rules he was to follow, Emilia was busy meeting Père at the bookstore in town he owned.

I remembered her cheeks heating when we met later that day and blamed it on the sun, but I knew better. She was smitten. He came out to check on her and made sure to bring books that she would enjoy. One thing led to another, they married and now had a child with a second on the way.

We left Joséphine in Emilia's care, knowing that she would need more than the three of us could provide—stability.

"D'Arque has since disbanded the Church of the Beast and is leading the townspeople on a less destructive path," Bastian informed us.

I lifted my hand above me and ran my hand through Soren's sandy, sunkissed hair and mused, "And he will continue going down that path unless he wants to be buried six feet under, his family thinking he ran off on them for a mistress, never to be heard from again."

"We check in on him yearly to ensure he stays that way, and we just saw him a few months ago. Relax, Rose."

"Humph. I should have let my shadows run rampant through his mind so that he would think twice before doing something absurd like the Reapings again."

"You did let them run rampant on the men who attacked Emilia and most of the council," Bastian reminded me.

I was about to give a witty retort when Soren took my hand and kissed from my wrist up my arm and across my shoulder. I moaned at the sensation that tingled along my body. Soren always knew how to calm the anger I felt whenever I thought about that town.

We heard Bastian make a strangled noise. Soren and I laughed, my body moving to the motion of his laughter. I replied coyly, "Is there something we can help you with, Bastian darling?"

I heard a growl and yelped as my legs were being pulled down the length of the bed. Bastian's face was between my widened legs. His mouth slowly kissed my ankle, and up to my inner thighs.

He shrugged, staring at me from lowered lashes, and said against the apex of my thighs, "I got a little lonely."

Soren had moved down the bed and continued his lazy kisses on my neck, gently nipping at my skin. This wasn't fair. They knew what this did to me and could feel the full effects at my core, my stomach tightened.

"You both are pure evil," I whimpered.

Bastian bunched my silk nightgown around my hips and kissed the bundle of nerves while Soren brushed a strap off my shoulder, exposing my breasts to the chill morning air. His hand lightly squeezed my breast. I sucked in a breath, my nipples pebbling under his touch.

It was evident that they were going to take their time this morning. I growled my displeasure over their pace and was about to demand that they hurry when my body spasmed and a sound escaped me that I had never made before. We were all stunned. Bastian looked up from between my legs and rubbed the stubble of his beard against my inner thigh and I made the same sound and movement again.

Eyes bright, he asked, "Are...you ticklish? Ren, I think our mistress is ticklish."

"Brother, I think you may be right."

This was headed in a direction that I wasn't going to enjoy. I couldn't remember the last time I was tickled and wasn't exactly delighted about this form of torture. I knew I was in trouble when an idea struck.

I used my shadows to push Bastian hard enough on his back and straddled his stomach. I leaned down and licked his lips as my shadows slipped under their trousers and tightly gripped their cocks. I smiled to myself at the sounds coming from their mouths, knowing how good it must feel.

I leaned back, and slowly lifted a leg over Bastian's stomach and stood, giving them a mischievously wicked grin. I knew they wouldn't be able to move while my shadows stroked them.

Bastian growled through clenched teeth, "Thea... Don't you dare run."

"We will chase you, Rose."

"And will punish you for this."

I turned and ran down the stone steps leading to the sandy beach and ran as fast as I could, using my shadows to help propel me forward. I dared not look behind me and pumped my arms as fast as they could go. The wind whipped my long, brown hair around my face.

I was laughing and almost ran straight into the path of a descending bird. I stumbled to a stop and saw birds chirping off in the distance, but there was one that flew next to me—a crow. I paused for a moment and lifted an arm toward it, and surprisingly, it perched on me. It was staring at me intently, cocking its little head back and forth before lifting its wings and flying away.

Fly away, my little bird. Fly away onto your next adventure.

I forgot all about our game of chase and barely turned when Bastian abruptly wrapped his arms around me, picking me up, and spinning me around.

I squealed, "Set me down right now, Bastian Corleone!"

"Brother, she used your entire name. She must be furious with you," Soren teased, barely out of breath as he caught up with us.

"She must be, Ren." He dropped me on the warm sand without warning.

I huffed as I turned over to lay on my back, arms braced underneath me to hold me up slightly. I glared at them as they stood over me, blocking out the sun that had fully peaked over the mountain range, illuminating them in a halo of light. They looked like gods.

"Calathea. Rose." Soren started, kneeling on the ground to my right.

"Everhart. Corleone." Bastian finished, kneeling on the other side of me.

I loved it when they used my full name. My married name. Loved that it bound me to them in ways I had only ever dreamed of. My shadows yearned for it just as much as I did and answered them by illuminating my eyes to the vibrant periwinkle they both had come to crave.

We spent the rest of the day in each other's arms. I thanked their god for bringing them to me. For giving me the gift that I didn't know I needed.

My story was a thing of nightmares, chaos, and murder, but also of love.

A fairytale. A tale as old as time.

Acknowledgements

There are so many people I want to thank for helping me bring this book to life. First and foremost, I want to thank my readers for taking a chance on my first book. Your support means everything to me, and I hope this story resonated with you in unexpected ways.

To my best friends, Regina and Chynna, who read the original draft and still saw the potential this story had! You both are my biggest cheerleaders and have kept me going when I wanted to give up. Regina, thank you for always asking me about the book, gobbling up every detail, and being willing to listen to twenty-minute-long voice memos droning on about updates. Even if it was something you had heard a million times. Chynna, thank you for spending your small amount of free time helping me catch all the tiny details and being someone I could bounce ideas off of. I am so grateful to have you both in my life.

Thank you to my beta readers—Nathalie, Aimee, and Anandi—who gave me valuable advice on how to make my story even better. You were also essential in giving me the confidence boost I needed when I wasn't sure if people would enjoy the story and resonate with my characters.

Mom, there are a million things that you thought I could be one day. I am sure that a dark romance author wasn't one of them, but I am very thankful for you. You have never once made me feel like what I am doing didn't mean anything. Your words of support have meant everything to me. I love you so much! I hope I continue to make you proud.

Rachel, your designs blew me away when I saw them on Instagram for the first time. I knew I HAD to get one done by you. As a newbie author, I had no idea what I was doing and you made the process incredibly easy and enjoyable. And wow! You created an absolute work of art!

Now, I need to thank a very special person in my life. Someone who I have only known for about two years; not long, but who is now vital to my life—Erin. Erin, I truly don't have the words to express how much you have affected my life. Your constant guidance, advice, late-night sessions, and expertise have been an essential part of my writing experience. This may be my book, but you took care of it as if it were your own and helped me mold it into something I never could have imagined it could be. For that, I will always be thankful. You aren't just my editor, but a dear friend. I have said it before and I will say it again—I am keeping you forever! You are never getting rid of me. I am so excited to continue taking you on this wild journey with me. Cheers to the Dream Team!

About the Author

Bria Rose is a Disney enthusiast turned dark romance author. She once dreamed of being rescued by a prince, but now yearns for a morally grey 6'5" alpha male who would burn the world for her. When she doesn't have her head in a book she is a boudoir photographer, scuba diver, travels the world, and is currently learning French.

Learn more about Bria Rose on authorbriarose.com. Join her newsletter to receive exclusive content, giveaways, updates, and special deals.

Social Media Accounts:
TikTok @authorbriarose
Instagram @authorbriarose
Facebook @authorbriarose